The Relationship Bargain

Bretta Elaine

<u>Before You Read</u>

The Relationship Bargain is a steamy contemporary romance that features strong language and explicit sexual content. For modification or steamy spoilers please see the dicktionary located in the back of the book.

This one is for the feral girlies.
Stay fierce.

Chapter One

Sutton

Everything is perfect.

From the floral arrangements dangling in cascading beauty. To the last pin in my hair.

It's a dream come true.

A dream I painstakingly planned and saved every dime to afford.

Countless hours of stress and tears were poured into the vision. Everything accumulated to this perfect moment.

Only it feels wrong.

Something isn't right.

I scan the room, trying to find what's out of place. What minor detail I might have forgotten. Nothing.

Not a single thing.

It's just nerves. Cold feet. It's perfectly normal.

"You look stunning." Vivian wraps me in a hug, carefully lifting her neck high to avoid touching her face on my stark virginal-white gown. "You ready for this?"

A shaky breath puffs past my soft, pink-painted lips. "Yeah, totally."

Vivian peers at me with unbelieving eyes. As my best friend of twenty-plus years, the woman knows me better than she knows her left tit. She opens her mouth to say something, but right then, my mom walks up, interrupting her.

"Viv, you just missed your cue," my mom says, pointing at the open doors.

She curses and skips to the door, only to halt and resume walking like a composed woman as she turns into the doorway.

With slow steps, Mom and I make our way just outside the doors.

I'm so glad she is by my side, walking me down the aisle. She's the only parent I've ever had. She had me at such a young age and then struggled for years while she finished school and somehow managed to take care of me without any help from my loser of a father.

So it was an honor to have the woman who took on the role of both mother and father give me away today.

The music is idyllic, romantic, and powerful.

A sweat breaks out across my forehead as I take my first steps into the room.

It's everything I had imagined.

I smile wide, loving how magical it all feels.

My mom squeezes the hand she's holding. She looks so proud, with a gleam of tears in her eyes. Everything about her radiates her warmth and love for me.

She is the epitome of beauty. Her hair is swept into a sophisticated chignon, and she's wearing a lilac silk gown that makes her shine so brightly.

This day is as much for her as it is for me, and for as long as I can remember, I've always wanted nothing more than to bring her the joy that's radiating from her eyes.

"I'm so proud of you, Sutton," she whispers as we stroll down the aisle, smiling at all the people who showed out to celebrate my marriage to Dillon.

"Thank you, Mom." I smile, even as my stomach drops with every step closer to where Dillon stands with the minister, with Vivian and Jake flanking them on opposite sides.

He's as attractive as always. Everything about him is polished, with his crisp dark suit and hair slicked back, but somehow, he's still slightly disheveled. His tattoos peek out of the collar of his suit in a way that usually makes my mouth water. But today I feel nothing.

We stop before the altar, and Mom leans in, wrapping her arms around me for one last hug. "I love you and will always be proud of you." She pulls back, looking right into my eyes with a seriousness that hadn't been there moments ago. "No matter what."

I hesitate, dipping my chin in acknowledgment. "I love you too."

The music trails off as Dillon grasps my hand, turning me away from my mom to face him. The sound of my heart pounding fills my ears as we walk the last few steps.

Heat fills my body as every inch of the silk-and-lace woven dress scratches my skin like it's made of itchy wool.

I tug on my straps with my free hand as we turn toward the minister.

"Love is a funny thing. You never know where you'll find it or how it will happen. It just does. You can't plan it. Can't force it. It is a force that we have no control over," the minister says to the crowd. "That's what makes it so special. Such a precious gift. It is once in a lifetime. It is an out-of-control force that can lift and destroy. It is beauty in destruction. It is the most important thing we give to others. Because even though we can't control who we love, we can choose to give that love or take it away. And it's in that choice that something magical happens. Today, Dillon and Sutton have given their love to each other willingly. Today, the two vow to share their lives and souls until death. Today, we celebrate the uncontrollable force that brought these two together."

With every word, every syllable, my heart cracks a little more. Because this isn't the amazing, magical feeling he speaks about. Our relationship, our love, is nothing like what he described.

As I peer into Dillon's eyes—his bloodshot eyes, for fuck's sake. He couldn't go one day without getting high, could he?—I feel it. The pull in my gut.

The something that is wrong.

It isn't a flower or strand of hair out of place.

It's the person I agreed to marry.

The line of sweat that had only been on my forehead is now dripping down my face.

Great.

Just great.

I glance back to Viv, only to find a supportive smile on her face. She hates Dillon and hates that I've been so insistent on marrying him. When I first told her we were getting married, she laughed and then broke into tears, begging me to reconsider. But once I told her my mind and heart were made up, she did everything in her power to support me. Even now, I know she has her reservations, but she's kept them to herself instead giving me the gift of her friendship.

Taking a deep, controlled breath, I turn back to Dillon and the minister.

"Dillon, do you take Sutton to be your lawfully wedded wife, in sickness and in health, as long as you both shall live?"

He looks my body up and down once more with his red eyes, biting and licking his lips, and says, "I do."

"And you, Sutton, do you take—"

The sound of my blood rushing through my body drowns out the words he's speaking.

I can't do this.

I can't be with him.

Oh, how Vivian is going to have a field day with this recent development.

"I do," I say, the words tasting wrong. I want to take them back. To rewind to a moment before and undo it.

My hands shake as we're instructed to exchange rings. Sweat coats my palms, and I almost fumble his ring.

Once again, Dillon doesn't notice my demeanor is wrong, taking my lack of grace as excitement. He leans in, whispering as he slides my ring on my finger. "Don't worry, babe, we can have our first fuck in a few."

It takes everything in me not to cringe away from him. Does he really think I want our first time as a married couple to be here? That I want to mess up the masterpiece that is my hair and makeup for a quick round in a closet, with my friends and family only a few feet away? He knows how hard I worked on this wedding. How I wanted everything to be special and perfect, and a lackluster screw before pictures isn't a part of it.

It's like my eyes have been pried open. How in the ever-loving hell had I ever thought this was a good idea? He can't even read my body language. He doesn't even try.

"I now pronounce you Mr. and Mrs. Oak."

Wrong.

Dillon leans forward, wrapping an arm around my waist as his lips land on mine in a claiming kiss.

Wrong.

Every part of this is wrong.

My heart pounds in my chest as we walk back down the aisle.

Hand in hand with Dillon, I force the smile to stay glued to my lips as we pass person after person clapping and cheering for us. The flash of cameras all around us almost pulls me out of my act.

I just have to hold it together until we're alone.

Once we make it down the aisle, we circle back into a room tucked behind the altar, where we will have a few minutes together before we are supposed to sign the licenses with our witnesses.

The moment the door closes behind us, Dillon's arms wrap around me in a familiar hug that used to bring me joy and warmth but now only feels heavy, reminding me of what I have to do.

I pull out of his arms. "Dill, we need to talk."

"Nah, babe. We need to get this dress off you."

The minister clears his throat to remind us we're not alone, and that we are in his workplace. A chapel. A no-fornicating zone.

Aiming a sleazy smile at the man, Dillon says, "You know how it is with newlyweds."

Much to my surprise, the man laughs. "Yes, yes I do."

"About the marriage license—" I begin, but the minister cuts me off.

"Yes, here it is. I'll go get your chosen witnesses, and we will get this thing signed and done."

I put my hand up to stop him. "Here's the thing. I'm not signing that. I refuse. I think this was a mistake." A massive weight lifts off me the moment the words leave my mouth.

"A *mistake*?" Dillon scoffs.

"Yes."

"A mistake is buying the wrong fucking brand of toilet paper. A mistake is taking a wrong turn. Saying 'I do' in front of everyone isn't something you accidentally fuck up, Sutton."

"I'm sorry. I realize this is unexpected. But I can't do this."

"You didn't think so five minutes ago when you said 'I do.'"

"Actually, I did. I didn't want to embarrass you in front of everyone."

"Versus embarrassing me *now*?"

"Look, the way I see it, we have some options."

"From my standpoint, your only option is annulment or divorce."

"Wrong, Dillon." I sigh, trying not to get frustrated with him. His anger is warranted. I did just drop a bomb on all our life plans. "I'm not signing the paper."

He huffs out a laugh. "So what? It's just a piece of paper. We're still married."

"No, no we're not. The paper is the legally binding part. Everything else is just a show."

He groans, pulling at the ends of his hair. "Stop being so fucking *dramatic*, Sutton. I get it, you want the excitement and drama to last, but now isn't the time."

"It isn't about excitement or drama, Dillon. It's about knowing that us being married is wrong. So, like I was saying before, we have options, and I will do whatever you would like. I'm willing to go to the reception and act like nothing has happened and pretend like it fell apart after. Or we can call it now."

"You'd be willing?" He laughs.

"Yes." I nod again.

"Or you can stop being a bitch and sign the paper," he sneers at me.

The blood drains from my face as I'm frozen in place. "I understand this isn't what you were expecting today, but treating me like shit isn't going to make me change my mind."

"Screw you, Sutton."

"Okay, to option two, it is."

"Do whatever you want. I'm out of here." He tears the ring off his finger and flings it at my feet before striding toward the door.

"Okay."

Stopping on the threshold, he turns back to glare at me. "Oh, Sutton? I fucked the stripper last weekend," he sneers before slamming the door behind him.

"Well, that went well," the minister says from behind me.

I had forgotten we weren't alone. Whirling around, I mutter, "I'm so sorry you had to witness that, sir."

He gives me a demur smile. "I'm sorry to tell you, Ms. Hale, that in the eyes of the lord, you are married."

"But legally, I'm not." I grin. Well, this is awkward.

He opens his mouth to continue, but I cut him off.

"And thank the lord for that. Because I doubt even God would want me to marry someone who spoke to and treated me the way you witnessed. Now, if you'll excuse me, I have a reception to ruin." I walk away with my head held high and my fingers clenching the sides of my dress.

As I swing open the door, Viv and my mom almost topple right into me, only being saved by Nate, Vivian's husband and all-around dreamboat of a man, quickly wrapping his arms around them.

"Any chance you guys are going to pretend like you didn't hear everything and let me have a couple glasses of champagne before you start in on me?"

They straighten, glancing at each other.

"I have no idea what you are talking about," my mom lies, giving me a quick hug before turning to walk away.

Nate and Vivian stand off to the side. Vivian is practically bouncing in her nude heels as she smiles at her husband.

"Who's ready to get drunk?"

Both of their hands shoot up.

Chapter Two

Cooper

I twirl the beer in my hand, bringing it to my lips as I read Nate's millionth message. This is the problem with having a happily married best friend. All he wants to do is hang out with his wife. So when we hang out, Vivian is there, which isn't an issue. She is amazing. I love the two of them together. Honestly, I couldn't be happier for them. But it's her best friend Sutton that's the problem. The woman and I go together like fire and gasoline. Not that Nate cares. No, the little shit wants us all to be one happy family.

He's been badgering me about going to that damn wedding for weeks now, and my answer has always been the same. No, with a mixture of something like "Sutton doesn't want me there. She only invited me so you wouldn't be lonely while she made your wife her maid for a day." Or "I don't like weddings."

All true. She didn't want me there as much as I didn't want to be there. Everyone knew that she and Dillon getting married was a horrible idea, but no one would man up and tell her.

No one but me.

And we see how that worked...

She still went through with it like the stubborn idiot she is.

I haven't even spoken to her since that day three months ago when I decided enough was enough. Every time she showed up when we were out, I would sneak out, not wanting a repeat of that explosive night.

So instead of spending my Saturday night with my friends, I'm drinking alone in my dark apartment. Wallowing.

I have enough stress on my plate as it is without adding Sutton marrying a total loser into the mix.

The email from work is still up on my computer screen. Hell, it's another reason I'm drinking tonight.

Cooper,

Thanks for your contribution to Jorge's gift. I know you haven't been with the firm for long, but I'm glad to have you as a member of this firm/family.

I'm looking forward to finally meeting this amazing girlfriend we've heard so much about at Jorge's retirement party.

-Mr. Avery

Astor and Avery Financials

Well, shit.

Scrubbing my face with my hand, I sigh as my stomach bottoms out for the tenth time tonight. *How the hell am I going to spin myself out of the web of lies I've weaved?*

See, I might have told an innocent little white lie in my job interview about being in a committed relationship when the board made it clear that they were only considering a candidate who was settled down and held the same family-first values as them.

I was so desperate to get out of my soul-crushing teaching career that I might have made up a girlfriend. And maybe I panicked after getting the job and never got up the nerve to set the record straight once everyone began to pester me with personal questions.

Yeah, so basically, I screwed myself. Because now they all want to meet this amazing woman who I've talked up to them.

I'm seriously contemplating packing a bag and taking the next flight to Canada to start over with a new identity when my phone pings with another text from Nate. I open it to find a picture of Sutton walking down the aisle. She is stunning. Her poise is ethereal in the ivory-laced wedding gown. My chest aches at the sight of her. I zoom in to examine every last detail of her. Torturing myself further like the dumbass I am.

Another ping.

I scroll to the next photo from Nate. It's of Sutton and Dillon walking hand in hand. She's smiling, but it isn't bright. It doesn't fill her face.

It's wrong.

That isn't Sutton's happy smile. Or her overjoyed smile.

Fuck, it isn't even her mischievous smile.

No, this smile is something I've never seen before. Sutton should be over the moon with love and happiness. Instead, everything about the picture is wrong. And I'm not talking about the fact that Dillon the Douche is walking beside her.

Nate answers on the first ring with a laugh. "Oh, so that got your attention."

"Keep your gloating to yourself and tell me what the hell is wrong with her."

"Never going to believe it."

"We'll never know if you don't start moving your lips."

"It was like something out of a movie, Coop. She walked in, looking like a beautiful bridal version of herself. But the moment she made it up to him, it was like there was a massive shift in the air. Like something changed in that instant. She no longer had that same Sutton spark she always has. But I thought she was nervous. She's marrying Dillon, so of course she's nervous. The man is mediocre at best, and she is selling herself short by tying herself to him. Even as she said 'I do' and walked past Viv and me, she seemed smaller. But that's not what makes this entire thing so crazy. What does is what me, Viv, and Sheryl, Sutton's mom, overheard when we went to sign the license."

My footsteps speed up as I pace my living room, wondering what the fuck happened. Scared of what might have happened. "Stop dragging it out for dramatics and tell me."

"Sutton refused to sign the license."

I freeze. "She what?"

"Yeah," he says, laughing again. "She said the whole thing was a mistake, and she refused to be legally married to him."

"Shit."

"Yeah. Coop, you should have heard the nastiness he flung at her when she stood up for herself. It took everything in me not to burst into that room and punch the prick."

Abandoning my pacing, I plop onto my couch and run my hand through my hair. "Is she okay?"

"Yeah, I think so. Viv is feeding her alcohol at the moment. So she will be for at least tonight. But I still think you should come. For moral support, that is."

"Wait, are you guys still at the wedding?"

"No, don't be stupid," he gripes. "We're at the reception, and so are a lot of other people who are curious about what's going on."

"You've got to be kidding me," I groan.

"Like I said. You should get down here. Your support is needed. Also, I will probably need your help to lift the two of them into a cab by the end of the night based on how much liquor is currently being consumed."

Fuck. Pain shoots through my jaw with how hard I grit my teeth. "I'll be there soon."

I don't bother to put on a suit or brush my hair. Instead, I place an Uber order, down the rest of my beer, and head to them.

It doesn't take long to find the trio of idiots I'm searching for once I arrive at the reception. They're huddled at a table in the back, forgoing the bride-and-groom table front and center. From the way they're slouched, I can tell each of them has had their fair share of booze tonight. I walk past groups of guests milling around the dance floor.

Floral arrangements hang from the back of every chair in a whimsical yet elegant manner. It screams Sutton.

One thing is for sure, though—it doesn't scream Dillon at all. The only thing that looks even remotely like him is some of the scowling faces from across the room.

As I approach their circular table covered in a cream tablecloth, Sutton catches a glimpse of me and groans. "Come to gloat?"

I toss my hands up. "I haven't even said anything."

"You didn't have to. You said it all months ago."

I bite back the remark itching to leave my lips about me being right about this wedding. About her and Dillon.

"Have a drink with us," Nate encourages, waving me over to where he's sitting with Vivian in his lap.

He passes me a beer from their secret stash of booze they have slipped beneath the table.

I raise an eyebrow in question at the hidden hooch.

"Dillon's family and friends have made less than friendly comments when we go to the bar."

"So hoarding it like teenagers was the solution?"

Vivian and Nate both nod as Sutton scoffs into her glass of clear liquid, sucking the substance down without hesitation. No flinch or grimace. I'd have thought it was water if I hadn't just watched her refill her glass with vodka.

My stomach threatens to roil as I stare at her.

"He's judging me again," Sutton grumbles, giving me the stink eye.

"Who's up for a drinking game?" I ask, taking a seat across from a glaring Sutton.

A group of scowling guests pass our table on their way out of the reception, which has slowly been emptying over the past two hours. Sutton fumbles her glass, splashing vodka onto the table where we've been drinking our feelings and talking about anything other than the elephant in the room—Sutton's untimely breakup.

Vivian wraps her arms and legs around Nate like a monkey trying to cling to a tree for dear life. "I love you."

"I love you too, Cherry." He smiles at her with a look that makes my heart crack with jealousy.

"I want you to do that thing with your tongue that I love tonight. You know, the one where you—"

Wide-eyed, Nate clamps a hand over her mouth. "Okay, kids, time to pack it up and go home."

"On it," I agree, pulling out my phone to order a ride.

"He's always so embarrassed when I start to talk about his sexual prowess." Viv presses a kiss into his neck.

Looking up from my phone, I ask, "Sutton, where are we dropping you off? A hotel? Your mom's? Home?"

"Go to my newlywed suite? No, thank you. And no way in hell am I going to Sheryl's. She'll just want to talk my ear off about everything that went down, what went wrong, and blah, blah, blah."

I hold her glossy stare, her chestnut eyes lacking their normal mischievous glint that I love. "You've really thought about this?"

"Nope. I just know my mother, and she's a talker. And right now, that's the last thing I want to do."

"So home it is."

She cuts her gaze back to me in a glare that's sharp enough to kill. "Whatever, just get me out of this hellhole of a wedding party, stat."

"Are you done pouting and ready to be a runaway bride?"

Rolling her eyes, she shoulders past me, purposely hitting me as she stalks out the door. I'm on her heels, with Viv and Nate trailing behind us, making noises that sure as shit sound like sucking face. I don't bother to look back to make sure because, honestly, even though I love the shit out of those two idiots, I'm not in the mood to see a happy couple right now.

The moment the SUV pulls up, Vivian practically pushes Sutton and me into the back so she can sit in the middle row with Nate and continue to make out like they'll never have the chance again.

"Ugh," Sutton groans, closing her eyes and throwing her head back against the seat.

"What? Don't tell me, you plan to be bitter now?" I whisper in her ear.

"No," she scoffs, and I pin her with a knowing look until she spits out, "Fine. Maybe a little. I don't plan on it after today. Is it so wrong to want this night, of all nights, to not have"—she gestures to Nate and Viv panting and dry humping—"that?"

I glance at them and wince. "They are very passionate."

She nods. "They could tone it down."

"They could. But also, why should they? Nate and Vivian aren't responsible for your feelings. And they sure as shit didn't cause your wedding to be... unsuccessful."

"Can you just *once* be on my side?" Sutton asks, turning to watch the beautiful chapel and attached reception hall fade into the background.

Silence lingers between us. Only the sounds of Matchbox Twenty playing on the radio and Viv and Nate's kissing filling the SUV.

I reach across the seat and squeeze her hand, drawing her gaze away from the chapel of broken vows and down to where we're connected as I whisper, "I'm always, always on your side, Sutton. Whether you realize it or not."

My hand only lingers against hers for a moment before I pull away without another word until the car stops at Viv and Nate's house.

The two untangle for long enough to shout their goodbyes before stumbling up their driveway, leaving us to move into the now-evacuated middle row as I give the driver directions to Sutton's house.

Chapter Three

Sutton

Shit. Shit. Shit.

Cars line my driveway and down the street, and music blares through the walls of my house.

People are spread all over the lawn, with beer bottles and red plastic cups scattered around their feet. They stumble and laugh just as I was moments ago.

"What the fuck is this?" Cooper straightens from his slouched drunken state.

"He's throwing a party." I huff out a laugh. "Great."

"Dillon?"

"Yeah. Who else, Sherlock?" Of course he would do this. A little "fuck you" to me from him. Dillon isn't exactly known for being mature and diplomatic. I'm honestly shocked that I'm surprised by his acting out like this. When I first met him years ago, this kind of recklessness and wild behavior was what drew me to him. He was fun and made me feel alive at times.

A chorus of laughter draws my attention to the side of my house, and my mouth drops open as a group of guys pick at my garden, probably choosing which rose bush to piss on. Nate just planted those and will be so pissed if they die within weeks. But instead of whipping out their dicks as I expected, they laugh and kick over my decorations. "Hey, that's my gnome. That's my *favorite* gnome."

"Forget the gnome, Sutton. Why is he here?"

I drop my forehead to the window. "Because he lives here."

A curse leaves his lips as he runs his hands through his hair.

"My sentiment exactly."

Dillon moved in with me a few months before the wedding. We had waited so long to make our cohabitation official because of his lease and his touring schedule. And his roommates/bandmates needed him there to pay his share until they found something better.

At the time, it seemed like that was never going to happen. Week after week, month after month. They still hadn't found shit. Until I found it for them. A small three-bedroom house for rent, with a garage for their band's equipment and a price tag they couldn't deny.

After that, Dillon packed up what little he owned and moved in. Honestly, that first day he showed up should have been a red flag. He didn't have boxes or suitcases. Just trash bags full of clothes and albums. I asked about his other things, like furniture or towels, anything else besides clothes and music. And he said, "Oh, that was all my bandmates'." Everything in that house, in his room, wasn't even his...

I don't know why it bothered me so much, but it did. Like, he didn't even bring a toothbrush. I didn't get into the specifics on that, but it sounded like the band shared way too much. Maybe even a communal toothbrush. Which makes me want to gag at the thought alone.

"So are one of you going to get out, or what?" the driver asks as the two of us stare out the window, watching the crowd gathering at my house.

"I guess I could go to the honeymoon suite since Dillon isn't using it. But I think it might be too late to check in... Do you think they'd make an exception for me since I'm clearly a bride? Or maybe since I didn't actually get married, maybe they'll feel sorry for me? Or Sheryl's. Either way, I'm not gonna be staying here."

"No. Take us to the last stop," Cooper demands.

I don't miss the odd looks from the Uber driver at my run-away-bride getup or the sideways glances from the other tenants in Cooper's building as we stumble into the elevator.

Playing into all of their wondering glances, I lean into Cooper, giggling and running my hands all over his warm chest to the nape of his neck.

When the doors open, Cooper grabs my hand and pulls me out behind him as I wave to our nosy audience.

"Great. Now they're all going to think I'm a home-wrecker," he grumbles, tugging me to his door as he fumbles with his keys in his other hand.

"Oh, please. As if anyone would believe you could possibly pull a woman like me."

A click sounds as he twists the key in the lock, opening the door. "Remind me why I brought you home with me?"

"'Cause I'm an emotionally distressed woman, and you thought I was easy prey?"

Ignoring that last comment, he asks, "You want something to drink?"

I nod, running my fingers over the edge of his couch as I follow behind him. "Whatcha got, Glasses?"

He pinches the bridge of his nose—something he seems to do quite often around me. "I'm not even wearing my glasses right now."

"So? Still a nerd either way."

"Red wine or beer?"

"Wine me," I demand, reaching my hand out as if he already has my glass ready.

Cooper's forearm is enchanting as he works the corkscrew with gentle pressure. His hands look strong. Not in the same way Dillon's are. Dil has calluses from playing guitar, but Cooper's look soft and smooth, like they would glide over my skin perfectly.

I take the glass of dark wine from him greedily and down it, not caring that my head is already swimming from the previous drinks and the sexy thoughts of Cooper running through my mind.

Cooper stands there, staring. Waiting for me to tell him what to do.

The glass clinks as I plop it in the sink. "Can I lie down?"

He sips on his water before responding, "Yeah." Angling his head in a "this way" gesture, he turns and strolls down the hallway back to what I suspect is his bedroom, and I follow a few steps behind.

His room is everything I expected it to be.

Plain and understated.

So perfect for Cooper.

His walls are a light, millennial gray that matches the gray blanket meticulously folded over his king-size bed. The walls are noticeably bare, and the only furniture adorning the space, other than his bed, is two nightstands and a tall dresser.

I stand quietly in the doorway as Cooper digs through his dresser, finding sweatpants and a T-shirt. He hands the clothes to me before showing me to the bathroom connected to his room.

"Thanks," I whisper, slipping through the door.

When I arrived at the chapel earlier and put my gown on, I asked my mother to place my clothes and things in her car to drop off at the hotel later. In the flurry of not having the night I had planned, I completely forgot about my shit and let my mom leave with everything, including my phone and a change of clothes.

Normally, I would've taken every opportunity to snoop in someone's bathroom, especially Cooper's. I would have crossed my fingers and hoped to find a prescription for Viagra and a box of extra-small condoms next to a tube of hemorrhoid cream. But not tonight.

Tonight, any petty thoughts of making fun of Cooper are missing.

Instead, my head is swimming with thoughts of how I barely managed to escape the worst mistake of my life.

While pulling out the remaining pins from my hair, I sneak a glance in the mirror. My perfect wedding dress still looks pristine. It wasn't marred by the day like I was. Hell, if it weren't for the glassiness and sadness in my eyes, I'd look like a blushing bride with my flushed cheeks.

Silk and lace slide over my skin as I pull off my wedding dress and leave it in a pile on the floor, then slip into the huge clothes Cooper loaned me. I'm practically drowning in his shirt and the pants. Yeah, those aren't going to work. I skip the pants, leaving on the shirt that falls to my knees and nothing else.

When I open the door, Cooper is sitting on the bed, waiting for me with a glass of water and two pills. His gaze falls to my bare legs, and he frowns.

Rude.

"Why no pants?"

"Why no regular-people-sized clothes?"

His warm hands graze mine, sending an electric pulse through me as I take the water and pills from him.

"My clothes are fine. I can't help that you are miniature."

"Lies. I am, like, five foot five. That's average."

"Sure it is."

I glare at him over the water before I swallow the pills and drain the glass, hating how sweet he can be at the same time as being an ass. Setting the empty glass down on the nightstand, I climb into the bed, burrowing myself in the middle of Cooper's massive bed. The subtle familiar scent of bergamot fills my nose.

"Where are you going to sleep?" I ask while fluffing the pillow behind my head.

"The couch is calling my name." He walks to the door, then hesitates for a moment before he looks back, opening his mouth like he wants to say something but doesn't. Instead, he just flicks off the lights.

"Goodnight, Cooper," I whisper as my heavy eyes close and exhaustion pulls me under.

The light from the window glares into my eyes, burning away the last bit of peaceful sleep I was holding on to. I roll, twisting the blankets over my head to block out the annoying brightness. A thrumming pain spears into my forehead with the movement, and I still.

Nope.

No more of that.

Fuck hangovers and their stupid symptoms.

I'm not moving another inch. Take that, consequences of my actions.

I'm seconds away from drifting back off when a loud clanging noise jolts me up, and the pain sears through my head again.

Cooper.

Slowly, I crawl out of the cocoon of blankets I've wrapped myself up in while sleeping, then shuffle down the hall to where the intoxicating smell of food is wafting from. It also happens to be the same place the head-splitting noise is coming from. Once in the kitchen, I find Cooper standing in front of the stove, hunched over and holding his head.

Sans glasses and hair unruly, Cooper is the picture of perfection, even when he looks like he's about to keel over.

I push that thought away, not needing my head to be clouded with thoughts of Cooper's hotness when I just dumped my fiancé at our wedding yesterday.

"You couldn't have waited to get up until a more humane time, could you, old geyser?" I groan, sliding onto one of the bar stools and lying my head on the island's cool stone.

He takes a deep breath, then exhales loudly. "It's two in the afternoon."

"Well... You could get some better curtains."

"And you could sign the marriage license like a normal person."

I glare at him, wishing his head would explode. "Remember that time you tried to kiss me?"

"Remember that time you *did* kiss me?" he shoots back. God, did I ever. It was the first night I had met him. I was beyond drunk on expensive baby-shower champagne, and he was the most attractive thing I had ever seen. It didn't help that he played white knight to me while our best friends went home together. I made my move the moment he pulled up in front of my house, practically eating his face. He had to pry me off him.

Like pulled away and pushed me at the same time to get me off him.

So naturally, I did the logical thing and scurried away as fast as I could, like a kid caught stealing an extra piece of cake.

I was humiliated.

Scratch that.

I'm *still* humiliated.

And I've been pretending it never happened ever since.

"Making up stories now? That's pretty pathetic. Almost childlike. Did you learn that move from some of your students before you abandoned them to become a finance bro?"

His nostrils flare and I know my hit landed. Turning back to the stove, he picks up the spatula, pushing food onto the two plates sitting on the counter beside him.

"Remind me why I let you stay with me?"

"'Cause the elderly always pity youths like me. Taking us under their wings and trying to mold and nurture us into well-rounded adults." I smile, taking the plate of greasy bacon and runny eggs from him.

"How many times do I have to tell you I'm only thirty-one, not eighty-one, so can you cut the shit?"

"Practically the same thing."

He sighs and sits beside me, shoving forkful after forkful of food into his mouth until his plate is empty.

I know why I'm being a grumpy bitch, but why the hell is he?

Normally, I poke, he pokes.

I jab, he jabs.

We do this dance back and forth until one of us, aka me, is crowned victor. But today he just gave up. Hardly a fun fight.

Chapter Four

Cooper

The ride back to Sutton's house is painful.

Excruciating, even.

She hasn't spoken a word to me except for a semi-polite yes or no after breakfast, which is starting to creep me out.

Sutton isn't nice or polite.

No, my Sutton is a force of nature to be reckoned with. She gives me more shit than I even know how to handle, and I admire her for it.

Not that she's *my* anything.

But this demure, quiet creature beside me is something I have no idea what to do with.

Snark and sass, I can handle anytime.

Quiet and letting me lead? Fucking weird.

I toy with the radio dial in the truck, switching the sensual sounds of Hozier to some backwoods country music that she hates. Hell, the only reason I have the station programmed into my truck is to annoy the shit out of her on the off chance I have to take her home.

The singer's twang fills the cab of the truck as he croons about his love of beer, cut of shorts, and God.

I glance in her direction, waiting on a bated breath for the insult she's sure to spit out at me as usual, but nothing comes.

Not a peep.

Sutton sits there without a sound. Not even an overexaggerated eye roll. Hell, she doesn't react at all.

Two songs play through without her acknowledging a thing.

I had to bite my tongue not to say something once the first ended.

"Fuck it," I gripe, turning the radio off and pulling off the side of the road. "What's wrong with you?"

"Hmm?" She turns to me. "What do you mean?"

"I mean this"—I gesture to her—"this silent and agreeable bull-shit you're doing."

Her brown eyes are full of that fire that I know and love. "I'm trying, Cooper."

"Trying what? To be a bigger pain in my ass than usual?"

Sutton's jaw drops. "Are you kidding me?"

"No, drop the act. It's weirding me out."

Shaking her head from side to side, she scoffs. "Of course, nothing I do is right. You don't like me as myself. You don't like me when I go out of my way to be agreeable. Why don't you just admit it already, Cooper, and make everyone's life easier? You don't like me."

Shock slams into my chest like she physically punched me, and I rear back at her words. That can't be what she thinks. Can it? For once, I'm cursing the large interior of my truck. I wish she was closer so I could tug her over to me and shake the crazy out of the woman. "You can't possibly think that?"

"Please take me home so we can both be put out of this misery already."

"Sutton—"

"Please."

I bite the inside of my cheeks and nod before pulling back out onto the road.

Five painful minutes later, I pull up and park in front of Sutton's trashed lawn. Beer bottles and cans litter almost every inch of the lawn, and the grass reeks of hops and vomit.

"Shit, Sutton." It's all I can get out as we make our way through the wrecked sidewalk to her door.

A sniffle sounds from her direction, and I look down to find her wiping away a tear.

"No, no, no. Please don't cry, Sut. I can't handle your tears."

She scrunches her face as if she's trying to hold back the tears filling her eyes from falling any further.

"Come here." I wrap my arms around her, and she buries her face into my chest. Her hands fisting the back of my shirt.

"I'm sorry," she weeps into me.

"Shhh," I say, rubbing circles into her back. "You have nothing to apologize for. It's going to be okay."

"How?"

"I'm not going to leave until we get this place picked up."

"You don't have to stay..."

I pull back so she has to look up at me. "Yes, I do. Friends don't let other friends clean up this kind of mess alone."

"But we aren't friends," she whispers, batting away yet another fallen tear.

I try to ignore the tightening in my chest at her words. "I might not be your friend, Sutton, but you're mine."

Her lips part a little at those words as she stares at me, stunned.

"Okay, now show me where the recycling bin is, and I will get started on the front lawn while you assess the damage within."

The recycling bin is overflowing by the time I have the front lawn cleared. And sweat drips from my brow as I shut off the water, having power washed the grass and pavement to the best of my ability before calling it quits.

I'm not sure if the scent of stale beer and vomit is gone or if I'm immune to it after the hour I spent ankle-deep in it.

"Sutton?" I call out while walking through the front door to her living room, which smells just as bad as the lawn had. Trash bags are piled by the door, filled with aluminum cans and, sadly, the remnants of pillows and picture frames.

"Sut?" I call again.

"In the guest bathroom," she yells from the back of the house.

Navigating my way around the bags of trash, I make a mental note to pile whatever didn't fit in her garbage bin into my apartment dumpster to get rid of. When I reach the back bathroom, I find Sutton on her hands and knees, scrubbing at the floor with her ass pointed straight at me.

Gone are my oversized sweats she had worn home. No, now she's in nothing but a pair of my boxer briefs and a tiny sports bra that leaves little to the imagination.

I swallow the lump that always seems to form in my throat when I see her.

Pushing aside my growing arousal, I clear my throat. "Lawn's finished."

She pauses her scrubbing, lifting onto her knees and turning her head to look at me. God, she is beautifully sinful-looking in that position. My mind reels with images of her on her knees before me like that, but with my cock getting ready to be buried between those two plush lips.

"Were you able to remove the skeevy slut aroma?" she asks.

I shake off the fantasy of her as I lean against the doorframe. "Unfortunately, the scent of desperation and poor decisions might linger until the next rain."

"Shit," she groans. "Why couldn't Dillon have trashed the honeymoon suite like the idiot I expected him to be?"

"That's Dillon the Douche for you, always keeping you disappointed."

She lets out an exhausted, halfhearted chuckle. "That he does."

"Where do you want me now, boss?"

"Cooper, you really don't have—"

The sound of the front door slamming and glass bottles crashing makes us jump.

We start toward the living room, only to find Dillon relaxing with his eyes closed, his ass on the couch and his feet propped up on the coffee table as if the place isn't completely ruined by his dumb choices.

I lean in closer and whisper, "Speak of the douche."

Sutton chuckles beside me as said douche opens his eyes and looks in our direction.

"Of fucking course he's here," he grumbles. He lifts his feet from the coffee table and places them on the floor as he stands. "I should have known it was about him."

Sutton's forehead scrunches in confusion. "Excuse me?"

I don't like it, not one goddamn bit.

But I hold still. Waiting, watching.

Sutton isn't a damsel. She isn't weak. She doesn't need me to fight her battles. And she sure as shit doesn't need me to make the situation worse by stepping in to help.

But that doesn't mean I won't the moment he looks like he's going to take it too far.

I'm ready for whatever that tool throws her way.

Sutton stays silent. Not moving an inch. Not showing one ounce of guilt for leaving him or fear of his reaction. No, she is a stone wall before him, unbreakable.

"Him. Cooper. The smarter-than-me asshole you've been secretly carrying on with." Dillon's eyes widen as he looks at me, then back at her. "Are you fucking him?"

Sutton's eyelashes flutter as she blinks.

Aiming a glare our way, he pops his knuckles. "You are, aren't you? He's the real reason you wouldn't sign the damn wedding papers. I'm right, aren't I?"

Unease spreads through my veins like wildfire at his behavior.

"Answer me, you bitch," he demands, his voice filling the room.

"That's it." I move to step between them, when Sutton steps forward, cutting me off by laying her hand across my chest.

"You finally figured it out. Congrats. Maybe you aren't as dumb as you think you are," she taunts with a laugh.

Huh?

I open my mouth to object, but Sutton lifts her hand, silencing me.

Surely she isn't insinuating what I think she is?

I freeze in place.

She did not just lie and use me as her scapegoat.

"I knew it." He spins on his heels and grabs a beer bottle from the table full of them, then chugs down the remaining liquid. "I asked you if there was anything going on multiple times, and you told me no. So I guess you're a cheating whore *and* a liar now, aren't you, Sutton?"

Still reeling from being officially dragged into their shitstorm via a lie, I don't have time to process the fact that he has questioned her about me on more than one occasion.

"I'm so glad I cheated on you during every out-of-town gig."

Despite the anger roaring through my chest and the bitter disgust coating my tongue, Sutton stands there showing no emotion. Not giving him a damn inch. She might not want to be with him anymore, but that sure as shit doesn't mean it doesn't sting to hear he was sleeping with other women.

"I mean, come on, Sut, you wouldn't even let me hit it raw." He gawks at me as if it's some insane thing. "Not even once."

"And it sounds like she was pretty fucking smart not to since you've been cheating on her this entire time."

He huffs out a laugh. "She letting you ride bareback?"

I ball my fist, taking a step forward, but Sutton steps in front of me, placing a hand on my chest. "He's not worth it," she mutters to me before turning to face him while leaning against my chest. "And for the record. I always let Cooper fuck without protection. I love it when his cum coats my insides."

This *fucking* woman.

My dick hardens at her words. The image filling my every thought until Dillon's red-hot rage boils over. He picks up a vase from the table and throws it against the wall, and I instinctively wrap my arms around Sutton and pull her closer to me.

"Get out," I shout, my menacing voice echoing off the walls.

"This isn't the end. I'll be back," he seethes before stomping out the front door. I don't move until I hear the rev of his car and watch through the window as he tears away down the road.

Sutton shakes as she clings to me for support.

"It's okay. It's going to be okay."

"How?" she cries. "How is this okay?"

"He's an asshole. But he's gone. This is *your* home. I'll help you pack up his stuff, and we will leave it out for him on the lawn."

"Okay."

I tip her head back until her beautiful brown eyes are staring up at me. "You aren't alone in this. You have me, Viv, and Nate. Speaking of which, why aren't those two assholes over here helping us clean this mess?"

"I gave them my honeymoon last night."

"You did what?"

"I transferred everything over to them." She shrugs as if what she did was nothing and not something extremely thoughtful. "They deserve a getaway."

"How did you do that without me noticing?"

"You didn't notice they were a little extra horny for each other?"

"Ugh. No. Those two are always all over each other, especially after a couple of drinks."

"Well, it was more than that. They knew they were going to get some extra romance on this weekend. And it brought out their inner wanton sluts."

I laugh. "Wanton sluts?"

"It's the perfect word to describe them."

"No it's not."

"Yes it is."

"No," I argue. "They are over-the-top, outrageously in love."

"Like I said, wanton sluts."

Chapter Five

Sutton

Hours later, the house is almost clean, and the fresh scent of Pine-Sol fills the air instead of body odor and bodily fluids.

My back aches from all the bending and scrubbing. I'm dying to take a bath, but both tubs are currently undergoing a bleaching of the century, and I can't even step foot into either bathroom without goggles or my eyes burn. So a bath is out of the question.

Cooper is working on hosing down the backyard and salvaging as many of my gnomes as he can.

A door slams, startling me, and I drop my mop. With a huff, I bend over to pick it up, but when I stand, I come face-to-face with Dillon.

"Let's stop playing whatever game this is," he demands, moving closer.

"I'm not playing a game."

He dips his head, trailing his nose along the column of my neck in a motion that used to set me on fire.

Now it makes my skin crawl.

Backed against the wall, I'm completely trapped by the man I once thought could be *the one*.

I'm not scared of Dillon.

Not really.

He's never been violent.

Verbally idiotic? Yes.

But I've always given it back to him as good as he gave it.

It's comical now that I've ended the relationship just how open my eyes are to the shit show that was us.

We were toxic.

Constantly fighting over everything.

The only thing we had going for us was our sexual relationship, and even that had been strained in the end.

So to have me pinned against the wall, rubbing up against me, trying to tempt me, is laughable.

It also makes me want to cry. Not out of embarrassment for him. But for myself. How could I have been with someone like this? Worse, how could I think marrying him was a good idea? I hate that I ever thought he was what I deserved.

And I hate that a small part of me still craves the chaos from our relationship.

God, my brain is the worst.

"You know you still want me." He trails his fingers up my arm and across my chest.

My breathing is erratic. Not from lust or temptation. But from anger. This man has done nothing but insult me, calling me every nasty name in the book since I called things off. He has proven to be a cheater and a liar. And he still thinks putting the moves on me is going to work?

As *fucking* if.

No, I'm pissed.

Like, about-to-kick-him-in-the-balls pissed.

So pissed the man would probably never have kids, pissed.

I turn my head away, looking out the window to the backyard. Maybe if I ignore his grabby hands, he will tire out and leave.

I don't have time to test that theory, though, because the front door bursts open and slams against the drywall, possibly even denting it.

"Get the hell off her." Cooper's deep voice cuts through the room as he storms over to where I'm flat against the wall. He yanks Dillon off me and tosses him to the side like he weighs nothing.

And hot damn if I'm not turned on by it.

He did it so effortlessly, it has me wondering what else he could do with that amount of ease.

Maybe toss me about in the bedroom.

I bet he could switch positions without slipping out with the grace of a porn star.

Damn it, Sutton. *No.* Stop thinking about Cooper that way.

It's *Cooper.*

The stupidly tall guy who shot you down the first time you met him.

Cooper Shaw, the same guy who makes fun of your favorite movies. The same man whose arms are looking mighty strong all of a sudden.

Oh fudge.

"You okay?" he asks me, stooping a little to look me in the eyes.

I blink away all lusty thoughts of him. "Yeah, Dillon was just—"

"Being a douche? Yeah, I could tell."

A smile tugs at my downturned lips. "Does he know how to be anything but?"

"Nah, it's his only setting."

Dillon scoffs, interrupting our fun. "You two are assholes. You know that?"

"Sure we are, douche." Cooper rolls his eyes and pulls me into his side as he spins to face the man who has outstayed his welcome.

Dillon's anger flashes across his face for a second as he stares at where Coop is holding me, but then he schools his expression into a mask of indifference. "You should know, Cooper, our girlfriend here was looking mighty thirsty moments ago... For me."

"Ew," I scoff.

"It's true," he continues on, "She was practically begging me to screw her."

I grind my teeth together. *That slimy, lying piece of shit.*

"Oh really? Is that why she looked like she was about to throw up as you had her trapped against a wall?"

"She wasn't trapped..."

"Make her feel uncomfortable like that again and I will break your arm."

I wrap my arm around Cooper's middle, grasping his shirt in my hands. He doesn't have to do this. In fact, I don't want him to do this.

"Coop, it's fine. Dillon was just about to leave, for good. Weren't you, Dillon?"

"Nah," Dillon replies.

"Yes you are. I want you to leave. Cooper wants you gone. No one wants you here."

"Well, that's too fucking bad for you and your new boy toy, Sutton, because I'm not leaving."

"Yes. Yes you fucking are."

Shaking his head, he laughs.

This dirty, two-timing son of a bitch has the nerve to laugh in my face.

"Yeah, that's not going to happen."

"I'll call the police."

"Try it, baby."

What the hell is going on here? Why would he encourage me to do something that might actually affect him? I eye him suspiciously.

Picking up my phone, he clears his throat.

"Oh, and don't forget to tell them whose name is on the lease. Or should I say *names*?"

My heart drops.

No. No. No.

How could I have been so stupid? How could I forget that I added this motherfucker to the lease two months ago?

A slimy smile pulls at his lips as he watches the realization dawn on me. "Oh, did you forget that I am legally allowed to live here?"

"I'll break the lease."

"You do that." He winks.

Anger zapping through my veins, I storm out of the room and call my landlord. It shouldn't be an issue. I've been renting this house for almost five years now. I never call and complain. I never ask him to do anything for me. I keep the place tidy and pay my rent on time every month. I am the perfect tenant. So imagine my surprise when he says, "Sure, but it will be five thousand dollars, and you will be forfeiting your security deposit."

It's a goddamn highway robbery.

I try to reason with him and explain that I don't have that kind of money.

But he doesn't care, saying it's just business, and it's up to me how badly I want my ex to leave.

Fuck. Fuck. Fuck.

There has to be some way to get this asshole out. Because I'm sure as shit not going to pay that ungodly amount.

My brain practically comes to a screeching stop.

Cooper.

It could work.

No, he'll never agree to it... But if he did...

Dillon hates Cooper. It's perfect. He'll never want to stay if Cooper is around.

Walking back into the kitchen, I find Cooper and Dillon sitting across from each other, giving the death stare. The tension between them is as heavy as usual, but this time, it feels different.

My little lie about being with Cooper has worked, and he's going along with it at the moment. So here goes nothing.

Dillon turns to me. "So how did that go?"

I hold my tongue but aim a hostile glare his way.

He snorts. "That bad? Looks like you're stuck with me, Sut."

"Get the hell out of her house."

"You need to mind your own business," he snaps at Cooper before turning to face me. "And no, I don't think I will." He stands, scraping his chair against the hardwood floors before grabbing yet another beer from the fridge and stalking off into the garage.

Not even a minute later, the sound of his guitar fills the house as he strums the tune of my least favorite songs of his.

Cooper flinches at the noise. "How in the hell did you put up with shitty music?"

"Honestly?" I shrug. "I have no idea."

"At least now you don't have to pretend to like it anymore," he offers with a smile.

"One upside."

I slump into the chair Dillon just vacated. "Ugh," I groan. "This situation is a nightmare."

"What did the landlord say?"

"Basically that I'm shit out of luck unless I want to pay him an obscene amount of cash and leave altogether."

"That's bullshit."

"I know."

"So what's the plan?"

I peek up at him from under my lashes to find him staring at me intently. "For you"—I point at him—"to move in with me"—I turn my finger at my chest—"and pretend to be my boyfriend to scare him off," I rush out.

"Come again?"

Chapter Six

Cooper

It's official, Sutton has lost her damn mind.

I always thought the woman was crazy. But this is next level.

It's one thing to pretend for a few minutes in front of the dickwad. But to pretend to be her live-in boyfriend? That's straight insanity.

Even if it weren't, it'd be a horrible idea.

We are like oil and water.

Every time we're near each other, we do nothing but fight. No one would ever believe it.

Well, Dillon the Douche did. But he isn't exactly the brightest bulb in the box.

Yeah, Sutton and I have this sexual tension between us that feels electric at times, but that isn't enough to build a fake relationship on, is it?

After Dillon stormed out and Sutton laid out her crazy idea, I needed a drink and space to think.

I got one of those things as I hopped into my truck, followed by a silent Sutton, and drove us to the closest bar I could find.

There's something about sticky floors and cracked vinyl that always brings me peace. Or maybe it's the alcohol that always accompanies these types of environments.

I order myself a beer and a stupidly sour lemon drop for Sutton. Grabbing our drinks, I turn and find her sitting in a booth near the back of the bar.

Soft rock filters through the speakers as I slide into the seat across from her and silently pass her the yellow concoction. Her brown eyes sparkle at the sight of her favorite drink.

Her golden-blond locks fall in front of her face as she leans forward to capture the tiny straw between her lips.

I take a large gulp of my beer, letting the cool liquid and flavor fill my senses before I plop my bottle back down and gawk at her. "You're crazy."

"Crazy smart," she sasses back at me with big puppy-dog eyes.

I shake my head at her hopeful stare. "It would never work."

"It would. Please, Cooper, please."

"What's in it for me?"

"What do you mean?"

"What do you mean, what do I mean?" I ask incredulously. "What do I get out of pretending to be your boyfriend?"

"Besides a clear conscience that you helped me get rid of a loser from my life?"

"Yeah," I scoff. "Besides that?"

"I don't know. Street cred?"

"*Street cred*?"

"Yeah, you get to claim you bagged a hottie like me. That will definitely throw you in a higher league of women."

I stare her down, an unamused expression coloring my face, and she crumbles. "Please, Cooper. Anything. I'll do anything."

And just like that, it hits me.

"Okay, I pretend to be your live-in lover until Dillon moves out. But I need you to convince my coworkers and bosses that we are madly in love."

It's perfect. I can use Sutton to solidify the web of lies I created at work. The heaviness that's been sitting on my chest, thinking about how to explain why my girlfriend missed yet another party, finally lifts. Sutton's proposition might be the answer to all my prayers.

"Cooper, be for real. You want me to try to convince people who already know you that I could fall in love with you?" She laughs. "They'll never fall for it."

"Not with that shitty attitude, they won't."

"I'm sorry. Us fucking is one thing, but love?" she wheezes. "No one will buy it."

"Then I guess you're shit out of luck, Sut." Twisting my body, I move to slide out of the booth.

Sutton grabs my hand. Her laughter gone. "I'll do it."

I quirk an eyebrow at her. "You'll do it?"

"Yes."

"You know that means you'll have to be nice to me, right?"

"Psh. We will have a love filled with teasing. It's our foreplay."

"Is it?"

"In the act, yes."

"So it's a deal?"

She sticks her hand out for us to shake on it.

This is a horrible idea... Logically, I know there's a huge chance this will all blow up in our faces. But my insides are vibrating with excitement at the chance to sell my lie as well as have an excuse to be near her.

I place mine in hers and squeeze. "It's a deal."

Sutton practically squeals with enthusiasm as she bounces in front of me. "Thank you, thank you, thank you, Cooper. You won't regret this. I am going to be the best fake out-of-your-league girlfriend you've ever had."

"You are going to be the *only* fake girlfriend I've ever had."

She eyes me with disbelief. "I highly doubt that."

When I don't budge, she flashes me that beautiful smile. "Come on, grumpy pants, you are a total nerd."

"Your point?"

"That you have most likely been this way your entire life. Am I correct?"

"Yes." I grit my teeth together.

"So it's safe to say you probably made up a fake girlfriend or two in high school, because I refuse to believe you have always been this hot."

My face lights up. "You think I'm hot?"

"You have a certain appeal," she says before taking a sip of her drink. "I mean, I don't see it, but I know your nonsexual life partner Nate does, and he obviously isn't an idiot when it comes to looks. Just look at that smokeshow of a ginger goddess he gets to call his wife."

"How is it you can insult and compliment me at the same time."

She beams again. "It's a gift."

I rub at my temple. "How is this going to work, anyway."

"Easy, you will pack a bag tonight and play house for a couple of days until Dillon hightails it back to the heavily smoke-ridden garage he climbed out of."

"I meant logically. Like, where am I sleeping? And will we have to hold hands and kiss?"

"Are you asking if we are going to have sex?"

Amber liquid flies across the table onto Sutton's face and hair as I choke on my beer. "Oh shit," I say, wiping the alcohol from my mouth. "I'm sorry, Sut. I—"

"Got a little excited about the thought of blowing something else all over me? I get it," she says, grabbing a napkin to clean her face off.

"Damn it, Sutton, you can't keep making comments like that."

"Why not? Besides, you're the one who brought up sex, not me."

"No, I sure as shit didn't, miss pervy."

"I'm not the perv. You're the perv."

"So mature, Sutton. What's next? 'I'm rubber, you're glue—'"

"You wish you could rub your glue on me."

"See?" I toss my hands up. "This will never work. You can't stop your stupid taunts for a minute to have a conversation about me doing you a favor."

"Oh, so now screwing me would be a favor. As if I am below you."

"Stop putting words in my mouth and listen to me, you infuriating woman."

Her eyes widen, but she shuts her mouth.

"I meant, how much of a show are we going to be putting on? And are we sleeping, sleeping, as in eyes closed, brains shut off, in the same bed?"

Her shoulders heave in annoyed defeat. "Yes. To make it convincing, I need you to sleep in my room with me. If you don't, he is going to weasel his way into the bedroom, probably while I am sleeping, and I don't feel like waking up to his dick poking me in the back."

"We are getting a lock installed on your door tonight. I don't care if I am there or not. That little shit isn't coming near you, awake or asleep. Understood?"

"Yes, Daddy."

I groan, frustrated that her smart-ass mouth has my dick twitching and she couldn't care less. Not wanting to give her comment any attention, I continue on. "Okay, what about outside of your bedroom? Do you think we will need to put on a show?"

She shrugs. "Honestly, he thought something was going on this entire time, and we clearly act like we hate each other, so we should be good to be normal."

"You sure?"

"Eh, maybe you could sit close to me on the couch while we binge SVU at night. Play up the occasional pet name. But other than that, I think we should be good."

"SVU?"

"Mariska is a national treasure, and you know it."

I nod. "I would never say anything negative about her holiness, Olivia Benson."

"You know SVU?"

"Oh, my dear simple-minded friend." I pat her hand. "You are looking at the owner of all twenty-five seasons on DVD and digitally."

"Shut up." She leans forward. "How did I not know this about you?"

"Um, because you never ask me anything. You only make fun of me."

She bounces a little in her seat again. "Oh my God, I think I'm actually excited for our sleepover."

After our drinks, we stop by my house to water my plants and grab some clothes, toiletries, and other essentials before heading back to Sutton's for the night. I hadn't thought much about our arrangement other than the overnight items I would need to bring with me to go straight to work in the morning.

But the moment we step into her house again, it all becomes real.

Sutton walks ahead of me, beckoning with her hand for me to follow. "This way, my lover."

"Lover?"

She shushes me with a cutting glare, placing her finger over her lips while ducking her head into the guest room, then the bathroom down the hall, before pulling me into her bedroom and shutting the door behind us.

"Yes, lover. We want Dillon to believe this charade, don't we?"

I laugh. "And you think calling me *lover* is going to get the job done? Come on, Sutton, I thought you were crazier than this."

She rears back, her brow crinkling with confusion. "What's that supposed to mean?"

"It means that the woman who once dressed as a man to spy on her best friend should know better ways to fool an idiot like Dillon than the word lover."

She rolls her eyes. "Whatever. Are you going to wear that to bed?" she asks, gesturing to my jeans and tennis shoes before climbing into the bed and pulling the covers up to her chin.

I shake my head, ridding myself of the inappropriate and inconvenient thoughts of her barely there pajamas.

Toeing off my shoes, I strip out of my jeans and pull my shirt over my head, leaving myself in a pair of black boxer briefs, which now feel entirely too thin to be sleeping next to her in.

Darkness covers the room as I turn off the bedside lamp and slide under the blankets, lying on my back beside her.

Sutton rolls onto her side and faces me, tucking her hands under her head.

"Do you think we can pull it off?"

Ignoring her question, I stare up at the ceiling. Glow in the dark stars dot the entire space, giving the room a slight green gleam. "What's with the childlike ceiling aesthetic?"

She lifts her shoulders in a halfhearted shrug. "It's something I've done in every bedroom I've had since I was a kid."

"Do you like space?"

"Not particularly."

"Are you scared of the dark?"

"No."

"Then why?" It seems like such a weird choice for her girly French provincial room.

"Nostalgia, maybe. It's something constant in my life. A reminder that the stars always shine. Even from millions of miles away, they are the same and different at the same time. They are a moment captured in time. My ceiling is a bit of my childhood captured for me to enjoy forever."

"That was entirely confusing and logical at the same time."

"Sometimes the youths can teach their elders."

Dragging my hand through my hair, I blow out a puff of air. "Just when I thought you were being normal, you hit me with an old joke."

"I can't stop, Cooper. It's ingrained in me, just like the gray hairs sprouting from your scalp."

Instinctively, I touch my hair, wanting to cover the exact streak she's referring to.

"Stop," she whispers. "It's kind of hot."

Eyeing her suspiciously, I weigh her words.

Sutton giggles. "I'm serious, you are going to be a silver fox someday."

"Are you saying that I'm a fox right now?"

"Don't let it get to that prematurely graying head of yours," she says sleepily. "Goodnight, *lover*."

"Night, Sut."

⚘

I've learned two things after one night of sharing a bed with Sutton Hale.

One, the woman is the biggest blanket hog I have ever met. I don't think I have ever frozen that much. And that's saying something. I once had to share a singular throw blanket with Nate while sleeping on a concrete floor at a house party in the middle of winter.

And two, Sutton has a case of somniloquy.

Yep. The woman is a big, fat sleep talker.

Not that I could actually take advantage of her sleep musings last night while I was shivering and shaking, freezing my balls off in her tundra of a bedroom.

I had just fallen asleep when Sutton's alarm went off, startling my tired self awake from my two blissful minutes of sleep.

Sutton stretches out, not caring that I'm beside her, punching me in the jaw as she does.

Okay, maybe she forgot in her sleepy state, but it felt intentional to me.

I groan in pain, slapping my hand to my now-throbbing jaw as she slips her scantily clad ass out of bed with a small "oops" before padding into the bathroom, closing the door behind her.

The sound of the shower and Creed spills through the cracks of the door, followed by what can only be described as the screeching that a cat makes when it's cornered in an alley, ready to fight to the death over a piece of thrown-out chicken.

Sweet baby Jesus, Sutton can't hold a single note of the '90s rock tune she's attempting to assault my ears with.

I pull a pillow over my head, hoping to block out the poison that is close to making my poor ears bleed.

Twenty minutes.

Twenty painful minutes, and she still isn't done.

No, she's getting louder, a feat I didn't even think was possible. But Sutton lives to amaze me.

But the longer I wait, the more the need to pee pounds at my bladder.

I heave myself out of bed, needing to answer nature's call before it answers me, aka before I piss myself.

Down the hall, I try the guest-bathroom door handle, turning it without luck. I turn it again and rest my head on the door right as it opens. Catching myself on the frame, I come face-to-face with Dillon.

"Cooper."

"Dillon." I glare back. "You done in there?"

"Oh, do you need in here while Sutton takes her hour-long morning shower?"

"Yeah," I let out a relieved breath. "I tried to wait her out, but—"

"She's taking forever?"

I huff a laugh. "So can I?" I attempt to step forward, only for Dillon to step in front of me.

"Ooh," he hisses through his teeth. "I'm actually not done."

"Seriously?"

He tilts his head and gives me a smile that has chills dancing across my skin. "Seriously." And then he shuts the door in my face.

That feels right.

That's the douche I've come to know.

I make my way back to Sutton's room and bang on the bathroom door.

"Hurry up, Sutton. I'm about to piss myself," I yell through the door.

"No can do, Cooper-roo," she shouts back.

Fuck it, I'm going in.

I place my hand on the knob and almost sob when it turns and the door opens.

Steam rolls out as I cover the side of my face closest to the shower and walk to the toilet, no longer caring about the weirdness that is me peeing while Sutton is in the room. I'm sure as hell not going to think about the fact that Sutton is less than five feet away from me, naked and dripping wet.

No, no, no.

I will not let the ridiculously infuriating temptress that is Sutton fill my mind with her folly.

I will stay strong.

And by strong, I mean I will continue to avoid looking in the shower's direction and will definitely not think about how the woman I agreed to fake date is currently sudsing up her body in the same vicinity as me.

Stop it.

Pee, you need to pee.

I lift the lid quickly, banging it on the back of the porcelain.

"What the—Cooper," Sutton yelps. "Get out."

"No can do," I tell her with my back facing her, pulling down the front of my underwear and letting go. Sweet relief fills me as I empty my bladder. Seriously, there is nothing like that first morning urination. I could bask in the elation of this moment forever if Sutton's shrill voice didn't ring out, interrupting me.

"Oh my God, you perv. Are you peeing? You are, aren't you? Ew. Why, Cooper, why?" she whines.

"Maybe if someone hadn't been taking an hour-long shower"—I pull my shorts back up—"I wouldn't have had to barge in on you to relieve myself."

"Gross. Don't say relieve."

"Now who's the perv, thinking about me relieving myself while you're in the shower," I tsk. "Naughty, naughty."

"As if I would ever—" Her words are cut off with a shriek that most definitely woke the neighborhood dogs as I flush the toilet.

Chuckling to myself, I move to the sink and quickly wash my hands, averting my gaze from the mirror directly in front of me with its fogged-up reflection of Sutton's naked body behind me.

I try my best not to look, but... I'm only human. A human man. And that pretty much means my dick will take over all logic at some point.

Some could argue it isn't my fault that my gaze trails up to the mirror for a second—more like a millisecond—to see the sensual outline of her curves; it's my biology's fault.

Yep. I blame science.

That pesky subject tried to screw me over years ago while growing up, and here it is, striking again, trying to make my life a living hell of hormones.

I walk out of the bathroom and immediately focus on getting ready for work. Right as I finish buttoning my crisp white shirt, the bathroom door bursts open to reveal Sutton wrapped in a large, fluffy pale-purple robe with a matching towel twisted on her head. Her skin is flushed red from the shower.

"Well, well, well. If it isn't the shower peeper."

"Don't you mean pee-er?"

She cocks her head to the side, causing her towel to slip slightly. She catches it with her hand, righting it but keeping her head to the side as she narrows her gaze on me. "No, I don't think I do, Tom?"

"Tom?" I ask, genuinely confused by the name. Did all that hot water fry her brain? "Should I call 911 and report a possible stroke?"

"Yeah, sure, do that. I would love to tell them all about how I caught you creeping into my bathroom with your hand in your pants while I was showering."

"I didn't see anything," I growl defensively.

She shrugs a single shoulder, walking to her closet before looking over her shoulder. "Sure you didn't."

I grab my tie off the bench in front of her bed, and for a brief moment, I think of all the things I could do with this tie.

Like strangle her to shut her up.

Or gag her and bind her to the bed.

Get it together, Cooper.

Now is not the time to think about this. No, now is the time to finish getting ready for work and then hopefully leave early. The thought of hanging out here before work has my skin crawling, but I will do it if Dillon is still here. There is zero chance I'm leaving Sutton alone with that creep after yesterday. I don't care if she doesn't think he would get violent. I'm not going to chance it.

So, unfortunately for me, I'll be sticking around until either Sutton leaves for the day or the guitar-strumming douche disappears.

Passing Sutton, I grab my bag of toiletries and head into the bathroom to finish getting ready. I make quick work of washing my face and brushing my teeth.

As I'm swishing water in my mouth, Sutton joins me at the sink, bending to retrieve her blow dryer from the cabinet. It's like nothing I've ever seen. It has a hairbrush-like extension attached to it that she drags through her wet strands.

I stand by in fascination as she makes quick work of her long locks and then moves on to her makeup.

Our eyes meet in the mirror, and Sutton quirks an eyebrow as she pauses her movements. "Do you always watch women shower and put their makeup on?"

"Nope, you're the first."

She glances down as her lips lift in a small grin. "I don't know whether to be flattered or concerned."

"Don't limit yourself to one emotion. Why choose when you could be both."

She snorts, her hands fidgeting with two lipsticks. "Which should I wear?" She holds up two almost identical shades of red. I pull both from her and examine the label at the bottom, reading the names of the shades.

"Maneater or Blood of Thy Enemy."

She gives me a single nod. "Which should I wear today?"

"Maneater seems fitting."

She smirks before swiping the color over her plush lips, rubbing them together before leaving me standing alone in the bathroom.

Grabbing one of the tubes she discarded, I remove the cap and twist the base to have the color appear just as she had done.

I lift the red shade to the mirror and hesitate for a split second. Sutton will probably hate this, but there's always the chance it could make her smile. And as much as she drives me crazy, I love nothing more than making that woman smile.

Chapter Seven

Sutton

I'm dreading going to work today.

I know I'll be asked a thousand questions about how the wedding went.

And I have no idea how to answer them.

Usually, I'd bullshit my way around a problem or a question I don't want to answer.

But there isn't a way out of this one.

Everyone in the building knows I was getting married last weekend.

They'll definitely notice when I walk in without a ring on that particular finger. And that I'm back a day early.

My dread was—and still is—running so high this morning that I burned myself not once but twice with my curling iron as I got ready and then completely skipped my normal cup of coffee.

Cooper thought I should take the days I already had scheduled off to plan out how to handle everything.

But I knew that wasn't how it would work. It would just be a few extra days for me to dread the inevitable.

And this morning with Cooper and Dillon was nothing short of a nightmare. While Cooper, being his normal, annoying self, acted as a shield from Dillon, I still had to put up with his constant questions and judgment of my life. And don't get me started on the video game console he just *had* to bring with him when we went to pick up more of his things for his extended stay. The man was already glued to the screen by the time I walked out the front door, taking advantage of the fact that he doesn't have to be at work until an hour after me.

My fingers tap on my steering wheel the entire drive to the office. When I pull into my assigned spot in the parking garage, I place the car in park. Closing my eyes, I grip the wheel as tight as I can.

You've got this. You are Sutton fucking Hale. You convinced a passionate man to play decoy boyfriend. You are capable of wonderful things. A few nosy Nellies are nothing. You've got this.

I open my eyes and release the steering wheel. My stomach churns and my heart feels like it's pounding so hard that it should be visible through my shirt.

Balling my hands into fists, I place them on my hips in a superwomanesque pose that Vivian taught me. She said it helps to increase confidence or something like that. Honestly, I didn't listen at the time; I was too busy laughing at her as she stood in front of me looking like she was about to save the city from an alien invasion.

But I'm desperate, so I hold the ridiculous pose for a solid four minutes as my racing heart slows down.

I've got this.

Glancing in the rearview mirror, I give my hair one last fluff.

At least I look good.

My hair and makeup are immaculate. I'm wearing the sexiest pantsuit I own without being indecent. And my heels are the highest I've ever worn.

I look better than good. I look hot.

Grabbing my purse off the passenger seat, I turn and open my door. Somehow, I manage to make it to the elevator without seeing one person from my company, which is a relief. The ride up is filled with people getting on and off. Some I recognize, others I don't. I smile at them all and try to ignore the obvious stares at my left hand—at the absence of a ring.

I'm only three floors away when the elevator opens and a woman from accounting walks on. Her eyes beam when she sees me. "Sutton, you're back early. Was the wedding as beautiful as you imagined?"

I nod. "It was, and you know there's no rest for the wicked, unfortunately."

The elevator numbers climb as we lift a floor closer.

"You'll have to show me pictures of the floral arrangements. My daughter is looking for a florist for her wedding and needs to see the big picture."

"I can do that." I don't mind showing pictures of the flowers and wedding setup. It was beautiful, and the people who worked endlessly on it deserve the praise.

Finally, the doors open to our floor, and I walk out as fast as I can without looking suspicious.

Keeping my head high and my eyes focused on where I'm going, I scurry through the main lobby, rushing past the hag Hadlee's desk and through the crowded cubicles. I don't glance in anyone's direction. But I can feel all of their eyes on me. Burning through me like lasers. Quickly, I drop my lunch off in the break room fridge before rushing back to the elevator and heading down to my office one floor below. When I finally reach my office, I close the door. Then throw my purse on the filing cabinet as I round my desk to slink into my chair. I bury my face in my hands and let out a silent scream.

A ping sounds from my purse. Followed by another and another, drawing my attention away from my meltdown.

I groan as I side-eye my purse from across the room before sliding out of my chair and onto the ground to crawl across the floor and grab it.

I'm not proud of the crawling. Add it to the pile of other things I'm not proud of.

Grabbing my purse off the cabinet, I dig inside for my phone. The screen lights up as I pull it out, finding the texts are all from the same person.

Cooper

You've got this.

Never forget that you are 100% terrifying. A little office gossip is nothing. Go out there and scare them shitless.

Also, if it helps, you looked smoking hot today.

My phone dings again with another message from him.

> Not in a pervy way. More like an appreciative way.

A laugh bursts through my lips. *What a goober.*

> It's fine. I'll take both the pervy and appreciative compliment.

> And thank you, Cooper. I needed that.

I can do this.

I lift myself off the floor and return to my seat. I'll take Cooper's advice and make them terrified to ask me any questions.

The plan works for the most part. I manage to go all morning without another peep from anyone. Yeah, I get the occasional double take when they don't see a sparkle shining from my hand. But for the most part, people keep their mouths shut.

It's refreshing.

But sadly, it doesn't last.

I'm a couple of steps outside of the break room when I hear it.

"I heard she's already shacking up with another man."

"I heard that her new husband caught them in bed together."

"Well, I heard—"

"You heard wrong," I interrupt them. Every head swings in my direction. I proceed to walk to the microwave, taking out whatever they had heating that smells like day-old tuna, and place my chicken-and-rice casserole inside. I place the timer for two minutes and then take a deep breath before turning around.

Three sets of eyes are glued on me.

I smile. "Anything else you want to say—to my face this time?"

Two of the women at least have the decency to look ashamed as they avert their gazes to the table.

But not the office bitch, Hadlee. No, Hadlee smiles brightly right back at me.

I hold her gaze for a moment longer before turning back around and gathering packets of salt and pepper for my food.

"Actually," she says, her voice freezing me in my tracks.

Don't. Don't do it, I mentally scream at her. Don't. You. Dare.

I spin around to face her, quirking an eyebrow. "Yeah?"

Don't. Don't. Don't.

"Is it Cooper?"

My throat bobs as I swallow. "Why?"

Her long red nails drum against the table. "Oh, I don't know. I just thought you would want to know that he was with Sarah this weekend."

I blink. There's no way Cooper had been with that woman. He told us all that he was done with her months ago. And Coop doesn't lie... Or does he?

Shit.

She's good.

The witch has already planted a seed of doubt in my mind.

Heat fills my veins, and I use everything in me not to react.

"Oh, poor Sutton. Did you really think he was sitting around pining for you while you planned your wedding to another man?" Her evil laugh bounces around the small room, ringing in my ears.

Of course I didn't think that.

Cooper is my friend-ish.

There was no pre-wedding pining.

Or was there?

Why else would she bring it up unless she noticed pining?

Was there pining on his end?

I, for one, am one hundred percent sure there was no such pining on my end.

Nope. No pining or lusting at all.

She's still laughing when the microwave buzzes, my food finished heating up.

I gather my things. Not bothering to spare Hadlee another glance.

Rage boils in my stomach as I walk out of the break room and back to my office to eat my food in peace.

I stood up for her with Vivian. I've been nothing but kind to her. For what? She's still the same horrible, catty woman as always.

I guess being a mother hasn't changed her personality.

Closing my office door behind me, I set my food down on my desk and wait for it to cool off.

My fingers itch as I peer at my phone.

I want to call Vivian and question her about Cooper and if she thinks he was—or is—pining or if he's a secret liar. But I can't. She and Nate are currently hungover from the trunk load of booze they consumed on the mini honeymoon I gifted them over the weekend. And the only reason I know that is because she sent me a questionable voice message this morning where she proceeded to vomit a minute in before crying about how she is never drinking again.

Cursing myself, I pick up my phone and dial the one person who can put this issue to bed for me.

"Hello." Cooper's deep voice fills the line.

"Were you with Sarah this weekend?"

"Define with?"

I gasp. "I can't believe you. Here you are playing house with me when you were just with her."

"Sutton—"

"Don't 'Sutton' me, you shady manwhore."

"Sutton, stop. I bumped into the woman outside of the gym the morning of your non-wedding."

"Oh."

"Yeah, *oh*. What is this even about?"

"Hadlee said—"

"Hadlee?" he laughs. "There's your problem. You listened to that wicked woman."

I groan, "I know it was dumb, but she goaded me by basically saying you were dicking down Sarah instead of pining for me."

"Did you want me to be pining?"

"What—I—that's not the point, Cooper. She got in my head. She made me doubt things even when we aren't real."

"Take a deep breath, Sut. I'm not with Sarah. I haven't been with her in months. We ran into each other and spoke for less than a minute the other day. You have nothing to worry about."

"I'm not worried."

"Oh, really? Then what is this call about?"

"It's about the fact that an alleged dalliance between you and that woman could make us look less credible and, in turn, cause Dillon to never leave and make you look bad at work."

"Don't worry about me, Sutton. I will be okay. But more importantly, so will you. Now, next time anyone decides to talk to you like that, remember you are HR. You can write them up."

"Holy shit. I can write them up for bullying." I don't know why I hadn't thought of that before.

Cooper's laugh rings through the line. "Feel better?"

"Yeah. Thanks again, Coop."

"Any time."

Hanging up, I find a new sense of confidence. Cooper wasn't with the slimy Sarah, and no one can talk crap about me without risking my wrath.

Exhaustion seeps through my bones as I leave work. My entire drive home is done on autopilot. I honestly don't know how I make it home without wrecking into something, but here I sit in my car, decompressing, seeing that Dillon's van is still in the driveway. But beside it is Cooper's truck.

I don't even make it out of my car before Cooper opens the front door and walks out to me. He pulls my door the rest of the way open and wraps his arms around me.

I freeze at the contact for a moment before sinking into his warmth with a sigh. Thank God for him.

"How did you know this was exactly what I needed?" I ask him with my face smooshed into his neck as I hold tight, squeezing him as hard as I can.

"I just knew. I don't know how, but I did," Cooper says.

He unbuckles my seat belt and gently pulls me from the car. Instead of setting me down, he taps my thighs, and my legs automatically wrap around his waist.

He walks around to the other side of the car, opens the passenger door, and grabs my purse before carrying it and me into the house.

"You've got to be kidding me," Dillon yells as Cooper moves us past him in the living room and down the hall to my—I mean, *our* bedroom.

He still doesn't set me down. Instead, he sits with me still wrapped around him like a crazy person.

"You okay?" he murmurs.

I nod into his neck.

"Are you sure?"

This time, I let out a cry that is part frustration and part sadness.

Cooper's hands leave the back of my thighs, moving to my back, where he draws pictures.

After about five minutes, he asks me to guess what he drew.

"A fairy drowning in the middle of a shark-infested sky-rise pool," I answer.

He pulls back to look at my face. "That was oddly specific."

I wipe my nose on the back of my hand. "Did I get it right?"

He grimaces. "Not even slightly."

"Well, what was it?"

"It was you perched on the edge of a building, with your hair billowing in the wind, looking like an evil, hotter version of Batman."

"Draw another. But this time, make it what you would spend your money on if you were Batman."

His finger traces up and down my back, exciting and relaxing me with his touch.

Sutton

SOS!

Vivian

Our usual spot in thirty minutes?

Make it twenty, and I promise to buy you a muffin, muffin.

Your bribery is accepted.

Fifteen minutes later, Vivian walks into our favorite coffeehouse that used to be home to our hour-long breaks when we worked together.

My heart is still pounding in a panic-induced race like it has been since Cooper comforted me last night, and I knew the second I woke up that I needed my favorite sounding board, Viv.

I bounce in my seat as I wave her over to the table I secured us.

She beams at me as she catches my hand frantically beckoning her over.

Stopping two feet from the table, she glares at me. "Where is my muffin?"

"No time for food when I've made a horrible mistake."

She gasps and clutches her purse to her chest. "There is always time for food, Sutton. Always."

I grip her hand and pull her into the chair across from me. "You'll agree once you hear what I've done."

The scowl on Viv's face falls. "Don't tell me you got back together with Dillon?"

"What? No. Ew. I would never."

She crosses her arms, leveling me with a stare.

"Okay, fine. I have before. But not this time. It's *really* done."

"You better mean it."

"I do. Trust me, the last thing I want is to get back with Dillon Oak."

"Good. Now, what could you have possibly done other than the d-bag that would have you calling an SOS the moment I got back from your honeymoon?"

I gnaw on my bottom lip for a few seconds before squeezing my eyes shut and letting the words tumble out of my mouth. "Cooper and I are pretending to be together to get Dillon to leave me alone."

Her eyes widen as she leans in. "What was that?"

"Cooper is temporarily living with me, and we are pretending to be madly in love to trick Dillon into leaving."

She sits there silently, staring at me for a good thirty seconds—so long that I consider calling an ambulance for her, afraid I shocked the woman into an early grave. But that bubble bursts when she laughs.

No, not laughs. Cackles.

The bitch is bracing one arm on the table while the other rests on her stomach as she cackles like a wicked witch she's clearly channeling.

"It's not funny," I hiss.

"You're right. It's hilarious."

"Ha-ha," I mock her, leaning back against my chair. "Laugh it up, but I am in deep trouble here."

She wipes at her eyes, the bitch having laughed so hard she cried.

"If by 'in trouble' you mean at risk of finally admitting your feelings for Cooper, then yes, you are in deep trouble."

I scoff. "I have no feelings for that man, unless you're counting the ones of utter contempt."

"I'm not." She shimmies her shoulders. "I'm talking about feelings of the sexy variety."

"Psh, never have I ever had such feelings for that man."

Viv gives me a smile that screams "bless your heart" as she pats my hand. "Sure."

"I'm not lying."

"Okay."

"I'm not."

"I know," she agrees, which only spurs me to dig myself even deeper in my defensive trench.

"I'm not lying. I've never once thought about Cooper in a sexual way. Nope, not once. Not even that time he was super sweaty, and his shirt was stuck to his muscles while he helped you and Nate move in together."

Viv nods slowly as I continue on.

"Like I would ever be attracted to someone who looks like Clark Kent with those ridiculous glasses. I mean, does the man even need them? I swear he can see fine without them."

"Sutton."

"What? Do you think he is wearing contacts the other times? Or maybe he is risking all our lives driving around as blind as a bat without his four eyes?"

"Babe, you just said he looked like Superman."

I rear back. "No I didn't. I said Clark Kent."

Her eyes crinkle in the corners as her lips form a flat line of a smile. "Same person, honey, and you know it."

"Ugh, whatever. I didn't ask you to meet me here to argue. I needed your advice on what to do about this weird fake relationship bargain with Cooper."

"I'm going to give you the same sage advice you always give me when I come to you with man problems—"

"Vivian Fisher, I swear I will cunt punt you if you say what I think you're—"

"Fuck him."

I toss my hands up in the air. "And you did it. That's it. Stand up and ready your hoochie of a coochie for the hit."

Still sitting, she withdraws her arms from the table to cover her crotch. "There will be no snatch slaps today," she declares in a high-pitched voice that turns multiple heads in our direction.

I sneer at them all except for my favorite barista, Kevin.

No, Kevin gets an apologetic smile and will soon be getting a fresh twenty placed in his tip jar.

I put my hands up in surrender and sit. "Fine, I won't hit you this time, but watch your back, Fisher."

"Sut, you can't threaten to pussy punch people when they tell you things you don't want to hear."

Bullshit, I can't. I'm Sutton Hale, and I can do whatever the hell I want.

The problem is, I probably shouldn't do whatever I want—like threaten my best friend's baby box. But what can I say, I'm a wild card like that.

"Fine," I cry out dramatically, resting my forehead on the table. "But I need genuine advice. I need Vivian advice, not Sutton advice. Clearly, the Sutton way isn't working since it keeps getting me into these insane situations."

"Okay, okay," she says, lifting my limp head from the table. "But I need you to start from the beginning and tell me everything. No details left out."

And I do. I spill my guts to her about it all. About sleeping at Cooper's. About the look on Dillon's face as he jumped to the most ridiculous conclusion, and how I couldn't help feeding into his delusions about Cooper and me. I tell her everything. Only leaving out the parts about how I felt sleeping next to Cooper and how his note on the mirror made my heart flutter like a fool.

"I lied. I did look."

My first instinct should have been to be pissed. Not only did he pull a peeping tom on me while I showered, but he used a thirty-dollar lipstick to write on the mirror.

I should have been screaming like a banshee in furry at him for using one of my favorite shades for something so dumb.

But I wasn't.

No, instead of getting pissed at the sight. My chest warmed.

And an odd flutter sensation filled my belly.

The idiot's confession gave me butterflies.

It was a secret I would take to the grave.

Chapter Eight

Cooper

"What kind of porn do you watch?"

Heat spreads through my throat as I choke on my coffee, coughing and spluttering. It has been like that for the past week and a half that we've been living together. Sutton asking me off-the-wall personal questions that she claims she needs to know to help her sell the ruse of being into me. "Sutton, you can't ask people questions like that."

"Why not? You can learn a lot about a person from their masturbation preferences."

"Yeah, a lot of personal things."

She gives me a teasing smile, leaning her elbow onto the kitchen counter. "So, tell me, what is it? Stepsister or babysitter?"

I shake my head. "Neither."

"Oh, come on, Cooper. If not those, then what?"

"Are you telling me you watch stepsister porn?"

"What?" She frowns. "Ew, no. I have much better taste than that. I happen to like double-penny porn."

"You what?"

"You know, a good old two d's going in at the same time. DP and I are like this." She twists her fingers together.

I sit there gaping. How did I not know this? Why *would I* know this about her? This is something deeply personal and so goddamn hot that my dick stirs awake.

My mind fills with flashes of her bent over, riding another man while I take her from the back. It doesn't help that I know what her ass feels like nuzzled into my crotch. Three nights in a row, I've woken up spooning Sutton with a boner, both of which I'm fairly certain she doesn't know.

I clear my throat. "Have you—I mean—is that something you're interested in, in real life?"

She shrugs a shoulder. "It's definitely something I like to read about and watch. Have I ever done it? Nope, never had the opportunity. All the guys I've dated in the past were more interested in threesomes with two women instead of two men, which blows my mind because most of them could barely pleasure one woman, let alone two."

"So, what I'm hearing is, you've had threesomes with other women." I rake my gaze down her body as an image of her with another woman takes over my fantasy.

She smirks. "Wouldn't you like to know?"

I nod eagerly. "Yes, yes I would."

Sutton hops up to sit on the counter. "Not until you tell me what kind of porn you like."

With a sigh, I close my eyes. "Do I have to?"

"Yes. It's the only way." Her legs swing back and forth with her anticipation.

I groan, refusing to look at her as I whisper the words. "Hentai."

A giggle escapes her lips. She slaps her hand over her mouth, trying to cover her obvious amusement as I lay my head on the table with a groan. "I knew you would make fun of me."

"No, no," she laughs, her hand coming over to rest on mine. "I'm not making fun of you, I swear."

"Your cackling isn't convincing."

Her laughter comes to an abrupt stop as she chokes it back. "I swear, I'm not. You just took me off guard with that answer."

Lifting my head, I sneak a quick peek at her. She stands there with a serious look on her face. Her cheeks pinched inward as if she's still trying to hold her amusement back.

"Okay, fine," I say, pushing myself back until I'm flush with the chair. I cross my arms over my chest, bracing myself for whatever crazy thing will fly out of her mouth next. "What does my preference tell you?"

She sits there quietly for a moment, pondering what it could mean. Her head tilts to the side as she narrows her eyes at me like she's studying me. "I think it means that you're a bit of a child at heart. With a great imagination."

I smile at that.

"Or," she says with a wicked grin, "maybe it means that you like to watch cartoons do it like a dirty pervert. Not that I am kink-shaming or anything, but..."

"I knew it was too good to be true. Can't you, just once, stop when you're being kind of nice to me instead of turning into the evil witch you are?"

She leans back against the kitchen cabinets as if she's offended.

"Oh, please. Don't even try to act offended. You love being mean to me."

Her lips lift again into an irresistibly devastating smile, which makes my heart stop. "You're right. I really do."

⚘

"Cooper, your two o'clock prospective client is here," Janice, the group secretary, says through my phone.

"Thanks. Send them on in."

A knock raps on my door before it opens, revealing a familiar face. Audra, Nate's older sister, and mine by default.

"Oh, look, it's my favorite of the Fisher siblings," I announce, standing to round the desk and wrap her in a bear hug.

She laughs, patting me on the back. "Please. Everyone knows you're obsessed with Nate and always have been."

"Okay, maybe a little. But you are my favorite female Fisher sibling."

"I'll take it."

"What are you doing here? Is this a social call? Because you didn't need to make an appointment to say hi."

She looks nervous as she sits in the chair. She's wearing clothes I've never seen her wear before—a nice dress, with a cardigan sweater over it. It's a far cry from her usual tube tops and high-waisted jeans or sweats or, hell, anything that allows her to move.

"This place is nice, Cooper. It looks like you upgraded. That old geometry teacher's desk has nothing on this one. What is this?"

Audra raps her knuckles against the desk. "Is it solid oak? Pine? Mahogany?"

"What I'm hearing is you know nothing about wood."

"I know about *some* wood." She chuckles to herself, and I shake my head, trying to ignore the obvious sexual innuendo.

"What are you doing here?"

She glances around the room, ignoring my question. "This is a nice office. Looks like they gave the new guy something sweet on his first day. Ooh, maybe I should look into changing careers like you."

I frown at her. "Trust me, you don't want to do that. It's not worth it."

She gives me a skeptical look and motions around the room. "Are you sure? Because I think it could be worth it to sit in a cushioned chair like that all day."

"Yeah, and in said chair, you'd have to listen to rich people tell you about how sad their life is. All the time. You'd hate it. You would loathe every moment."

"Maybe, maybe not."

Her nonchalance over listening to the rich whine about being rich concerns me. It isn't like Audra. She lives to make fun of the more fortunate. "Seriously, what are you doing here?"

Another nervous expression crosses her face. So un-Audra-like in the way she gnaws at her bottom lip and picks at her cuticles. Her eyes darting around the room.

She tucks her growing locks behind her ear and clears her throat as she looks me in the eye as if she's gaining all her confidence right there, psyching herself up to speak to me.

"Not a social call. I wanted your professional advice on starting my own business. Well, not my own, per se. It would be with my best friend Bel. We were thinking of opening a store."

"Do your parents know about this?"

"No, and I would like it to stay that way until I have everything planned out."

"Audra... Your mom and dad are going to flip. I love you, but this is going to kill them. Is that what you want? To kill your parents?"

"Dramatic much? Listen, I don't want to completely split myself off from Mom and Dad. I have a great business idea that would run in conjunction with the floral business."

"So this is going to be a joint business between you and your friend. Are you sure you want to get into business with a friend? As far as I've seen, it's not a good idea."

"Bel is the best. We're both super passionate about this idea, and it doesn't work without each other."

"What is the business idea?"

"It's floral preservation. We would use resin to create one-of-a-kind keepsakes for people. We even thought about hosting classes maybe once a week."

"You've thought this through?"

"I have." She dips her chin confidently. "I just need help figuring out the financial aspects. Bel and I have already started saving. But we have no idea where to begin."

I rub at my temples. "Have you thought about dancing? You love dancing. Why don't you do that on the side for a while if you need something other than your parents' business to keep you fulfilled."

"Dance for me is an escape. It's something I do for fun, and if I start using it as something to keep my career balanced, it will kill my love for it."

"I understand."

"Thank you. Before we go over everything and you get too deeply involved in helping me, I have one more request. Can you keep this between us?"

I nod. "I won't tell your parents anything until you're ready."

"Not Nate either."

"Okay, so you're not only asking me to keep secrets from your parents but from your brother too. You know he's my best friend. I can't and don't keep shit from him."

"Oh, he's no longer your best friend."

"If he's not my best friend, then who is?"

"It's obviously... You guys are obsessed with each other." When I don't immediately respond, she rolls her eyes. "My God, I swear you're like two dogs sniffing each other's butt. Stop pretending like you can't stand each other and admit that Sutton's your best friend, not Nate."

"That's blasphemy. Nate is my one and only. Don't get it twisted."

"Yeah, that's what every woman wants to hear. That the man they're in a relationship with considers his best friend his one and only instead of them." She slow claps. "Good job, Coop. I'm sure Sutton is going to love hearing that."

"She will say nothing. Because she still considers Vivian to be her nonromantic life partner, just like Nate is mine. And besides, Sutton and I are just faking it."

"Men are so dumb."

"Hey," I snap. "Insulting my gender isn't going to get you any help from me."

"I'm sorry. You are so smart. The smartest, even. I'm surprised Mensa hasn't snatched you up yet."

I let out an unamused laugh. "Okay, that's enough. Now, let's start with your financials and credit."

A grin splits across her face. "Thank you, thank you, Cooper. You're not gonna regret this."

She stays in my office for an hour, discussing her plans and what options she might have for her business idea. Do I agree with her idea of striking out on her own without her parents? Not necessarily, but who am I to stop her from following her dreams? I know better than anyone what being stuck in a job you don't want can do to you.

Chapter Nine

Sutton

"Be cool." I elbow Cooper as we walk across Toasted, my favorite breakfast spot, to meet my mother.

She's been blowing up my phone for the past two weeks, and I've been dodging her concerned calls with expert precision.

Cooper places his hand on my lower back, guiding me through the throngs of people and tables. The barely there press of his fingers into my soft cotton tee that is meant to be comforting has me spiraling in the opposite direction.

Cooper is voluntarily touching me. And it isn't for my mom to see. She hasn't spotted us yet.

No, he's touching me for some other reason, and it has me on edge.

I halt my movement and look over my shoulder at him. "Stop it," I snap at him through my fake smile.

His head tilts as he examines my face with confusion. "Stop what?"

"Touching me. It's inappropriate."

"I'm lost. What exactly is inappropriate about the way I'm touching you?"

I take a deep breath through my nose. "Nothing would be wrong if you weren't who you are."

A grin tugs at Cooper's mouth as his fingers gently move back and forth on my lower back. "What's so wrong about a boyfriend touching his girlfriend?" he asks in a flirty tone.

I lift a finger and point in his face. "Stop."

He doesn't stop. No, his smile only grows with the movement of his hand.

"Cooper," I growl through gritted teeth. "Stop."

His hand falls from my back, and I almost regret saying anything. Almost.

"Listen, my mom is no fool. She will see through your bullshit if you play it up too hard. Okay?"

"So what do you want me to do? Sit there silently like a monk?"

"Yes." I clap my hands together. "Do that, it's perfect."

He frowns down at me. "I was joking."

I turn around in time to see my mother catch sight of us. Her gaze narrows from across the room as she scowls.

"No time to change the plan," I whisper-yell at Cooper, grabbing hold of his sleeve and dragging him behind me until we're standing in front of the retro teal booth.

"Hello, Mother," I greet, opening my arms for a big hug. I had hoped to whisk her into a giant bear hug the moment I saw her and squeeze her so tightly that one of two things would happen:

she would either pass out from lack of oxygen and then wake up disoriented and forget all about why we're here. Or she would get lost in the magic that is my hug. I mean, a mother-daughter hug is something beyond special. Add in the fact that I am her only child and am growing up so fast, and she should be a goner in zero seconds.

She stands still, eyeing me seriously as she wraps her arms around my back and allows the magic of my hug to take place. Soon, the tension will leave her, and then *bam*, lost to the memories in no time.

I'm about to congratulate myself when she pulls away far too quickly for my only-child spell to have ensnared her.

"Oh, no you don't," I say, pulling her back into me.

"That's enough, Sutton." She disengages herself from me.

I grumble but let her go reluctantly.

She gestures for us to take a seat, and I slide into the booth across from her before Cooper follows.

My mother stares at me, waiting for me to speak first. It's a tactic she used to pull on me when I was growing up.

Well, that's too damn bad, because I've had years to perfect this game with her, and I refuse to be the first one to talk.

We can sit here all night for all I care.

Silence fills the space. And Cooper's gaze volleys between me and my mother.

Minutes pass without any sounds. Cooper stares at the menu through squinted eyes, pretending to look it over until he can't take it anymore and clears his throat.

"I'm going to use the restroom. Order me a number fourteen and a water if the server comes by before I'm back." And then he's gone. The man practically bolts from his seat and then rushes around a group of teenage boys, nearly knocking one of them out in his rush to get to the bathroom faster.

Once he's out of sight, my mom opens her mouth like she's going to concede and be the first to say something when a server stops at the foot of the booth.

"What can I get you lovely ladies to drink?" she asks with a charming smile. She's definitely going to get a big tip from me if she continues to interrupt like my guardian angel.

My mom replies with her usual brunch order. "A flight of mimosas and a Denver Omelet."

I smile. "I will have an orange juice and the sampler, please."

The woman smiles as she writes down my order.

"Oh, actually, can you make my orange juice with extra champagne?"

"You want a mimosa?"

"Yeah, an extra-champagney orange juice." I nod.

"Okay, got it, hun. Anything else?"

"Nope, that's it."

My mother clears her throat and eyes where Coop had been sitting.

"Oh shit, Cooper. I'm sorry, my boyfriend is in the bathroom, and he asked for water and a number fourteen, please."

The server takes our menus and walks off to grab our drinks and put our order in.

Deafening silence sits between us for the longest minute of my life before she blurts out, "It's because I never gave you a decent father figure, isn't it?"

"Huh?"

"The man jumping. It's got to be some sort of long-lasting negative effect of not having a father," she explains, stroking her chin contemplatively.

I rub my temples. "I have a dad, Mom." Albeit, I say *dad* in the loosest meaning of the word. The man might not deserve the title, but it's his nonetheless.

She opens her mouth to respond just as the waitress brings over our drinks. Mom immediately sucks down one glass and starts on her second as the poor woman watches in horror. "Do you want another?" she asks as my mom finishes her second mimosa and moves on to her third and final.

My mom smiles. "I'll take an orange juice with extra champagne."

The woman's eyes round, but she nods and walks away.

I sip on my juice, letting the alcohol swish in my mouth for a moment as I try to stall until Cooper gets back.

Where is he? Doesn't he know that he's my buffer?

A silent buffer, but still. My mother hates yelling at me in the presence of another. Hence why I always make sure Vivian is around after I do something particularly motherly rage-inducing.

She cocks an eyebrow at me, and I go rigid.

Shit, shit, shit.

She's going to explode on me. I can feel it.

I glance around the room, looking for the best way to flee, when I catch sight of Cooper striding back to the table.

I sag in relief as he sits beside me, pressing his thick thigh into mine.

With my focus on Cooper, my mother takes her opening. She reaches across the table and smacks my upper arm.

"Ow." I grab the spot she hit. It didn't actually hurt, but she doesn't need to know that. "Really, Mom? Was that necessary?"

"Of course it was necessary, Sutton. What do you expect me to do? My daughter runs out on her wedding two weeks ago, and already, she has a new boyfriend living with her. This is necessary, and thinking that it's not is crazy." She pauses, looking me up and down. "Are you crazy? I think so. Do you need me to check you into a mental institution? 'Cause I will. I'll do it, Sutton. Don't you worry. Is this some sort of early midlife crisis? I don't get it, Sut. I don't. But you need to explain it to me right now. Or we are on our way to a hospital to check you in for a lovely seventy-two-hour hold. Do you understand me?"

I sigh, slumping back into the cheap vinyl seat. "Yes, Mother, I understand. But I'm not crazy. You know what is crazy? You're questioning me about this instead of being supportive. Can't you be like everybody else's mom and be blindly supportive of my questionable choices?"

Her gaze narrows on me as her lips form into a tight line. It's her pissed-off look that always had me cowering as a kid. Not today, though. Today, I will stand my ground.

"Everybody else's mom would let their crazy-ass daughter run wild and go even more crazy. I'm not letting you get crazier. We have a family history of crazy, and I refuse to let it sink its claws into you."

I open my mouth, ready to fight her once again, but before I can get a word out of my mouth, Cooper leans forward with a big grin on his face, jutting his hand out. "Hi, I don't think I introduced myself. I'm Cooper. Aka the live-in boyfriend."

My mom stares at him. Not acknowledging his hand or his words.

Cooper clears his throat, pulling his hand back. "I'm sorry for any confusion our unconventional situation might have caused."

No, no, this was not the plan. He was supposed to be silent and look pretty.

Stick to the plan, Cooper. *Stick to the plan.*

"Why don't you clear a few things up for me, then, Cooper," she says in a calm yet scary voice that would scare anyone who didn't know her.

With a not-as-confident smile on his face, he says through his teeth, "You know how it is. It's"—he shrugs and waves a hand in front of his face—"stuff was"—he gestures up and down—"wow. And here we are. So yeah, it's kind of like that. You know?"

My mom and I glance away from Cooper to give each other a twin look of confusion.

"Wow, Cooper, that cleared everything up for her. I'm glad you spoke up at this moment." I pat him on the hand.

"Well, I'm glad he's at least trying. Unlike you, Sutton." She glares at me. "I've never, not once in my life, questioned your sanity until now. Actually, that's a lie. I questioned a lot of things about you growing up, and the fact that you're not a lesbian is one of them."

I scoff. "Excuse me?"

"I don't get it. You and Vivian would have been perfect together. It seems like a missed opportunity to me. I don't get it." My mom's forehead wrinkles.

"As I've said a million times before, Mom, sexuality isn't a choice. If it were, I would be all over Vivian, and Vivian would be all up in this perfect puss."

"Don't be so crass, Sutton, it's unbecoming."

I laugh. "Says the woman who told me to test drive the car before you buy it."

"I was talking motor vehicles, and you know it."

"Oh, okay. What about that time we went to see *Forgetting Sarah Marshal* when I was in middle school, and you said it was about time there was peen on screen?"

She rolls her eyes. "I don't remember that ever happening."

"Sure you don't."

My mom groans. "All I'm saying is I don't understand what's happening here. If you two had a romance brewing before this, why have I never heard of him before?" she asks, gesturing to Cooper.

I explain—well, *explain* might be a stretch.

I lie.

Because if I tell my mother the truth, she'll tell everyone she knows about our lie, which will somehow get back to not only Dillon but also Cooper's job, and then we'll both be screwed. But luckily for me, Cooper interjects again. "It's 'cause it's all new. We've been friends for a while now, but there's always been some underlying feelings. Right, Sutton?"

"Right..."

Just then, our waitress shows up and sets our plates in front of us, and once again, she's an angel sent from the heavens with her timing.

The conversations pause as we all dig into the delicious breakfast food.

Taking a massive bite of his pancakes, Cooper gives me a small side glance and wipes his mouth with a napkin before clearing his throat. "Anyway, the reason she's probably never brought me up, I can only assume, is because she'd gush over me, and you'd see right through her pretending we were 'just friends,' and she knows it. But also, she was probably afraid that if she did tell you about me, you would want to meet me, and I would become friends with you and eventually tell you all about the first time we met. She tried to make out with me, and I had to let the poor girl down. Gently."

She giggles. I mean, full-on giggles like a schoolgirl for him. She's eating his shit up, which is a blessing and a curse.

"I was drunk," I grumble, swiping Cooper's drink from his hand and taking a swig.

"That's why I turned you down, but we both know that's not why you made the move, baby."

My cheeks flame. That night was embarrassing enough the first time, along with what followed that day at laser tag. I didn't need that playing on repeat in my head for days.

Cooper's hand finds my thigh under the table, and he squeezes. "She likes to pretend that it never happened. But I don't. Because it was the first time we had ever met, and I knew then."

"Knew what?" my mom asks.

"That we were going to be more than friends someday."

I shake my head. "No he didn't."

He bites down on his bottom lip, tugging at the flesh as if he is debating what to say next. "I did. I can prove it."

"How?"

He pulls out his phone and scrolls through his and Nate's text messages until he finds what he's looking for. He passes the phone to my mom first.

Her face softens and her shoulders relax, and then she smiles at me as she passes it back to him.

"Show me."

"Ready to eat your words?"

"Whatever, show me."

He hands me the phone.

There it is, the night of Rian and Amy's baby shower.

Cooper

She's the one.

Nate

Sarah? Please no, man. I will organize an intervention for you. She is the worst.

Noted. But no, not her. Sutton.

Really?

Yeah, she's the one. I know it.

My heart pounds in my chest.

Cooper thought I was *the one* the first night we met.

Does he still feel that way?

I doubt it.

All we've ever done is fight since that first meeting.

He probably regrets those words.

I look from the phone to him. He gives me a small, shy smile as his hands fidget with the condensation on the sides of his cup.

I pass him back his phone as my mom asks, "Why didn't you guys start dating then?"

"Well, you see. Cooper was hung up on this chick named Sarah. Can you believe it? He liked a Sarah. He's a basic bitch."

My mom snorts. "Who are you calling a basic bitch? You dated a guitarist, Sutton."

"Don't forget how she almost married him," Cooper tosses out, and I poke his ribs.

He swats my hand away. "*Ow.* That's as basic as it gets. So keep your basic bitchiness to yourself and don't go pointing fingers."

My mom's eyes dart between us before she starts laughing hysterically.

Cooper and I turn our glares on her as we both say, "What?"

"Nothing. I think this is absolutely brilliant."

When neither of us responds, she continues on. "You two. You're gonna kill each other, but also, you're gonna fall so head over heels, it's perfect. I don't know what you two are doing right now, but I know it's some sort of scheme. But all I can say is you're perfect for each other. Sutton, baby girl, forget what I said about Vivian and you. This"—she gestures between Coop and me—"is the real deal. Willing to put money on it?"

"Mom, how many times have I told you to stop betting on my relationships? Gambling is an addiction. You don't want to be an addict, do you?"

My mom tips her drink back. "Whatever. If you need any help with whatever this is that you're doing, don't come running to me. Because if I even catch a whiff of your insanity, I will have you both committed. I don't know how I'll do it for you, Cooper, but I will."

"Mom, stop," I groan.

"Don't worry, honey. You two will still be together. I can make sure you share a little cell block. It will be pretty adorable, actually. I can see it now, you both in matching straitjackets."

"We aren't crazy, Mom."

"Sure. You aren't. Get your story straight, Sutton. People are going to have a lot of questions about a runaway bride and her new man she moved in not even a day after her failed attempt down the aisle."

"We get it."

"I don't think you do. Even with everything you've told me, your body language suggests differently."

"What's that supposed to mean?" I ask, trying my hardest and failing not to sound defensive.

She sighs, rolling her eyes as if I am the dumbest person she has ever met. "It means you two don't look very cozy. Actually, you both look the opposite. A kiss might sell whatever this is you're selling."

"A kiss?" Cooper asks, leaning forward onto his elbows.

My mom wiggles her eyebrows. "Kiss. Right now."

I throw my napkin on the table as I bark out a laugh, leaning back against the booth. "We aren't going to kiss just to convince—"

Cooper's hand is wrapped around the back of my head and his lips are on mine before I can even finish my sentence.

What the hell?

Cooper is kissing me.

Cooper is *kissing* me.

Cooper is kissing *me*.

And it's fucking spectacular.

I tense, hands flailing for a split second as I consider pushing him off me, but then I think better of it, relaxing and sinking into him as his tongue sweeps across my bottom lip, coaxing my lips open for him.

Everything inside me comes alive as his tongue rakes over mine. I clench my hands in his shirt, wanting to climb on top of him to get a better angle.

Cooper breaks the kiss, much to my displeasure. His eyes are still closed as he turns back to face my mother in the booth. I quickly let go of his shirt and do the same.

"If you continue to kiss like that, you won't have any problems convincing people." She stands and grabs her purse, winks, and then spins on her heels, leaving us to watch her as she walks out of the diner.

I lick my lips, not wanting to even glance in Cooper's direction. Do we address the kiss? Do I pretend like nothing happened? Do I pretend it didn't get my pussy throbbing? Because I'm not sure that is possible right now.

Cooper clears his throat. "Well, your mom is nice. I liked her."

So pretending it never happened, it is.

I grab my drink, suddenly thirsty, and suck down the remaining contents before reaching across the table to finish off the rest of my mother's mimosa.

With champagne courage, I respond, "Everybody does. She's really great. Especially when she's trying to have us committed to a psych ward. I mean, I don't get it. So what if we're being a little impulsive? That doesn't mean we need to be committed, right?"

"I don't know, it kind of sounds nice. Like a mini vacation with Jello. Maybe we should call her back and tell her we're interested."

"Interested in a trip to the looney bin?"

He hisses through his teeth. "I do have a lot I wanted to do this weekend, though. And if we left, Dillon would get the house." He shakes his head as if talking himself out of it. "We can't do it."

"No shit, Sherlock."

"But what if we have her commit Dillon?" He lifts his brow. "It's a good plan, right?"

I tilt my head to the side. "We could make him look crazier than he already is."

"Okay, let's brainstorm."

I pull a notebook from my purse and begin writing ways to make Dillon the Douche look crazy. Then I add a bullet point below it. "Okay, Cooper, shoot your shot. What do you think we do to him."

"I say we make him *think* we're doing stuff to him, and it makes him so crazy paranoid that he starts acting insane about everything, and then he doesn't know what to do, and he assumes that we are screwing with everything, so he's scared to go in the house until he can't take it anymore. He has to leave because he's terrified of us."

I clap my hands together. "I love it. I'm writing it down." I write *increase paranoia* beside the first bullet point before creating another one.

"What do you think about us making him shit his pants all the time?" I ask, chewing on the end of my pen.

When Cooper doesn't respond immediately, I look up from my paper to see him staring at the pen resting on my lips.

He clears his throat. "I love it, but how are we gonna do that? Because that kind of seems like poisoning?"

"It's not poisoning if he doesn't ask us what's in the stuff he's eating."

"Kind of still sounds like poisoning."

I shrug. "Sounds like a him problem. I say we buy a lot of stuff high in fiber and maybe we decide to get some of that colon-cleansing stuff." I smile. "Maybe you and I want to go on a cleanse. And so we just happen to leave it out. And he loves to eat and drink things that aren't his, so it's perfect."

Cooper crosses his arms and tilts his head as he looks me over. "Why do I feel as if you've thought about poisoning people with laxatives often?"

I beam. "Maybe I just think that shitty people deserve shitty things to happen to them."

Cooper nods as he waits for the bill. His eyes widen when he glances at the total. "What did you and your mom drink before I sat down?"

"Just the usual."

"The usual cost you guys sixty dollars in drinks alone?"

"What can I say, we have expensive taste."

Cooper doesn't reply as he stares at me with disbelief.

"Are you going to pay or should I—" I lift my purse.

Cooper pulls his credit card out of his wallet. "You are a menace." His voice is teasing and leaves no hint of actual anger.

"I don't know why you're looking so grumpy. You make so much more money than me. You're banking, and this is your first year at this new job."

Cooper opens his mouth to probably argue. I'll never know, though, because I add, "Hush, boy. The pay-wage gap is real."

He sighs, dropping his head back on the booth. "I can't with you."

"You can and you will."

He peeks at me with one eye. "Oh really? So willing, so easily."

"Please, that kiss told me everything I needed to know."

His brows shoot up. "And what was that?"

"That you, my sir, want me."

He leans in close enough to whisper in my ear. "That kiss was anything but one-sided."

Heat flames my cheeks as silence stretches between us.

With a smirk, Cooper gets up from the table, leaving me sitting there in shock.

Sutton

SOS!

Answer, you hoe bag. I need you. Now.

Vivian!

Vivian

Jeez, it took me less than five minutes to respond, don't get your panties in a wad.

Rude! I'm in crisis and you mock me. Shame, shame, shame!

My apologies, my lord. Please do tell me about your crisis, I am all ears.

Cooper kissed me.

Shut. The. Front. Door.

Now you get the urgency of the SOS?

Spill. Where? When? How?

At Toasted with my mom watching us.

...Your mom watched you two kiss?

Yeah, that's not even the worst of it. The psycho actually suggested it.

I feel like this needs to be a face-to-face conversation because WTF!

The usual spot?

I'll be there in twenty.

I grab my car keys from the dish by the front door as Cooper comes walking down the hall.

His eyes catch on the keys. "Where are you going?"

"Coffee run." I turn, opening the door.

"Hold on, I'll go with you. Just let me grab my wallet."

"No," I shout, slamming the door behind me and running to my car. I put the key in the ignition and begin backing out as Cooper stands on the porch, watching me with his arms crossed in disappointment.

I roll down my window and yell out "I promise to bring you back something" as I speed away as fast as my Volvo will take me.

When I arrive at the coffee shop, Vivian is standing on the curb with a muffin in one hand and a coffee in the other. The moment she spots my car, she jogs toward me. I pull into the closest parking spot, and she opens the passenger door and slides into the seat.

Swiveling her hips, she faces me. "When are you going to fuck?"

I rear my head back. "Excuse me? I'll have you know I will never, ever have sex with Cooper."

Vivian snorts. "Sure you won't, and I'm never, ever going to eat this banana nut muffin."

She broadcasts her point by immediately taking a bite of said muffin. My reflexes kick in, and I swat it from her mouth. The muffin flies at my windshield, crumbling into small pieces as we both gawk, speechless.

Vivian turns, the half-chewed muffin falling from her mouth as she gives me a bewildered look. "You slapped my muffin."

"That's what she said," I whisper, still shocked by my own actions.

"You slapped my muffin," she booms again with a glare.

"And I'll slap your crotch muffin if you insinuate that I would have sex with Cooper again," I yell back, hands flailing.

"I hope your car is filled with crumbs from my muffins forever. I hope you clean and clean but still find crumbs for years to come. I hope the ghost of banana nut muffins haunts you and this damn car until the day we die together."

"You did not just put a muffin curse on me. You know how much I hate cleaning a messy car." I stomp my foot against the floorboard.

"You bet your ass I did." She grabs the door handle, attempting to flee the scene of my crime.

"Oh, no you don't." I press the lock on the door, trapping her wannabe witch ass with me.

"Damn it, Sutton, you can't hold me hostage."

"Don't you want to hear the entire story?"

"No." She crosses her arms over her chest and turns to look out the window.

"Not even if I tell you if Cooper used tongue or not?"

The corner of her lips curves up, and she slowly turns to face me. "Tell me everything."

And I do. I tell her about our crazy plans for Dillon. About my mom's insane plan to have us committed. But mostly, I tell her about how Cooper's touch and lips were like water, and I was beyond parched.

My cell chimes with a text alert, and I freeze as I glance at it.

Cooper

> I thought you were getting coffee...

"Oh my God," I shout, throwing my phone at Vivian.

She reads the text, then looks up at me. "You don't think he followed you, do you?"

Oh shit.

"I didn't until you said that."

Is he here? Does he know I'm talking about him? How does he know?

My gaze darts from my phone to the parking lot surrounding us. I survey everything from the shrubs outside the coffee shop to the cars parked a couple businesses over.

I'm panicking.

Nothing to be alarmed at, just a small heart attack in the works over fear of being found talking about Cooper.

"I'm joking, you idiot." She laughs. "He's probably just wondering where in the hell his coffee is since you ran out like a madwoman and promised him you'd get him something."

"You think so?" I chew on my bottom lip.

"Yeah."

"Should I text him back?"

"Do you want to text him back?"

"Stop it. Be helpful, not annoying."

"I'll stop being annoying when you turn back into my bold and beautiful best friend again. Seriously, Sut, what is going on? Since when do you stress over a man?"

I sigh. She's right. I've never been unsure or insecure. I've always known who I am and go after anything I want. Guys don't make me nervous. They never have. I mean, they're just guys, and the majority aren't worth sweating over.

But Cooper is different.

I don't know how, but he is.

And almost every time I'm with him, I either embarrass myself or end up in a pissy mood for the rest of the day.

I close my eyes and lay my head back against the seat. "Since when have I had to fake a relationship? Clearly, I'm a hot mess going through something."

"Look, I understand."

I peek at her with one eye. "Really? You understand what it's like to go through with a marriage ceremony, only to refuse to sign the license at the end and have to enter into a stupid fake relationship bargain with a man you can barely stand to get your ex to move out?"

"No," she says, "but I have watched a ton of rom-coms, so I feel like I can speak on the subject."

"Um, okay..."

"Anyway, I think you need to take Cooper to town."

"Town?"

"Yeah, pound town. Your reluctance to admit your attraction to Cooper is what's causing these mini meltdowns."

"Ha-ha-ha, lies."

"Sutton, I think you like the guy and have since the moment you met him. But for some reason, you never gave him a chance. If you want my advice. Take the risk. Make a move." And with that, she's gone. Well, not gone-gone, but she does lean across me and unlock the car, then slip out to buy herself another muffin.

Take the risk. Make the move.

If only she knew. Her words replay through my mind on a loop, bringing up the memories of that first night. The night Cooper entered my life over a year ago.

I had maybe had two—okay, five—drinks too many. But in my defense, I needed every single glass of champagne that I drank after the disaster that was me knocking into the table of gifts.

I never failed at making a fool out of myself at Vivian's mom's fancy events. But I thought that time was going to be different. I mean, it was a baby shower; how much trouble could I possibly get into.

Apparently, a ton.

Add in Viv's mom making Vivian feel like shit, and we were a mess. So booze was an obvious must.

I made the executive decision to be responsible in all the ways by sneaking Vivian's phone from her purse and contacting her new boy toy to help get our no-longer-sober asses home.

Not long after, Nate walked in with another tall brunette man. He scanned the room, his gaze snagging on me for a moment as he smiled, and I waved, then pointed to a heavily intoxicated Vivian talking to Rian and Amy. Nate's gaze found Vivian instantly, and his face lit up with a big smile. Nate nodded to the man beside him, who followed his line of sight until he found me.

The man made his way toward me as Nate trekked off to Vivian.

I didn't bother to watch my friend anymore. Instead, I was captivated by the six-foot-something man with tousled brown hair and glasses who was grinning at me with a smile that warmed my skin.

"Hey, I'm Cooper," he introduced himself before taking a seat beside me. "Nate's best friend."

I licked my lips, then took another swig of the drink in front of me.

"And you are?" he asked.

"Wet," I muttered.

His eyes widened and his smile grew. "I'm sorry, what?"

"Sutton," I said with a wink. "The best friend of your bestie's new girlfriend."

"It's a pleasure to meet you, Sutton." He offered out a hand for me to shake.

I placed mine in his, letting his grip swallow me.

His hands were twice the size of mine, and I couldn't help the dirty thoughts that filled my mind as I wondered what else was big on his body.

"I'm sure the pleasure will be all mine later with hands like these."

Cooper laughed. "I see someone has been hitting the bottle a little hard tonight."

"Not so hard that I can't get you hard." I winked.

Redness crept up his cheeks.

Ladies and gentlemen, I've got a shy one on my hands.

God, that was hot.

It'd been so long since I'd been interested in someone who wasn't completely full of themselves.

Cooper cleared his throat. "So I think the plan is Nate is going to take Vivian and her car back to his place, and then we are together."

"You going to give me a ride?" I leaned closer to him, pushing my tits up to give him something special to look at.

He bit his bottom lip, suppressing a smile. "To your house."

"Okay, I'll let you give me a ride"—I lifted my fingers in air quotes—"'to my house.'"

Cooper chuckled, shaking his head at me as Vivian took a seat beside me, Nate behind her. He pressed a kiss into her hair before sitting beside Cooper.

"Nice to see you again, Sutton. Hopefully, you won't judge me too harshly based on the first time," he said with a shy smile.

I smiled, looking into my glass. "Oh, honey, trust me when I say you made a *huge* impression. And I won't forget it." I downed the last of my champagne as Viv reached across me, trying to grab the last bit of booze we had at the table. "Oh, no you don't, you beautiful, boozy bitch." I swatted her hand away as Cooper picked up the glass and emptied it.

Viv's gaze narrowed. "Who is this, and why do you both want me to be miserable?"

I trapped her hands between mine. "Babe, you're trashed." I paused for a moment. "But so am I. I called Nate off your phone to get us since we're both far beyond the point of driving."

Vivian practically melted. "My unicorn came to our sloppy rescue. Awe."

"And it turns out he was out with his friend Cooper, so here is the plan: Nate is going to drive you and your car back to your place or his. No one cares which one. And Cooper here is going to take me home in Nate's truck."

"Oh my God, Cooper? As in thee Cooper? As in Coop? As in Nate's nonsexual, or at least I don't think, life partner?" Viv practically bounced with excitement as she stood from the table to move between the two men before settling in Nate's lap.

"I like you," Vivian slurred with a smile.

Cooper did the same. "And I like you."

Nate wrapped one arm around her waist, pulling her back into his chest.

"Stop it. I'm trying to get to know your Sutton," Vivian said, pushing forward. "Tell me every embarrassing story you know about this one behind me. Because I need to knock him down a peg, you know? Like, I need him to be a skosh less attractive."

Coop scooted closer, his stare twinkling with excitement. "What level of embarrassment are we talking about? Like, called the teacher 'Mom' or masturbation stuff?"

Nate glared. "Don't you fucking dare."

Viv smiled, planting a loud kiss on Nate's lips before looking into Cooper's eyes and responding, "Masturbation."

We didn't stay much longer after that, seeing as Nate was not a fan of his best friend and new girlfriend joining forces to tease him. I, for one, would have loved to watch the two of them spill secrets all night. But alas, the soberest of us all was in charge and put a stop to it all.

I hugged Vivian, placing a hand on her back and pushing her closer to Nate, who wrapped an arm around her waist, pulling her to his side and down the sidewalk to where the valet had her car parked.

We watched them climb in as I asked, "You think those two will be okay?"

"Nate and Vivian?"

I nodded, trying to stand still and not sway the way my body was desperate to.

Don't move.

You aren't that drunk.

You are steady, like a tree.

No, trees move with the wind. You need to be like a wall.

A brick wall.

You will stand still and not stumble.

You will not fall, damn it.

"Yeah, Nate is the best person I know, and trust me when I say he is going to take better care of her than her mother would."

I snorted. "Good to know." Viv's mother was a raging bitch and the main reason the two of us drank like we did tonight. But that didn't feel like something I should be sharing with a stranger. No matter how attractive he was or if he made my pussy flutter with hope.

"Come on. I'm parked this way." Cooper tilted his head toward the parking garage down the street.

I barely made it ten feet before my drunkenness struck.

Turned out that willing yourself not to sway and stumble didn't work. I tripped over nothing as I tried to walk beside Cooper.

"Whoa there," he said, catching me by the shoulder and pulling me into his side.

"My hero." I fluttered my lashes at him.

"Are you good, or do you need to hold on to my arm?" he asked.

"I'm fine." I waved him off like he was being ridiculous for even suggesting I was too wasted to walk.

Which I wasn't.

I was practically sober.

Yep, I was a sober Sutton.

"You sure? Because a second ago, you seemed to lose your footing?"

"That's not what happened," I said calmly.

"I'm fairly certain it is."

"Nah, you see, I was actually stepping over something and over-estimated how high my foot would go, so when I went to bring said foot down to the ground, I miscalculated. Hence the almost-fall-like event."

"You were stepping over something?"

"Yep." I nodded so enthusiastically that the world around me started to spin for a moment. Slowly, I blinked, trying to right the world with Cooper being none the wiser.

"What was it?"

"What was what?"

"What were you stepping over?"

"Oh." I searched my mind for the most reasonable answer and blurted out, "A small family of mice."

"Mice?"

I wanted to slap myself across the face. *Mice?* What was I thinking? But it was too late to change my story. So I ran with it.

"Yes, there was a momma, pappa, and two twins all scurrying along our path, just trying to survive."

"Really? Because from my perspective, there was nothing but air."

"Of course it looked like nothing to you. Everyone knows that distance makes things look much smaller than they actually are and sometimes invisible to the naked eye."

"You're saying because of my height, I couldn't see the family of mice?"

"See, you get it. For a moment there, I was getting nervous that I was going to have to explain measurements and all that jazz, and to be honest, I'm not that great of a teacher."

"That your final answer?" He raised an eyebrow in question.

"Yes sir." My head bobbed in a one hundred percent sober manner.

"Okay, then. I guess I have no choice but to believe you."

"Thank you."

"Come on," he said, wrapping an arm around my shoulders and tugging me with him as he walked.

I shivered as the breeze hit me. The air had grown colder since the beginning of the baby shower, and I was deeply regretting not wearing a dress with sleeves.

Cooper's hand moved to my arm and began rubbing up and down, creating a friction of warmth on my skin... and in my pants.

I burrowed into his body, soaking up his heat. Hints of bergamot and pepper lingered on his shirt, and I wanted to drown in his scent.

I didn't say another word as we walked to the truck, mostly because I was too busy trying to figure out what brand of cologne he must wear to have my mouth water like this.

When we got to Nate's truck, Cooper opened my door and helped me into the seat before moving around to the other side.

He climbed in, closing the door with a gentle sweeping motion before turning the key in the ignition.

Letting the truck warm up, he buckled his seat belt, then turned to me. "Put your address into the GPS."

"Ooh, bossy. I like."

"Sutton."

"Cooper."

"I need you to put your address in so I can drive you home."

"Fine." I leaned forward and pressed my fingers into the truck's touch screen. It took me two attempts to spell my street name, but I finally got it, and I turned to Cooper, smiling. "Huzzah, I did it."

Cooper's deep chuckle filled the cab of the truck as his eyes roamed my face.

"Your eyes are very pretty."

"Thank you." He blushed and turned away from me, backing the truck out of the parking space before driving out of the parking garage and onto the street.

"Spectacular, even," I added, resting my head against the back of the seat.

"What makes them so spectacular?"

"They remind me of shimmering pools of water."

"My eyes are an amber brown."

"I didn't say it was clear water."

A smile quirked up on his lips as he turned left.

My attention jumped from those bright eyes to the way his hands gripped the steering wheel. His long fingers lifted to allow the wheel to slide back into its original position. But it was the way his thumbs swept back and forth across the leather that had my breath hitching and me squirming in my seat.

If I kept moving like this, my body was going to get the wrong idea.

I bit my lower lip as my core throbbed.

Too late.

God, I was horny.

But not regular, run-of-the-mill horny.

I was horny for *him*.

For this mesmerizing man.

I wanted to pull those black frames off his face and do deliciously bad things to him.

"Sutton?"

"Huh?"

"I said we're here."

I turned away from him to look out the window, and there was my small house. Not a light in sight. I sighed, chastising myself for once again forgetting to turn on something to not only keep the burglars away but also help me not break anything as I made my way through the clutter that currently was my living room.

"Walk a girl in?"

Cooper smiled. "Sure." He pulled the key from the ignition and hopped out of the car. Not sure if I should wait on him or not, I opened my door and stepped out, not remembering how high the truck was from the ground.

I fell, only to be caught by Cooper's strong arms once again.

"Let me guess, mice?"

"Nah." I shook my head. "Baby opossum. The thing looked feral but fierce."

The grin on his face only grew as he helped me right myself and followed me to my doorstep.

"So," I said, rocking back and forth.

"So…"

"Think we should exchange numbers?"

His brows quirked.

"So you can text me to tell me you got home safely."

"I'm not the one who went on a champagne bender tonight, Sutton."

"That Vivian sure is wild, am I right?"

He gave me a knowing look but still pulled out his phone and asked for my number. I rattled it off, and he repeated it back to me. "I'll text you when I get home."

"Or…" I stepped closer to him. "You could come inside."

"Sutton…"

I stepped even closer until there was only a small breath between us. "I thought you were going to give me a ride." I winked at him suggestively.

"In the truck," he said, hitching his thumb in the direction of said vehicle.

"We can do it in there if you want, but I prefer to be able to stretch out more."

"You're drunk, Sutton."

"I'm barely tipsy."

"You almost fell two times."

"There were extenuating furry circumstances."

He sighed. "I can't."

"Come on, Cooper." I ran my hands up his hard chest, relishing in the feel of his muscles tightening under my palms. I lifted onto my tiptoes, my lips brushing against his. "You know you want to."

He didn't pull away. He didn't do anything. So I took my shot and latched my lips on to his.

His hands found my shoulders, and he pushed me a few inches away. "Not tonight. Not when you're drunk."

The sting of rejection slammed into me as I stumbled backward. My ankle rolled in my heels, causing me once again to lose my balance as my back hit my door with a thump.

Cooper stepped forward, but I put my hand up. "I'm fine."

"Sutton, I..."

"You can leave now." I turned around, careful to keep my weight off my now-aching ankle. Slipping my key into the lock, I opened the door wide enough to slip through and shut it without another word.

"Goodnight, baby opossum," he said, as I waited there silently with my back to my door until the sound of his footsteps disappeared, followed by the purring of the truck's engine drifting down the road.

Sliding to the floor, I pulled my heels off my feet and threw them to the side.

"I'm such an idiot," I groaned, burying my face in my hands.

Chapter Ten

Cooper

Two and a half hours later, Sutton finally reappears.

Her keys jingle in her hand as she steps through the front door and stalks over to where I'm sprawled out on the couch.

She juts her hands out, thrusting a melted iced coffee in my direction. "Here."

I sit up, eyeing the drink with caution.

"Just take the damn coffee, Cooper."

I don't know what's up with her. She's acting like a crazy person. From running out of the house earlier like a serial killer was in her house. To acting awkward as fuck with this coffee.

Honestly, I assumed she wouldn't get me anything after her sprint away from me.

I stand, taking the condensation-covered cup from her. "Thank you."

She glances down and around the room. Hell, she looks anywhere but at me. She's been like this since we had brunch with her mother.

Something is off.

And it's making me nervous.

I miss my usually sunny, albeit snarky, Sutton.

I don't like this version that won't look me in the eye and challenge me.

I'd like to think it was the brief kiss we shared earlier today.

I hadn't planned on kissing Sutton. But the older Ms. Hale was a force to be reckoned with, just like her daughter. And she was right.

No one was going to believe us if there weren't any real physical interactions between us.

Sutton wouldn't move on from her fiancé that quickly and not be so wrapped up in the man that she couldn't keep her hands off him.

No, she would be all over me. So the kiss was the least we could do to sell the lie.

Problem is, I've been dreaming about kissing Sutton since the first moment I saw her.

She was drunk and fumbling but also so damn cute.

And when she flirted with me, it made me feel something I hadn't since my first crush in high school.

I've tried to ignore the feelings that've been eating away at me for the past year or so we've been in each other's lives.

Tried and failed.

I've lied to myself by convincing myself it was nice to be flirted with by a beautiful woman. That it was flattering.

But God, did that kiss make the truth rise to the surface, whether I liked it or not.

Fuck, I hope it's eating her the same way it's eating me.

The moment our lips touched, I was gone. What was supposed to be a chaste kiss quickly took a turn into something more. She was intoxicating, and I couldn't get enough.

And now all I want to do is take her mouth again. To wrap my fingers up in her blond strands and yank her to me.

Cautiously, I bring the cup up to my lips. Hoping it wasn't tampered with.

She would smirk or bounce on her toes if she did something to the drink, right? *Right?*

But she doesn't do either. Instead, she focuses on her feet.

Closing my eyes, I give the drink a chance.

Hazelnut flavor fills my mouth as I take my first swig. The coffee is only partially watered down, but other than that, it tastes normal.

It tastes like my usual hazelnut iced latte.

Smugness and caffeine fill my veins. *She knows my usual.*

Her eyes finally move from the spot on the wall she's been staring at, and she watches me as I gulp down the drink. She licks her lips as her gaze falls to my throat.

I make a point to drink every drop while she's standing right in front of me.

Peeling the cup from my lips, I say, "Ahhh."

"You didn't have to drink it all right away."

"I was thirsty. Someone had me waiting for hours."

She blinks up at me innocently and gives me a small smile and a shrug. "Oops."

I set the cup on the coffee table and take a step closer to where she stands. "What took you so long?"

"Lines." She clicks her tongue, shaking her head.

"Lines?"

"Yeah, they were super long."

"Long lines made it take over two hours for a coffee?"

"They were huge. Astronomical, even. Out the door and down the block. I think maybe there was a celebrity or something in there."

"A celebrity?"

"Maybe. Who knows? Not me and definitely not you."

I laugh. This woman is insane. Certifiable. Maybe her mother was right about needing to get her committed.

The only problem is I like her brand of crazy.

"I feel like you're lying to me, baby opossum." I take another step, bringing us almost chest to chest.

"Too bad you can't prove it." She juts out her chin in confident defiance.

I brush my fingers down her forearm, and Sutton sucks in a breath as goose bumps trail behind my touch. I stop when I reach her wrist, running my thumb over her pulse.

Her heart is pounding as she shifts on her feet, trying to yank her wrist from my grip, but I don't budge.

"Why did you run out of here so fast earlier?"

"Cooper, please," she whispers, her eyes pleading with me to leave it alone. To drop it. But I can't. I won't. I have to know if it was about the kiss. If she's feeling the same things I am.

It's crazy to think I might affect her the same way she affects me. Especially since she just left a man at the altar. But if there's even a sliver of a chance, I'm going to take it.

I've waited too long. Have let her brush me off for too long. Tonight, I'll get some answers.

"Answer the question."

Unease fills her eyes, but she opens her mouth. "I—"

The front door bursts open, and Dillon struts in, giving both Sutton and me a cocky smile before he turns to hold the door open for someone.

Long, toned tan legs fill the room first before a face I'm all too familiar with. Both my and Sutton's jaws drop as Sarah, my ex-girlfriend, walks into Sutton's living room.

I drop Sutton's wrist but don't move away from her.

Now, I expected him to bring home a new woman every night, trying to get under Sutton's skin, but this—her—I wasn't expecting. It's not just a poorly calculated move against Sutton. No, this is a strike against the both of us.

But not for the reasons he probably thinks.

I'm not sure if Sutton will be jealous. But I know that's what he is going for.

But for me, it's more annoyance. No envy, jealousy, or insecurity. I don't care if he is seeing my ex.

That relationship ended a long time ago.

Admittedly, I dated Sarah for way longer than I should have. We were fun. The sex was good. But the spark died long before I ended things with her.

I had taken the coward's route out, too. I told her it was her friendship with Hadlee that was the problem. That I couldn't be with a person who knew what Hadlee was doing to hurt my friends and stayed silent.

It was true, but it wasn't the entire truth.

But it *was* an excuse to leave.

I had been complacent.

The relationship had run its course.

And I hate to admit it had been feeling that way since the moment Sutton had blamed her tripping on rodents.

Sarah comes to a halt when she sees Sutton and me. "Cooper?"

I open my mouth to reply, but Sutton beats me to it. "Sarah." Her tone is anything but friendly.

"What are you doing here?"

Again, Sutton speaks for me. "He lives here… With me."

Anger and annoyance radiate from her. And she looks as if she's going to snap. I can't tell if it's because of Dillon or because of me. I don't even care if it isn't about me, as long as it isn't over Dillon. That's a lie, I do care. I want her to be jealous over me.

Sarah's eyebrows shoot up. "You two live together. Like roommates?"

Dillon smirks, his eyes glued on Sutton's face.

"If roommates mean two people who are sleeping in the same bed every night, fuck like rabbits, and are in love, then sure. Roommates," I toss out.

Sutton pulls my hand into hers, intertwining our fingers.

Sarah's gaze drops to our linked hands, and her face falls. "Oh, when did this"—she gestures between us—"happen?"

Dillon opens his douchebag mouth and chimes in, "Sutton left me for him." He frowns at her, and Sarah gasps and strokes his arm to comfort him. He then turns his attention back to us. "But oddly enough, even with these thin walls, I haven't heard anything that sounds remotely sexual coming from the room you two share."

Sutton sneers. "Been listening, perv?"

He shrugs. "Just find it odd, is all. Guess the grass isn't always greener, is it?"

Sutton rolls her eyes. "It's ponds vs. the ocean. One mirky and dirty. The other is vast and full of wonders you can't even imagine. There's no comparison."

"Whatever." Dillon closes the door behind Sarah and stalks off to his temporary room.

Sarah watches him for a moment, then moves to follow before stopping directly in front of me. Her eyes soften. "I don't have to go with him, Coop, if you don't want me to."

Sutton rears her head back as if she's been slapped. "You did not just proposition my boyfriend in front of me."

Sarah's attention darts to Sutton, then back to me. "Cooper?"

"And she can't stop herself, can she?"

Fighting a smile, I tighten my hold on Sutton's hand and step behind her. "Dillon's room is the last door on the right."

Her eyes widen as she swallows down her embarrassment and walks away. Sutton and I don't move a muscle until the door closes and the familiar sounds of Dillon's music blare through the walls.

"Can you believe the nerve of that hussy?"

"Total trollop," I agree.

She shifts nervously, her eyes darting back to Dillon's room, and my stomach bottoms out. She's pissed that he brought her home. Her anger was for him.

"You weren't—I mean, you didn't want to take her up on her offer, did you?"

I stare at her, perplexed.

"Shit," she mutters to herself, untangling our hands and stepping away from me. "Don't tell me Dillon's little revenge worked on you?"

She can't be serious.

I wait for her to laugh or something, but she doesn't.

Dear God, she's serious.

"Are you high?" I ask. It would explain her weird behavior today.

"What? No, of course not."

"Then why on earth would you think I give two shits about Sarah?"

"I don't know, you guys were together for quite a while."

"Yeah, on and off. Just like you and the douche of the century over there. Are you still hung up on him?"

"What? No!"

"How?"

"What do you mean, how?"

"How did you just drop all of your feelings for him within a split second."

"Drop it, Cooper."

"No, I want to know since you seem to think I'm still hung up on someone I ended it with when Viv and Nate were broken up."

Her throat bobs as she swallows. "I don't want to talk about this right now."

"Well, I don't like seeing you upset that the asshole brought home another woman when I am supposed to be your boyfriend, but here we are."

"I'm not upset about him. I'm upset about her." She flings her hand out toward that door down the hall. "I'm upset about you." She slaps a hand over her mouth like she didn't mean to say that last part.

"Me?"

She groans in frustration. "Yes, you. You just stood there mooning over her like a damn idiot. You made me look stupid. And I *am* stupid. This is never going to work. We should call it now because no one is ever going to believe we are a thing. Not with you staring at your ex like that and def not when Dillon doesn't even believe we are sleeping together."

Frustration pumps through my veins as I rub a hand down my face. "You want him to believe it?"

"Obviously."

"Fine." I grasp her by the arm and pull her back into her bedroom, slamming the door behind us. I flip the lock and stride to her bed.

She eyes me warily as I climb on top of her bed and bounce. The bed squeaks under my weight.

"What are you doing?"

"Convincing him."

"By bouncing?"

I shoot her a frustrated glare. "By creating a sensual auditory experience for anyone who might try to listen."

"Are you saying what I think you're saying?" She jumps to sit beside me on the bed.

I grin. "Sutton, can I fake rock your world?"

"Yes, yes, yes," she moans out with a sly smile.

The music coming from down the hall gets quieter, and Sutton motions with her hand for me to continue on.

"Does Mommy like Daddy's cock?" I ask, sounding breathy as I bounce up and down.

"Ew," she laughs. "Mommy and Daddy?"

"Shhh," I say in a hushed tone, pressing a finger to her lips. "Just go with it, trust me."

Sutton then climbs onto her feet and jumps on the bed, causing it to bump the wall even harder. "Yes, Daddy. More, more, more."

Disgust fills me, and I fake gag, whispering to her, "You were right. It's awful."

I grunt and groan as Sutton begins to slap my thighs to create the perfect combination of sounds.

"Oh yeah, right there, Mommy. Don't stop."

"I won't stop until you've filled me with your sweet seed," she yells, jumping faster and faster.

We're both panting in no time, which only helps to sell our little charade.

Soon, we're both screaming each other's name in fake pleasure with a long, exaggerated sigh as we finish.

We collapse on the bed, side by side and panting.

A door slams down the hall, and I know it worked.

Sutton lifts her hand up, and I slap it. "Good work."

"Don't tell me you high-five after sex?" I ask, both curious and apprehensive.

She wiggles her brows like a madwoman. "You'll never know."

Laughter bubbles out of her until she's laughing so hard her face turns red and she can't speak, only squeaky wheezes falling from her lips.

I love the insane amount of joy that something so ridiculously childish can bring her.

Chapter Eleven

Sutton

We're a sweaty mess. And as much as I hate to admit it, I had fun. Cooper is fun.

He still has me on edge, though.

I know I'm the one who talked him into this entire fake-dating situation, but how much is he getting from it compared to me?

I'm getting a live-in buffer and fake boyfriend to scare off my ex. All Cooper's getting is the occasional arm candy at work events.

It just feels fishy.

Cooper hauls himself up from the bed and strides toward the closet, then riffles through his duffle bag and picks out a shirt and sweatpants.

I don't mean to stare.

But I can't tear my attention away from him as he tugs his shirt over his head to reveal the most intoxicatingly toned chest and stomach I've ever seen.

Abs.

Cooper has abs.

How did I go this long without knowing this stupidly hot fact about him?

Oh, I know how. I've avoided him like the plague at all times, ensuring I'd never catch a glimpse of his deliciously taut torso.

Call it self-preservation, because with a body like that, I'm bound to catch something, and God, do I hope it isn't feelings.

Ha! What a stupid thing to think.

I would absolutely never, ever catch feelings for Cooper.

The more I say it, the more I can convince myself of its truth. Right?

"See something you like?" Cooper asks, his tone light and flirty.

I lick my lips and give myself three more seconds of staring before I have to look away.

One. His skin looks smooth like a baby's.

Two. I wonder if he would let me count his abs... with my tongue. I could start on the first row, going horizontally. Then, when I reach the edge of the back tattoo, I could—

Three. A tattoo? No, it can't be. Stuck-up math teacher turned finance bro Cooper would never.

My eyes widen like saucers as I ask, "You have a tattoo?"

Cooper peers over his shoulder, then smiles at me. "I don't know, what do you think?"

"I think you're too lame, Mr. Four Eyes, to deface your precious, perfect skin."

"Four eyes? Really, Sutton? You couldn't have done better than my elementary school bully?" He opens his arms wide in a challenge as he beckons me over. "Why don't you come see for yourself."

Swallowing down my desire, I push off the bed and stalk over to him. I spin my finger in a circle, motioning for him to turn, which he does with a wry grin that makes my stupid heart skip a beat.

Why does he have to be so pretty but also so annoying?

On his left shoulder, trailing down his back and peeking out beside his ribs, is the most intricate geometric design I've ever seen. There are flowers and math symbols I recognize, along with ancient Greek-like statues.

It's a piece of art.

I can't help myself as I reach out and trace the lines over and down his back. Cooper stills at first but soon relaxes as I continue to draw my finger over the black ink.

"It's beautiful."

He clears his throat. "Thank you."

"Did Nate design it?"

His throat bobs as I continue to assess him. "He drew it, and an old friend from college, who now owns his own shop, tattooed me."

"When did you get it done?"

"About three years ago. When did you get yours?"

"How did you know I have a tattoo?"

He turns to face me, giving me an *are you joking* look. "Sutton, it's visible anytime you wear your hair up."

"Oh." He's right; the small tattoo isn't exactly a secret, but still, I don't like how he knew something about me that we had in common and I didn't. "I got it when I was twenty. It was a dumb, drunken impulse that I can't seem to regret."

"What's it of? I can't ever see it well enough."

I don't answer. I don't *want* to answer. In this moment, I'm embarrassed. So instead, I pull my hair up and off my neck to show him.

"I don't get it. It's hands holding an apple."

An unwelcome flush heats my cheeks. "Yes."

When I glance over my shoulder, Cooper is tilting his head as he studies the small drawing inked on my flesh.

"I feel like I've seen this before."

Dropping my hair back over my neck, I step out of his reach. "Weird. It's one of a kind."

"What does it mean?" he asks, genuinely confused.

"Oh…" I pause, trying to come up with anything other than the truth. Cooper waits patiently for me to answer. "That apples are precious to me," I blurt out.

"I don't think I've ever seen you eat an apple."

"You don't know everything about me." I try to walk around him.

"I think I know enough." Confidence radiates off him. "I know that you have horrible taste in music."

I scoff. "I do not." My music taste is impeccable. In fact, it's downright amazing. He's simply jealous because he's a mindless listening machine to whatever new crap is milled out by the music industry every five minutes.

"I know that you secretly like having me around."

"You would think that, wouldn't you?"

He flashes me a not-so-subtle grin. "You know what else I think? I think you liked having my hands on you more than you're willing to admit yet."

"You wish."

He licks his lips, stepping closer until his bare chest presses against mine. "Maybe I do."

His hand splays against my hip. I release a haggard breath as I fight against my instincts to climb his body and capture his mouth with mine.

"Would it be so bad if you admitted this attraction isn't one-sided?"

I could do it.

I could confess that every time he's in the room, my eyes search for him in the crowd.

I could confess that my heart speeds up just a little whenever he speaks to me.

Or maybe I could admit that whenever he accidentally grazes my skin, my core throbs with want.

I could do all of those things.

But I won't.

I can't.

It's better this way.

It's better for the both of us to remain as we are.

Cooper looks down with hope and lust in his gaze. And I hate him for it.

I don't need him confusing me like this. Making me want things that can never happen.

"I—I can't."

His shoulders fall, along with his hand. The glimmer of hope leaves his face as he backs away from me, shaking his head.

"One day you won't be able to fight this anymore."

"Stop lying to yourself, Cooper. This"—I gesture between us—"is never going to happen."

The corner of his lips tugs up in a smirk. "I can't wait to prove you wrong."

He turns and walks out of the room, his thick back muscles flexing with every step. He leaves me alone to hate the fact that I can't have him.

I toss and turn all night thinking about him. Cooper slipped into bed an hour after he left me stunned into silence.

I wish I could say that, in that time, I didn't let his words get to me, but I did. I let them fester in my brain as he slept silently beside me.

I didn't understand how he could fall asleep that easily after throwing down a claim about the two of us being more than this. More than a bargain of convenience.

Just when I've finally tired myself out by running through every possible scenario I might encounter with Cooper, my alarm goes off, startling me awake.

I slap a hand over it and cover my head with my blankets. I want to dig a hole in my bed and burrow into it while I cry myself back to sleep. But the squawking starts up again only moments later.

"Sutton," Cooper groans. "Turn it off."

"I'm trying," I whine as my hand flails out, blindly trying to find the dumb button.

Suddenly, the noise stops, but my hand hasn't made contact with anything other than air. I pull back the blankets to find Cooper scowling over me.

"Next time press the damn button."

I grit my teeth. "I was trying."

He closes his eyes and huffs as he walks to the bathroom, slamming the door behind him.

The sound of the shower starting has me sitting up.

That son of a bitch is stealing my bathroom time.

Fine, then I'm going to make coffee.

Leaning my hip on the counter while I wait for the pot to fill, the perfect idea pops into my head.

I take two oversized mugs out of the overhead cabinet; I make them identical, with tons of creamer and a splash of coffee.

Before I can stop myself, I open my junk drawer and dig around until I find what I want. Two packets of the white powdery goodness. I clutch the MiraLAX packets to my chest with a smile. This is about to get so much better.

I tear them open without another thought and pour their contents into the coffee remaining in the pot. Grabbing my hand mixer, I stir that powder in until the evidence has disappeared.

Loud, thumping footsteps that I'm too familiar with clamor my way, and I shove the empty packets back into the drawer as Dillon walks into the kitchen.

He eyes me up and down as he moves closer. "You don't look very refreshed after all those fake orgasms. The lies keeping you up at night?"

"I didn't fake shit, Dil."

He huffs a laugh. "You forget just months ago, I was the one making you come. I know what it sounds like when you get off."

I tilt my head to the side and sip on my coffee. "Do you, though?"

"Yeah."

"Hmm, sure."

His gaze narrows. "What is that supposed to mean?"

"Oh, nothing. Just maybe you don't know what it sounds like when I climax as well as you thought."

Dillon looks like he's about to lunge when Cooper walks in wearing nothing but a towel, water still dripping down his taut, toned muscles. He completely ignores Dillon as he steps up to the counter and stares at the other made-up cup of coffee. "This for me?" he asks, picking it up.

I nod.

Cooper gives me an appreciative smile before taking a sip of the overly sweet coffee. His face contorts for a moment, but he glances up at me and takes a big gulp.

Dillon sneers as he flings the cabinet open and looks for his favorite mug. Little does he know, I broke it the day he trashed my home as revenge for us not getting married.

I turn to Cooper and whisper, "Quick, kiss me."

What? he mouths.

"Do something. Or he is going to be suspicious."

He pinches the bridge of his nose. "Fine." His hands snake out, one going to my lower back and the other wrapping around the nape of my neck as he closes the gap between us, and his mouth crashes down on mine.

His wet body melds with mine as I open my mouth and let his tongue slip in.

My body comes alive the moment he touches me—every inch of me heating as he takes my mouth in a kiss that feels anything but fake.

I can't help but wonder... if this is how he kisses when it's fake, what would it be like when he meant it? When it was real.

"Disgusting." Dillon's voice interrupts us. I pull back, glancing back at Dillon as he picks up the pot and pours the rest of the liquid into two mugs.

Cooper lowers his head into my neck, nuzzling me. I giggle as droplets of water fall from his hair and down my shirt.

"Oops, looks like I finished the pot, and you both are stuck drinking that crap Sutton calls coffee." He smirks as he backs out of the room.

We don't untangle ourselves from each other until we hear the bathroom door shut.

"What is he doing up at this hour, anyway?" Cooper asks as he steps away to lean against the counter.

"Eh, he's basically like a night-shift worker. This is his bedtime. Being a musician, he mostly kept an opposite schedule from me, working nights and sleeping during the day. So it isn't unusual to see him up at this time. Coffee has, like, zero to no effect on his weird brain. He can and does drink it until he falls asleep without a problem, which is why I knew he would take the bait."

"Bait?" He pauses with his cup inches from his lips. "Did you?"

"Yep." I nod with a massive grin as I pull the MiraLAX packets from the drawer.

"You're crazy." He laughs, picking me up and bouncing me against his still-damp chest.

"Stop," I squeal. "Your towel is going to fall off."

"You'd like that, wouldn't you?"

"You wish."

He places me back onto my feet and grips the towel around his waist as it slides down, revealing one of those delectable V's that every woman loves.

My eyes are glued to that spot as he says, "Kind of seems like you wish." And then he's gone, leaving me once again to think about how I actually do wish that.

Chapter Twelve

Cooper

Last night brought back so many memories of when I first got to know Sutton. Of her rejecting me. I couldn't help but think about the first time I ever met Dillon and the instant hatred I felt for him.

Antsy, I shook my knee the entire drive.

Because I was going to see her.

Maybe it would be the day Sutton finally listened to my explanation. Maybe it would be the day we squashed this misunderstanding and became friends.

My heart was pounding as I hopped out of the truck and followed Nate and Vivian to where they stopped in front of Sutton's car.

Nate elbowed me in the ribs, and I knew instantly what he was trying to convey.

The douche was present.

I had heard bits and pieces about the man but hadn't gotten to put a face to the shitty reputation.

All hope I had for mending things with Sutton was squashed the moment I saw him. Dillon the Douche. I knew what to expect. A dickhole of a man who wasn't worth anyone's time.

I was prepared for that.

What I wasn't prepared for was the surge of jealousy I felt the moment he touched her.

As we walked into the building, I kept waiting for her to look at me, to say something nasty that I knew she didn't mean.

But she didn't glance in my direction once.

Instead, she kept her eyes straight ahead.

Inside, we checked in and got our gear.

Dillon's hand swept over Sutton's lower back as we listened to the woman relay the instructions.

I barely heard a word the woman said as my attention was glued to his hand. His hand that moved too far south while in front of others.

Sutton jumped a little and shot him a scowl.

But she didn't move away. She stayed glued to his side, even when her gaze met mine. She gave me a sneer of a smile, and I couldn't help the butterflies that took flight in my stomach.

This woman had a control over me that she was goddamn clueless to.

I was gone for her.

From the first moment I laid eyes on her gorgeous face, I wanted her. But it was everything else that made me crave her. She was wicked with her words and wit, and I was putty in her hands for her to mold or throw away whenever she pleased.

We split up into two teams, and logically, I should have known I wouldn't get to be with her, but it still filled my body with disappointment as she chose Dillon and his equally douchey friend Jake to team with.

The game began, and my adrenaline spiked as I sprinted out of the light into a dark corner, watching, waiting for their colors to light up near me. It didn't take long until a blue light bounced into view, and when I say bounced, I meant it.

Sutton was skipping with her gun swinging at her side. There wasn't a care in the world on her face as she just smiled, moving along the neon path. That was until I stepped out in front of her with my laser gun pointed directly at her.

She came to a screeching halt with a frown pinching her brows together.

"I just want to talk," I said, lowering my weapon to my side and lifting my hands in mock surrender.

"No, thank you." She glared, brushing her shoulder against mine as she passed me.

I followed her into a darkened alcove. "Please, baby opossum, just hear me out for once." I grazed my hand down her arm until her hand was in mine, pulling her to a stop.

"Cooper," she gritted through her teeth, but she didn't pull away from me. "How many times do I have to tell you not to call me that?"

I grinned, leaning in closer till my lips were a whisper away from her ear. "At least once more."

She sucked in a deep breath and closed her eyes. "Please stop calling me that. It's ridiculous and semi-insulting."

"How is it insulting? They're feral and fierce, just like you."

"I can't do this with you right now," she said, trying to step around me.

"I need to explain to you about that night."

"I don't want to talk about it."

"Tough shit. I'm sorry."

"Can you please drop it? I'm begging you," she pleaded, her eyes shining up at me so brightly, even in the hazy maze.

"Just let me explain..."

"Explain what?" a voice called out from behind us.

We both jumped at the interruption.

"Shit," she muttered under her breath.

I hung my head. There went my shot to talk to her alone.

"Nothing," Sutton said quickly, moving out from behind me and walking over to him.

I spun to face them.

She wrapped her hands around one of his biceps and began to tug him in the opposite direction.

"No." He yanked his arm from her grasp. "I want to hear what he has to say."

Sutton silently pleaded with me to keep my mouth shut. Her eyes growing wide.

"Nothing. It was nothing," I said before walking past him.

He threw his arm out in front of me, effectively blocking my path. I glanced at him questionably.

"No, I want to know what you two were talking about."

"How about it's none of your fucking business," I said, pushing his arm down.

He blocked me again, this time by stepping into my path. "That's where you're wrong. If it has to do with Sutton, it's my business."

My brows shot up as I glanced at her to see if she was going to let this asshole talk for her.

Sutton averted her gaze to the ground, and I clenched my fists.

Dillon tracked the movement and laughed. "You didn't think you had a chance with her, did you?"

I tilted my head to the side and stared down at him. I had a good three inches on the man, not to mention a good amount of muscles compared to his lean frame.

I didn't dare chance another glance at Sutton. Her silence was telling enough. She was going to let her little shit of a boyfriend talk down to me as she stood by and watched.

I wouldn't bother to fight him on this.

If she wanted to continue to pretend like nothing had happened that night, I would do it.

Not because I cared about what the immature asshole thought.

No, I would do it for her.

Because for some stupid reason, I cared about her.

But that didn't mean I was naive.

No, I got the message.

Screw whatever romantic fantasies I had about us.

There was no us.

Today made that crystal clear.

"Can I leave now?"

"Not just yet." He pulled his laser gun up and fired at my chest with a stupid-ass grin on his face. "Now you can."

It was childish.

And I wished I had thought to do it first.

"Thanks," I grumbled, stalking out of the dark hall and down the ramp back to where we started.

Nate and Viv were cozying up to each other as I approached. "You guys ready for round two?" I said, my tone clipped.

Nate opened his mouth but didn't say anything before he closed it.

"Yeah, just let me go grab the guns," Vivian said before running off to wherever they had left them.

We made our way to our starting mark and waited for the next game to begin.

I ran, sweat tickling my brows as I made it my mission to get Dillon out for the next two rounds.

I left Jake to Nate and Viv. I knew they had their own issues going on with the other team.

I smiled with every shot. The redness that crept up his neck and filled his face was priceless. So was the vein bulging from his forehead.

Despite my best efforts, Sutton wasn't spared.

I had tried hard not to shoot her. No matter how pissed I was at her for not interrupting him, for dating a guy like that, I couldn't shoot her.

Even though they were toys and not real, it made me queasy to take her out. That being said, I did end up shooting her in the end. But only because Dillon used her as a human shield.

Game or not, who did that to their girlfriend.

Neither Sutton nor I spoke another word to each other for the rest of the time. Dillon spewed hatred at me, which I answered with my middle finger more than once.

I left that day feeling more pissed off than ever.

No matter how much I tried to work out the anger that lingered, I couldn't rid myself of it. It was as if I was infected by it, and the only thing that made it relent was seeing her.

I hated that she was both the disease and the cure.

That she alone could hurt or heal me.

Chapter Thirteen

Sutton

Cooper wipes his hands down the front of his jeans before taking his key from the ignition and slipping it into my purse.

"Are you okay?" I ask, turning in the leather seat to get a better look at him.

It's been a week since the fake sex and the intense kiss that followed it. Cooper has been flirty, but he's also remained distant. He'll only touch or kiss me in the presence of Dillon. And I can't tell if that's what I want or not anymore.

He jerks his head up and down. "Yeah, of course."

"Really? Because I've watched you rub your sweaty palms on your pants three times since we got in the truck."

His head drops forward with a groan. "Fine. I'm nervous as fuck. These people in there are a lot."

"Coop, it's just a work party. They're just your colleagues."

"Just my colleagues," he scoffs. "Those people are hounds, sniffing around for anything and everything out of place that they can gossip about and use to their advantage."

He's right. I know enough people in the business circle to know they're worlds different from his previous teacher coworkers.

"Are you nervous about us? About the bargain?"

"Yes. No. Maybe."

"You didn't need to bring me if having me here with you was going to give you an ulcer."

"It's not you. You are the only thing even remotely calming." He pulls my hand into his clammy one. My first instinct is to pull away, to avoid all physical contact with him unless it's a thousand percent necessary. But I don't. Instead, I let him lean on me, just like he did for me the other day. I wrap my finger around his, and Cooper smiles at our joined hands. His thumb sweeps back and forth over my hands. "It's them. When I first started, I panicked. They're all settled in their relationships and careers, and there I was, switching careers in my thirties with no romantic ties. So I lied and said I was in a relationship."

"You didn't exactly lie. You've been in a long-term partnership with Nate for the better part of twenty-something years."

He laughs while staring out the window as person after person files into the building.

"If this place, this lie, is giving you this much anxiety, maybe it's not worth it."

"It is," he disagrees, his voice steady as every trace of anxiety seems to have vanished. "I needed to get out of teaching. It didn't bring me joy anymore. This job gave me a fresh start with a salary that is almost triple what I was making before."

"Cooper, I've seen your place. You live so freaking modestly that it annoys me. What the hell are you doing with all the extra money you've started to make?"

"I'm saving it."

"For what?" I press, scooting closer to him as if my proximity will force him to open up more.

He taps on the door handle, turning to look out the window as he says, "My parents. I want to help them retire."

"They don't have a 401k? Scandalous." I clutch my imaginary pearls.

His lips clamp together, fighting a grin. "No, they do, but it just isn't enough for them to retire anytime in the next twenty years. They both work for the public school system. Dad is an elementary gym teacher and Mom is a high school guidance counselor. So, as you can imagine, they aren't making bank. And on top of that, they helped pay for my college."

And just like that, I think a layer of ice has melted off my heart for Cooper. "That's very selfless of you."

"Not really. They were the best parents I could have ever asked for. I mean, the two of them are saints. Seriously, they volunteer two weekends a month at a local food bank. They rarely yelled at me growing up, even when I was a teenager doing dumb shit, like setting off the smoke detectors in the middle of the night because my dumbass lit up a joint in my bedroom without opening a window."

"They didn't yell at you for that?"

"Nope. They sat me down and attempted to discuss the dangers of marijuana with me. Then they confiscated my stash and made my high ass a grilled cheese."

"They sound amazing. Now, let's go in there and secure your saintly parents their retirement by being the most sickeningly in love couple these people have ever seen."

He takes a deep breath, hesitating as his fingers flex on the handle.

"You got this, Coop. Just be yourself."

"You want me to be myself. The same self you consistently complain about?"

I slap his thigh with our hands still connected. "That's the one. Now, time to go out there and dazzle everyone with the perplexing question of how a below-average man in height and looks like you got a smoking-hot girlfriend like me."

A genuine, almost panty-dropping smile graces his lips as he lets go of my hand and opens his door.

Now that I've gotten his nerves under control, I need to focus on mine. My heart is pounding as I hop out of the truck and meet Cooper at the front. With my hand in his again, I wrap my other around his bicep—his very *large* bicep—almost clinging to him.

I've been to hundreds of parties like these. Heck, I thrive in these situations. But the need for this to all go right for Cooper has me stressing about every move I make. I won't let my own anxiety ruin anything for him, though, so I straighten my spine as we walk through the doors of Astor and Avery Financials.

The entire enormous lobby has been transformed into a tropical getaway. Bright flowers decorate every corner. Palm trees and tall blades of grass are set up for a photo booth with a professional photographer. Beautiful floral arrangements, pineapples, and coconuts adorn the room. Bamboo-like chairs and tables are scattered around, with people gathering in front of them.

"Wow," I sigh, my eyes darting all over the place to take in the grandeur theme. "What kind of party is this?"

"It's a retirement party for Jorge. All I know is he is packing up and moving to the beach next month, and I'll be inheriting some of his clients, including Mr. Tillan."

"Lucky man. Looks like he is going to paradise."

"He basically is," Cooper replies, placing his hand on my lower back and guiding me through the few people standing between us and Jorge.

The older man beams at Cooper as they greet each other. Cooper might've only joined this company a few months ago, but it's obvious how much they all love him and consider him one of them already.

"You must be the man of the hour. I'm Sutton, Cooper's longtime partner in crime and occasional lover," I announce, shaking the older man's hand.

His eyes twinkle with amusement. "Occasional lover?"

"Only when he's being extra good." I wink.

Jorge slaps Cooper on the back. "You've got a keeper with this one, son. Don't let her go."

Cooper sucks in his bottom lip with a grin. "I don't plan on it."

And just like that, my panties want to leave my body again.

Could the man cool his sex appeal for one night?

Pump the breaks.

One night is all I ask.

"So, Jorge, I hear you're leaving us for some tropical paradise?"

Jorge's posture melts as if just imagining his near future has all the tension leaving his body. "Ah, yes, it's always been my dream to live on the beach. Starting next month, I get to make it a reality in Maui."

"Maui. Hot damn, Jorge, do you need an occasional lover?"

Cooper frowns as everyone else laughs.

"I'll tell you what, Sutton, if my wonderful wife of forty years decides she is done with me, I will give you a call."

I smile. "I'm counting on it. But something tells me she isn't gonna give up living in paradise with a catch like you."

Jorge is soon whisked away into conversation with another group of Cooper's coworkers.

"He was nice," I tell Coop.

"Do you need to flirt with every man you meet?"

"Every man?" I scoff. "I also charmed the ladies as well, thank you very much."

"Sutton..."

I roll my eyes. "You're being dramatic, Cooper. I wasn't flirting."

He stares at me in disbelief.

"Okay, fine. Maybe with Jorge. But can you blame me? The man apparently has Maui money. I was trying to get us a free vacation."

"*Us*? I don't recall you angling for anything for *us*."

I tsk. "Your old age is starting to show, Cooper. That noggin of yours isn't remembering what it should."

He pinches the bridge of his nose before letting his shoulders relax. "Want to see my office?"

"Yes." I bounce with excitement as he leads me out of the crowded room down a long hallway past an open office space that looks like FTW's cubicle land, or basically all other office buildings.

Cooper stops to show me abstract art that litters the walls. It's a nice change from the offices that only have self-promotions or achievements covering every inch of space for potential and current clients to see.

I tilt my head at a particularly interesting painting. Black, white, and red are smeared across the canvas in a haphazard way that feels anything but intentional. "Sometimes I think artists are making fun of us all."

Cooper glances away from the painting. "How so?"

I huff out a laugh. "You can't honestly say this is good, can you?"

He shrugs. "Beauty is in the eye of the beholder and whatnot, so who am I to say it isn't."

"You're such a *nice* guy."

"What's wrong with being nice?"

"Nothing... unless you count being boring."

He smirks. "Fine, it's ugly."

"Ha! I knew you didn't like it." I point at him.

He chuckles, returning his hand to my lower back and leading me away until we stop at the third door from the end of the hall.

He pushes open the door before leading me inside and shutting it behind us.

I run my finger along the edge of the large mahogany desk as I take in the space. "Fancy."

"Mm-hmm."

"Did you bring me in here to show me your new, fancy desk, or..." I tease.

"Or what?" He moves to stand right in front of me. His chest flush against mine.

"You tell me," I say, my breath becoming short. "Or better yet. Why don't you show me."

His eyes glue to my mouth, and his Adam's apple bobs. Heat swirls in his amber-brown gaze like a wildfire raging through fall foliage.

I wait in frozen anticipation, my breath quickening as he leans forward. Is this really about to happen? Is Cooper going to kiss me? And not for the bargain's sake?

And at this very moment, I know I want him to kiss me.

God, do I want him to kiss me.

The warmth of his breath lingers on my lips when he pauses mere inches from my mouth.

He reaches forward, his hand grazing across my cheek and down to the nape of my neck. Tingles erupt down my spine as I close my eyes, letting the sensation of his touch overwhelm my senses.

"Sutton, I—"

I don't want to hear it. I don't want to know what he might say, because all I want is his mouth pressed against mine.

Throwing caution to the wind, I close the gap between us, pressing my lips to his in a kiss that's anything but gentle.

Cooper quickly parts his lips, and I waste no time swiping my tongue across them.

He tastes even better than I remember, and it's a flavor I want to drown in.

Our tongues dance, rolling against one another in a sensual rhythm that makes my core ache with desperation for friction.

Sensing my need for more, Cooper's grip on my neck tightens, and he pulls me closer until there's nothing between us but our clothes. My hands lace in his chestnut strands, tugging at the edges as I demand more.

His other hand finds my hip, and he crushes me against his growing erection.

I let out a sigh of pleasure at the feeling of his cock hitting that perfect spot between my legs.

Yes, yes, yes, I want to yell as he angles his hips upward and I unabashedly rub myself all over him.

God, he feels so good. Too freaking good.

Cooper's touch falls from my neck to my ass, where he palms me through my dress, kneading my flesh with a groan. "You're so fucking sexy," he husks, pulling his lips from mine and trailing them down my jaw to my neck, where he lavishes that special spot that has me dripping in no time.

I bump into the desk, and Cooper lifts me, settling between my thighs. "I bet you tell that to all the women you have sprawled out on your desk."

"Only you," he snickers. As he pushes my dress up so my panties are my only barrier, he hikes one of my legs around his hips and grinds his erection into me, finding that sweet pace that has me rushing to the finish line in seconds.

"Right there," I pant, holding his head in the crook of my neck.

The heat coiling deep inside me erupts like a volcano as I come. My nails dig into his scalp as I throw my head back, letting the pure pleasure light me up. Every inch of my skin burns from Cooper's touch.

My heartbeat is erratic as he pulls his head back to peer into my eyes.

Neither of us say a word. Instead, our mouths fuse together again. I regain control of my limbs and reach for his belt just as a knock raps on the door.

We break apart like two teenagers who've been caught by their parents. Frozen, we listen.

"Cooper," a deep voice calls through the thick door. "It's time for the group photo with Jorge."

Cooper wipes his mouth with his finger, those same long, delicious fingers that had been holding me steady just moments ago. Oh, how I hope they'll leave small bruises in their wake as a reminder that this was real. That this wasn't a figment of my imagination. "Be right there," he hollers, his voice tight and clipped.

We both sit there staring at each other for a long, torturous moment before he finally releases his hold on me to grip my hands that are still clutching his belt. "Sutton," he starts, but I cut him off by tearing my hands from him and jumping off the desk.

I fix my skirt and run my fingers through my curls while Cooper stands there observing me. His expression a mixture of confusion and concern.

"You're staring," I singsong.

"And you're absolutely stunning after you come."

I blink, unsure of how to respond. I open my mouth and close it twice before finally spitting out, "Is a thank-you an appropriate enough response after dry humping your fake boyfriend to completion in his office?"

Cooper snorts with laughter, stepping closer to me. "I'll take anything you give me." His lips brush mine in a feather-soft kiss, and then he's gone, leaving me alone in his office, staring at my new favorite desk.

Chapter Fourteen

Cooper

We leave the party sometime after the group photo and cake. I was both bummed and relieved that we didn't end up running into my boss. I wanted to show Sutton off to everyone in the office. But I also wasn't looking forward to having to lie about us.

Neither of us say a word as I drive us back to her house. The silence must finally unnerve her, though, because she reaches over and turns on my stereo, then presses a few buttons to connect the Bluetooth to her phone. Seconds later, the familiar sounds of Creed fill the air.

I can't help but chuckle at her choice.

Sutton shoots me a look that I'm sure is meant to intimidate, but it merely makes me want to wrap her in my arms.

I listen to her humming along with every song, so thankful that she doesn't start that horrible squawking she calls singing.

When I pull up to the house, we find the driveway empty besides Sutton's white Volvo.

She looks down, fidgeting with her nails, picking off the pristine opal color she perfected only twenty-four hours ago.

"Do you want to talk about it?" I ask, palming my keys.

Her nose crinkles. "Do you want to?"

I release a heavy, shaky breath, my nerves ramping up at the anticipation of what we need to do. "Not particularly. But I feel like it's the mature thing to do."

She scoffs. "Since when are we mature?"

"Since you came all over my desk only hours ago."

Sutton's hand flies to her chest. "Cooper Fisher—"

"Not my name."

"What a dirty mouth you have."

"You love it." I smirk.

A flush rises to her cheeks. "Maybe I do. Not like you're going to do anything about it."

"You don't think so?" I lean across the seat until we're sharing the same breath.

She shakes her head with a daring smile before grabbing my keys, jumping out of the truck with a laugh, and running to the front door.

It only takes me a moment to spring into action behind her, chasing her into the house as she flings the door open and sprints to her bedroom.

Once in the room, I slam the door behind me and wrap my arms around her waist from behind.

Sutton laughs, throwing her head back against my shoulder.

I spin her around, and she pounces, her lips landing on mine in an instant.

Tongues and teeth clash as we rip at each other's clothing, Sutton throwing my jacket off and fumbling with the buttons on my shirt, while I slip the shoestring straps of her dress off her slender shoulders, then tug the zipper at the back of her dress down.

It falls to the floor, and she stands before me in nothing but a tiny black lace thong and a pair of matching heels.

She finishes with my shirt buttons and pushes it off me as I kneel before her. My hands glide down her curves until I palm her ass, leaning forward to press a kiss to her navel before continuing my descent down her luscious legs to her feet as I help her out of the shoes.

I glance up at her, heat filling her gaze as she demands, "Take off my panties."

My fingers trace the edge of the lace as I lean forward, burying my face in her heat. She gasps as I rub my nose along her covered slit before doing the same with my tongue.

She smells and tastes intoxicating. I want more. I want to taste her without anything between us. As I pull the thong down her legs, she steps out of it, and I bury my face back between her thighs. My tongue flicks at her clit, causing her to pitch forward.

Her little pants egg me on as I suck and lick at her pussy.

"More," she begs.

I pull back, resting my chin on her stomach. "You want more?"

She nods quickly as her chest heaves with her rapid breathing. She's a fucking sight to behold.

I flick her clit once more with my tongue before standing. Sutton whimpers at my action.

Laughing, I promise her, "Don't worry, baby, I'm not done with this pussy just yet."

My dick presses into the soft curves of her stomach, and she gasps as I press two fingers inside her dripping cunt.

"Fuck, Cooper," she moans, throwing her head back.

"You like the way my fingers stretch your tight, wet pussy?" I thrust them in and out while my thumb rubs slow circles on her throbbing clit. Her walls clench as I add, "You like me talking about your greedy cunt while I finger fuck you, don't you?"

She grabs my neck, pulling my lips to hers for a rough, breath-stealing kiss.

I pick up my pace, matching the rhythm of her tongue against mine.

Sutton's legs shake, only encouraging me to move my fingers faster.

I tear my mouth from hers and watch as she pants against me, her nails digging into my neck and wrist as I work her body into a frenzy.

I slide my hand that's still tangled in her hair to her neck and squeeze. Sutton's eyes widen as she comes apart on my hand. Her pussy clamps down on my fingers and her back bows. I can tell she's fighting not to look at me as her orgasm racks her body. She's magnificent. It's everything I remembered and more.

Watching her come is something I never want to forget.

It's pure magic.

The sight of her convulsing for me has me fighting the urge to follow like an inexperienced nitwit.

I remove my fingers from inside her and release my grip on her throat, loving the sound of her panting for air.

"So goddamn beautiful," I groan before licking them clean.

Sutton stares up at me, her chest still heaving and eyes glassy from her orgasm.

I expect some sort of smart-ass reply or even a thank-you. What I don't expect is for her to drop to her knees and lick up the bulge in my pants.

Even through the slacks, my cock twitches from her touch. She makes quick work of the button and zipper, pushing my pants down my legs for me to step out of. Her hand rubs against my straining erection still covered with my black boxer briefs.

I hiss at the contact. "Stop playing with it, Sutton."

She bats her lashes up at me as her fingers work their way into the waistband. "But I like watching you squirm," she teases, leaning in to run her teeth over my covered shaft.

"Fuck," I groan.

She pulls my underwear down, releasing my cock, and immediately gets to work. Her hands wrap around the base while she flicks her tongue against the tip.

My hips jerk forward, urging her to suck me in. And boy, does she deliver. Sutton's pouty lips wrap around the head of my cock, proving the most intense suction I've ever felt as she pulls me further back into her throat.

"Goddamn it, Sut, your mouth is heaven. It feels like fucking heaven. Keep sucking my cock deep down your throat, just like that," I demand, and she hums, the vibrations from her throat only adding to my pleasure.

I don't even last five minutes before I'm pushing her magnificent mouth off me and tossing her onto her back on the bed.

The mattress dips under my weight as I crawl over her, bracing my hands beside her fanned-out hair. She smiles up at me as she wraps her legs around my hips and rubs her wet center over my cock.

I bend down, capturing her lips with mine in a breath-stealing kiss. "I need to be in you right now."

"So get inside me," she demands against my lips.

"I need a condom."

She reaches down and grabs my cock, notching it at her entrance. "I have an IUD... If you want to go without."

I pull back to meet her eyes. "You sure?"

"Yeah," she laughs, pushing her hips forward, taking my tip inside her.

"Fuck," we both groan as I slide further in.

"You feel like my own personal heaven. It's like you were made for me."

"Shut up and fuck me," she commands in a breathless voice.

And that's all the encouragement I need. I pull back until I'm almost completely out of her before snapping my hips forward. Sutton gasps, clutching my shoulders, and I repeat the movement.

"Again," she begs.

I continue to pound into her as she meets me thrust for thrust.

Being with her, fucking her, is like nothing I've ever experienced.

Sweat slicks our bodies within minutes as that familiar tingling hits the base of my spine.

I don't want this to be over already, but there's no way in hell I'm going to stop. This—she—is everything I've ever wanted.

"I'm going to fill this cunt up with cum, Sutton."

"Do it."

I spill inside her as I continue to drive in and out of her clenching pussy. The pleasure is unlike anything I've ever known. She writhes under my body, grasping my biceps as her orgasm continues to crash through her, wave after wave as she moans my name.

My heart pounds as I pull out of her and lean back on my heels. Thick spurts of cum slowly leak out of her still-pulsing cunt as she reaches down and trails her fingers through the mess of our pleasure. She coats her fingers, all while staring me straight in the eyes before bringing her fingers to her lips and sucking them clean with a moan.

"Shit," I groan. "You're gonna make me hard again if you keep doing that."

Sutton smiles up at me. "That's the point."

"How can you still want more after that?"

"How could I not?"

I lean down and capture her face in my hands as my lips crash down upon hers. "I never said I didn't. I just might need a second to catch my breath."

"Have you ever done any breath play?" A smile tugs at her puffy lips as she stares up at me beneath her long black batting lashes.

"Performed or received?"

"Either. Both?"

I trail a hand from her face down to her neck and lightly squeeze. "I've choked a woman or two for the sake of pleasure."

"But never been choked?" she asks as she flips us over to where she's straddling me.

I shake my head. "No, never."

Sutton rubs her drenched pussy over my already hardening cock. "Can I choke you while I ride you, Coop?"

"Baby, you can do anything you want to me."

She swivels herself, hitting the crown of my cock with her clit over and over as she works us both back up into a frenzy. My hands fall to her waist, and she lifts onto her knees, lining herself up to sink down on me.

"Fuck," I grind out as she slides down my shaft, enveloping me in her sweet, wet, hot embrace again, with her hands braced on my chest.

Sutton moves up and down, riding me at a slow, rhythmic pace, steadily chasing that euphoric bliss she knows is just up ahead, waiting for us both. She slides her hands further up my chest until one is resting on my shoulder and the other is wrapped around my throat, constricting my airway.

It's a new feeling. Something exciting.

I look up from where my eyes had been glued to her bouncing breasts and into her half-lidded gaze. She's a goddess, compressing my throat while taking everything she wants from me.

As my lack of oxygen starts to hit me, she moves faster and faster. My hips pound up, matching her every thrust. I'm on the verge of exploding again, and so is she.

"Don't stop," she demands. "Don't you dare stop."

I don't. Even as my lungs burn and my body fills with heat, I continue to push up into her until she shatters.

Sutton arches forward, her movements stopping, and she releases my throat as she spasms around my cock, crumbling my last shred of resistance. My release spills from me faster than ever. Black dots cloud my vision as I gasp for air.

Sutton collapses onto my chest, her lips brushing against mine in an exhausted kiss. Our skin is sticky with sweat, and the heady scent of our fucking fills the air.

It's perfection.

She is perfection.

"Amazing," she whispers against my mouth.

"Sensational."

"Out of this world." She giggles, sliding off my chest and settling on my side. "So, were you scared?"

"That you were going to kill me?" I ask, stroking my fingers through her sweat-dampened hair. "No, I trust you."

As the words tumble out of my mouth, I realize I do. I trust this incredible woman with everything.

My body, life, heart, and soul. She can have it all. Use it all. And I'd be happy.

"Thank you." Sutton buries herself deeper into the crook of my neck, letting out a sleepy sigh.

"Oh no," I say. And it takes every last bit of resolve I have to sit up, pulling her with me. "You and I both need to clean up before we pass out."

She grumbles something that sounds like *fuck off* before attempting to flop back onto the bed.

"Ah, ah, ah," I laugh, dragging her out of the bed with me. "There will be no UTIs on my watch. Get your sexy ass in that bathroom and wash up."

"But what if I like the feeling of you dripping out of me?"

"Sutton," I groan. "You have to stop torturing me like this."

"Fine." She pouts and slinks off into the bathroom, shutting the door behind her.

While she's cleaning off, I change the sheets on the bed. I'm tossing the dirty ones into the laundry room when I hear the slamming of a car door.

I glance out the window, my mood changing instantly.

The douche is back.

Every time I think that cockroach is gone, he manages to weasel his way back and ruin my mood.

Not giving a fuck that I'm stark-ass naked, dick still covered in my and Sutton's cum, I walk back through the house, passing him as he walks into the living room.

I'm not hiding anything from this prick anymore. Sutton isn't his. She's mine. And the fucker needs to get it through his thick skull that he isn't welcome in our lives.

Dillon doesn't say a word as I pull two bottles of water from the fridge and make my way back into Sutton's room. She's already nestled into the clean sheets, with an arm laid across my pillow.

I set the bottles of water on the nightstand beside her and go into the bathroom to take a quick shower.

Toweling off, I turn off the bathroom light. I don't bother with clothes as I climb into bed beside her. Immediately, she scoots closer, nuzzling into my side as I wrap an arm around her.

"You took too long," she whispers.

I glance to see her eyes still closed. "I took less than five minutes."

"That's five minutes too long. I couldn't sleep without your stupidly hot, big body next to me."

"Well, I'm here now. So shut up and sleep."

She nods and falls silent for several minutes until she eventually whispers, "We really should do the mature thing and talk about what this meant or means."

"What do you want it to mean?"

She shrugs. "That we are just having fun."

My throat constricts.

Fun.

She just wants fun. Of *fucking* course she does. Just last month, she was prepared to be Mrs. Oak, and now she's free from the dickhole. Obviously, she isn't ready to jump into a new relationship.

"I can do fun," I reply.

Sutton squeezes my hand, and seconds later, she's lightly snoring against my skin.

Chapter Fifteen

Sutton

My heart slams against my chest as I'm startled awake by a loud screeching. Grumbling, I roll over to the sound of my alarm going off. The beeping feeling simultaneously all too soon and like I've had enough sleep to last me a lifetime. Stretching out in bed, I'm reminded of last night with every move of my beautifully sore muscles.

Of the world-shattering sex Cooper and I had.

It was like nothing I had ever had before.

Yeah, I knew we had off-the-charts chemistry.

But he made up for all of our wasted time. It was like we were both jacked up on lust-laced Viagra.

Not that I'm complaining.

I'll never complain about being that thoroughly spent.

I mean, shit, I don't think I've ever come that hard. Not even when I DJ on my favorite solo night of the week, Masturbation

Monday. Not that I've gotten to celebrate that particular day in a while. And now that Cooper and I are fucking—have fucked. God, I hope it's going to be for more than one night—I don't foresee needing such a night anymore. Not with having a horny Hercules in bed who is more than willing to match my high sex drive.

And while I now know he can deliver an orgasm like no other with his mouth, the two of us coming together in such a primal, hungry way was something more. Something about last night was different.

Shutting off my alarm, I roll over to find Cooper's side of the bed already empty.

It's only six a.m., and the man is already up.

I admire and hate him for it.

Can't he be a normal human being for once? Be a little lazy and not wake up before the sun to get his morning run in or whatever he does.

Groaning, I push myself out of bed and into the shower. Every drop of water on my skin reminds me of how good last night was. The feeling of Cooper's body pressed so firmly against mine as we brought each other past the brink of pleasure.

I trail my hands over my body, imagining Cooper slinking into the shower with me for another round before I have to head to work.

Get it together, Sut. Now is not the time to be horny. You have work to do.

I shake off all sexual thoughts of Cooper and his cock, trading the mental images for the least sexy things I can think of, like my grandma when she was on oxygen, smoking as she would say mean things to my mom every holiday. Nothing kills a lady boner like a hacking bitch of a grandma.

After I shower and blow-dry my hair, I slip into a modest wrap dress and heels before running a coat of mascara over my eyes and brushing bronzer on my cheeks.

In the kitchen, I find Cooper sitting at the table, his hair mussed and glasses sitting on his face. Two plates sit in front of him, one with half-eaten eggs and bacon and the other full of the same, plus avocado toast on the side, while his gaze is focused on his laptop.

"Is that for me?" I ask, sliding into the chair beside him.

"Who else would I feed?"

I shrug. "Maybe the other woman you're seeing."

He looks up, taking off his glasses. "There is no one else. Only you."

"That's what you say to all the girls."

He grabs my chin, turning my face to his as he leans in closer. "There is no one else. Do you understand?"

His brown eyes give no hint of jokes or lies. I nod, and he dips his mouth to mine, pressing a tender kiss that I want to savor forever onto my lips.

He loosens his grip. Kissing me one more time before letting me go. "Good. Eat up, baby."

I tear a bite out of my toast. "Since when did you get so nurturing?"

He looks me over curiously. "I've always been this way. Maybe you're just starting to pay attention."

"Please," I laugh. "I let you coat my insides with your baby juice, and now you are obsessed. Admit it."

The corners of Cooper's lips turn up into the most painstakingly beautiful grin. "Oh, I am a thousand percent obsessed. But that doesn't change the fact that I have always tried to take care of you, whether you let yourself see it or not."

"Bullshit," I tease. "Until we changed our relationship into a physical one, you were nothing but a pain in my ass."

He shakes his head, standing up to scrape his plate off into the trash before placing it in the dishwasher. "Okay, believe what you want. You're wrong, but okay."

⚘

I can't help but think about Cooper's words for the rest of the day.

"I have always tried to take care of you, whether you let yourself see it or not."

There's no way it's true.

Until recently, he was nothing more than Nate's annoying friend, albeit super hot, but still *very, very* annoying friend.

Memories fill my day as I try to concentrate on my job. Phone interviews with potential employees fall flat because all I can think about is him.

Has Cooper always tried to take care of me?

I mean, yeah, he's driven me home multiple times when I've been drinking.

He always carries my things for me.

Whenever I'm having a bad day, he always tries to make me smile.

Sure, Cooper is the first one to go along with my schemes when they involve pranks.

And yes, I guess he did let me stay with him without a second of hesitation the night of my failed wedding.

He stayed and cleaned my house with me when he could have bolted the moment he dropped me off.

And he agreed to pretend to date me to get Dillon to leave.

Fuck, he didn't have to do any of that.

He never had to do any of those things.

Yet he did. He's always been there for me, even when I was being a bitch to him.

Even when it would have been easier for him to stay out of it. He's stood by my side, being a rock for me to lean on.

How have I never noticed everything he does for me?

Have I been so caught up in my own world and embarrassment that I wrote him off completely when he's always been there for me?

"And that's how I landed the biggest project of my career," the voice says through the phone, breaking my thought process.

Shit, I'm in the middle of interviewing someone.

I clear my throat, thankful this is a preliminary phone interview and that they couldn't tell I had drifted off into a Cooper thought bubble. "That's quite the accomplishment. Please be sure to pass that story along during your next interview with the partners."

"My next interview?" the candidate asks. "So that means I did okay?"

I laugh. "Of course. Your resume is outstanding, and based on our conversation, I see no reason why I shouldn't push you through to the next step." Honestly, unless he said something insane during my daydreaming, there's no reason not to. He's a great candidate for the position, and I'd love nothing more than to fill this position with someone of his talents.

"Thank you so much, Ms. Hale. Thank you."

"You're very welcome. Be on the lookout for an email to set up your next interview."

After hanging up the phone, I immediately send out a text to Viv.

I arrive at the coffee shop only a few minutes before Viv. I spot her the moment she bounces out of her car, bounding toward the coffee shop without a second glance at her surroundings.

Sticking my fingers in my mouth, I let out a loud, ear-piercing whistle. But she doesn't stop.

I groan. *This woman.*

I whistle again without success.

Taking a deep breath, I let out the turkey call I thought I'd never have to use again. In college, we would use the sound to alert each other to an unattractive suitor's approach. It was a call that said "come to me right now."

She stops dead in her tracks, glancing around the parking lot for where the sound came from.

I let out the gobbling noise again, ashamed that I still have it in me.

Her gaze finally lands on me after twenty seconds of looking around, and she immediately frowns as she stomps toward the alley behind the café.

When she gets closer, I wave for her to continue walking toward me until we're both standing behind the giant black dumpster that reeks of rotten food.

"Seriously?" She eyes my outfit. "Camo and a bird call..."

"I'm trying to be incognito."

"And the nasty, trash-ridden alley?"

"Same reason, duh."

She sighs as I stick my hand out with the coffee I got her.

She takes it without question and pulls it up to her lips. "Spill."

"I don't know where to start."

She takes a long sip of her coffee. "How about we start with the fact you've recently had sex?"

My eyes widen. "How did you know?"

"Please." She rolls her eyes. "You have a big-ass hickey on your collarbone that you're hiding horribly, and your lips are puffier than normal, which means either they've been getting sucked on or you've been sucking on something."

I blink back my shock. "He gave me a hickey?" I look down at my chest and *yep*, just as she said, there's a fresh love bite peeking out from under the strap of my camo dress. "That motherfucker."

"Sooooo?" Her face lights up with a teasing smile. "Care to share?"

Nerves prickle up my arms, all the way to my chest, as I blurt out, "I had sexual intercourse with Cooper Shaw... More than once."

A wicked grin overtakes her face as she leans back against the grimy dumpster and busts out laughing.

"Vivian, it's not funny."

She continues to laugh. "Yes, yes it is."

I groan, covering my face with my hands. "Fine, laugh it all up. I know it must be *so* freaking funny that Cooper and Sutton have been doing the naked tango."

"That's not what's funny about it, darling."

"Then what is?"

"The fact that it took you so damn long to get there."

I squint at her. "I'm not following."

"Sut, since when are you nervous about telling me you've been sleeping with a guy?"

"Never," I say matter-of-factly, because it's true. I tell Viv every raunchy, debauched story I can.

"Why do you think that is?"

I drop my head and stare at my hands, my fingers fidgeting and twisting together. "'Cause it's Cooper... And me."

"Because it means something to you."

"Pshh." I wave her off. She always has to make things into something more than they are.

"Admit it. It's more than sex, isn't it?"

I swallow. "I don't know."

She waits, silently staring.

"Fine. It's so much more. It's confusing and terrifying. When I am with him, everything feels right."

"Then why are you confused and scared?"

"Because you've seen the guys I date. Hell, I almost married Dillon. My judgment in the romance department is a little flawed."

"Do you think Coop is like those other guys?"

"No. He is nothing like them. He's the complete opposite. Which is the problem. He's kind and dependable. He looks after me. And don't get me started on the way that man knows how to use his body."

"I'm still not seeing the issue here."

"The issue is me. I'm going to fuck it up. He's too good, and I'm just Slut-ton."

"Oh, Sut." Her eyes soften, and she leans forward, taking my hands into hers. "It's okay to be scared to mess up. But it's not okay to let that fear hold you back from someone amazing like Cooper."

I take a deep breath. "I don't know how not to be scared."

"It will pass the more you let yourself enjoy what's happening."

"Okay."

"Okay, now tell me everything." She swats my hands excitedly.

"I think I have a breeding kink."

Chapter Sixteen

Sutton

"This is the last time," I say between pants. It's a lie. I know it. He knows it. But it's one I have to tell myself. And I have, every time my fingers have held on to his thick shoulders. Every time I have felt his breath on my skin. And every time I have wrapped my legs around his waist. And every single time, it has been a lie.

Damn, he feels so good. It's like an addiction. I'm a junkie, and he is the only thing that can make me feel good. I crave him, even though I know I shouldn't. It's hard to explain because I also can't stand him. But at moments like these, those thoughts go out the window because my body takes over.

He laughs into my neck, letting the heat of his breath caress my skin as his hips thrust himself into me over and over again. The sweet sensation of him being inside me is a pure pleasure like I've never known before.

"Stop lying," he says as his hand reaches between us, finding my bundle of nerves. His fingers move in circles, and I can't think as my orgasm builds. "You love the way I fuck you."

"Shut up, Cooper, you're killing my orgasm by talking," I growl before pressing my lips to his. Our tongues tangle together as he continues to drive into me. I'm about to break, I can feel it, but I don't want to. I want to continue to enjoy this for as long as possible. My body, though, has other ideas.

He laughs into my mouth as my release hits. My body shudders, and I pull his closer to mine. My nails dig into his back so hard he hisses in a mixture of pleasure and pain but never stops driving into me. My back arches, trying to steal every last bit of ecstasy from him. His movements slow as I feel him come inside me.

He rolls off me, grabs my face, and kisses me like I'm his salvation. The smile on his face is contagious when he lies back. "Sutton?"

"Hmm?"

"What are we doing?" he asks, his eyes closed, with one hand over his chest and the other tangled up in my hair.

"We are going into a post-orgasm coma. A cuma, if you will."

He chuckles, and the sound has my body revving up for round two. "Not what I meant, and you know it."

I roll onto my side, trailing my hand over his chest and tracing the definition of his body until I'm grasping his hardening cock in my hands. "You almost ready for round two?"

He sucks in a sharp breath before looking at his phone. "We have thirty minutes till we have to be across town, or Viv and Nate will kill us."

I sit up to straddle him. "I can work with that, can you?"

He grabs hold of my hips and sinks me onto his hard shaft. "You bet your sweet ass, I can." And we begin our dance again.

We end up arriving at the party fifteen minutes late. Mostly because round two ended up with us screwing like Olympic athletes. I don't think I've ever been that flexible. God, was it delicious. I don't even care what Vivian says, some things are more important than being on time.

Like my vagina's happiness.

And nothing makes it happier than when it's riding Cooper's cock or mouth.

We're both still straightening ourselves up as we ring the doorbell. Coop looks disheveled in a handsome way that makes me want him again, and I hate him for it.

I, on the other hand, look like I've been at the gym. My hairline is drenched in sweat and my lipstick is now a slight stain around my mouth.

"We smell like sex," I mutter to him before the door swings open, and sweet Vivian scowls at me.

"Oh, look, if it isn't the best friends who promised they would arrive early to help me set up for the party." Her voice is laced with sarcasm. "Please do come in." She holds the door open for us to pass.

Coop and I glance at each other before cautiously walking into the house.

She glances at our hands with pursed lips. "Empty-handed, too, I see," she tsks before spinning away, leaving us alone in the entryway.

"This is all your fault," I hiss at Cooper as he takes my jacket off me and places it in the hallway closet with his own.

"Yeah, like you weren't a complete and willing accomplice in our tardiness."

"Okay, here is the plan. You are going to tell Nate that you had a raging case of diarrhea, and that's what kept us. He will discreetly tell Vivian, and she will pity me for having to be around you in your current condition."

"What?" he balks. "I am not pretending like we were late because I had the shits."

"Why not? It's completely believable."

His mouth falls open as his eyes bulge in horror. "No it's not. Why would you say that?"

"Coop, baby." I place my hand on his cheek. "You are the most at risk out of every person I know to get a raging case of bubble guts."

His eyes widen and his mouth drops open. "No, no I'm not."

I give him a thin-lipped smile. "Okay."

I make my way through the house, passing Audra and Viv's brother in a tense game of Jenga before making it outside to the gorgeous patio that never ceases to amaze me.

It's an absolutely gorgeous backyard.

From the pergola that holds twinkling lights to the fire pit and hammocks. Nate and Viv's yard is an outdoor paradise.

One that, from Viv's stories, I know is home to lots and lots of sexy times.

Luckily for me, though, I know my bestie knows how to Lysol a place before a party.

I spot Nate by the grill and make my way straight for him, grabbing a kebab from the plate he just filled and shoving a delicious piece of meat into my mouth. "Sorry we are late, Natey boy." I thumb over in Cooper's direction. "Someone was having some tummy issues."

Nate sighs. "Cooper, I told you not to try that sketchy hardware store's sushi."

Cooper doesn't say a word, but he does glare at me.

Serves him right, though. He caused my best friend, my person, to be ticked at me all by tempting me with his wickedly delicious body. The least he can do is take the blame without letting them know what we were actually doing.

"Need any help?" I ask, not waiting for his response as I take the plate of meat and bring it to the table that has dish after dish of food laid out.

"As much as I would love the help, I know Viv would like it more." He points to where she's at in the kitchen, with a blender and what looks like multiple pitchers of margaritas.

"On it." I salute him before sauntering past a still-silent Cooper with a grin on my face.

From a few steps away, I hear Cooper say, "I didn't have any gastrointestinal distress. She is lying."

"Bro, don't lie to me."

I can't contain my laughter as I make my way inside the house to Viv.

"I'm the worst," I admit, hugging her from behind.

"The absolute worst," she agrees, leaning into my embrace. "You want to tell me what the hell had you coming in after everyone else?"

"Cooper was on the pooper?" I offer up.

A smile breaks across her face. "Nice try. I could tell by the fading lipstick smeared across Cooper's face and neck that the two of you were late not because of his guts but because he was all up in yours."

I scoff, immediately turning on the sweet southern accent I adapt when I can't be bothered to be serious. "Vivian, I am a lady."

"A lady of the night," she snickers.

"Those are fighting words, my friend. Take 'em back."

"I shan't."

I glare.

"Tell the truth. You were late because you were too busy knocking boots with Coop," she implores with her big eyes staring into me.

"Shhh." I fold my arms across my chest and glance around us. "There were no boots being knocked."

"Sure, there wasn't," she says disbelievingly.

"But there was a certain snake in my garden."

Vivian barks out a laugh so loud that everyone around us turns to see what's so funny.

I hold up a hand. "Just telling her about Cooper's upset tummy. This one loves potty humor."

A couple of onlookers grimace, while others smile before returning to their conversations. But it's Audra who pauses, giving me a look that screams suspicion as she walks over.

"Take it to the grave, Fisher," I hiss at Viv before Audra wraps her arms around me.

"Now, what are you psychos actually laughing about? Because I know it isn't Cooper's bowels."

"Nothing," I spit out a little too fast to be casual.

Vivian and Audra share a look.

"So, Sutton, you and Cooper finally gave in?"

I rear my head back. "I don't know what you are meaning?"

She laughs as Viv shakes her head, pouring margaritas into cups for us.

"Babe, you look like you were just fucked six ways to midnight, and Cooper has this glow about him that can only come from coming."

I sputter. "I—I."

"Oh, give it up, babe. She knows."

"Well, she does now that you said that." I frown.

"Nah, I knew the moment you two were walking up the sidewalk."

I cant my head. "Were you spying on us?"

"Spying is a strong word from a stalker like you."

"Harsh," I whine. She isn't wrong, though. Last year, I put on a disguise and watched over Viv as she ended a doomed relationship with a busy doctor she had been trying to rebound from Nate with. And Viv, well, she straight up attempted to stalk Nate when she realized she wanted him back. The girl drove around town looking for him, attempting to stage a run-in before he finally found her in the end. "But true."

"He smacked your ass, and you smiled."

"So?"

"Wait, she smiled?" Viv chirps, handing us both a plastic margarita goblet with sugar lining the rim.

"Yeah." Audra nods, taking a sip of her drink. "Like big, megawatt, 'he is the sun in my rainstorm,' 'I would let this man do anything to me' smile."

"Huh," Viv says, taking a sip.

"Huh? What, huh? What does that mean?" I ask.

Vivian claps me on the shoulder. "It means you're screwed, my friend."

Audra laughs. "It means Cooper and Nate's dream of getting married to best friends is finally in the works."

"Whoa there, cowgirl, no one said anything about marriage. We are just sleeping together."

"And living together."

"Yes, but—"

"No buts about it. You guys are a couple."

A belly-shaking laugh rips past my lips before I argue, "No, we are *faking* being a couple."

"Are you, though?" Audra squints at me.

"Yes," I say, exhausted with this line of questioning already.

"Is the sex fake as well?"

"No."

"Do you two spend time together when no one else is around?"

"Yes?"

"It's not a trick question," she teases.

"It sure feels like a trick," I tell her.

"The only ones playing games are you and Cooper as you pretend to not actually be together."

I shake my head, desperate for her to understand. "It's really not like that."

Audra holds up her hands. "Okay, I'll stop. Just do me a favor and think about it. About what you actually feel for the man and what you want, and do it before either of you falls too deep to be saved."

And with that, she takes her drink and walks away.

"What the hell?" I give Viv a questioning look.

She shrugs her shoulders. "I think she has a point."

"No you don't."

"Yeah, babe, I really do. You and Cooper are an item, whether you admit it or not."

"Ugh, you are supposed to be on my side." I glare while tipping back my margarita. Alcohol is the only solution to this conversation.

"I am."

"No, because if you were, you would be agreeing with me."

"So being on your side means lying to you?"

I nod. "When the occasion calls for it, yes."

Viv shakes with laughter as she grabs two pitchers and gestures for me to do the same. "Come on, my man and your *fake* man are waiting not so patiently."

Across the yard, Cooper and Nate are standing by the grill with beers in their hands as they watch us place the three different pitchers of margaritas on the table. I fill my glass back up and grab another of the strawberry-flavored one before following Viv over to them.

Nate wraps an arm around Vivian's shoulders the moment she pulls up beside him. It's sickeningly sweet. Honestly, I am surprised she is still gulping down margaritas and not barefoot and pregnant already. It's coming. I know it. And they both know it. It's only a matter of time before their twosome involves a mini Fisher.

I thrust out the strawberry margarita to Cooper. He looks at the drink and then back up at me before hesitantly taking the drink.

"Thank you." He smiles, setting his beer on the counter beside the grill and taking a drink of the tequila concoction.

Feigning nonchalance, I shrug. "Figured you would rather have some flavor."

Chapter Seventeen

Cooper

She brought me a margarita.

Sutton Hale actively chose to get me a drink because she thought I might want it.

Do I like margaritas?

Fuck no.

But I drink it anyway.

Because Sutton got it for me. And I wasn't going to turn down anything she was offering me.

Hell, I'm so gone for her that I would probably take any scraps she gave me.

It was such a sweet gesture that is normally hidden within the walls of her home that I was nervous when she first tried to hand it to me, thinking it was some sort of trick like we've been playing on Dillon.

But it's not. So I drain the tequila-doused drink for her, and I do it with a smile.

"Are your parents here?" she asks, eyes wandering around the yard of crowded people for them.

"Nah." I shake my head. "They couldn't come tonight."

"Why?"

"Some school function that they couldn't get out of." Sometimes it feels like my parents live for their job and nothing else. It was their passion that pushed me into teaching, which, don't get me wrong, I loved. But it wasn't something I could do for the rest of my life.

"How long are you two going to be keeping up the dating *charade*?" Nate asks, his eyes darting between us.

"As long as it takes. Dillon still hasn't gotten the hint that he isn't wanted at her house. At this rate, I'm afraid he's never going to get it."

"Nervous you're gonna be stuck with me for longer than we bargained for?" Sutton raises a brow.

"Petrified," I lie. I'm damn near ecstatic that I get to be with her longer than we planned. I'm nowhere near ready for this thing between us to be over.

"As you should be. I am quite the hostile bedmate."

"I agree, very demanding and aggressive."

She shrugs a shoulder. "I see no issue with knowing what I want and how I want it. It's called being decisive."

"It's called being domineering."

Vivian's voice breaks through, reminding me we aren't alone. "Ooh, Sutton, are you a dom in the bedroom?"

"What can I say, I'm a lady in the streets and a freak in the sheets." She winks at me.

That's no lie. Sutton's love of my cum coving her body is something I never knew she'd be into. Fuck, I never thought I would be obsessed with seeing it drip out of her or drench her perfect skin.

She's a surprise that I never want to forget.

"More like sheet stealer. Every night, I have to snuggle up to her just to get some warmth because she steals every damn blanket on that bed."

"Well, maybe you shouldn't sleep with a fan blowing on your damn face and you wouldn't be so cold," Sutton fires back. And God, does it turn me the fuck on. Her sass has my dick ready to take her again.

Nate chuckles into his beer. "How have you two not killed each other yet?"

"We've found creative outlets to help rid ourselves of the frustration," Sutton replies, wiggling her eyebrows.

Nate's eyes widen as they shoot to me. "Cooper. A word, please," he says as he walks away.

I groan. "Great." I look at Sutton. "Now look what you did. He's about to have my ass for keeping this from him."

"Please, Nate doesn't know shit."

Vivian and I shake our heads.

"Oh, he just figured it out," Vivian says with a frown. "And once he is done laying into Cooper about keeping this secret, he is going to come for me."

"If that's so, why is he pulling you into a private area to talk?"

"Because he doesn't want to embarrass you," I offer.

"My husband is sweet like that."

"As if talking about my sex life would ever embarrass me." She laughs.

"It should. You used to sleep with Dillon," I say as Nate calls my name. I sulk toward him, leaving Sutton with her jaw dropped in shock that I just said that to her.

I follow Nate into his shed, where his lawn mower and other landscaping tools are kept. He swings the door shut behind us, leaving us in pitch-black darkness.

"If you wanted your seven minutes in heaven, you missed your chance, buddy. You're a married man, and I can't do that to Viv. Even though I think she would enjoy watching it happen at least once," I joke, needing to fill the silence.

"Really?"

"Yeah, I think she would find it hot."

Nate growls as his hands find the front of my shirt, sliding down my chest to rest over my pecks. And for a split second, I wonder if he is going to kiss me. That is, until he takes hold of my nipples and twists.

I let out a shriek that can only be described as something similar to the noise a cat makes when it's in heat. My hands cover his as I attempt to get him to release his hulk hold on my sensitive nubs. Nate releases me after about five of the longest seconds of my life, pushing me back a step as he does.

"Why?" I cry, covering my nipples with my hands.

A click sounds, and light fills the space, illuminating an angry Nate before me. "Because you kept this from me. What the hell?"

"I'm sorry," I whisper.

"How long?" he whisper-shouts.

I stare at the floor, not wanting to meet his gaze.

"How long, Coop?"

"Since my work party."

He lets out an exasperated sound. "Why didn't you tell me? Based on the way Viv acted out there, she definitely already knew. So why didn't I?"

"I didn't know Vivian knew. I should have known Sutton would tell her, but she was so adamant on pretending like we were just faking it for Dillon and my work."

"So you aren't faking it?"

I groan, running my fingers through my hair. "Fuck if I know anymore. All I know is I love every moment I am with her. She makes me laugh with her weird-ass old-person hobbies, and the sex, God, the sex is like nothing, *nothing*, I have ever experienced in my life."

"Does she know all that?" he asks.

"The sex part, yes. The rest, I'm not so sure."

"You should tell her."

I roll my eyes. "Of course you'd think a heart-to-heart is the answer."

He laughs. "That's because it is."

"I don't want to ruin it if she doesn't feel the same."

"What if she does, though? And you ruin it by being a little chickenshit?"

"What happens if she doesn't feel the same way, huh? Did you think about that? Our little friend group won't be the same."

"That's probably something you should have thought about before you stuck your dick in her."

"Stop acting like you're mister logical over here. You lied to Viv for months about the extent of your relationship with Hadlee."

"I'm telling you to be honest because of that. You saw what that lie did to us, to me. I almost lost Vivian because I was scared to tell the truth. Don't be like me."

"But you're my best friend. I love being like you."

Nate glares at me. "Do yourself a favor and be honest with Sutton about how you feel. Don't think about me or Viv, we can handle whatever the outcome is."

"I'll think about it."

Nate turns the light back off as we walk out of the small shed and make our way back to where Sutton and Vivian are waiting with big smiles on their faces.

"What took you guys so long?"

"Nate was practicing his disappointed dad act on me."

"Oh, we thought maybe you guys were kissing." Vivian raises her eyebrows suggestively.

Sutton nods in agreement. "Yep, and Viv was very upset by that idea."

Nate wraps his arms around Vivian, holding her to his chest. "Baby, I would never do that to you."

"Oh, she wasn't upset over you two potentially swapping spit. She was upset that she wasn't invited to watch."

Nate jerks his head back to look down at a smiling Vivian.

"Told you," I tease with a laugh.

"Whatever, you are all insane," Nate says, squeezing Vivian tighter.

"For a moment there, I thought it was about to happen," I tell them.

"What the hell? What about that in there made you think I was going to kiss you?"

"Well, for starters, you took me into a confined dark space, and then you slid your hands down my chest."

"You did?" Vivian's eyes twinkle.

"Tell her the rest," Nate says.

"And then he twisted my nipples so hard I thought I was going to die from the pain."

"Now I'm even more shocked you didn't have a boner when you walked out of there," Sutton says with a devilish smile on her lips.

"Stop it." Nate holds up a hand. "I'm learning too much about everyone's sex lives and fantasies than I ever wanted to know."

"But, Nate, I thought you didn't want any secrets between us?" I smile.

"Fuck all of you," he gripes, then looks at Viv. "But not you, baby. I love you."

"I love you too," she says, reaching up on her tiptoes to kiss him.

Sutton and I glance at each other like we usually do when the two start their sickeningly sweet declarations of love.

"I'm hungry. Are you hungry, Coop?" she asks.

"Starving. Let's see if Nate managed not to overcook the meat this time," I mutter as we both slink off in the direction of the food.

"I heard that, asshole," Nate shouts from behind us.

"Yeah, yeah." I wave him off and pile food on my plate beside Sutton.

We both have two plates filled with meat, corn, and every side dish imaginable by the time we sit down.

"Do you think we overdid it?" I ask her, looking at the massive amount of food between us.

She scoffs. "Speak for yourself, Cooper."

Sutton tears meat off a kebab and begins aggressively chewing her food, all while scowling at me. "I swear if you make one comment about how much I'm eating, I will skewer you."

I hold up my hands. "I wasn't planning on it. I was going to say that I wish it was my meat you were shoving into your mouth right now."

Sutton stops mid-bite. She slowly pushes everything off the wooden stick onto her plate until it's clean of food. And then she stabs me right in the dick.

"Ow." I jump, covering my dick with my hands. "First my nipples, now my cock. Why does this barbecue hate me?"

"What?" she says innocently. "I thought it was what you wanted."

"I can't believe you tried to castrate me."

"Wrong word, Cooper darling. You mean make you a eunuch." She grins, grabbing another kebab and taking a bite.

I grumble to myself about how scary she is and inch my chair away from hers. Sutton stops me, placing her hand on my thigh.

My heart speeds up as she slowly moves her hand up and down in a torturous rhythm that has me panting for more. Every time she goes up, she draws a tiny bit closer to my cock.

She places her hand over the growing bulge in my jeans and squeezes. "I'm sorry for stabbing you."

"Are you apologizing to my dick?"

"Yeah, I don't want him to be mad at me later when I need him."

"Him? *Him?* You mean me? I am the owner of said cock that you are currently teasing."

"Cooper, shhh. I am trying to apologize," she shushes me, turning her attention back to my crotch again. "I promise to give you extra kisses to make it better tonight. Does that sound okay?"

My dick jumps a little in response as I curse myself for reacting to her like this.

She pats my crotch and turns back to her food as if she didn't give me a boner at a barbecue.

I'll make her pay for this later tonight. She thinks she can just kiss it and make it better? Nah, she's in for a rough awakening.

We leave the truck at Nate and Viv's, opting for an Uber since both of us had our fair share of booze at the barbecue.

Silence fills the tiny back seat of the Kia Soul as our thighs touch.

"So," Sutton mutters.

"So."

"Our friends know."

"That they do."

"Do you want to talk about it?"

I glance at her from the corner of my eye. "About our friends knowing that we are sleeping together?"

She huffs, "Yes."

"What about it?"

"Do you think it's going to get awkward when we…"

"When we what, Sutton? When we break up?"

"Can't break up when we aren't actually together."

My jaw hardens as I grind my teeth together with a nod. "Right."

Every time I feel like there's something real happening between us, Sutton has a way of reminding me that it's all temporary. A show for Dillon.

The problem is, I'm not even sure she actually believes that. Lately, it's felt more like she's trying to convince herself. I wish she'd let herself give into this, to us. To try it for real. Stop hiding behind the wall of how this started and admit to herself that it *is* happening. That we are a thing. That we are something bigger than the small uncomplicated box she wants to shove us into. And we always have been.

Sutton's hand covers mine. "You look mad."

I don't respond. Just turn to stare out the window, watching as we draw closer and closer to her house. We're only a few streets away now. I need to hold it together as long as possible.

"You are mad. Why?"

I don't respond.

"Coop, come on. What's wrong?" she asks as the Uber pulls up in front of her house.

I climb right out, holding the door for her as she sits there staring up at me.

"Honey," the middle-aged woman driving says, "You told the man you're sleeping with that y'all aren't a thing. I don't even know y'all, but I know why that fine man is upset."

Sutton sputters for a moment, her mouth opening and closing as she searches for the right words to say before settling on "thank you" and scooting out of the car.

I smile at the woman, thanking her for the ride, and shut the door before storming up to the front door with Sutton trailing behind me.

"Cooper."

I don't turn to her. Instead, I continue to move, placing my key into the lock and turning it.

"Cooper, stop."

My hand stills on the handle.

Sutton wraps a hand around my forearm. "Talk to me, *please.*"

I sigh. "What do you want me to say, Sutton? That I'm cool with us being nothing more than sex? Is that what you want to hear?"

She says nothing. Just stares up into my eyes.

"Well, if it is, tough shit. I'm not okay with it."

Her chest rises and falls rapidly. "What does that mean? That this"—she gestures between us—"is over?"

"Is there even an *us*? You seemed quite sure that there wasn't in the car."

"Coop, please don't do this."

"Do what, Sutton? Tell you that I want more? Fine, I won't. Because it already is more. It always has been more. You're just too damn scared to admit it to yourself for some reason."

She sucks in a breath as I wait for her to say something. Anything. But she's speechless yet again.

I shake my head and turn the doorknob. "Never mind, Sutton. You win," I say in defeat, walking into the house and leaving her on the porch. I flick on the lights in the living room, thankful that at least Dillon isn't here to watch her absolutely clam up and deny her feelings for me.

I make my way into the bathroom and turn on the shower, needing something to do to get my mind off her and the lack of conversation she's willing to have with me.

Stripping out of my clothes, I drop them in a pile and step into the shower, letting the hot water fall over my body. I tip my head toward the ceiling, squeezing my eyes closed as I try to block out the memories from moments ago.

Seconds later, the door to the bathroom opens, but she doesn't say a word, so neither do I. I let the sound of water fill the air around us as I wait for her next move. She pulls the shower curtain aside, and the heat from her body brushes against mine as she steps inside with me.

"I'm sorry," Sutton mutters.

I swallow, turning my head to the side to look at her from over my shoulder.

"I suck at this."

"You really do," I agree.

She lets out a strangled laugh. "I'll do better." She wraps her arms around me, resting her head against my back. "I promise."

I can't help myself. I pull her around me so her front is wrapped around mine as I hold her tightly against my chest. "Do better at what?"

"At being an us."

I rear my head back enough to look down at her. "Us?"

Sutton gnaws on her bottom lip like she's nervous. "Yeah, I mean, I'm not ready to label it as more, but I am open to it... With you."

I answer her by tangling my fingers in her now-wet hair while dropping my lips to hers.

Chapter Eighteen

Sutton

Our mouths crash into each other as our hands fumble with urgency to roam freely, grabbing and caressing every inch of each other. Placing his hands under my ass, he lifts me up, and my legs immediately wrap around his waist. My core slides against his already hard erection.

A flush rises through my limbs from the small amount of pressure made by the tip of his cock sliding against my clit as he pushes my back into the tiled wall behind me.

"You and that cock will be the death of me if it doesn't get inside me right fucking now," I groan as he hits my clit just right.

"As you wish." Cooper reaches down and positions himself at my opening. I slip my tongue into his mouth, stroking his as he slams inside me. "So damn perfect."

"Cooper," I gasp, grabbing his shoulder as he pounds his cock inside me. The intensity of his thrusts is almost painful.

Crying out his name, I break around him. My pussy clamps around his dick, causing him to growl into my ear and move even faster as he chases his release.

I dig the heels of my feet into his ass, helping to push him even deeper inside me.

"Fuck," he pants into my ear as he relentlessly thrusts, then continues kissing me as he fights the urge to pour every piece of himself into me.

Pulling back to look at my face, he cups my cheeks. "You, Sutton Hale, are like no one else." He kisses me again, and my arousal and need for him ramp up once more.

He must sense my need for more, because suddenly, Cooper spins me around, placing my chest on the tile before sliding my legs apart with one hand. At the same time, the other rubs tight circles into my throbbing clit.

His cock rocks against my ass as he drags his teeth across my shoulder, stopping to kiss my skin before he bends to rub the thick tip of his cock through my ass cheeks.

I laugh, arching my back and grinding my ass against him. "Never going to happen, Coop."

"Someday, baby, someday," he promises. "But for now, I want to feel that pussy, still soaked with my cum, grip me so fucking tight till I see stars."

"Please," I beg.

He runs his mouth up my neck, kissing me as he plunges his cock into me. I buck my hips back to meet his rhythm until both of our releases are building fast.

Cooper presses his fingers down on my clit before giving it a light squeeze that causes me to erupt. My legs spasm underneath him as he grips my hips, pounding his hard dick into me. "Don't stop. That feels so—" My words are cut off by the second wave of pleasure that crashes into me.

A long hiss escapes his lips as he bites my shoulder. Pain mixes with pleasure as he fills me with cum once again. Slowly, he pushes in and out of me until we're both completely sated.

Pulling out, he releases his teeth from my skin, kissing the spot before turning my head to the side to capture my mouth as cum leaks down my inner thighs. I want him again; I want to feel him move inside me until I can't feel my legs.

"How did I go so long without you in my life?" Cooper asks as he pulls us under the now-lukewarm water stream. The heady scent of his body wash fills the air as he pours it on his loofa and then begins to wash me.

"I keep asking myself the same thing. I never knew it could be like this."

Lathering soap between my thighs, he asks, "Do you mean the sex or—"

Warmth rushes to my face. Biting my lip, I close my eyes. "Both."

His hands frame my face as he stays quiet, waiting for me to open my eyes. When I do, I find him staring down at me with an intensity I've never seen before. "I feel the same."

"You do?"

He nods, and I try not to let the tears that are begging to be cried fill my eyes.

We're both dripping wet as he carries me out of the bathroom. My legs wrapped around his trim waist as I grind my pussy over his hardening cock.

"Sutton, baby, you better watch it."

"Or what?" I ask, circling my hips.

Cooper's eyes dance with mischief as he smiles. "Lie on your back with your head hanging off the bed," he commands. His tone leaves no room for argument. Not like I want to. Seeing him like this, in control, is insanely hot.

Anything Cooper does is hot.

Seriously, the other day, he was reading, and my panties were drenched. Then there's how he puts his hand on my lower back when we're walking side by side... It's like lady Viagra to me.

I do as he said. My head dangles off the back of the bed as my naked body is presented to him.

"Open wide, baby." He strokes his hard cock as his gaze roams over my body.

I open both my mouth and my legs.

Cooper chuckles. "Such a good girl. But right now, baby, all I want is that smart mouth to suck my cock," he says as he moves closer until he's standing above my head.

Slowly, he dips the thick crown between my lips, and I swirl my tongue over him before clamping my lips around him with a moan.

He's delicious.

My favorite flavor.

An indescribable combination of salty and musk that drives me wild.

He pushes in another inch, letting me slide my tongue all over him to coat him in my saliva before he pushes in a little more. Repeating this until he's almost hitting the back of my throat.

He pulls out completely and begins to pump himself again.

"Such a good girl," he croons, caressing the side of my face. "Now I want you to be a dirty girl and let me fuck this face until I'm choking you on my cum."

I nod as I open my mouth for him, a new eagerness filling my bones.

Smirking down at me, he wastes no time shoving his cock back into my mouth.

His pace is punishing as he hits the back of my throat. I wrap my hands around his strong, muscular thighs, bracing myself as he fucks my face. Cooper is pushing me to my limits, and I love it.

He brings out a new side of me sexually that I didn't know existed. I love it when he dominates me. When he takes what he wants without remorse or shame. It's the biggest turn-on. Because even as he brutally chases his own pleasure through my body, I know he'd never hurt me. That he's challenging me. Pushing me to the edge of pain and pleasure.

And God, does it feel fantastic.

Seeing how much I do to him—how I affect him—has my pussy drenched and pulsing for him.

Cooper moans as he pushes himself into my throat until my nose touches the base of his cock.

My eyes water, but I don't tap out. I'm not about to quit something that makes him feral for me.

More moisture pools between my thighs, and I squeeze them together. This is torture, and I never want him to stop. The hungry look in his eyes when he pulls his cock out of my mouth to give me a moment's reprieve before thrusting back in has me wondering if I can get off just by bringing him pleasure.

"You take me so good," he grinds out.

I hum my appreciation as I circle my hips, needing something to help the building need.

Cooper leans over my body, running his hands across my breasts. He tweaks my nipples, sending a scorching trail of heat to my core, and I moan, arching my chest up for him to do it again.

"You like that, huh? You like when I play with these pretty tits while you choke on my cock?"

I can't reply while his cock pushes further into my throat, but he knows he's right.

"What about this pretty pussy? Am I going to find you soaking with need?" he asks as one hand leaves my breast, trailing down my stomach, straight to my pussy.

Cooper's fingers sweep through my wet folds, and he hisses. "Does this pussy need my attention, baby?"

He pulls his dick out of my mouth again, and I breathlessly reply, "Yes, please, Cooper. I need you."

That's all it takes. Cooper leans over my body and drags his tongue through my center, lapping up my juices.

God, he's a master of eating me out. One lick, and I'm about to come. I work him in my hand, still trying to catch my breath, which feels impossible when he begins to suck and flick my clit.

"Right there, baby," I whimper, trying to lift my hips closer to his mouth.

He pulls his mouth away, and I cry out in frustration, but his fingers quickly take over, circling my clit. "I want you to come while I fill that pretty throat of yours."

I open my mouth as wide as I can and take him back into me, letting him set the pace once again. "That's it, baby," he praises me as he leans back down and takes my clit between his lips.

It's almost too much, too quickly. My legs shake as I try to focus on my breathing while I suck and lick Cooper's cock with the same enthusiasm he's showing my body. But it's all for nothing because the moment Cooper pushes two fingers inside me, I'm done.

My orgasm slams into me like a freight train, leaving my body a quaking mess. Pleasure fills every inch of my skin as Cooper continues to fuck me with his mouth and fingers, never stopping.

"I love watching you come," he says, giving my clit one last kiss before he stands back up. "But now it's my turn."

He pulls at the back of my neck, making me arch more as he pushes even further back, opening my throat for him. I gag, and Cooper lets out a string of curses before he attempts to pull back out, but I move my hands from his thighs to his taut ass and hold him in place for a moment.

"Fuck, Sut." He pulls back before diving back in, thrusting in and out of my mouth again rapidly.

His cock throbs, and I know he's close. Cooper's muscles are rigid as he comes with a groan that has my pussy aching to be stuffed. His cum fills the back of my throat, and I swallow it down with every spurt.

We're both breathless as he pulls his cock from my lips. He peers down at me with a content, blissful smile, and my chest fills with warmth at the sight.

I reach up, hoping he'll give me what I need, and he does.

Cooper drops to his knees and spins my body around, pulling me off the bed and onto his lap before kissing me.

His lips and tongue taste of my release as he thrusts them into my mouth, and it only makes me want him more. I tangle my fingers in his hair, holding him as close as I can.

"Will I ever get enough of you?" he asks, pressing a soft kiss to my lips before trailing them down my jaw and neck.

"I hope not," I say, wrapping my arms around him and squeezing him to me.

His heart is still pounding from his orgasm. I love feeling his skin against mine. His heart beating with mine.

Cooper drops his head on my shoulder. "Can we do that every day?"

I laugh. "What, give each other mind-blowing orgasms, or you fucking my face?"

He kisses my throat. "Both."

I sigh. "I think it can be arranged."

His head lifts. "You didn't hate it?"

"What, you choking me on your dick?" I raise a brow.

"Yeah?"

"Did you not notice how wet that made me? It was fucking hot."

"You're so perfect," he growls, grabbing my chin in his hand before slamming his lips down on mine.

I moan into his kiss, knowing it'll be the start of round two.

Chapter Nineteen

Cooper

Gag. Someone destroyed our guest bathroom toilet last night.

Ew, who do you think did it?

No idea, but they didn't even bother trying to unclog the mess they made.

Cooper, your stomach was mad messed up last night until it wasn't…

Lie.

Nate

It's okay, Coop, friends tell each other these kinds of things. Besides, you owe it to me after lying about the thing with you and a certain blond "friend."

Sutton

Are you talking about us boinking again? Get over your sexual attraction to Cooper, man. It's not going to happen.

Vivian

Sutton's right. But so is Nate, and as his wife, I am entitled to know everything he knows about you.

Sutton

And as her best friend, I am also, by default, entitled to know the same things.

Cooper

That's not how that works.

Sutton

Sure it is. Now fess up.

Vivian

Tell us. Tell us. Tell us.

Nate

The tribe has spoken, Cooper. You have no choice but to share with the group.

Sutton

Ooh, I think he is scared.

Vivian

Probably embarrassed.

Sutton

Come on, Cooper, fess up to being the party pooper already.

Cooper

FUCK you guys.

Nate

Did you or did you not clog the toilet at my house?

Cooper

Why am I friends with any of you?

Sutton

That doesn't sound like an admission of innocence.

Vivian

She's right. You sound very guilty.

I didn't even piss while I was there, and you all know it.

Do we, though?

YES! Yes, you do. I did not clog your damn toilet.

Me thinks the gentleman doth protest too much.

Cooper has left the group chat.

I'm on cloud fucking nine.

Sutton and I are doing this. Whatever this is. All I know is that she is acknowledging that it's more than the sex. That we are an us. Maybe not officially, but that doesn't make it any less true.

Walking out of Sutton's room, I'm greeted with the usual morning sounds of Sutton and Dillon arguing. It's been like this for weeks. The two of them go back and forth every morning. It's childish and immature, but I love seeing the look in his eyes when he loses the verbal sparring match with her, which is every day.

Sutton has her back to me as she faces the douche who's sitting on the couch with both arms extended across the back as he gives her a smug grin.

I lean down, giving Sutton a quick kiss as she hands me one of the two cups of coffee she's holding. It's become a new routine for me to shower first while Sutton makes our coffee, then sneaks a laxative into the rest of the pot.

She gives me a conspiratorial look just as a gurgling noise fills the room.

I quickly glance at Sutton as the corner of her lip tilts up for a second before going flat again.

Dillon slowly sits up, his breathing becoming heavier.

"You okay?" I ask as he places a hand over his stomach, his forehead bunched.

"Fine." He swallows, leaning forward and gripping the edge of the couch.

"Okay, like I was saying, stop stealing our—"

The noise pierces the room again, and my eyes snap to Dillon's hands now back on his stomach.

"Seriously, Dillon?"

"What? It's not like I'm doing it on purpose," he shouts.

"Okay, well stop stealing our food."

"I'll stop stealing your food when you stop being such a bitch."

I bite my tongue. I know if I react to his name-calling or attitude toward her, it will only fuel him into doing it more. He's like a teenager. The more you tell him no, the more he wants to do it. Which is why he's still stealing our food and is now about to shit his pants due to the high fiber and healthy dose of laxatives Sutton's been adding to the leftovers.

Sutton rolls her eyes. "So never?"

Dillon smirks at her, but it's less effective as he also wipes sweat from his brow.

You'd think by now, the man would've begun to build up a tolerance or learn to avoid the drink or food that keeps causing him gastrointestinal distress, but alas, Dillon isn't the brightest tool.

He sprints out of the room only moments later as Sutton chuckles to herself.

"What's got you so happy this morning?" I set my mug down and pull her against my chest.

"I stole all the toilet paper from his bathroom." She grins maniacally.

"Damn, baby, you're vicious. Remind me never to cross you."

Chapter Twenty

Sutton

Lights flash above us everywhere. The crowd clapping their hands together and cheering at loud volumes. My ears can't stand it, and I turn to Cooper. "You don't actually like this shit, do you?"

A grin sweeps over his face as he gazes down at me. "Why? Don't you?"

I look him over. "You cannot be serious. What about me looks like I love the smell of beer and body odor?"

"I don't know, something about you screams team sports, like high school cheer."

"Screw you. They wouldn't let me on the squad."

His eyes gleam with excitement as he twists in line to look at me. "Did you try out? Tell me everything. Did you lack school spirit? Could you not do the splits? Not flexible enough? Tell me! Oh, was it the attitude? Not cheery enough?"

I scoff, taking his nasty beer and chugging it down. "I'll have you know I am plenty flexible. Plenty."

The past few weeks, we've made more of an effort to explore our relationship outside of sex, and that includes date nights. Some I've planned and some he's planned. Tonight is a Cooper-planned night.

The sun beats down on us as we squeeze through row after row of people to find our seats, people standing in the white foam of the beer that's sloshed over their cups as we pass by. I can't tell you how many knees I've bumped or accidental ass grazes I've had.

I say accidental, but I have a feeling some of those men did it on purpose.

Our seats aren't the best in the stadium, but they also aren't the worst. We're smack dab in the middle.

I glance around, finding everyone wearing the same red-and-black gear as Cooper. The same Willow Hill Wyvern logo stamped across their shirts and hats. "This is my first game."

"I couldn't tell," Cooper deadpans as he eyes my tight jeans and stilettos.

"I'm just saying, be prepared to be peppered with questions by the pesky baseball newbie."

"I'm looking forward to it." He smiles, leaning down to kiss me just as a voice behind us calls out his name.

"Mr. Shaw?"

Cooper swivels to look at the person.

"Oh my gosh, it is you," a middle-aged woman with hair that is teased to the heavens and boobs that are too perky to be natural peeking out through her voluptuously cut jersey squeals in delight.

I scowl. This floozy interrupted my kiss.

"Mrs. Weatherby. How are you?" Cooper says with a soft smile that should only be for me tonight.

"It's actually Ms. now." She pouts, holding up her very empty ring finger for him to see.

"Oh, I'm sorry to hear that. I hope everything is good with Jaxon."

"He's missing his favorite teacher, but other than that, he is great. He is going to be starting football this fall. I'm very proud."

I zone out the rest of what she's saying as I rest my hand on Cooper's shoulder. The woman ignores it. Not caring at all that she's flirting with the wrong man. *My* man.

I have half a mind to knock Coop's beer on her overflowing cleavage, but that would bring more attention to her tits, and that isn't a risk I'm willing to take.

"Coop, baby," I purr, interrupting the woman mid-story about her son being gone for the weekend at his dad's.

I see the game she's playing. Well, two can play that game, MILF.

"Yeah?" He turns back toward me, giving me his whole attention.

The woman frowns and her forehead crinkles as if she forgot I was here.

"Can you explain to me why that man is doing that?" I ask, pointing at the field.

"Which one, Sut?"

"The one in the tight pants."

Cooper bites his lip to keep from smiling. "They're all wearing tight pants."

"Oh, well, why are they doing that with the bat?"

"Batting?"

"Is that what the swinging thing is?" I blink up at him.

He eyes me suspiciously before nodding and turning back to that woman. "I'm sorry, Deb, we will have to catch up another time. My girlfriend apparently needs a major lesson in baseball."

"Oh, yeah, sure," she mutters, finally looking to where my hand is on his thigh. She smiles and turns back to the field.

"Happy now?" he asks.

"Very." I smile, pulling his mouth down to mine.

His lips are cold from the beer, but the kiss still manages to light my skin on fire.

"Do you really not understand the basics?" he whispers.

"Oh no, I do. I was just jealous you weren't paying attention to me."

"Oh, my sweet baby opossum, I'm always paying attention to you."

"Really? Because from where I'm sitting, it looked like you were enthralled by the hot mom's bosom."

"The only bosom I'm enthralled with is yours."

"You're just saying that."

"I'm not." He shakes his head. "Pinky swear."

"Good." I slap his knee and turn back to the field.

Surprisingly, I enjoy myself. The game ends up being pretty exciting. The crowd goes wild as the players race around the field, throwing the ball from base to base as a player from the other team sweeps through them.

I glance over to see Cooper's face lit up with excitement as he stands, shouting at his team.

The player shoots forward to home base as a Wyvern player throws the ball to the catcher. The stadium falls silent as we all watch the opposing player slide into the plate just as the catcher's glove clamps down on the ball, tagging him out.

I can't help myself; I jump up too, getting lost in the excitement along with everyone else.

Cooper wraps his arms around me and lifts me up as he screams in triumph.

I laugh as he jumps up and down, jostling me against him.

The rest of the game goes on like that. Cooper expressing his love of the game like a child who got told they are going to Disneyland, and me basking in his excitement and joy.

Our walk back to the car is a long one. My feet and legs ache as I try to keep up with Cooper's long strides. But I'm failing.

"Ugh, my feet hurt," I whine.

I slam into Cooper's back as he comes to a halt.

He spins to face me, crouching as he motions up with his hands. "Piggyback or face-to-face?" he asks with a no-nonsense look.

"Face-to-face. That way I can see how much you regret carrying me."

"I won't regret it."

I bark out a laugh. "I give it one block before you need to set me down."

"Is that a challenge?"

I shake my head. "More like a bet."

"And what do I get if I win?" he asks, running his hands down my outer thighs as he squats and lifts me up. A small squeak leaves my lips as my legs instinctively wrap around his waist, my arms doing the same to his neck.

"Hmmm," I say, pressing a ghost of a kiss to his lips. "Is the knowledge that you were right and I was wrong not enough?"

His left eyebrow quirks up. "You'll admit I'm right?"

"Only if you can carry me more than one block."

"I can do better than that, baby. I will carry you the entire way back to the car."

"Bullshit. There is no way you can lug my heavy ass that far."

Determination sparks in his eyes as he says, "You're on. Prepare to sing my praises."

"Okay, sure."

We're halfway to the car when I rest my head on his shoulder. "I never knew you were so into baseball."

"There's a lot you don't know about me, Sutton."

"Like what?"

"Like when I was twelve, I thought for sure I was going to marry Keira Knightly."

"Solid choice."

"I thought that if she could only see me, it would be love at first sight for her like it was for me. So I wrote her a letter explaining all of that in *extreme* detail and sent it off with my phone number and a picture of me attached."

"Let me guess, she never called."

"Never," he sighs sadly, and I can't help but feel a little joy at his preteen despair.

"Which movie sparked your obsession?"

"*Pirates of the Caribbean.*"

"So that's what you're into? Delicate woman turned dirty pirate?"

"I think we both know what I'm into."

I wiggle my eyebrows. "Oh, do we?"

He nods, giving me a wink.

"You best be talking about me."

"What do you think?"

"I think I need you to say it clear as day. I'm a little insecure after watching that hot mom drool all over you."

He stops walking and repositions his hands from under my thighs to my ass. "To clear up any lingering ridiculous confusion, I am into you and you alone."

I glance at his lips for a second. "No hot-mom fantasies?"

"None."

I smile.

"Unless you count the ones where I knock you up."

My breath catches in my throat. I know we both love it when he comes inside me, but holy shit. The thought of him actually putting a baby inside me has my pussy throbbing.

"You like that I think about fucking a baby into you?"

What the actual hell?

Why am I getting so turned on by that? Oh, dear God, I have a breeding kink. No, scratch that. I have a breeding kink with Cooper and Cooper alone.

I swallow. "I don't dislike it."

"If I dipped my hand into these tight jeans, would I find you wet from the thought?"

"Yes, but not just from the thought, from the way your hold on me has my jeans rubbing me in all the right places."

He inhales sharply. "God, I can't wait to get you home."

"Well, get a move on, then." I dig my heels into his back, and he starts walking again.

Not five minutes later, Cooper stops again. "I think someone owes me some praise." He smiles at me as he drops me on the hood of my car.

I look around. "Wow, Cooper. You did it. You carried me. My hero." Sarcasm laces my voice.

"Excuse me?"

"What would I have done without you?" I ask, tapping my finger on my chin. "Oh yeah, walked a mile in high heels."

His eyes narrow. "You played me."

"Like a violin, baby."

"Ugh," he groans. "So, you never thought I wasn't strong enough to carry you a mile?"

"Oh no, I definitely thought these biceps would give out on block number three, but I was desperate to get the toes off the ground."

"Man, I thought I was doing something."

"You were doing something. You were saving my feet from complete and total destruction. You are my hero."

"Yeah, yeah," he says, pushing out from where he's standing between my legs.

"Oh, no you don't." I grab his shirt and pull him closer to me. "Thank you for carrying me for over a mile. My feet and I applaud you."

"You're welcome," he grumbles, looking over my shoulder.

I wrap my legs around his hips again, trapping him against me as my hands rub up and down his biceps. "It was super hot the way you took care of me."

"Really?" he asks, still not looking at me.

"Yep. Every woman dreams of a man treating her like you just treated me. Even if you only did it because of a challenge and not out of the goodness of your heart."

He pins me with a glare. "I was going to carry you before you made it into a challenge, remember."

I smile up at him. "Did you plan on carrying me the entire way before, though?"

He huffs out a defeated sigh. "I would have carried you until my arms gave out."

My eyes find his as I curl my fingers into the hair at the nape of his neck and drag his mouth to meet mine.

There are no words for the amount of gratitude I feel toward him. For the warmth that fills my veins when I look at him. For the overwhelming desire that floods my senses when he says things like that.

My tongue meets his instantly as we lose ourselves in yet another kiss. Nothing can ever compare to his lips touching mine. To his tongue tangling with mine. To his hands kneading my flesh.

I groan into his mouth when his fingertips dig into my hips as he presses us closer together.

My pelvis tilts forward just as a horn blares beside us. Cooper rips his mouth from mine and glares at the person who had the audacity to interrupt us.

Chapter Twenty-One

Sutton

"Come on, Bella, really? You automatically assumed it was pregnancy, not that you undercooked that chicken or are stressed from your wedding and your new husband refusing to sleep with you."

It's the first night in a week that we're both home at a decent hour and Dillon is nowhere to be found. The plan was to relax, shove some food into our faces, then meet our friends for drinks.

We took over the living room with a plate full of homemade marry-me chicken, made by Cooper, on top of spaghetti straight from the box, boiled by me.

It was a group effort to make dinner. But one of us is clearly more talented than the other, and I have zero complaints about that as I shove my second helping of chicken in my face while Cooper chuckles and shakes his head without taking his eyes off the TV.

"And are we supposed to believe that Mr. Virgin Eddy lasted long enough in bed to not only bruise her up but also destroy the entire bed, feather pillows included? Yeah fucking right."

Cooper picks up the remote, turns down the volume, and faces me. "Why are we watching this entire damn saga if you hate it so much?"

I rear back and scoff. "I don't hate it. I freaking love this shit."

"You've literally done nothing but talk crap about it since the moment we turned it on."

"So?"

He laughs. "It doesn't sound like you like it in the tiniest."

"Please, we both know my love language is shit-talking," I say, snuggling in closer to him. It's true. If I love something, I poke at it.

Cooper raises an eyebrow. "Oh, so that's why you're always picking on me. It's your way of expressing your love for me."

My lips thin. "Wrong. It's due to the fact your face screams 'make fun of me' on a daily basis."

"Sure it does." He smirks. "Are you ever going to tell me how you ended up engaged to that loser, anyway?"

I groan. "Please don't make me."

"Come on." He nudges my knee with his. "I won't judge you..."

I look at him skeptically.

"Any more than I already have. I'm just curious how someone who romanticizes a sparkling vampire almost marries a wannabe Tommy Lee."

"Tommy Lee is a drummer, not a guitarist or lead singer."

He waves me off. "It still fits."

"What even made you think of this?"

He gestures to the TV and sits quietly, waiting for me to speak.

I toss my hands up. "Fine. You want the sad, pathetic story?"

"Yes."

"Dillon was about to turn twenty-six..."

"So?"

I inhale. "So he was going to be kicked off his parents' insurance."

He rears back. "Do not tell me you agreed to marry that douche to get him health insurance."

I shrug. "It felt right at the time."

"Did it?" he asks softly.

"I don't know. I felt like marriage was the obvious next step in life."

"Did he at least get down on one knee?"

I cover my face with a pillow, but Cooper pulls it away.

"Are you trying to embarrass me for being a complete and total idiot? Because don't worry, I've already got you covered on that front."

He stands from the couch and moves in front of me, crouching until he's eye to eye with me. "I'm not trying to embarrass you. I promise. I just want to understand why someone as confident, smart, and beautiful as you would ever want him."

"I can't explain it. At first, he was fun, and that was the appeal. Then it was toxic, but I craved the excitement of not knowing where our days and nights together would lead. Eventually, that all led to a familiar comfort of sorts. Does that make sense?"

"Kind of," he consoles.

"Can we change the subject, please?"

"Sure..." He sits back down, pulling me into his side and turning back to the TV just in time to see a certain car drive out of the shot. "Wait, is this movie why you drive a Volvo?" he asks, exasperated.

"Did you not just hear about how safe they are?"

"From a fictional vampire... You bought a car on a fictional vampire's advice."

I pat his chest with a bless-your-heart look. "He's over one hundred years old, Coop. I'm fairly sure he knows a thing or two about cars that we don't."

"He isn't real."

"He is to me, in my heart."

Both Viv and Audra are already sitting at the booth near the back of the bar when we arrive. I bolt toward them the moment I see them, leaving Cooper to find Nate and get us drinks.

Sliding into the booth, I grab the drink in front of Viv and down it before grabbing Audra's and doing the same.

"Whoa there, boozy. Slow down," Audra scolds.

"Seriously, Sutton, what's gotten into you," Vivian chimes in, her brows furrowed in concern.

"You mean besides Cooper?" Audra cackles.

"We made it official," I squeak.

Both of their jaws drop.

"Official, official?" Viv asks.

I nod. "Do you guys have anything else to drink?"

"Hot damn, it's about time," Audra cheers. "But why do you look so deer in headlightsy right now? Shouldn't you be all filled with love and whatnot?"

"Deer in headlightsy?"

Viv nods in agreement. "She's right. You have this strange look in your eye like you are about to freeze or run for the hills."

I sigh. "I'm not gonna run. But—"

"No buts," Audra proclaims.

"I agree, no buts. You like him. He likes you. You're already aware you two match on a physical level. So why the flighty eyes?"

I let my head fall to the table. "I don't know. I guess I thought you guys were going to roast me a bit more for it."

"So you needed liquid courage to tell us you are in a committed relationship with the man you've been banging for the past couple months?"

"Yeah?" I cringe.

"Well shit, either we are doing everything just right as friends or possibly everything wrong," Audra contemplates, reaching for her empty drink. "I need a refill. Want me to refill yours, Viv?"

Viv shakes her head. "Nate's getting it for me."

"You?" she asks, pointing to me.

"Cooper promised to be my bitch tonight, so he is on it."

"Ugh, I hate you both for reminding me how single I am that I have to get my own damn drinks," she snarks, stalking off toward the bar.

I turn to Viv. "So."

"So?"

"You gonna tell me why you're drinking virgin Shirley Temples tonight, or am I going to have to guess?"

"Maybe I just wanted a booze-free night."

"Maybe. Or, hear me out, maybe you are—"

"Shhh," Viv whispers as she slaps her hand over my mouth.

I dart my tongue out to lick her, and she immediately retracts her hand in disgust.

"So?"

She looks down with a sheepish grin. "Yeah."

"Yeah?" I ask, tears welling in my eyes.

She silently nods.

"Vivy. That's amazing!" I wrap her in a tight hug. "I take it not everyone knows."

She pulls out of my death squeeze. "We haven't told anyone yet."

I beam. "So I'm the first person to know."

"Yes."

"Fuck yes! Wait... Were you planning to tell me first, or am I just too smart to fool?"

"Did I plan on telling you tonight? No. Were you always going to be the first person we told? Yes. Well, you and Cooper, obviously."

"This is so wild. My best friend, a teen mom."

"I'm not a teenager, Sut."

"Shhh, it's okay, honey. I will make sure he does right by you and marries you."

"Once again, not a teen, and we are already married."

"Good thinking. That's exactly what you should tell people if they ask."

Vivian laughs, and I shut my mouth as Nate, Audra, and Cooper slide into the booth with us. Cooper hands me my drink before resting his palm on my thigh.

Vivian leans over to whisper in Nate's ear. He looks up at me with a big grin, and I smile back, overwhelmingly happy for them.

Our night is filled with drinks and laughs. Apparently, the shock of Cooper and I being a couple is minuscule to these three. They all look at us like we are dumb for even announcing it, as if it was obvious to them.

"Do we want to do another round?" Cooper asks the group.

"Nah. I'm out," Audra says, standing while typing into her phone. "Bel wants to meet up around the block for a round, so this fifth wheel is out."

With Audra gone, Nate clears his throat. "Okay, apparently, the cat is out of the bag. So we can discuss."

Cooper and I both turn toward each other. "You knew?" we both say at the same time.

I glare. "I just found out before you sat down. How long have you been sitting on this secret?"

He scoffs, rearing his head back. "Not that I need to explain myself to you, but I just found out when I heard Nate ordering his booze-loving wife a nonalcoholic drink before watching the bartender like a hawk as she made it."

"Damn it," Viv exclaims. "That drink gave away everything."

"Maybe try not only drinking booze around us and we won't be able to guess instantly next time," I joke.

Vivian shrugs. "I make no promises."

"Okay, so back to the important stuff. How far along are you? Because wasn't it just a couple weeks ago that we watched you drinking margaritas like a fish?"

"Yeah, so about that…"

"You've got to be kidding me. You knew then? But how? I watched you drink."

"But did you?" Nate asks.

Both Cooper and I nod. "Yeah, we both did."

"You remember how I made multiple pitchers of margaritas?"

"Like you usually do?"

"Well, I made the first one with zero alcohol before anybody showed up. And it just so happened to be the one I had all night."

"But how could you be sure? They weren't labeled."

"The handle was a different color, but also, I put so much tequila in the others that there was no way I could accidentally drink it anyway."

"You sneaky bitch."

"When did you guys find out?"

Nate is practically glowing as he says, "The week before the barbecue."

"We are pretty sure we conceived on the honeymoon you gave us, Sutton."

My shoulders soften. "I'm the reason this perfect angel is going to be born?"

"Um, I wouldn't go that far," Cooper says before sipping on his beer. "I think them being horn dogs had something more to do with it than you."

"And Cherry getting her IUD removed months ago probably had something to do with it," Nate offers.

"Nope. It was the romantic setting my fleeing the altar provided you both with." I raise my glass. "To the baby growing inside Viv."

"To the baby," we all cheer, clinking our glasses together.

Nate and Viv start talking about when they plan to tell their families as Cooper leans down to whisper in my ear, "Fleeing the altar?"

"Yes, I was practically a runaway bride."

"Um, from what I recall, you went through the entire sham of a ceremony to that creep before dumping him."

There's a bite to his tone that has me concerned.

"Cooper, you can't seriously still be annoyed."

"Why the hell not? You went through with the ceremony, Sut, and now the guy won't leave you—us—alone. Of course I'm annoyed. I'm actually fucking livid."

I sigh because he's right to be annoyed. Hell, I'm annoyed by it as well. "Can we talk about this at home?"

"Look at them, waiting to have a fight till they get home," Vivian interrupts.

"Practically married already," Nate teases.

"And with that, I think I should be getting this grandpa home. It's well past his bedtime, and you know how he gets when the sun goes down."

Cooper grumbles as he slides out of the booth to stand. "Knock it off with the elderly jokes. Someone is going to think you're ageist."

"How can I be ageist if my boyfriend is an elderly man?" I climb out of the booth to stand beside him.

Frustration contorts his face as he runs his fingers through his hair. "Why am I into this?"

"'Cause I am irresistible, baby. Don't fight it." I smile up at him.

Cooper grabs my hand and waves with his other at our friends. "Okay, see you later, Mom and Dad."

"Love you," I call out as Cooper drags me away.

Chapter Twenty-Two

Cooper

The moment we leave the bar, we hop into an Uber. I'm expecting us to go straight home but soon become suspicious when we head in the opposite direction.

"Where are we going?" I ask the driver.

The man scoffs, "To the location provided to me."

I open my mouth to tell the man off for not only taking us somewhere other than where we requested but also for his shitty attitude when Sutton places her hand on my leg.

"We aren't going home yet, Cooper. I need to pick something up."

Our driver stops in front of the Yard Barn. Gesturing with his hand for us to get the fuck out. I glare at him through the mirror as Sutton scoots out of the back seat and I follow her. The man throws up a middle finger before speeding out of the parking lot and back onto the street.

"What an asshole. You better leave a bad review."

"Why? He was just having a bad night."

"A bad night? A bad night doesn't give him the right to be an asshole."

"No, but finding out his boyfriend was cheating on him earlier tonight does."

"How did you know that?"

She sighs, pulling out her phone and tapping on the Uber app. "He messaged me before picking us up and told me he was sorry he wouldn't be his usual bubbly self if there was a male passenger and that he was sorry in advance for being a bitter bitch due to being cheated on."

I grind my teeth. "Fine. I'll give him a pass just this once."

She leans up to kiss me on the cheek. "You're the best. Now help me find some yarn."

Sutton grabs my hand and hauls me into the yarn superstore behind her.

I'm immediately assaulted by the store's bright fluorescent lights, followed by wall after wall of yarn.

It's everywhere. Thick yarn, thin yarn, yellow yarn to rainbow yarn, you name it, this store has it.

I never knew there were so many yarn options. Everywhere I turn, there's something new and different, not that I can tell the difference.

"What exactly do you need yarn for?"

"To knit the baby a blanket." She looks at me as if I'm an idiot.

"What do you think about these colors?" She holds up two blues that are practically the same.

"I like blue."

"So does Viv. I was thinking one yellow and one blue and then a mixture of shades of both."

"What about pink and the other blue?"

"I want it to fit our friends, not the stereotypical gender colors." Again, she looks at me like I'm a fumbling dumbass.

I toss up my hands. "Hey, no need to get testy. It was just an honest question, Grandma."

Sutton's eyes widen as she slaps her hand over my mouth, looking around frantically. "Shhh. You can't say that word in here."

I push her away. "What word? Grand—"

She cuts me off again with a closed-mouth scream.

"You can't be serious. Why can't I say Grandm—"

"No, I don't want to see the needle in your pants, sir," Sutton says so loud, there's no chance in hell that the entire store didn't hear.

"What?" I whisper-yell at her.

She winces. "Sorry."

Our gazes are locked as an older woman in her seventies hobbles around the corner and into our aisle. "I couldn't help but overhear. Need some help?"

My mouth gapes like a fish, opening and closing. Did Sutton really just cause this poor woman to think I was trying to expose myself to her?

When neither of us reply, the woman smiles gently at me. "Young man, what kind of project are you working on?"

Glancing at Sutton, I silently beg for help. She just glares at me while I buffer. That's the only explanation for what my brain is doing.

"Umm," I begin, trying to formulate an answer just as another older woman steps into the aisle.

"Oh, young people need some assistance?"

I shake my head. "Oh, no thank you. I think we've got it covered. Don't we, Sutton?"

She smiles, nodding her head enthusiastically.

The women both look at each other with doubtful expressions. "Really?" asks the first. "Then what are you making?"

"A baby blanket," I reply.

Both look disapprovingly at the yarn Sutton's still holding. "Not with that yarn, you aren't," the second woman says with the click of her tongue, taking the yarn from Sutton's hands and placing it back on the shelves. "Now, let me show you what I used for my great-grandbabies' blankets, not this new-age organic excuse for yarn."

The first woman grabs the cart from Sutton as the second locks elbows with me and begins to lead me away.

I glance back at Sutton, begging her for help.

She just hangs her head and mouths, *This is why we don't say the G word here.*

Two hours later, Betty and Ethel finally let us go, but not because they're done with us. No, because the store is closing. In fact, they force us into exchanging numbers so we can contact them for more advice on the blankets.

I'm sad to say I let those grannies force me into buying everything they wanted me to. They were very persistent saleswomen for people who didn't work in the store. At one point, Sutton snuck off, claiming to need to pee, only to go grab the yarn she had been looking at the entire time and snuck it into the cart under the piles of essentials Betty and Ethel said we had to have. I wave goodbye to my new older friends, as Sutton pulled me into our Uber. As we sped away, Sutton lectures me on how to conduct myself properly in any type of craft or hobby store.

Chapter Twenty-Three

Sutton

"Aye yo, Malibu, is that you?" a deep voice calls out.

Cooper cringes. "Great." His eyes close as he drops his head back in frustration.

Tonight is the first night we've been out in a week. Cooper and I have been filling in alongside Nate and Vivian at Fisher Landscaping almost every night this past week to help out Miles and Delia since a few of their employees came down with a stomach bug and they were in desperate need of hands. Do I have a green thumb? No. Do I have any kind of landscaping experience? If a riding lawn mower counts, then yes. If it doesn't, then no.

So needless to say, we're in desperate need of a relaxing night out.

A tall man with shaggy brown hair stops at our table. His face beams with joy as he says, "It is you." He punches Cooper's shoulder. "I almost didn't recognize you without the—"

"Yeah, it's been a long time, Greg."

"What's it been, fifteen years?"

"Fourteen, but who is counting."

"Damn." He shakes his head. "I can't believe it's you, Malibu, in the flesh. Where's your boyfriend? What's his nuts?"

I almost question the boyfriend comment, thinking maybe Cooper has a much more adventurous side to him that I haven't seen. Just the thought of Cooper with another man has me squirming in my seat. But then I realize this is a man he knew in high school, so he's most likely talking about Nate.

Cooper clears his throat and gives Greg a tight-lipped smile. "Nate's at home with his wife."

Suspicions disappointingly confirmed.

"No shit? Your boyfriend married a woman. Unbelievable. I always thought the girls you two dated were some sort of front to hide your love for each other."

"Alas, it was not."

Greg turns his eyes to me, finally noticing there's another person at the table. "And who might you be."

"Sutton, Cooper's girlfriend."

Greg's gaze roams down my body, settling on my breasts for a good seven seconds before he seems to remember we can see him. "Damn, Malibu. You did good."

Ew.

I already didn't like this man, but his blatant checking me out is another strike against his already failing likability.

Cooper glares at him with disgust.

"Greg," a man calls from the bar. And the asshole turns his head, giving the man a thumbs-up.

"Well, looks like I've gotta boot, scoot, and boogie," he says, throwing his thumb over his shoulder. "See ya around, Malibu."

I wait till the man is completely out of earshot before I lean my forearms on the table. "Malibu?"

"Stop."

"Come on, Coop. Tell me!"

"No."

"Why not, Malibu?"

"Because it's embarrassing."

"Pssh, even more reason to share with me. You know I live for the cringe."

"Sutton, will you please drop it?"

"Nope." I sip on my drink, waiting for him to go on.

"Okay, if I tell you, will you promise not to ever call me it?" His eyes implore. He's serious. Whatever the story behind the name is, it bothers him.

I squeeze his thigh. "I promise."

He huffs out a long breath. "Okay, so growing up, I was super into trying and experiencing new things."

"You still are."

He grins. "True, but it was different then. I wouldn't just try something new. I would immerse myself in it. I would learn and experience everything I could. I would adapt aspects of things into my personality."

"That doesn't sound like a bad thing. Isn't that basically what we all do every day? We find something we like. We do it. We enjoy it. We share it with others? What did you get super into, surfing? And they called you Malibu for that? That doesn't seem so weird or anything to be embarrassed about."

He grumbles something quickly under his breath.

"What was that?" I lean in closer to him.

"I said it was for the movie *Malibu's Most Wanted*."

"You liked that movie that much? I mean, it's fun to watch, but..." I aim a confused look at him. "I don't get it?"

"No, I was super into basketball."

"I'm not seeing the connection here."

"My favorite players all happened to be black men. They were, still are, my idols. And I wanted to be just like them."

"Okay?"

His cheeks flush with embarrassment as he says, "I got my mom to buy me a durag."

The corners of my mouth tilt up.

"I wore that thing every time I played any sport. I was determined to believe that it was going to make me a great, like them. Hell, I even wore it to bed."

"That's the cutest thing ever. I bet it smelled like crap, though."

He laughs, "It did." He takes a sip of his beer. "It was all fine and dandy until some kids at school started calling me Malibu's Most Wanted. At first, I didn't even realize what they were saying or that they were making fun of me for wearing it. I just thought it was cool, like my idols."

"How old were you?"

"Eleven or twelve, I think."

"That's so shitty."

"Yeah, it was. I got so tired of the constant teasing and *Malibu's Most Wanted* references that I just stopped wearing them."

"Those little fuckers bullied you out of wearing something that you loved."

He glances away, his smile replaced with a glum expression that tells me he is lost in negative memories.

Red-hot rage fills my veins. I jump to my feet, letting my anger for the small child version of Cooper take control as I storm across the bar until I'm beside Greg.

"Sutton," Cooper yells after me. "Stop."

But it's too late. I tap on the tall shaggy-haired bully's shoulder, waiting for him to turn around.

He does, and when he sees me, a triumphant smile graces his face.

I bat my lashes up at him before glancing down at my cleavage. His gaze follows mine, just as I wanted.

With his gaze now locked on my breasts, I cock my balled-up fist before slamming it into his stupid jaw.

Pain ricochets from my fist through my arm.

"Fuck," we both cry out at the same time.

Cooper is there in the next heartbeat. "Sutton, what did you do?"

Tears stream down my cheeks as I just raise my hurt fist up with the assistance of my other arm.

"The bitch punched me, that's what she did," Greg shouts.

Cooper spins so fast, putting his back to me as his demeanor shifts from one of concern to something still. "Watch your mouth."

Greg huffs out a laugh. "You can't be serious. She just broke her fucking hand punching my face, Malibu."

I leap forward. "And I'm about to break the other," I seethe, fighting to get around Cooper to teach that shit a lesson.

"You two need to leave. Pay your tabs and get out," the bartender shouts over the crowded room, pointing to both me and bitch-ass Greg.

Cooper nods, reaching into his back pocket to pull out a couple of twenty-dollar bills and then sets them on the bar. Placing his hand behind my back, he leads us back to our table to grab our jackets and my purse.

I sniffle the entire way to the truck as we walk in silence. Cooper buckles me into the passenger seat and then rounds the truck. I can barely see him through the tears clouding my vision as he climbs in, closing the door and turning in my direction.

"Are you okay?" His voice is quiet.

I sniffle again, wiping my nose with my undamaged hand while shaking my head. "No," I cry out.

"Oh, baby," he coos, reaching across the seats to pull my good hand into his. "Why did you do that?"

"Because he was mean to you."

"That was when we were kids, Sut. It doesn't matter now."

"No, not just when you were kids. He did it tonight. Multiple times. I can't. I won't stand for someone treating you like that."

He kisses my hand. "You are so sweet to defend me. I really, *really* appreciate it, but can we both agree that violence wasn't the best method?"

"Not the best method? Did you see the way his face lit up bright red from my skilled punch?"

A soft smile tugs at his lips. "Yes, I bet his jaw is going to hurt for days. But I'm also worried about your hand."

"I think I broke it," I whine.

Cooper leans in and kisses my forehead. "I do too. Now let's get you a professional opinion on that."

I swallow. "Okay."

⚘

"Yep, it's broken," Dr. Bryan Asshole says as he walks into the ER room I'm waiting in.

"No way. I call bullshit, Dr. Asshole," I murmur sleepily. They gave me a good dose of some pain medication when we first came in, and ever since, I've been walking on cloud nine.

He slowly shakes his head. "It's Athule, but you already knew that, Sutton."

Cooper smiles at him apologetically. "Sorry, she's a little high from the meds."

Dr. Asshole just shakes his head with a tight smile.

"Nah, Coopy, it's not the drugs. It's him. I called him that when he was dating Viv back in the day." I motion for him to come closer, and he leans down as I try to whisper to him. "You need to stop being so nice. He's basically your best friend's enemy."

"Baby, Nate doesn't have enemies."

"He should. And if he did, it would definitely be the guy who dated his wife when they broke up for a hot minute."

Cooper sighs, rubbing his head with his hand as he straightens. "Does this mean she needs a cast or something?"

"Yes, she will need to contact an ortho in the next few days for an appointment. They will do more x-rays and most likely proceed with a cast from there."

"Why does she have to wait?" Cooper asks.

Asshole, MD walks over to the bed and points at my hand, which is twice its normal size. "The swelling. We can't cast it until it goes down."

Cooper nods in understanding while I just stare up at him in awe. He is so damn beautiful. From those full lips to the glasses that cover my favorite amber eyes.

I'm happy to have him in my life. To have him with me now.

I sit up in the bed and reach out for his hand. He looks at me and smiles while pulling my hand to his lips for another kiss.

"Give it to me straight, doc. It was my extreme strength that broke my hand."

"No, it was an unskilled fist. You tucked your thumb, the number one thing you're not supposed to do when punching someone."

I hold up my bad hand. "Sorry I'm not an expert on physical violence. Unlike you."

Bryan's eyes turn to slits as a tight smile forms on his face before he turns his attention back to Cooper. "A nurse will be in shortly to go over paperwork with you guys."

"Thank you," Cooper says.

I wait until the door closes. "You were being too nice to him."

Cooper laughs. "You were being too mean."

"No, I wasn't even close to being as mean as I can be."

Cooper sits on the bed and hands me my phone. "Do you want to call Vivian and tell her?"

"Oh my God, yes," I squeal in delight as I struggle to use only my left hand to navigate my phone to her number.

She picks up on the first ring. "Hello."

"Hold on to your panties, Viv. You are never going to guess who Cooper and I just ran into."

"Who?"

"Are your panties secured to your body?"

There's a moment of silence before Viv replies, "Yes. Secured and ready for potential panty-blowing-off news."

"Bryan."

"Who?"

"Bryan. Dr. Asshole. Don't tell me he was so boring that you already forgot about him. Let me just refresh your memory. He was a dud you dated to pretend you could move on from Nate."

Viv chuckles. "Ah, that Bryan. Honestly, I just erased him from my memory. Where did you guys run into him?"

"The hospital. He's my doctor."

"The hospital," she yells. "Oh my God, Sut, are you okay? What happened? I'm on my way. What room are you in? Do you need blood? I will donate blood."

"Hold on, Mother Teresa. I'm about to be discharged, so no reason for you to come here."

"Fine, I will meet you at your house. What do you need? Food? Medicine? A new blanket?"

She doesn't even give me time to respond before she says, "Never mind, I'm just going to get you them all," and then hangs up.

"Well, sounds like we are going to have a Viv-shaped third wheel tonight in our bed. Hope you are prepared for how she hogs the covers," I tell Cooper as his fingers furiously type away on his phone. "Wait, who are you texting?"

He glances up at me. "Vivian and Nate are blowing up my phone right now."

"Let me see."

He passes the phone to me, and I see two threads filled with messages from the past five minutes.

Nate

You guys ran into that dick-bag Bryan?

Was he as hideous as I remember?

Please tell me he's at least balding.

Answer me, Cooper, or I'll tell Sutton every deep, dark secret you have ever shared.

"Ha," I yell out in triumph. "I knew they were enemies."

Cooper

Yes, we did run into him. He is Sut's doctor tonight. And yes, he's hideous, basically a mix between an orc and a troll.

And don't get me started on his hair. His hairline might still be in place, but man, it's so thin you can see his scalp. I give him another three years before he is completely bald.

You're a good friend.

And you're a shitty one. Don't you dare threaten to spill my most sacred secrets ever again.

Noted.

Secrets.

I wonder how much I'd have to bribe Nate to get him to spill a few for me.

Ooh, maybe I can enlist Viv to use her body to pry them from him.

I stash that plan away for another day as I open up the thread between him and my best friend.

Vivian

Cooper, what did you do to my best friend?

Cooper

Excuse me?

No I will not, not if you are the reason she is hurt.

Vivian, I would never do anything to hurt Sutton, and you know it.

…Okay, you have a point. Sorry. I love you and I know you would never hurt her, it's just… I go feral for my people.

You and Sutton have that in common.

So tell me what's going on? Why is she in the care of Dr. Athule?

She may have broken her hand while punching a man in the face tonight…

Was that man Dillon?

I wish.

Why on earth would she do that, then?

You'll have to ask the untrained fighter when you see her.

"You didn't spill the beans to Viv about what happened."

"Of course not. I know you, Sut. You'll want to make a big production about it."

My chest aches. He does know me. "Thank you."

Chapter Twenty-Four

Sutton

I've never felt like such a badass and idiot at the same time. But breaking my hand on some jerk's jaw while standing up for my man has a way of making me simultaneously awesome and foolish.

My hand throbbed for the last couple of days until I got in to see the ortho for my cast. Did I choose the prettiest purple plaster that is normally reserved for children? Yes, but that's only after they claimed they didn't have any designs. I mean, come on. They have a plethora of colors but no designs? Boring.

Cooper had driven me to my appointment, even holding my unbroken hand as they smoothed the weird material over my hand and wrist.

"Stop pouting," Cooper says as he turns the steering wheel in the direction of home and not my favorite breakfast place.

"I wouldn't be pouting if you would get me a treat for being good during my doctor's appointment."

"You're really laying it on thick today."

"I don't think I understand what you mean." I cross my arms over my chest and stare out the window.

"Sure you don't, *baby* girl."

My jaw drops as I spin to face him. "Excuse me."

"You heard me. I think you're acting a little childish, Sut."

"I am not."

"Are so."

"Am not," I fume. "How dare you spew such ludicrous lies."

"Sut, you asked for a dino cast and are now pouting 'cause you aren't getting rewarded for behaving like an adult."

"Okay, maybe I'm being a tiny bit childish. But that's only because I was scared. And we both know I don't cope well with... well, anything."

He reaches over and squeezes my thigh, his fingers dipping between my legs and staying there. "I know, that's why I already ordered your favorite from Toasted."

My lips pull up into the biggest grin. "You did?"

"Yes." He rolls his eyes. "You were a very brave girl."

"I was, wasn't I?"

Cooper shakes his head.

"The dino cast would have been dope, and you know it."

"You would have been the most popular girl in the office with a cast like that."

I sigh. "They really should invest in cast designs—for the children."

"Yes, for the children."

I wake up hours after going into a mini food coma to the sound of Vivian arguing with someone. Rubbing my eyes with my good hand, I climb out of bed and pad toward the sound.

In the living room, I find Viv, Nate, and Cooper sitting on the couch glaring at Dillon as he stands in front of the TV.

"Stop being a douche and move. This is the best part," Viv says, waving her hand in a shooing motion.

"Nah, I don't think I will." He smirks. "Besides, this show is garbage."

I glance at the TV to see the newest dating show, *Now or Never,* playing. It's a complete rip-off of *The Bachelor,* but that doesn't stop me or my friends from bingeing the hell out of it.

"Seriously, Dillon? Isn't it enough to be living here unwelcome? Now you're blocking people from the simple pleasures of reality trash TV?"

Dillon raises his hands in the air. "I should have known you all would like trash. It's very fitting."

Passing by him, I make my way to Cooper, plopping myself in his lap. Dillon's eyes flare with rage, and I can't help but smile. That is until he laughs. "Real mature, Sutton," he says, stalking off toward the front door. "And I know you guys have been fucking with my body wash," he yells before slamming the door behind him.

I frown. What triggered his attitude change? Looking down at where Cooper's arms are wrapped around mine, I gasp. Flowers cover my cast, with small dinosaurs in the middle of the blooms.

"When? How? When?" I ask to no one in general.

Cooper chuckles behind me as Vivian says, "While you were sleeping, Nate put his talented hands to work."

I glance at her. "But how did you know?"

"Cooper enlisted us. He told us all about your fixation on the dino pattern."

I glance over my shoulder at him. "You made sure I got the dinos?"

He nods. "I made sure you got your dumb dinos."

I smoosh my lips against his in an over-the-top peck. "Thank you."

I turn to Nate and gush, "I love it."

"You're welcome. I'm not going to lie, it was a bit of a challenge. Not only is drawing on cast difficult, but Sutton, you move in your sleep more than any other person I have ever met. Not to mention the sleep talking."

"Do you watch people sleep often, Nate?"

Cooper leans further away from Nate. "How often have you watched me sleep?"

"Every chance I get."

Cooper laughs. "I thought so, you creep."

"Wait," I say, holding up my good hand. "Let's circle back real quick. Did you say sleep talking?"

"Yeah." Nate nods. "You wouldn't shut up about some spider monkey."

I gasp. "I do not talk in my sleep." I glance at Cooper and Vivian for confirmation, and they give me a "you bet your ass, you do" look.

"Okay, enough about the creepy sleep watching and talking," Vivian beams. "I want to know what you guys have been doing to Dillon's body wash."

Cooper and I glance at each other, big toothy smiles plastered across our faces.

"Nothing," we declare in unison.

Vivian and Nate both give us a disbelieving look.

"Bullshit," Nate says. "You two look guiltier than a dog who just ate your food."

Cooper looks his friend in the eye. "We haven't done a thing to his body wash."

I bite my lip to keep myself from laughing. "His shampoo and conditioner, on the other hand…"

Their eyes spark as Cooper adds, "I might have switched his expensive haircare with Mane 'n Tail."

"The horse stuff?" Vivian asks. "I thought his hair looked shinier."

I glare at Cooper. "I told you it was making his hair healthier."

Cooper tosses his hands up in frustration. "How was I supposed to know that?"

"Maybe if you listened to me."

Cooper opens his mouth to argue, but Nate cuts him off. "How else have you guys been torturing him?"

Cooper and I dive into detail about everything we are and aren't doing to Dillon. How his paranoia is increasing every day, and we can only hope that soon, it will be enough to drive him out the front door for good.

He's already too scared to try anything that isn't sealed shut, which is perfect. The other day, I watched as he installed a new knob on his door so he can lock it as he leaves. Little does he know, Cooper and I are now enrolled in an online lock-picking course. Are we about to become locksmiths just for prank's sake? You bet your ass, we are.

There's no limit to what we'll do to get Dillon to leave.

Okay, that's a lie. We won't cause him any physical harm. It's our one rule.

And oh, how I despise it.

After a while, the guys head out to go watch a new band play at a dive bar a few blocks away, while my still-on-pain-meds ass and Viv's tired, pregnant one chill on the couch.

I gnaw on my bottom lip as we watch the perfect women fly around the world for a handsome yet mediocre man.

"Okay, spill it," Viv demands thirty minutes into the show.

"Oh, thank God, I thought I was going to have to watch the entire episode before you demanded more details."

"Who do you take me for, a common acquaintance? No, I'm your ride or die. Your bestie for the restie. Your nonromantic life partner. So spill."

"So the tricks and everything are working pretty well on Dillon. He is almost to the point of breaking—I think. Soon, he should be too scared to try anything in the home. It's perfect. Maybe that will get him to leave us alone, maybe it won't..." I take a deep breath before rattling on. "Maybe we are gonna be stuck with him forever. I sure hope we aren't. I just want to be alone. I want my home to be mine again. And I kind of want it to be Cooper's too. But that leads me to an entirely different problem."

She stares at me for a moment. "Go on."

"I still don't know how to go about asking my fake boyfriend to be my actual boyfriend, let alone to move in with me for real. Would he even do it? Would he give up his apartment? I mean, he's pretty much given it up for now. He's been living with me for, oh my gosh, two months now. I mean, that feels pretty much moved-in to me. Like, why should he bother with paying his rent when he doesn't even live in that fancy storage container? He should just move in here permanently. But what if Dillon never leaves? Maybe we should just move into his apartment. I don't know what to do, Viv. Help me."

"Since when do you get so frazzled over a man?"

"Since this is the first time I have ever felt like my heart is going to explode if he doesn't want me."

She grins.

"What?" I ask.

Viv's grin grows even bigger as her shoulders slowly move forward and backward.

"Why are you shimmying? This doesn't feel like a shimmy moment."

"You love him," she singsongs. "Sutton and Cooper, sitting in the tree, k-i-s-s-i-n-g."

I roll my eyes. "More like f-u-c-k-i-n-g."

She quirks an eyebrow. "Notice how you didn't deny the love part?"

I clear my throat and look back at the TV. "I noticed."

She squeals. "This is perfect. Now all you two need to do is rip out that IUD and let his little swimmers invade your lady cave."

"That's all?"

"Well, you guys could get married if you wanted, but I wasn't sure how you feel about having another wedding so soon."

I sigh. "I want it all, Viv. The dress, the flowers, Cooper."

"Okay, so let's get you a dress and some flowers." She pulls out her phone and calls Audra.

"Hey, Audra, we need flowers ASAP."

"What are you doing?" I hiss.

Vivian smiles, placing the call on speakerphone.

"What's the occasion? And can't Nate just pick you some from your over-the-top flower beds?"

"Nah, it's not for me or your brother. It's for Sutton and Cooper's wedding."

"Vivian Gertrude Fisher," I scream and pounce at her, trying to take the phone from her.

She stands, dodging me just barely.

"She's crazy, Audra. It's all lies," I continue to yell as I chase my best friend into the kitchen while she laughs.

Audra's chuckle comes through the phone. "So, I take it Cooper isn't aware he is getting married."

"No one is getting married," I shout at the same time Vivian says, "Not yet."

"Ohhhkay," Audra says, "how about when Sutton and Cooper agree on the marriage, we circle back to the flowers. Until then, just tell me what color theme so I can get to designing."

"She's an autumn."

"But last time she did more of a pastel-like spring."

"Exactly," Vivian cheers triumphantly. "And last time, she was just delusional."

"That's rich coming from the woman currently planning a wedding for two people who aren't even officially dating."

Audra barks out a laugh. "Um, if you two aren't together, then I am a walrus."

The two of them proceed to make walrus noises until Audra hangs up five minutes later.

Moving back to the living room, I press rewind on the remote as I sink into my favorite spot. The old cushion nearly swallowing me with its worn-in age.

"Don't be mad," Viv pleads as she lays her head in my lap.

On instinct, I comb my fingers through her hair. "Too late, I'm pissed."

The front door opens, and Cooper strides in, followed by Nate.

"Pissed about what?" Cooper asks.

Viv opens her mouth, but I slap my palm across her mouth before she can utter a word.

"About Vivian having an excuse to eat more and me not."

Cooper eyes me. "Do you want to have the same excuse? Because that can be arranged." He winks.

Vivian's eyes snap up to mine as if to say, I told you so.

Flustered by all their eyes on me, I spit out a nonsensical jumble of words. "No. We couldn't. Shouldn't. Well..."

I can't answer the question.

Cooper just laughs and heads off into the kitchen while Nate leans down to pull Viv up into his arms for a hug.

Cooper drops a small plastic bag in the kitchen before returning with a beer and a bottle of water, handing the latter to Nate.

"Why are you back so early, anyway? It's only been, like, an hour. I thought you were going to see a band."

Cooper glances at Nate. "Well, you see, what had happened was, it turns out Nate has pregnancy brain."

I cock my head to the side. "That's not a thing for men."

Nate shakes his head. "It is."

I scoff, "Viv, talk some sense into your husband."

She tilts her head contemplatively. "Maybe he does, I don't know."

"Nope, not real." I stand my ground.

"Okay, maybe it's not pregnancy brain in the most traditional of ways. But my mind has been extra preoccupied with Viv—"

"Nothing new there," Cooper cuts in.

"—and the baby."

Viv sighs all dreamily—because of course she does.

I almost do too, and he's not my husband.

"Fine. You can have 'pregnancy brain.' But seriously, please don't tell anyone else that. Just say your thoughts are consumed by your wife and the child she is creating. The other way is just weird."

Nates looks like a puppy that's just been scolded. "Fine."

"You can still say it," Viv whispers to him.

"Anyway, why are you back so early?" I ask again.

Cooper clears his throat. "Yeah, so pregnancy brain over here got the dates mixed up."

Nate nods. "No band tonight."

"But we did get to enjoy some slam poetry."

"Ooh, slam poetry." Viv bounces excitedly. "I've never heard it performed."

"Consider yourself lucky," Cooper mumbles under his breath.

"Did you have a favorite poem or performer?" I ask.

Cooper sits in the chair beside me. "I don't know. I think my favorite had to be the one about vaginal discharge."

"Vaginal discharge?" Viv and I say at the same time.

Cooper grins. "Oh, you heard me right. It was about how amazing and complex the fluids expelled from the vagina are."

Viv grimaces while I smile brightly. "Do go on. Tell me more."

"The performer was deeply passionate about the assorted colors and textures being a metaphor for how people aren't so different from discharge. We all come from a vagina."

"Except for the cesarean babies," I argue.

"They don't count, obviously."

I gasp, my hand flying to my chest. "I'll have you know I was born via surgical removal."

"It's okay." Cooper pulls my hand from my chest to his. "I still think of you as a person."

"Thank you. I was genuinely concerned." I smile before turning to Nate. "What about you, Nate?"

"Cesarean as well," he deadpans.

"What was your favorite?" Viv asks. "Was it the vagina one too?"

His lips form a tight line. "I'm not quite sure I had a favorite."

Cooper laughs. "Don't lie. You had a favorite. Tell them."

"Yeah, Nate, tell us."

"Tell us. Tell us. Tell us," Viv and I chant.

He blushes but says nothing, just stares at Cooper with enormous eyes.

"Come on, baby," Vivian pleads. "You know if you don't tell us now, we will only become more annoying with time."

I bob my head in agreement. "She's right. If you don't tell us, we will be relentless in our pursuit to find out the truth, no matter how long it takes."

"If I tell you now, you're going to make fun of me for years."

"Very possible." Vivian trails her hand up and down his thighs.

Nate opens his mouth like he's going to finally tell us, but Cooper beats him to the punch.

"His favorite was about sweat."

"Sweat? I don't understand." Viv's brows crinkle.

"He said it was super sensual, and it made him want to jump Viv's bones once they get home."

I burst out into laughter as Nate stands, lifting a hand out to Viv. "You ready, Cherry?"

"Absolutely," she says eagerly with a look that can only be described as massively horny.

"They are totally going to get sweaty tonight."

"Without a doubt."

Chapter Twenty-Five

Cooper

...Why are you texting me from the other room.

Will you make me something to eat.

There it is.

Please!

I push the door to Sutton's bedroom open with my foot as I carefully balance a tray with an ice-cold can of Sprite and a plate of dino nuggets and french fries in one hand and her favorite blanket from the couch in the other.

The woman sits up so fast, her nose crinkling as she sniffs the air. "Is that what I think it is?" she asks, her eyes growing wide with excitement.

"A meal fit for a toddler? Why yes, Sutton, it is."

She reaches out for the tray. "I'm too hungry to care about your insults right now."

I sit the tray in front of her and throw the blanket at her feet, watching as she bites the head of a dinosaur off while shoving a french fry into her mouth at the same time.

Back off, ladies and gentlemen, she's all mine.

"After you eat, do you want me to help you wash your hair?"

She finishes chewing what's in her mouth before responding, "You'd do that for me?"

"Of course."

After we wrap her hand up in a makeshift cast cover made from trash bags and duct tape, I start a shower at the scalding-hot temperature I know she loves. My skin will hate me for it, but for her, I'd burn every inch of myself.

I help her strip out of her clothes and watch her perky ass as she steps under the spray of water.

I shudder as my cock threatens to harden at the sight. God, she's beautiful, even sweaty and covered in ketchup.

She pokes her head out of the clear shower curtain and asks, "Aren't you coming in?"

I clear my throat. "Yeah, I just need to grab one thing first." Pulling my phone out of my back pocket, I put on the last band I ever thought I'd willingly listen to, Creed, as I shuck off my clothes, leaving them in a heap with Sutton's.

I take my time massaging her coconut-and-vanilla shampoo into her scalp, then scrub her down with a body wash with the same scent. Then comes the hard part—shaving. I'm so nervous I'm going to cut her until Sutton points out that I have more experience than her as I shave my face. With that confidence boost, I help the woman clean up, removing any remaining hair from her underarms and legs. Luckily, my girl likes to get Brazilian waxes for her harder-to-reach areas.

Once she's satisfied with how well I washed and shaved her, we get out, and I blow her hair dry, following her explicit instructions. Her eyes close as she leans against my chest, completely relaxing into me.

With her hair finally dry, we both opt for sleep, piling into the bed nude as we snuggle against each other.

Sutton falls asleep almost immediately, muttering random words like *"with arms wide open, Renesmee"* and *"glasses liar."* Whatever that means. I smile as I drift off thinking about what wildness must be going on in her mind.

We've only been asleep for a couple of hours when my phone starts buzzing incessantly. Which can only mean one thing.

A group chat.

Aka the bane of my existence.

I reach over Sutton to steal my phone from the charger, readying myself to tell off whoever woke me up, but that all changes when I read the texts.

Mr. Avery- Hey, group. Sorry to be texting you all so late, but I just got word that Jorge passed away earlier today.

Unknown number- You're kidding?

Unknown number- But he just retired.

Mr. Avery- I know, it's horrible.

Jim- What happened?

Mr. Avery- Dawn, his wife, said heart attack.

My breath hitches. He just retired not even two months ago.

So many questions fill my head. Was it preventable? Did he have a prior cardiac history? Did he ever make it to his paradise in the sun?

He was so full of life. My own mortality comes rushing in with a wave of anxiety. Will I end up like him, dying before I ever get to enjoy my life to the fullest?

Sutton stirs beside me. "What's wrong?" she asks, turning to face me.

My phone continues to light up with more incoming texts from my coworkers, but I silence my phone and set it down on the bedside table before hugging Sutton and burrowing my head into her neck.

"Cooper?"

"Jorge had a heart attack."

"The man whose retirement party we went to?" she asks gently.

I nod.

"Is he okay?"

I breathe her in, letting her familiar scent soothe my aching heart for a moment, unsure of how to answer that question. "He didn't make it."

"I'm sorry." She presses a kiss to my hair and strokes her good hand down my back until I fall back asleep.

\#

A week later, Sutton stands by my side at the back of the packed sea of white fold-out chairs as we watch Jorge's casket being lowered into the ground.

Sutton wipes a stray tear away.

"Baby," I whisper, pulling her into my chest. "We can go if you want. It's almost over."

"I just hate that he didn't get to live his dream. He waited his entire life for paradise and never got to experience it."

"It's horrible."

"It's horse shit," she sobs, pulling back to look me in the eye. "I don't want to be like Jorge. Waiting for the right time. Pushing off my wants and dreams for the hope that they will still be there one day."

"Then don't, Sutton." I swallow, peering into her red-rimmed, glossy eyes.

With that, she reaches up on her toes and presses her lips to mine. It's soft and sweet and too short for my liking. She pulls back to look at me and declares, "I want to stop pretending."

"Pretending?" I ask as a mixture of fear and hope courses through my veins, lighting every inch of my skin on fire with anticipation of what she'll say next.

She nods. "I don't want to pretend this"—she gestures between us—"is fake in any way. None of it was ever just for show. I want to call it what it is."

"And what's that?"

"Real."

I squeeze her tighter to me before leaning down to capture her mouth with mine. "This is real," I promise between kisses. "The realest thing in the world for me."

\#

After the funeral, a wake is held for Jorge at his favorite bar that's just a short walk from the A&A offices. Billiard tables and dart boards line the back of the bar, with games already in progress as Sutton and I walk in.

The room is packed with a mix of black suits and dresses and various tropical-printed button-ups in honor of Jorge. I notice everyone from the office is there minus my boss. He told another coworker that wakes weren't his thing and apparently dipped out after the funeral.

Sutton and I mingle, each taking a shot in Jorge's memory before being whisked off to play a round of darts. We listen as coworkers and family friends of Jorge step up on the stage to share a fun memory of the man. His wife, Dawn, is smiling with tears in her eyes at every little anecdote shared.

We stay for almost two hours before leaving, stepping out into the rain that started falling while we were at the wake. And of course neither of us has an umbrella.

Sutton and I laugh as we race down the street to the parking garage across the street from A&A where we parked.

We make our way up the ramp to where my truck is, and I round the vehicle and open the passenger door for her, only for Sutton to wrap her arms around my stomach.

Her embrace calms every ounce of anxiety that's been coursing through my veins. I can do this. I can get through anything as long as I have her with me.

Droplets fall from her lashes as she looks up at me. She has never looked as beautiful as she does right now.

A smile curves up on her lips. "What?"

I lean in, placing a kiss on her lips. "I love you."

She sucks in a breath through her nose, the smile that was there falling as she locks her eyes with mine. "I love you too."

"I love you so much that I would lie to spare your feelings. And I do."

She shoots me a questioning look, and I can't help but smile as I add, "I hate the way you make my coffee."

"But you always have two cups every morning."

"Yeah, because you made it for me."

"That's sweet of you, but I don't want you drinking something you don't like. Just tell me how to fix it, and if it makes you happy, I'll make it differently."

"You would change your recipe for me?"

"Baby, I would change my life for you." She swallows harshly, then says, "Confession. I make coffee you hate on purpose."

"What? Why?" I laugh.

"At first, it was to get back at you for being so tempting. But then it just became routine to make it, and you never complained, so I figured you must not mind as much as I initially thought."

I don't care that she purposely makes me nasty coffee. I don't care about anything other than the fact that Sutton Hale loves me. She *loves* me. And I love her.

Chapter Twenty-Six

Sutton

"Tell me something nobody knows about you," Cooper demands with one arm draped over my shoulders, holding me close to his side. Ever since the funeral a few days ago, the two of us have become even more inseparable.

We've been sharing more than ever, desperate to learn everything about each other. Neither of us is afraid of showing how much we care and crave the other.

"Something nobody knows?"

He nods. "Not even Vivian."

"Okay, um, let me think." I scramble to think of something, anything, that no one else knows but can only think of the really, truly weird shit. I nibble on my bottom lip. "Promise you won't tell anyone?"

"Of course. This stays between us."

I hesitate for a second before letting it all spill out in a jumbled rush. "Sometimes when I get a rotisserie chicken, I eat it over the kitchen sink with my bare hands while I fantasize about being a powerful lord in medieval times."

He stares at me for a beat, his mouth opening then shutting before he finally decides on his words. "First of all, I love a good hand-eaten rotisserie chicken."

I laugh.

"And second, why are you a lord and not a lady?"

I side-eye him before heaving out a sigh. "When you think medieval warrior, do you think woman?"

His cheeks flush pink and he swallows. "No."

"Exactly. We are always taught men are powerful, physically and mentally. They are the leaders. Even in modern times as we step away from those 'traditional' roles, the titles of those in power still set us apart. We still think of a lady as being a lord's wife. Not someone of her own strength or power. So I refuse, even in my fantasies, to be called that. Instead, I choose the title that holds the power."

Cooper stays silent as if he's pondering my words.

I expect him to laugh or make fun of my tangent, but he doesn't.

"Do you want to add anything, or has my TED talk given you something to think about?"

He licks his teeth. "Can't it be both?"

"Sure, but I am kind of feeling a little exposed here."

He shakes his head, reaching out a hand to squeeze my shoulder. "Sorry, I just wasn't expecting all of that when I asked my question."

"What can I say, I live to surprise."

He grins. "That you do."

"So?"

"So?"

"Don't you have something you want to tell me?"

"Oh yeah, thank you for sharing."

I slap his toned stomach. "It's your turn to share, you dummy."

Cooper laughs. "Okay, fine, I'll tell you if you keep those chicken tearers away from me."

I scowl at him but place my hands under my thighs as I wait on him to hopefully share something of equal or greater embarrassment.

"I didn't know what foreskin was until I was, like, seventeen."

"What?" I bark out in disbelief.

"Yeah, I'm circumcised—"

"Yes, Cooper, I am well aware your peen is cut."

His gaze narrows. "As I was saying, as you know, I am circumcised. But when I was growing up, I didn't know that circumcision was even a thing. I just thought that was the way a penis looked naturally."

"You didn't know? Did you not look at the other dicks in the locker room?"

"Why do I feel like you're trying to get me to admit to checking out men?"

"Because I was. But also, it's a valid question. Did you notice something different about the other guys?"

"Nope. Every guy I grew up with that I had seen naked looked just like me."

"That's wild. Normally, there is at least one straggler in the group."

"Well, not at my school."

"How did you figure it out?"

He rubs at the back of his neck, looking away from me. "I think you already know."

I cackle. "It was porn, wasn't it?"

Hanging his head in shame, he mutters, "Yep."

A shrill scream echoes from the guest bathroom down the hall. Cooper and I turn toward the sound and glance at each other.

"Do you think…?" I ask, curling my feet under me on the couch. "Yeah, I think."

The bathroom door whips open, and a fully nude Dillon storms out and stomps toward us, trailing water in his wake.

Cooper's hand flies up to cover my eyes. "Dude," he yells. "Put on some clothes in front of my girlfriend."

A growl-like sound leaves Dillon. "You mean my ex-fiancée."

"Yeah, like I said, *my* girlfriend doesn't need to see your teeny weenie, so go put on some clothes."

I can't see the look Dillon's giving Cooper, but I can only imagine it's one meant to kill.

"It's only teeny because someone used all the hot water."

A small chuckle leaves my lips. "Um, I hate to point out the obvious, Dil, but neither Cooper nor I have showered today, so there's no way we used up all the hot water."

Cooper hums in agreement. "Yep, looks like that petite pecker is all yours… Now, if you would please put some clothes on, my arm's getting tired."

"I know one of you had something to do with this," he accuses, anger lacing his every word before he stomps off in what I assume is the opposite direction.

Cooper drops his hand from my eyes.

I give him a long sideways glance. "Was that necessary?"

"Covering your eyes? Absolutely. One hundred percent neces-sary. No girlfriend should be seeing another man's peen in person while we are together."

"So seeing a man's peen when you aren't around is a-okay?" I tilt my head, pondering his meaning.

"Negative, baby opossum. I meant porn is cool. Look at all the penises you want online."

"Oh, no in-person showing. But the professionals online are free game."

He gives me a matter-of-fact nod. "You get it."

"Okay, just to be clear, does this mean I can interact with sex workers online or just watch?"

"Do you want to interact?"

"No. I just want to know where our boundaries are."

"Ah," he says, understanding. "I think watching porn is cool, great even. I love it."

"I bet you do, perv."

He sighs, but the corners of his lips curve up into a reluctant smile. "But interaction, like chatting or paying for special videos, is a no-go for me. Is that okay? Or is it too much?"

I tap my pointer finger on my chin, pretending to ponder his question. "I think it's a fine boundary that I agree to."

"You do?"

"Yeah? Do you think I am out here striking up online relation-ships with adult performers?"

He shrugs. "Anything is possible. But mostly, I want our rela-tionship to have open communication. That means if you don't like a boundary of mine, you need to speak up so I can know and reevaluate how I feel on the situation."

"How are you not married with 2.5 kids?"

He chuckles. "You've met me. You know how I am."

"Yeah, super freaking amazing, and not just in bed. With communication and romance. I just—I don't understand how no one has snatched you up yet."

"Sutton..." His cheeks flare to a deep red that reminds me of the flush that flows over his skin when he fucks.

Swallowing down my overactive libido, I tell him, "I'm serious, Coop, you are the whole damn package, plus some."

After a few moments of silence, I can't help myself. "Was it actually small?" I ask, finally remembering my original question to him.

"Dillon's dick?"

"Yeah?"

"I guess that depends on what his dick looked like prior to his ice shower."

I roll my eyes. "Why can't you just answer me?"

"Because I have no frame of reference for Dillon's dick." *Which is funnier, his dick being shriveled from the icy water, or it being average and him being super self-conscious about it?*

"I bet I can find a picture of it," I tell him, pulling out my phone.

He snatches it from my hands. "I swear to Jesus H. Christ, if you have a dick pic from Dillon still on your phone, I am going to lose my shit."

"Ew, no," I hiss, offended by his pseudoaccusation.

His glare tells me he's still suspicious.

"Ugh, a little trust would be great." I snatch my phone back from him. "I still have access to his cloud." I smile slyly at him.

"Sutton... That seems wrong. Like an invasion of his privacy. We shouldn't..."

"Found one."

"Let me see." He scoots closer to me, peering over my shoulder to get a good look at Dillon's ding-a-ling's not-so-glamorous glamour shot.

We both burst into laughter at picture number one, and it doesn't stop from there.

"Why is he gripping it like that?" Cooper wheezes, clutching his stomach.

"I don't know. I don't pretend to understand the penis pictures, I just admire them."

He sobers beside me. "Admire them?"

I swat at his shoulder. "You're so sensitive."

"No I'm not," he grumbles, glancing at the picture of Dillon grasping his dick like a thin water bottle.

I suck my lips in to fight the grin threatening to form on my lips. My baby is jealous. And damn, do I like it.

Is that crazy?

It feels crazy.

Jealousy is supposed to be unattractive.

But nothing about Cooper could ever be considered anything but ungodly attractive.

I savor every second he shows any ounce of jealousy over me. As if I'm someone worth fighting over.

It's dumb. But it gets me so hot and bothered.

Chapter Twenty-Seven

Cooper

"Would you ever be interested in being pegged?" Sutton asks so casually as she takes a bite of her pancakes while scrolling through social media.

I nearly spit my coffee out on her. "Excuse me?"

She glances up from her phone, completely unconcerned about the droplets of coffee now covering the table. "You know, a little anal action. Would you be into it?"

My brain stalls, unsure what the correct answer is.

"Don't look so horrified, Cooper. You literally can't answer the question wrong."

"Before I answer, why do you want to know?"

She laughs. "Because I'm clearly interested, duh. I've always wanted to fuck a man, and damn if you don't have a perfect ass for pounding."

My dick stirs awake at her confession. "You want to fuck me?"

She nods, her eyes trained on my face as she studies my expression.

"In the ass?"

Again a nod.

"With a strap on?"

She gives me a glare that says *obviously*. "And with my fingers."

My dick is fully awake now. The fucker is clearly interested in what she's saying, even if it scares me shitless.

"Good to know," I tell her, lifting the coffee mug back to my lips and taking a long draw from it.

"So, is that something you might be interested in exploring with me?"

I arch a brow at her.

"Or have you already done it before?" Her smile drops slightly as if the thought of me trusting another with something so vulnerable upsets her.

"No, I've never let anyone even touch me there before but you... But to answer your first question, I'm interested in trying anything and everything with you."

Her face brightens. "Really?"

I nod, and she hops out of her chair and climbs across the table until she's in my lap, kissing all over my face.

"I promise I'll take such good care of you, Cooper. I promise."

I chuckle. "I know, baby. I know. But does this mean I can have your ass too?"

Her smile turns devious. "It's been yours since day one. Even when I pretended to hate you. All you had to do was ask."

Fucking hell.

I groan as she wiggles said ass into my hard cock.

"Unless you want me to fuck that round ass right now, I suggest you stop rubbing it over my dick," I groan as she circles her hips with a little more pizzazz than is needed.

"You two are disgusting," Dillon gripes, interrupting us with revulsion written over his face as he walks through the kitchen to finish off the pot of coffee I made for Sutton and me. "Anal talk at eight in the morning is a little skanky, even for you, Sutton."

Sutton just rolls her eyes, ignoring the jab. I, on the other hand, don't brush it off as easily.

"If you think it's so gross, why don't you try leaving?"

Dillon's lips curls. "Nah, I kind of like interrupting you guys every chance I get."

"It reeks of desperation, Dill, and that's a very unattractive look," Sutton says, reaching across my plate to grab a piece of bacon.

"And slut isn't an attractive look at all, Sutton, but here you are, day after day, sporting it."

I go rigid. Every muscle, every fiber of my being is begging me to stand up and teach this little shit a lesson.

To pound my fist into that shit-talking mouth.

To forget everything and get justice for her.

I'll go against my own morals in a heartbeat if it means shutting him up.

But I don't.

Sensing the shift in my mood, Sutton strokes my neck with her hand that's still wrapped around me. Her fingers move in a calming up-and-down motion that relaxes my body into hers.

Dillon huffs as he leaves the kitchen and pads back down the hall to the spare bedroom he's been calling home.

"We need to get him out of here already."

"I know. But what else can we do? Our constant PDA hasn't scared him off yet. So what do we do?"

"Fuck if I know. But his ass needs to be gone in the next week or so, or I am going to end up beating him into a pulp, Sut."

"I know, baby." She rests her head on my shoulder with a sigh. "God, I hate him. He ruined our perfect morning."

I tip her chin up with my finger until her gaze meets mine. "He may have ruined an opportunity, a blip in time. But trust me when I say my morning isn't ruined. Nothing can be ruined as long as I have you."

A goofy smile breaks out on her lips. "Cooper Dale Fisher, you are smitten with me."

"Yes. But that isn't my middle or last name."

Her face scrunches. "I think I would know the middle and last name of the man who has been blowing my back out every night."

"But do you? Because those aren't them, sweetheart."

She pats my chest with the leftover piece of bacon in her grasp. "Sure. Just like you and Nate have never frenched."

"Um, we haven't."

"Okay, whatever you say." She winks, standing from my lap and walking her barely covered ass into the hall.

"I'm getting concerned that you aren't joking and that you don't actually know my name, Sutton," I call out after her.

"Stop trying to trick me, Coop. I won't fall for it."

I pick up my now-cold coffee, taking a sip before cursing the fact that I have to leave for work in a few minutes. It's one of the things I miss about being a teacher. Summer break.

Sure, I worked part-time with Nate and his dad every summer, fixing up lawns I could only imagine owning in my wildest dreams, but I still had somewhat of a summer.

Now, I'm a nine-to-fiver with no summer vacation in sight due to me being the newer guy at work.

Do I miss the low pay and general bullshit from teaching? Hell no.

But I think I'll always crave those weeks of stress-free bliss when I only had to think about myself.

I finish my coffee and head over to top myself off before jumping into the shower, only to remember that Dillon the Douche finished the pot and didn't bother to start another one.

Just another reason to hate him.

First, he insults Sutton.

Then he drinks the last of the coffee and doesn't start another pot for the rest of us.

It is official; the man is irredeemable.

I crack my knuckles, needing to release some of the pent-up rage for that man.

The noise from the shower being turned on down the hall catches my attention. Sutton must be in there.

My dick once again jumps at the thought of her stripping out of those barely there sleep shorts she was torturing me with just a few minutes ago.

A quick shower with Sutton might cool me down.

Who am I kidding? A shower with Sut would do the opposite of cool me down. It would make every inch of me feel like it is on fire.

But afterward, I'll feel as I always do, like nothing is important. Like the world could fade away, and I would be okay because she graced me with her body and attention.

Chapter Twenty-Eight

Cooper

"What the hell am I supposed to put on this?" I groan, lying my head against the back of the couch. The company sent out self-evaluations moments before it was time to go home, and they're due by the end of the week.

"What's the question?" Sutton asks, setting her knitting down on her lap.

"What areas of your performance do you think you could improve," I read off the computer sitting in my lap.

I've already reached the maximum performance for my role, if you ask me. When Jorge retired, I took on over fifty percent of his clients, as the rest of my coworkers already had a full client load.

"Oh, I've got it. Hand me the computer." She motions for me to pass it to her. With the computer in her lap, she types away while chuckling under her breath before she hands it back to me.

I frown as I read the words she chose.

Nothing. Because like my mother always says, I'm perfect just the way I am...

"Sutton, I can't put that."

"Yes, you can and you will."

"Please be serious for a minute, baby. I need your HR experience, not your extensive bullshitting repertoire."

Sutton's chest heaves. "They are one and the same. I promise you, Coop, I'm being dead serious. These questions are a trick, and you need to answer them with complete confidence."

"My mother would never say that," I mutter under my breath.

"Well, mine would, and you deserve to be told that as well."

"I don't think they are going to find me putting that I am perfect too cute."

She shrugs. "They might not. I am telling you, if you put that you have any area that needs to be improved upon, they will use it against you as a reason not to give you a higher raise."

"That's bullshit."

"That's corporate bullshit," she supplies.

"So I lie and say I have nothing that needs to be improved upon."

She gives a curt nod. "Fake it till you make it, baby."

"Our new motto?"

"You bet your tight ass, it is. Want to play video games when you're finished?"

God, how I love this woman.

I'm looking over my answers one last time when I get an email alert that SluttonHale69@gmail.com has sent me something.

I look up from my computer to find her knitting.

Suspicious, I open the file and am quickly directed to a survey form.

Cooper's Boyfriend Evaluation

1. As a boyfriend to the absolute king/ruler of your heart that is Sutton Hale, how would you rate your overall performance on a scale of one to ten?

2. If you could buy Sutton one pair of shoes, which would you buy?

- Red stilettos with gems covering them to look like they are from the *Wizard of Oz*.

- Lavender stilettos with bows on the toes and heel.

- Black stilettos with chrome spikes.

- Trick question. You would buy all of the above.

3. Rate your performance in the bedroom.
- Poor (Sutton is faking every orgasm).

- Okay (I've only made Sutton come on accident).

- Average (could be better, could be worse).

- Above average (I only come if Sutton comes at least twice).

- Excellent (I take that pussy to pound town and give it unlimited orgasms).

Bonus: Tell the truth, do you honestly need glasses?

I laugh as I fill it out, answering, 10, All of the above, Excellent, and Wouldn't you like to know?

I make a mental note to make her one as I close my laptop and place it on the coffee table. Picking up one of the controllers, I turn and toss it into Sutton's lap, then power on the other as I pull up Mario Kart on the PlayStation.

A few days later, my boss calls me into his office.

"Cooper, please have a seat." He gestures toward the chairs, smiling at me from behind the desk. "Listen, I got your self-evaluation back and thought it was time we had a chat."

Shit. Shit. Shit.

My palms immediately slick with sweat.

"Sir, I—"

"Ah, hold it right there, son. We loved it. You've been an exceptional member of our team since day one. And since gaining the majority of Jorge's clients, you have stepped up."

Holy shit. Sutton's bullshitting worked. "Thank you, sir."

"So here's the thing, we have a senior position available, and based on your performance and go-getter attitude, it's yours."

I sit up straighter.

"That is if you're interested."

"I am. I'm *very* interested," I tell him eagerly.

He laughs. "Hold your horses, son. The position won't start for a few more weeks, but I will email you the details regarding duties and pay, and if you are still interested, let me know."

I nod enthusiastically. "I most definitely will. Thank you, sir." I shake his hand, on cloud nine. I can't wait to tell Sutton about this. She's going to be so excited to tell me I told you so.

Chapter Twenty-Nine

Cooper

Phase two of our plan—or as I like to call it, *the douche gets douched on*—is set and ready for tonight.

It's been weeks since we've done anything new to Dillon, so we're both itching to find another way to annoy the man out of our lives.

Sutton prepped for the prank the only way she knew how. By spending two hours taking an "everything" shower. Why the woman needs her entire body to be as smooth as a baby's bottom to prank her ex is beyond me.

I wish I could say she's doing it for me. But that'd be a lie. I'd love that woman if she had hair coming out of her eyeballs. And I'd sure as hell still want to fuck her. So a little hair and sweat don't bug me. Hell, I've fucked her while she was smelly and sweaty after going on one brief walk around the block. The woman is so out of shape it's insane. I tried to take her on a jog with me the other day, and she tried to pass out when we weren't even a block down the road. I should've known better. Most days, the driveway has her winded.

I glance at my watch one more time. I swear if she doesn't hurry up, I'm going to lose it. We're gonna be late for when his band plays, and then the plan will be pointless. We'd have to wait another week before we could do it again.

"Come on, Sutton. You're taking too long," I yell. "Do you even want to do this?"

"How can you even question me? Do you know how much time and money I've put into this prank?" she asks as she steps out into the hallway. Her long golden-tan legs shimmering in the dimly lit hall. I suck in a breath as I trace from her feet in those high heels, all the way up to her short leather mini skirt. She's wearing a shimmering triangle halter top that barely covers her breasts and leaves her back completely exposed.

She's a radiant god.

And I can't wait to get her back home to fuck her senseless.

I don't say a word as I continue to stare at her. She looks in the mirror in the hallway one last time, ruffling her hair a little bit to make it messy, and then smiles at me. "What?"

"You look... hot."

Her smile grows, and she glances back in the mirror. "I do, don't I?"

"Always so humble, baby opossum." I stand and make my way over to her.

Her gaze narrows in frustration. "Why won't you drop the baby opossum shit?"

Resting my chin on her shoulder, I peer at her through the mirror. "The better question is, why would I ever drop it?" I shoot back.

"I hate you."

I smile and press a kiss into her neck. "No you don't."

Sutton's phone pings with a text alert. "Oh shit, is that the time?" she asks, staring down at it.

"Are you kidding me? I told you what time it was not even ten minutes ago when I told you we needed to leave."

"Lies." She scrambles out of my embrace and moves faster than I've ever seen her do, sprinting into the kitchen to grab the two stuffed extra-large tote bags. "A little urgency would be nice, Cooper," she says, throwing one of the bags at me.

I rub my forehead with my free hand. *The things I do for this woman.*

After getting stuck in stop-and-go traffic, we pull into a parking spot two blocks from the club.

Killing the ignition, I turn to her. "You ready to stir the pot?"

She worries her bottom lip. "You don't think it's too much, do you?"

"Sut, baby, it's a little late to be having second thoughts."

She huffs a laugh. "I'm the king of second thoughts."

"Yes, but one was about marrying the loser, and today is about getting him out of your life."

"Sounds like the same thing to me."

I take her hand in mine, lacing our fingers together. "What are you nervous about?"

"That we might do actual harm to him instead of making his life harder."

"This won't affect his career negatively."

Even as she nods her agreement and understanding, her brow creases with worry. "What if we get in trouble?"

"We won't. We covered our tracks. It won't hurt him, but most importantly, it won't hurt us."

"You're sure?"

"A million percent. But if you want to call it off, we can. It's okay."

She takes a deep breath. "I just need a shot of something strong."

"Okay. Booze for my baby, coming right up."

Vivian and Nate are inside waiting for us as we flash the bouncers our IDs and let them search our bags.

"Finally," Vivian shouts at us over the crowded room. Behind her, Nate is busy hanging a banner with the band's name hand-painted on it. We spared no expense when it came to advertisement.

Vivian races around the small foldable table she and Nate brought, almost knocking Sutton over in a giant hug.

"Sorry we're late. I was trying to look the part of vixen vendor."

"And you delivered." Vivian wiggles her brows.

"Thank you, my fair lady." Sutton curtsies to Viv, then turns to me and demands I get her the shot I promised before she pisses herself from nerves.

Unsure if she'd actually anxiously urinate, I oblige, not wanting to have to race home to grab her new clothes.

Most men would've laughed off a comment like that, thinking it was a joke. But not me. No, I've learned not to play around when it comes to three things with Sutton.

Food, blankets, and bodily fluids.

There are some risks I'm not willing to take.

I grab Sutton a shot of vodka and a lemon drop while only getting a bottle of water for myself. If things go wrong tonight, not that I think they will, I want to be levelheaded, just in case.

When I make it back to the table, Sutton grabs the shot, giving me a quick thank-you before tossing it back.

She hisses through her teeth. "That's the stuff. It burns like the courage of a thousand men going down."

I tilt my head to the side. "Did you mean—"

She pats me on the chest. "You bet your tight ass, I did." She hands me back the shot glass in exchange for her lemon drop. With a quick sip, she sits the drink down. "Now let's finish setting up before Muzzled Velocity takes the stage in a few."

"As much as we want to stay and watch you both make a fool of d-bag Dillon, Viv is getting tired, so we are going to call it a night," Nate says, draping his arm over Vivian's shoulder.

"Boo. You can't bail. We haven't even made our first sale yet." Sutton stomps her foot at Viv.

Vivian's nose crinkles. "Sut, I told you I didn't want you to act like a child for practice."

"But Vivian..."

"But nothing." Viv glares as Sutton crosses her arms.

Nate and I glance at each other in confusion, then turn our sights back to our *colorful* ladies.

"Fine." Sutton rolls her eyes. "Leave."

"I will. I'm tired."

The two of them stare at each other for a tense moment, and then Sutton smiles and wraps Vivian in a hug. "See you tomorrow?" she asks.

"Same time as usual," Vivian replies cheerily before spinning on her heels and dragging Nate along behind her.

"Do I even want to know?" I ask, reaching for the bags on the floor.

She shrugs. "Probably not, but I'm going to tell you anyway. Viv's a little nervous about the actual mom thing and isn't sure she can be an authority figure, so I'm helping her in the only way I know how."

"By being a brat?"

"Exactly," she exclaims with a small bounce in her step.

I toss a bag of shirts in her direction, and she catches it.

"Seriously, how are we not going to get sued for these?" She laughs, pulling the first shirt out of the bag.

The shirt reads, "Dillon the Douche, not recommended by nine out of ten gynecologists." The other is a picture of Dillon's face on the tip of a sex toy, and underneath, it says, "Dil-do."

"Because we are donating the profits, minus the cost of production, to said douche's move-out fund. Also, I put the vendor's license in his name," I tell her with a smirk as I fold each shirt into piles based on designs and size.

The shirts are so funny, I almost want to keep one for myself. But that would mean owning something with the man whose face I despise on it. I'm not sure it's something I am ready for. And with Sutton's latest track record for stealing my clothes, the shirt would end up being hers in no time.

We're finishing setting up our makeshift table when Dillon's band takes the stage.

The now overly familiar sounds of their songs blare through the air.

Beside me, Sutton bobs her head, humming the tune.

I glare at her, but she just grins. "What? It's catchy as hell."

"I hate that his music isn't complete and total trash."

"Trust me, I get it. It only makes me more annoyed with him. Like the man is talented, so why does he have to suck so much?"

"Right? If I didn't know him, I might—" I gag. "—be a fan."

She laughs. "It's a hard pill to swallow, isn't it?"

"You have no idea."

"Um, I used to be the man's biggest fan... Some might have even called me a groupie."

"Please don't remind me that you've had sexual relations with that man."

She clicks her tongue. "Jealousy isn't attractive."

"You literally told me last night that Chuck Bass's jealousy in *Gossip Girl* was the hottest thing that's ever existed."

"That was Chuck... You, sir, are no Chuck."

"And thank God for that," I mutter.

"What was that?" She angles her head. "Are you saying you aren't as crazy obsessed with me as Chuck is with Blair? Do I not drive you crazy with the intensity of your love for me?"

"You drive me crazy, alright."

"I'm choosing to believe you meant that romantically."

I hum at her and continue to straighten our merchandise.

It doesn't take long until Muzzled Velocity's fan girls start swinging by our table, loving the stupid shirts.

Not a soul seems to care that they're a blatant dig at the lead singer of the band.

No, our drunk clientele find them absolutely hilarious and buy them up before the next band has even taken the stage.

Sutton is as shocked as I am when people ask if we have an online site or an order form.

I am half tempted to make one. But instead, we promise to be at their next local show with more shirts and maybe a new design or two.

I'm folding up the table as Sutton tears down the sign, taking sips of her third lemon drop of the night.

Out of the corner of my eye, I spot Dillon's sweaty beet-red face as he eyes a shirt on a girl walking past him.

I twist my back to him, blocking Sutton in the process. The last thing we need is for Dillon to see us here.

Would it make him realize how far we are willing to go to get him to leave our lives? Maybe. But it could also end in me being punched in the face, and I, for one, am not a fan of that outcome.

No matter what, the shirts will piss him off, and the money from the sales will be placed into his move-out fund, so he will eventually know we are responsible. But I'd prefer it didn't happen in a crowded bar where one or both of us could be arrested, depending on how he decides to react.

But by the sound of his angry voice booming over the music, he is livid.

"Time to go." I swat Sutton's ass.

She giggles but doesn't fight me as I guide her out the door.

Chapter Thirty

Cooper

Sutton's eyes widen as the medical assistant picks up the circular saw. She scoots closer to me until she's sitting in my lap. "Don't let them cut my hand off, Cooper." Warmth spreads through my chest as she turns and tucks her head into my neck.

This morning, she had been buzzing with excitement to come to this appointment.

The four short weeks she had to spend in a cast had apparently been the longest of her life.

Not that I had noticed. Every day, she would beam up at me as I helped her wash, dry, and fix her hair. Even painted her nails twice.

Heck, in my eyes, it seemed like she liked having the cast. Liked having me dote on her more than usual.

Not that I plan to stop.

I enjoyed every extra moment we got to spend together due to her cast.

If she still wants me to help with her hair, I will.

If she needs me to do her other hand when she's painting her nails, I will gladly volunteer.

Cast or no cast, I don't plan to give up any of the time we gained.

I chuckle as I rub a hand down her back. "No one is going to cut off your hand. But how about you sit still so the nice woman can get that stinky thing off you, because that odor isn't doing good things for you."

Sutton rears back on a gasp. "Take it back."

I shake my head. "I can't. It's true. You smell."

"No I don't." She turns to face the poor woman bearing witness to her crazy. "Do I?"

The woman winces.

"Oh my God. I do," Sutton whines, letting her chin fall to her chest. "Just put me out of my misery." She juts her hand out to the woman.

"Don't worry, though, everyone smells after having a cast for a few weeks. It's normal. I promise."

"But does everyone have a hot man tell them that nasty fact?"

I smile. It doesn't matter how many times Sutton tells me how attracted to me she is. I will never get used to it.

The woman positions Sutton's arm on the small worktable. "Only the lucky ones." Then she flips the switch at the bottom of the saw, turning on the circular blade.

Sutton jerks her arm back and shakes. "I can't do this." She looks at me, her eyes getting bigger and bigger with fear. "I won't do this."

I grimace at the medical assistant, who has flipped the off switch on the saw and is staring at Sutton patiently. "Maybe you could walk us through the process."

"Sure," she says. Her voice sounds sweet but rehearsed as she gives us a spiel about how it doesn't hurt at all. The only thing Sutton will feel is some mild vibrations as it works through the cast.

"It won't cut me?" Sutton eyes the saw warily.

The woman shakes her head adamantly. "Nope. Watch." She flips the switch again, and the blade begins to spin as she takes it down to her fingers.

Sutton lets out a yelp as she closes her eyes. But I watch as the blade does nothing. "Open your eyes, baby opossum."

"No, thank you, I would prefer not to see dismembered fingers today."

"No dismemberment here."

"What about blood."

"None of that either."

"Are you lying?"

"Would I lie to you?"

She contemplates that for a minute before peeking one eye open cautiously. When she sees there's no blood, she opens up both eyes. "Witch," she accuses the only slightly amused medical assistant. "Does your employer know you are practicing the dark arts in their fine medical establishment?"

"Listen, honey, do you want the cast off or not?"

Sutton's face scrunches in debate before she lays her arm back out on the table. "Fine. Do it."

The saw starts up once more. The woman has it mere inches from the cast when Sutton mumbles, "Please be a good witch."

The saw cuts through Sutton's cast within moments. She cringes, wincing the entire time, only peeking through one eye as she holds on to my thigh, squeezing for dear life. Her grip is sure to leave a bruise, but I don't care. I'll wear whatever mark she gives me with pride.

With the cast removed, Sutton gets one last lecture over violence never being the answer, but if she must punch, not to tuck her thumb in her palm again.

We've only made it into the lobby before she's pulling me into one of the two family bathrooms. The light flickers on as she locks the door behind us.

"A bathroom in a healthcare facility?" I ask, not at all feeling turned on by the setting. "I mean, if you want to, I will. But it feels nasty, and not in the sexy way."

"Ew." She slaps my chest with the back of her arm. "No, I need you to help me try to wash the stench off."

She scrunches her nose in disgust as she holds her previously casted hand as far away from us as possible.

My hearty chuckle bounces off the bathroom walls. "It's not that bad."

Her eyes narrow. "Not that bad. *Not that bad.* Cooper, this thing smells like a family of mice burrowed into my fingers and died."

"I think you're exaggerating."

She shoves her hand under my nose, and I gag. It's undeniable. The smell is putrid. And either we get rid of it now, or she is going to be riding in the bed of my truck trying to air that thing out on the way home.

"See," she whines. "I'm gross."

"Come on." I pull her over to the sink, being careful not to touch the skin where her cast had been. I don't think the smell can transfer to me, but I'm not about to test that theory.

Water spurts from the faucet as I turn it on and stick her hand under the warm stream. Next, I push the soap dispenser ten times, gathering more soap than any person should ever need into my hands. But if I'm going to scrub that radiating stench, I'm going to have enough soap that, hopefully, my bare skin never comes into contact with hers.

Sutton fills her hand with soap as well, and we both scrub. She takes her palm, and I take the outside of her hand. It's a group effort, but after five minutes, we rinse away the suds, and I pat her dry for the moment of truth.

Lifting her hand to her nose, Sutton inhales, never once making a face of disgust or pleasure.

"Is it gone?"

She bops her head from side to side. "For the most part. It still doesn't smell right, but there isn't a lingering smell of death any-more. So I'd call that a win."

"Come on." I grab her non-smelly hand and pull her out of the bathroom. "You can air it the rest of the way out on the way to your surprise."

Chapter Thirty-One

Sutton

"Seriously?" I ask, staring at the giant skeleton hanging from the ceiling.

"What?" Cooper asks innocently.

"Did you bring me to a museum? You know I hate to learn," I whine.

A deep, hearty laugh slips past his lips as he shakes his head. "I do know that, but just wait. I think you're going to love this version of learning." He tugs at my hand, pulling me through the lobby toward a smiling woman.

"Welcome to Dino Dig, Willow Hill's number one and only paleontology-themed attraction. How many?"

Cooper holds up two fingers and says, "Just us."

"Perfect." The woman beams. "Have either of you had the pleasure of unearthing our amazing faux fossils before?"

Faux fossils?

We both shake our heads.

"Well, sit tight and watch the video overhead for instructions while I grab your gear," she says before spinning on her heels and heading into the room behind her.

I glance around the room one more time before the TV overhead starts. "What exactly are we doing?" I ask as a dinosaur with glasses appears on the screen and begins to walk us through the steps of uncovering dinosaur bones. The cartoon dinosaur doctor explains every tool we'll be provided with and how to use them appropriately.

When the video finishes roughly five minutes later, I turn to Cooper, tears welling in my eyes. "You brought me to dig for dinosaur bones?"

Worry fills his bright brown eyes as he rubs the back of his neck. "I thought you'd like it."

I don't say a word. The warmth radiating through me from the sweet gesture of him knowing I love dinosaurs and finding a dino-themed activity for us is more than I can voice.

I throw myself at him, wrapping my arms around his neck as my legs tighten around his waist. "You brought me to dig for dino bones."

His arms are around me in seconds as he huffs out a laugh. "Fake ones... But yes. Do you like it?"

"Duh, Cooper. As if I would lie to spare your feelings."

He tilts his head to the side as if he's examining me. "You wouldn't, would you?"

"Nope," I say adamantly. "And neither would you...Except for when it comes to coffee."

"I wouldn't?" he asks, his voice laced with amusement.

"Nope, you aren't the lying kind."

He makes a hissing noise through his teeth and frowns.

"No," I gasp. "Don't you dare disappoint me by admitting to being a deceiver."

"I don't know if I would call myself a deceiver. That seems a little extreme. It's more like a fibber from time to time."

"I don't believe you."

"Well, you best believe it, 'cause it's the truth."

"I need an example."

"An example?"

"Yeah, a reference that illustrates you being the worst by being a teller of untruths."

"Untruths?"

I wave my hand in front of my face. "It sounds nicer than lies."

"I told my mom that I was out of town on a business trip the last three times she's called."

"You did?"

"Yeah." He rubs the back of his neck like the answer makes him a little uncomfortable.

My jaw hangs open in shock.

My perfect Cooper is admitting to a flaw.

And God, does that somehow make him even more perfect in my eyes.

His willingness to tell me the truth is refreshing as fuck. "Wait a minute, how do I know you aren't lying about being a liar?"

"You are just going to have to trust me."

I scowl at him. "I don't like this."

"I know you don't. But please believe me when I say I've never lied about anything important or anything that could hurt you."

The woman returns to the room and brings us both a bucket filled with all the tools we'll need, along with an apron to cover our clothes if we wish. We both accept them eagerly and follow her down a long hall. She stops before a set of metal doors with a rainbow film covering the windows.

"Whenever you're finished, just leave your tools on the bench inside the door," she says, leaving us to ourselves.

Cooper pushes open the door to an expansive space filled with dirt and sand, surrounded by shady trees and benches for rest.

"It looks like a giant sandbox," I whisper as I take it in.

"You ready to *dig* in?" he asks, snickering at his own cheesy joke.

I swing my shovel around in my hand. "Let's do it."

***

It doesn't take long before I have a good two-foot hole in front of me, along with five different-shaped bones.

"How the hell are you so good at that?" Cooper asks from across the room. He wipes away the sweat forming on his forehead with his forearm. A small smear of dirt takes its place, and I can't help the way my lips curve up.

He is devastating.

And he is all mine.

Every day, every moment we're together, I wonder how I ever could've gone without him.

How could I ever have thought that I deserved the scraps of a relationship that I had with Dillon?

His gaze narrows. "Why are you looking at me like that?"

"Am I not allowed to admire you?" I flutter my lashes at him.

"No." He scowls. "Not when it looks like you've been working at digging a shallow grave."

I wiggle my eyebrows. "You scared?"

"Terrified."

I roll my eyes. "I would never hurt you."

"You're the only person who could."

My chest squeezes as I drop my shovel and push my hands into my dirt-covered thighs to stand. I walk over to him and drop to my knees. "You never have to worry about that. You are one of my people. And I never hurt my people. If you need proof, I'm sure Viv can give you a glowing reference."

He licks his lips, biting down a grin. "I'll call her." And then he goes back to excavating the small bone he's been working on for the past twenty minutes.

I sit on my heels, taking a quick break just to watch him work. The muscles in his arms flex with every gentle movement of his hands.

I run my hands through the dirt and sand, letting the tiny grains sift through my fingers to stop myself from reaching out and touching those mesmerizing muscles.

We work for hours, uncovering and gently removing faux bones until our hands are aching.

At the end of it all, I have my small bag of faux fossils in one hand and Cooper's in my other. I'm practically skipping with delight.

"I think we should display our treasures."

"You want to display our fake bones?"

"You don't?" I ask, bewildered by his lack of sentimentality for our date.

Cooper lets out a dramatic sigh, then smiles. "Fine, we can create a display of our 'bones.'"

"Ooh, we can have the bones circling this picture of us digging side by side."

"You're describing a pagan altar."

I shrug. "Maybe I want to worship us as a couple."

"As you should," he says, leaning down to kiss me.

Today has been unexpectedly perfect.

Every day with Cooper is perfect.

The love he shares with me is something I never thought I would have.

Chapter Thirty-Two

Cooper

"That was honestly the best date I've ever had." Sutton squeezes my hand that's resting on her thigh.

"Are you trying to tell me our funeral date didn't do it for you?" I ask.

"It was definitely... memorable," she jokes. But in actuality, that was a day I'll never forget. It was the day she dropped all pretenses on what she and I were doing. It was the day she let all her fears wash down the drain.

"And here I was believing every date with me was the best date of your life."

"Nothing compares."

"Stop trying to flatter me."

"No flattery. It's true. Being with you is like nothing else, no one else."

"That can be easily taken in a negative direction."

"Could, but it's not. You are the best man I've ever been with."

"Thank you. You're the best woman I've ever known."

"I know."

"Once again, the lack of modesty you have is impressive."

She winks at me. "It's a gift. Like my ability to take your cock champion."

My dick hardens. Today wasn't supposed to be about sex. But when is it not about sex with Sutton. Her body is so damn addictive. No, *she* is addictive. I'm obsessed with her wit and mind as much as I am with the captivating curves that come naturally to her.

I groan. "Baby, are you trying to give me a boner while I drive."

She smiles coyly, wrapping her blond locks around her fingers. "Don't you like it when I get you all wound up?"

"Not when I can't do anything about it." I grip the steering wheel until my knuckles turn white.

"Who said you can't do anything about it?" She unbuckles her seat belt, pushing up the center console before sliding closer to me until our thighs are touching.

"What are you doing?" I glance at her for a quick moment before bringing my eyes back to the road.

"What you and I both want," she purrs, rubbing a hand down my thigh, then back up and across the crotch of my jeans.

My cock jerks at the graze through the denim.

"Sutton," I warn, grabbing her wrist to still her movements.

"Cooper," she mimics me before squeezing my hard length.

I suck in air through my teeth as she leans up to kiss my neck. "Let me make you feel as loved as you made me feel today."

I smirk, amusement and lust lacing my voice. "By giving me a handy while I drive?"

"To start with, yes. But I was thinking afterward, we might try something a little more special. Something you've been dying to try with me."

"You don't mean..."

She nods, nuzzling my neck before trailing kisses to my ear. "I do."

"Baby, I want that so bad."

"Fuck, fuck, fuck," she yells, her body tensing.

I lean forward, capturing her lips with mine. Pulling back, I stare into her eyes. "You can do this."

She shakes her head violently. "I can't, Cooper, it's too much."

"The painful part is almost over," I promise her.

She closes her eyes and nods. "Just do it. I can take it." It's like she's talking to herself more than me, but I push forward anyway.

"Done," I tell her.

"Really?" she asks in a quiet, strained voice.

"Yes." I smile. "If you cut back your eating out to two times a week, you could save thousands, and I mean tens of thousands a year."

Sutton lets out a pitiful cry. "I don't want to, though."

"Yes you do. Remember the goals you set, Sutton."

"Fuck the goals," she declares, standing from the table. "And fuck financial planning."

"Sit your soon-to-be financially stable ass back down, baby opossum."

She crosses her arms and narrows her gaze at me. "Gah, why are you so damn hot when you're bossy?"

"Because you have daddy issues." Guilt pangs at my stomach for joking about a potentially sensitive subject. She has opened up a little about having an absent father but made it seem like it was no big deal because she didn't really know anything different.

She scoffs but then gives me a sheepish grin. "True."

"Anyway," I say, pretending like her outburst didn't happen. "If you cut back on eating out and—"

"*And?*" she screeches.

"—and your spending on clothes."

"Cooper, be realistic here."

"I am being realistic, Sut. You don't need new shoes every month."

"But they're pretty."

"Yeah, a pretty penny. Cut them out of your spending, along with the copious amounts of takeout and cocktails, and you will be able to save enough for a generous down payment on a house within the year."

"Now you're just being crazy. I don't spend that much on clothes and food."

I look at her bank transactions, then back at her. "Really?"

"Fine," she huffs. "Maybe I do. But I like those things. They bring me joy. You don't want me to be joyless, do you, Cooper? Do you?"

"Sutton, you are the strongest, most stubborn woman I know. If you really want to buy a house, you have to save. It might be hard, and it might make you feel down at times, but you can do it. I know you can."

She lets her head hang forward in defeat. "Fine, I'll cut back on the shoes and eating out."

"Good."

"But what if I see a pair of beautiful pumps that are whispering to me about how much they love me and want to feel my feet?"

"If shoes are talking to you, we might need to take your mom up on that hospital vacation she keeps threatening."

She smacks my chest. "I'm serious, what if I see something I *really* want."

I sigh, pinching the bridge of my nose. "Then you wait a week, and if you still want it in a week, you buy it."

Sutton pops up from the chair, jumping onto me as she wraps her legs and arms around me. She tightens her legs around my waist as she frames my face in her hands and presses kiss after kiss all over my face. "You are the best boyfriend!"

"All I said was you could still buy the shoes if you *really* wanted them."

"Nope," she argues. "You gave your support on the shoes. My precious shoes."

I laugh. "Okay, Gollum." Smacking her ass, I grip her waist as she detaches herself from me. "Now let's talk about retirement."

She throws her head back with a groan. "Why did I agree to this torture."

"Because you love me." I smile, leading her back to her seat at the kitchen table.

"Yeah, yeah," she mutters but sits and lets me counsel her on the stock market.

Chapter Thirty-Three

Sutton

With my hand finally healed, I'm determined to make tonight the night of both Cooper's and my dreams.

Everything is ready.

I have the perfect atmosphere set.

I have Cooper's favorite video game queued up and his favorite food on the way.

Candles are lit, providing not only romantic lighting but a scent that has me itching to take my clothes off and seek release.

And in our bedroom, I have a variety of dildos that will strap into my underwear. I already know he isn't even going to consider the large and extremely anatomically correct ones. But I still lined them up on my dresser for a variety, along with my fresh bottle of lube that was recommended online for this exact type of intimacy.

I'm getting giddy thinking about how I'm finally going to get to own someone's ass. Not just any ass, though.

My favorite ass.

Cooper's perfect round ass.

I sigh just thinking about it.

The sound of the front door opening has me bounding into the living room, ready to pounce on my man. "Baby, I hope you are ready for a night of fun and fucking?" I come to a halt when I find Dillon standing in the doorway with his arm around a woman. "Oh, it's you." I let disappointment and disdain lace my words.

Dillon rolls his eyes. "Kara, this is my ex, Sutton." He gestures at me.

The beautiful brunette's scrutinizing gaze rakes down my body. "The one who refuses to leave your house?"

I scoff. "His house? Dillon, what kind of horse shit are you feeding this poor woman?"

His relaxed posture pisses me off as his face twists with a wicked grin. "Nothing but the truth."

"Sure," I say, stepping out of their way. "Stay out of the living room, please. Cooper and I have plans."

He and the girl share a look. "See."

She frowns, rubbing her hand down his arm. "I can't believe you were telling the truth."

"I don't blame people when they don't believe me. If it wasn't happening to me, I wouldn't believe it either."

"Do you want me to stay and make you feel better?" Kara asks, still stroking his arm.

Dillon nods with his bottom lip jutting out. "I'd like that," he says, placing a kiss on her burgundy lips. "My bedroom is the last door on the right. I'm going to grab us a drink, and then I will meet you in there."

We stand in silence, watching as she struts down the hall into his room, shutting the door gently behind her.

"Seriously, Dillon." I spin to face him. "What did you tell that poor woman to trick her into coming here?"

"Like I already said, the truth," he says, stalking off toward the fridge.

"Which is?"

He pulls the door open to examine the inside. "That you left me at our wedding for another man and moved him into our home the next day."

I sigh. He isn't wrong. I did do those things. But only to get his dumbass out of my life.

Every day he is still here makes me question my sanity.

The lack of respect alone should have been enough to make me leave his ass years ago.

Sometimes, I would, but it was a temporary thing. We always found our way back to each other like two toxic magnets.

But I didn't see it then like I do now.

It didn't matter how much Viv or my mom would point out how problematic the relationship was; I didn't care.

At the time, the constant push and pull from being with Dillon made me feel alive.

It was thrilling.

Exciting, even, until it wasn't.

Until I was about to tie myself to a man who didn't see me as an equal. As a partner.

He only saw me as someone who could do something for him, giving nothing in return.

Dillon grabs three of the special IPAs I picked up for Cooper out of the fridge with a smirk.

"You know those are for Cooper." I glare.

His shoulders square as the corners of his lips turn up into a sneer. "Here I thought he and I shared everything."

My jaw snaps closed as he saunters away to his room, slamming the door behind him.

I am fuming.

So caught up in thinking about how he's going to ruin everything I planned for Cooper that I don't even hear him come in.

His lips brush my cheek as his arms wrap around my waist, startling me.

"Jumpy much," Cooper laughs.

I turn in his embrace. "I missed you."

"I missed you too," he says, leaning down to kiss me before pulling away far too quickly for my liking.

"Go change into something comfy, then meet me on the couch."

He eyes me suspiciously but starts down the hall until the doorbell rings. He turns and changes directions, heading to the front door.

"No," I say, knocking into him and pushing him back toward our room. "I've got it."

He opens his mouth, looking like he's going to argue, but then closes it and does as I asked. I rush to meet the delivery guy, grabbing our food before Cooper can spoil one of his surprises by being helpful.

I let go of my thoughts of Dillon, which is hard to do when I can hear music and moans coming from the guest room, but I do. He won't ruin anything for Coop and me. I will make sure of that.

I set up the sushi like a buffet on the coffee table, adding two clean plates and chopsticks in front of them.

I rarely eat sushi because Viv is not only allergic but also because it reminds her of her cheating high school boyfriend and the friend that he cheated on her with at a sushi restaurant.

But damn, do I love it. My mouth is practically watering as I line up rows of rainbow rolls, spicy tuna rolls, shrimp tempura rolls, and uramaki rolls.

Cooper strides into the room as I set the dips out. "What is all this?" he asks, taking in the spread of his favorites.

"A little something special for my something special." I smile, patting the couch beside me.

He sinks into the cushion. "Are you trying to butter me up?"

"Absolutely," I tell him as I place some rolls onto my plate and sit back. "Try to enjoy it."

"I enjoy any and everything when it's with you."

That's what I'm hoping.

⚘

The rest of the night is perfect. The minor hiccup with Dillon the Douche forgotten.

Cooper and I laugh and gorge ourselves on enough sushi to feed a family of four and annihilate some teenagers on his favorite video game.

After, we clean up our mess from the food.

I'm rinsing off the plates as Cooper puts the few leftovers in the fridge.

He kisses my cheek. "Thank you for tonight. It was the perfect end to a long day."

"The night's not over yet." I wiggle my eyebrows.

He moves to stand behind me. His hands trailing up and down my body, caressing me through my leggings and leaving a trail of goose bumps in their wake. It's as if his touch lights a fire in my core that only he can handle.

Breathlessly, I finish washing the last dish, rinsing it off with lightning quickness that almost guarantees it will need to be rewashed tomorrow.

But I don't care.

The only thing that matters at this moment is his hands on me.

I lead us down the hall and into our room, locking the door behind us.

Coop slowly turns me before pushing me onto the bed. His body covers mine in an instant.

His lips meet mine in a frenzy of want and need. Our tongues clashing, eager to touch, tease, and please each other.

I waste no time in pulling off Cooper's shirt, followed by my own. His hands grasp my breasts, tugging gently on my nipples as my core throbs in desperation.

With his hands still massaging my breasts, Coop kisses and licks a trail down my neck to my chest and further until he meets my leggings. I expect him to pull them off right away. But instead, he kisses the waistband before moving to the center of my thighs, where I'm drenched for him.

He presses his face between my thighs and breathes in. A shudder runs through me as his nose nudges against my clit through the fabric.

"Stop playing with me." Desperation laces my every word.

"What do you want? For me to devour this delicious pussy?"

I nod enthusiastically.

Cooper groans, his face the picture of seduction. "I know you do, baby." He yanks my leggings off my body before resuming his place at my aching center. "And your wish is my command."

Cooper's mouth is on me in an instant. He isn't gentle or slow as his tongue works me into oblivion. My hips jerk and my hands bury into his hair as his tongue thrashes against me.

He slips two fingers inside me and presses against my walls. The action sends tingles racing down my spine as I explode. Bursts of color fill my vision as Cooper continues to eat me out until I'm begging him to stop.

I watch as he grins, leaning into me, giving me one last lazy lick.

"You are so *damn* breathtaking," I pant.

"So are you, Sutton, especially when you're coming on my tongue."

I yank at his hair, pulling him up my body until his lips are on mine again as I flip us.

Straddling him, I grind my wet pussy against his still-covered cock.

He grabs my hips, grinding me hard against him. He's rock hard, and the feel of him against me has my body ready for round two.

I lean down. "Can I fuck you tonight?" I whisper as I nip his earlobe between kisses.

"Yes," he rasps.

"I'm going to make you feel so good, baby." My lips trail down his throat, where I lick and suck as he swallows. I shove his pants down past his thighs, and Cooper kicks them off the rest of the way.

I palm his cock as his breath speeds up before I slide down his body to lick the tip, then suck him into my mouth. He flexes his hips, thrusting into my mouth as I circle my grip on him up and down. He's getting close, I can feel it. From the way his thighs tremble to the tightening of his abs.

I release him with a pop, and a groan of frustration rumbles from him.

"Roll over and get on your knees for me."

Cooper's heavy eyes peer at me with hesitation before he does as I asked.

I knead his calves. Caressing every muscle and planting my lips on it before moving on to the next as I make my way up his legs to his ass.

I sprinkle kisses over each perfect cheek before dipping a finger between them. He sucks in a breath as I move my finger up and down, then circle his puckered hole.

Slowly, I bring my mouth closer and closer to my fingers, listening to his breaths, feeling his pulse speed beneath my touch until I'm there.

I swipe my tongue against his tight rim, and Cooper's moans fill the air, growing louder as I reach around to grab his erection.

"Holy fucking shit," Cooper hisses through his teeth as I continue to flick at his hole.

"You like that, baby? You like my tongue licking your tight ass?"

It's word for *dirty fucking* word what he whispered to me the other night when I let him pound his thick cock into my ass.

"Yes," he pants.

"Have you been prepping for me like we talked about?" I ask him, squeezing his cock as I jerk him.

"Yes." He nods wildly, looking both excited and nervous.

I rub my fingers over the tip of his leaking cock, covering my fingers in his precum as I continue to squeeze him with my rotating fist. With my fingers now slick, I trail them down his length, over his balls, and across his taint, causing a shiver to run across his skin before I slide them up and down the crack of his ass.

His breath hitches as I touch his hole. "Pass me the lube, baby," I demand.

His hands fumble around the bed until he finds it and passes it to me. He turns, looking over his shoulder, his lust-filled gaze watching my every move as I flip the cap of the bottle up and coat my fingers.

I lube up a finger as I circle his tight hole, just like I've done multiple times before, sliding it in. Cooper clenches around me, but I push further, not stopping my attention to his cock until he relaxes. "Are you sure you want to do this?" I ask again.

"Yes. I want to do it with you."

I slip another finger inside, loosening him up even further until I'm moving them easily, in and out. My clit throbs as I watch him writhe with pleasure.

"Roll over," I command as I remove my fingers from him. Cooper does as I ask without a word.

"Such a good boy," I praise him as his cock becomes eye level with me. I flick my tongue against the tip, causing him to moan my name. "Are you ready?"

He nods, a look of lust and trepidation filling his face.

"We can stop at any point, okay?"

"Goddamn it, Sutton. I get it, consent is key. But the longer we talk about it, the more nervous I'm getting, so will you just fuck me already?"

I grin. "Someone is greedy. But luckily, I love to give." I grab the lube from the bed and slather the dildo up, as well as Cooper's ass again, to be on the safe side, before I line the dark-purple dildo up again his ass, letting the tip brush his entrance.

Cooper swallows, and I lean over to press one last kiss to his heart before I push inside.

He tenses as his hands wrap around my forearms.

"It's okay," I coo. "You can do it. Just relax."

"Easy for you to say," he bites back.

"Have you forgotten, my lover, that I've been on the receiving end of this too?" I quirk an eyebrow. "Relax," I demand as I stroke his cock again.

And he does. Cooper's muscles release as he focuses on the pleasure my hand is bringing him, and I push in a little further.

Inch by inch, the tension in Coop's face disappears until I'm fully seated inside him.

The friction against my clit is delicious. Every thrust brings me closer and closer to the edge of bliss. I pick up my pace, chasing that beautiful high that only Cooper can give me.

"Fuck, fuck, fuck," Cooper says through gritted teeth.

I slow my strokes. "Do you want me to stop?" I ask breathlessly.

He laughs. "Fuck no, Sutton. I'm about to fucking burst."

A wicked grin graces my lips as I grasp his hips and thrust into him repeatedly like my life depends on it.

Cooper explodes first, his cock shooting cum all over his stomach in thick spurts. The sight of his climax is enough to push me over that last edge as I grind my hips into him, hitting my clit just right.

My legs shake with my release as a weightlessness takes over my heavy limbs. I fall forward onto Cooper's stomach, becoming a boneless, blissed-out mess.

"Holy shit," Cooper pants as he wraps me in his arms.

I'm speechless, so I nod against him, not caring that I'm most definitely getting cum in my hair. I will gladly let myself be covered in this man's release any day, as long as he continues to make me feel like this.

As our heart rates come down and our breathing evens out, Cooper asks, "Sut?"

"Yeah?"

"Can you please take the dildo out of my ass?"

I laugh, and Cooper tenses.

"Stop. Laughing. You're making it move."

Which only makes me laugh more.

Cooper squirms away, practically shoving me off him in the most gentle way he can until I relent and sit up, pulling my hips back until the purple dildo slips out of him.

I stand up on my semi-Jello-like legs and slip out of the dildo-holding underwear. "Stay here," I command him, as I turn around and stalk off into the bathroom.

"Aren't I supposed to be taking care of you?" he asks, leaning up on his elbows but staying on the bed.

I turn on the faucet, letting the water warm as I quickly pee and clean myself up before wetting a washcloth and heading back to the bedroom.

He looks gorgeous as he waits for me. The red flush from his orgasm still coloring his skin and the sheen of sweat shining from his skin. But it's more than his perfect body.

It's the shy smile on his lips.

It's the loving and appreciative gaze.

It's his trust.

It's *him.*

I stop in front of him, stooping down to give him a quick, reassuring kiss. It's tender and simple but filled with so much affection. I pull back and gaze into his eyes. "Are you okay?"

He swallows and nods. "Yeah."

I press another kiss to his lips before bringing the washcloth to his abdomen and cleaning him off, then moving further down and gently cleaning around his ass.

"Hey, Sut?"

"Yeah?"

"You have cum all up in your hair."

I reach up to touch my hair, finding the sticky mess. "I do."

"Let's take a shower."

"Nah, let's take a bubble bath."

He groans. "I barely fit."

"We'll make it work. Besides, it will be good for that sweet ass to soak in the warm water."

I stand, pulling him up with me and into the bathroom.

Cooper turns on the water and fills the tub while I search for the perfect salts to relax and heal. Once I find them, I sprinkle them in and motion for Cooper to get in the tub first. He winces a little as he lowers himself into the water.

I feel a brief twinge of guilt for causing him any physical pain, but I also feel a weird sense of pride for making his ass sore. "Is this how men feel?" I ask, stepping into the steaming water and sitting between his legs.

"Huh? I'm not following."

"I feel oddly happy that your ass is sore because of me. Is that how men feel after they get guts deep?"

He chuckles, wrapping his arms around my middle to pull my back flush against his chest. "Yes, I guess it is."

Cooper kisses my shoulder before resting his chin in the crook of my neck.

"Did you like it?"

"I think you know I did."

"I mean, I know it made you come, but did you like it, and would it be something you'd like to do often?"

For a moment, silence stretches between us until he admits, "I liked it. It was intense as shit. Seriously, I came so hard, I might have blacked out for a quick second. But... I don't think it's something I want to do often... Is that okay?"

Something in his voice makes my chest crack, and I spin around to face him. Water splashes over the tub's edge, but I don't care. The only thing that matters is Cooper and making him understand.

"Cooper, of course it's okay."

"You won't be mad or disappointed?"

"No. It means so much that you were willing to try this with me. To trust me with your body. It was never about the actual pegging, Coop. It was that you were open to experiencing something new with me. If it's not something you're into, then it's not for us. It's that simple. We tried. We enjoyed it. But that doesn't mean we ever have to do it again."

His eyes drop to the water as he dips his chin slowly. "I feel bad. Like I'm letting you down."

My heart cracks a little at his admission. "Baby, you just fulfilled a fantasy of mine. You could never let me down."

"So you would be okay if I never want to do it again?"

I nod. "You never have to do anything you don't want to do."

His shoulders relax as he leans in to kiss me. "You're perfect."

Heat rises in my cheeks. It's ridiculous. I'm sitting naked in a bath with the man, but him calling me perfect makes me blush. I turn back to face the faucet but melt into him as he holds me against him in the warm water until we're both pruning.

Chapter Thirty-Four

Sutton

One hundred forty-six minutes.

That's how long I've been in corporate team-building hell. And it's not even my company. No, I'm at Cooper's employer's idea of a wonderful bonding opportunity.

In my experience, the only thing these types of events do is bond the employees in group hatred of the management team that dreamed them up.

"Come on, Cooper's girlfriend, you can do better than that," a rowdy redheaded man with bright, flushed cheeks yells at me as I try to pin the tail on a two-dimensional Eeyore after spinning in a circle with my forehead glued to a baseball bat ten times.

"Shut up, fire crotch," I snap.

The man tosses his hands up. "Cooper, your woman isn't being a very good teammate if she can't take a little criticism."

I stab the tail on Eeyore's stomach as my own rolls, the world around me still off-kilter. "Sutton. My name is Sutton, you jackass. And maybe I would have a better attitude if the worst person on this team wasn't shouting his critiques of me when he couldn't even do the egg-and-spoon race before the booze started flowing."

This night would have already been hard to get through normally, but apparently, A&A loves to supply their hardworking professionals with alcohol.

So not only are we split into teams to compete in elementary school-style relays, but now more than half of the company and significant others are behaving like children.

I am ashamed to say I am one of those childish people. But it's not completely my fault. Blame the bartender for making the best lemon drops I've ever tasted.

It would have been a sin to just have the one... Okay, three. I've had three.

"Cooper, did you hear the slander your woman just slew at me?" he slurs.

"That's it." I pluck the earrings from my ears and lunge at him. Cooper's arms snake around my middle, and the taut muscles in his forearms flex as he holds me against his body. Picking me up, he carries me across the lawn, away from fire cheeks, and places me on a stool.

I hop down from the seat, and Cooper blocks me as I bounce off his chest. "Come on, Cooper, let me just take one swing at him. I promise not to tuck my thumb."

"While I'm glad you have learned the proper punching form, I can't let you get into a fistfight with my coworker."

I tilt my head and give him the biggest puppy-dog eyes I can muster. I even jut my bottom lip out a bit. "Please. You know you want to take his misogynistic ass down a peg too."

He smooths my hair back away from my face. "First, just because a drunk man cannot remember your name doesn't make him a chauvinist. And second, give Warren the Woman Hater a break. He was mugged a couple of weeks ago by a woman of the night."

I pause, blinking up at him. "Your coworker was mugged by a prostitute a couple of weeks ago?"

"Yeah," he says like it's no big deal.

"Why am I only just now hearing about this?"

His broad shoulders lift an inch. "It must have slipped my mind."

"It must have slipped your mind?" I say incredulously. "Unbelievable." I stomp off in the direction of the bathroom to make a dramatic exit but also because my bladder is close to exploding.

"Don't be mad at me," Cooper yells after me across the lawn, not caring who hears or sees our little lovers' spat.

"Too late," I yell back over my shoulder. "Good boyfriends don't keep juicy gossip to themselves."

I make my way into the bathroom. Sitting on the toilet, I stare into my glassy, semidrunk eyes in the oddly placed oversized body mirror directly across from me. I finger-comb my hair while peeing. Rich people have the weirdest decor placements, but strangely, my intoxicated ass is liking it right now.

I finish up and quickly wash my hands, but when I open the door, I come face-to-face with the last person I expected to see tonight—Dillon.

Well, not Dillon *exactly*. But a large framed photo of a younger him, his dad, and his godfather, Ken.

That's weird. Why would Mr. Avery have a picture of Dillon and—oh my God.

Ken is Mr. Avery. Mr. Avery is Ken... Dillon's godfather, who was at my wedding.

Oh shit.

I've got to get out of this house fast—before Mr. Avery sees me.

Rushing down the hallway, I pull out my phone and shoot a quick text to Vivian.

Sutton

S.O.FREAKING.S!

Vivian

Really? Again, Sut? The corporate hellscape that is team bonding can't be that bad.

Cooper's boss is Dillon's godfather!

Sounds like a mess. Address, please.

I stop right as I make it outside and quickly shoot off a text with the address, then pocket my phone just as Cooper spins me around to face him.

He's so damn handsome in the twinkling fairy lights that fill the mansion's backyard.

Leaning up onto my tiptoes, I brush my fingers through his messy hair before capturing his lips in a kiss that's anything but innocent or workplace-appropriate. There might also be some ass-grabbing on my part.

A few whistles sound off around us.

Coming to my senses, I unlatch myself from his delicious, soft mouth. I glance around the yard to see multiple sets of eyes on us. My cheeks flush with embarrassment. Not just for myself but for Cooper. But thankfully no Ken in sight.

"It's time to leave, you big doofus. Our besties are coming to get our alcohol-loving asses." I spin on my heels, pulling Cooper behind me as I weave us through the crowded house and to the front door. I'm almost there when the door opens, forcing us to stop walking and come face-to-face with the person I've been trying to avoid.

Standing in the doorway, Ken Avery holds two cases of beer as he stares at me with confusion, the wrinkles on his forehead becoming more pronounced. His eyes widen as his gaze flicks to Cooper standing beside me, then down to our intertwined hands.

"Mr. Avery." Cooper's grin widens. This is the moment he's been waiting for. "This is—"

I panic and mutter the first thing that comes to my mind. "No time for chitchat, unfortunately. The pharmacy closes in thirty minutes, Cooper. If you want your anti-diarrheal medication, we must leave now."

Now both men are staring at me in shock. I take the opportunity to squeeze past Mr. Avery, dragging Cooper with me.

When we are halfway down the driveway, Cooper pulls me to a stop. "Seriously, Sutton? Bathroom jokes in front of my boss?"

"I'm sorry. I panicked, and it just slipped out." I wince. It's a poor excuse, but we *had* to get out of there.

"It just slipped out?"

"Yes."

"Whatever. Let's go sit in the truck while we wait on Nate and Viv to get here."

We walk in silence back to his truck. I close the door and turn to him. "I'm sorry I got all white-girl wasted on you in front of your colleagues and embarrassed you in front of your boss."

He doesn't say a thing. Just leans in to kiss me softly.

Pulling back an inch, he rests his forehead on mine. "I forgive you."

"You do?" I ask hopefully. If he can get over me telling his boss he has the shits, maybe he can get over something like his boss being a close family friend of Dillon's.

"Thank you for being your crazy, irrational self. I couldn't have done this night without you," he breathes.

"Any time," I whisper back. I need to tell him about Dillon and Mr. Avery's connection sooner rather than later, but I'm buzzed on alcohol and lust, and my brain only wants one thing. His mouth back on mine.

I wrap my hands around his neck, preparing to pull him closer for another kiss, but a loud knock startles me.

I jump, smacking my forehead into Cooper's.

We both groan in pain.

"Are you okay?" he asks, pulling back and placing a hand on my head.

I nod, fighting back the sting of tears. "I knew your head was thick, but damn, Cooper, that's some next-level shit."

He chuckles, checking me over one last time before looking over my shoulder to see who the interrupter is.

"It's our favorite dumbasses."

"Viv?" I call out.

"Present," she hollers through the window. I glance over my shoulder to see her face pressed up against the glass as Nate stands behind her.

"Open the door," Viv commands through the window.

"No," I yell at her. "Can't you see I'm trying to suck Cooper's soul from his mouth?"

"You can do that later," she calls back.

"I hear it works better when you suck it from the dick," Nate offers up.

Cooper's chuckle fills the truck as I turn around to glare at him.

"Because you chuckled, there will be no soul-sucking tonight."

He stops laughing and lets out an exasperated sigh. "Way to go, Nate, you cost me a blowie. Who even invited them?"

"I did, you idiot." I push on his chest.

We exit the truck and make our way over to where Nate parked. Vivian opts to sit in the back with me, while Cooper takes the passenger seat.

We take off, heading to the nearest Taco Bell, much to my and Vivian's delight. With our tacos and Cinnabon delights in hand, we head home.

"Spill," Vivian whispers over her taco.

I glance up to where Nate and Cooper are chatting about whatever the hell men talk about, making sure they aren't listening before answering.

I tell her about stumbling into the picture of Dillon and Coop's boss and our hasty exit that was thwarted by the awkward run-in with Avery.

"Are you going to tell Cooper?"

"Do I have to?"

She gives me a stern mom stare.

"Fine," I grumble. "But I'm waiting until we get home."

"Good," she says with a single nod before glancing up to where our men are still gabbing but leaning so close together that their hands are almost touching. "Think they're going to kiss?" Viv wiggles her brows suggestively while taking a very unladylike bite of her sugary dessert.

"I think there is a fifty percent chance they'll probably kiss goodnight."

She lets out a dreamy sigh. "Maybe if we're really lucky, they'll do it in front of us."

"We can only dream."

Chapter Thirty-Five

Cooper

Chapter Thirty-Five

Cooper

\#

Sutton and I stumble into the living room, laughing and kissing as I pull the key from the door. We are so caught up in each other's bodies that we don't notice the boxes piled by the door until Sutton backs into one and windmills her arms in an attempt to stay vertical.

I snake an arm behind her back and haul her to my chest.

"What the fuck?" she mutters, spinning to take in the cluttered living room.

There's junk everywhere.

Boxes are stacked all around the room. Some taped closed, others filled with things sticking out.

We both pause and turn to each other.

"You don't think...?"

I nod. "Yeah, I think so."

She squeals as she jumps into my arms and kisses every inch of my face.

I spin her around as she shouts, "Huzzah."

"Typical," Dillon's raspy voice sounds from the other side of the room.

Sutton and I stop spinning to face him. He's carrying his guitar case in one hand and a pillow in the other. He wears his usual look of arrogance and disdain as he stares us down, but this time, there's something else in his expression. Maybe a hint of defeat. Maybe even sadness.

He's finally doing it.

He's leaving.

I want to shout for joy.

To scream my happiness for the entire world to hear.

But I don't. I don't say a word. I won't, either.

I won't risk him changing his mind out of spite.

So instead, I step out of the doorway and let him pass me.

He doesn't do his usual shoving his shoulder into mine or his douchey remarks. He doesn't make a single sound until he reaches the door.

"I'll be gone in the morning... You win."

I turn to look at him.

His hand rests on the door handle. "You've got Sutton and the house. Congratulations." And with that, he steps out.

Sutton quickly drags me down the hall and into her bedroom. She wastes zero time before she pounces on me, knocking me back onto the bed.

She straddles my thighs as she leans down to run her mouth over mine. "We did it."

"One more night and we're free." I run my hands up and down her curves, savoring every touch.

"It feels surreal," she admits. "I never thought this day would come."

"Me either. But I'm so damn happy it did."

We've been waiting months for this day. Well, even longer if you count months of my pining after her from afar.

We can finally just be together without having to look over our shoulders every second for her scorned ex-boyfriend. We're free.

Sutton sits up, and I brace myself on my forearms. She's radiant. Her face beaming with pure happiness as she stares down at me, pushing her golden locks out of her face.

She's mine. All mine. Some days, I have a tough time wrapping my head around that fact. That the woman I'm obsessed with—who I love—feels the same.

I don't know what I did to deserve her, but I'll never take it for granted.

She wiggles her brows. "Victory fuck?"

Chapter Thirty-Six

Sutton

We finally did it.

Dillon is gone.

Cooper and I are finally free.

Now, what that means for us going forward... I'm not sure.

But what I am sure about is that I love Cooper with my entire being. And tonight I'll ask what we are going to do moving forward.

When we woke up this morning, I expected at least one nasty run-in with Dillon before he was gone for good. But I was pleasantly shocked to find every last one of his belongings was gone, along with a couple of my things, like my coffee machine and all the coffee, as well as a couple of my throw pillows and the shower curtain for the guest bathroom.

But I couldn't find it in me to care.

He left. Not only that, but after months of an awkward stalemate, he left peacefully.

He could have my pillows and coffee maker for all I cared.

I was finally free of the nightmare that was life with Dillon Oak.

To honor the victory, I stop into Cooper's favorite steak house, Rare, to place a to-go order on my way home from work.

Eating delicious steaks and potatoes seems like the perfect way to celebrate being Dillon-free. It should also soften the blow of his boss being the godfather to the demon who has been making our lives hell.

I knew I should have told him about the connection last night, but I couldn't. We were both so happy to see those boxes. I didn't want to put a damper on the mood.

"I want you to tell me the truth," a voice demands behind me. A voice I know all too well.

Dillon.

I sigh, spinning the barstool I'm sitting on to face him. "I thought when you moved out that would be the end of me seeing you." I frown. "I guess not."

"Stop playing stupid games and be honest."

"What are you talking about, Dillon?"

"I'm talking about it all. You leaving me last second at our wedding. To shacking up with that loser, Cooper."

"I tried to be honest with you, and look at how that turned out, Dillon. You threw a party and trashed my house. You called me names."

"Of course I did. You dumped me at the fucking altar," he hisses through clenched teeth as he steps even closer to me.

"And you admitted to cheating on me. That's not love."

He scoffs. "And what you have with Cooper is?"

"Yes. He is my everything. I would never hurt him, and he would never hurt me."

His jaw tightens. "When did it start? And don't lie. I'm sick of lies."

I take a deep breath, hoping that admitting this to him won't be a massive mistake. "Nothing happened until after we were already over."

"So you did lie?"

"Yes and no. Neither of us acted upon anything until after our relationship ended officially."

"Officially?"

"We both know it was over long before I left you."

"I didn't think that."

"We weren't even sleeping together anymore."

"Because you wanted to wait until after we were married."

"Yeah, and I think that time without the physicality of our relationship showed me that was all we were to each other. Just a warm body."

"So you replaced my body with another as soon as you could?"

"No. I think I always had feelings for him. But I never took the risk of acting on them until I knew we"—I motion between us—"were one hundred percent done."

"I knew it. I fucking knew it. How many times did I say something was going on between the two of you?"

I sigh. "I understand why you might be hurt by this."

He laughs, slipping into the empty seat beside me.

"Don't forget, though, Dillon, you cheated. That's pretty shitty."

"So I had a few one-night stands. That's nothing compared to you being in love with another man."

There's no point in arguing with him. He'll forever make himself the victim in our situation instead of taking half the responsibility for things like I have.

"Think whatever you want, Dillon. Hopefully, you can move on."

"You'd like that, wouldn't you," he sneers.

"Yes," I say, exasperated. "I would."

"Just tell me, why the lies? Why pretend to be a couple?"

"Well, first of all, we aren't pretending anymore. And second, I thought it was super obvious I wanted you gone."

"What did he get out of this arrangement? Besides a wet pussy?"

My blood boils. I imagine myself leaping off my stool and shoving my newly done manicure into his eyes. But alas, I don't do that.

No, instead, I do nothing.

I don't react. I know that's what he wants—to make me mad. To make me act crazy so he can look like the good guy.

So I smile. "He had his reasons."

Dillon laughs. "He wasn't in it for the sex. That must be a blow to your ego."

"Yep," I deadpan. "I'm terribly offended that my boyfriend didn't use me for my vagina. How will I ever cope?"

He stands, pushing his chair back with a scraping noise that has every patron in the restaurant turning our way. "I hope you and Cooper get everything you deserve," he says before turning and leaving.

While the words might have sounded like well wishes, I know better. I know Dillon.

Heat flames my cheeks as people continue to stare at me. I raise my hand and wave at them before turning back to the bar and ordering a lemon drop and a loaf of bread to keep me company while I wait.

Even though I'm thoroughly embarrassed by his outburst and will never be able to show my face in this restaurant without a disguise, I feel lighter now that he knows the truth.

Maybe the complete truth was all he needed, and now he'll leave me alone for good.

Chapter Thirty-Seven

Cooper

I am beyond excited to get home. All day, my head's been else-where. It's been at home with Sutton. She's consumed my thoughts more than usual. Electric energy courses through me at the sheer enjoyment of knowing tonight is our first night alone. Our first night officially done with the king of douches, and I plan to bask in every second of it.

I've just pulled into Sutton's driveway after work when my phone rings. I pick it up without even bothering to look to see who's calling; it can only be one person—the only person in my life who hasn't gotten the hint that texting is my—and almost every other person on this planet's—preferred method of contact.

Taking a deep breath, I grip the steering wheel. "Hey, Mom."

"Hey, baby, how are you?"

"I'm good."

A beat of silence passes before she finally says, "So, Sutton..."

"Yeah..."

"I like her."

I smile. We had dinner with my parents a few nights ago, and Sutton managed to charm them both as I knew she would. It meant the world to me that they were as in love with her as I am.

"Me too."

"You needed someone like her."

"Nah, I needed her."

"Awe," my mom coos on the line. "My baby is in love."

"Madly," I confirm.

"And she knows?"

"She is more than aware."

"Good. All I ever want is for you to be happy in every aspect of your life, and it sounds like you are getting there."

"Thanks, Mom."

She's silent for another moment.

"Mom?"

"I have something to tell you, but I don't know if it's anything or not."

"What is it?"

"I saw Sutton a bit ago... She was having dinner with some attractive yet dirty-looking man."

My blood boils. *Dillon.*

"That's her ex, Mom."

"Oh... And you're okay with that?"

"Not really, but I'm sure there's a good explanation for it all. He didn't take the end of their relationship well."

"Okay. Well, if you ever need to talk to me about anything, love life included, please call."

"I will."

At that, we hang up.

I'm not going to get mad. I'm sure Sutton had her reasons for meeting up with the man we just got rid of and not telling me. There has to be a good, reasonable explanation. Maybe her cell was dead, and she couldn't call me.

I'm going to walk inside and calmly ask her about it.

Opening the front door, I'm prepared to do just that, but all that changes the moment I find her lounging on the couch, laughing as she stares at her phone with a glass of wine in her hand.

I slam the door behind me. "Did you meet up with Dillon?"

"Wow, no hello, how are you? Or even a quick kiss. The romance sure does fade quickly."

"Did you see Dillon today?"

Her gaze narrows. "How did you know that?"

"Better question, why?" I work my jaw.

"Don't you think you're being a little dramatic?"

"No, I don't. But scratch that, the real question is why did I hear about it from someone else and not you?"

Sutton rolls her eyes. "Because he bombarded me when I was picking up takeout for our dinner, and I texted you earlier."

I pull up my texts. The last message from her was the side-eye emoji three times. "This? This is you texting me about it?"

"Yes. That clearly means I'm giving someone the side-eye, aka Dillon the Douche. Who else would it be about?"

"How on earth was I ever going to guess that, Sut?"

"I don't know, with logic. Gah, it's like you don't even know me."

"That's because you have the personality of a horny teenage boy and a rodent."

Her mouth gapes in shock. "Rude."

She knows it's true. I groan, scrubbing my face. "I'm sorry. I don't know why I'm being so jealous."

"Because you love me," she yells and hops up and into my arms like a monkey as she wraps her legs around me tightly.

"Don't worry about Dillon. Don't worry about anything. You and me, we are rock solid. Like your dick will be shortly."

I snort. "I'm sorry for overreacting."

"It's okay. I would probably react the same if I heard you spent time with Sarah."

"I would never."

"Good." She presses a kiss to my lips. "Now let's enjoy one of the first nights alone without you-know-who and have wild sex in the living room."

I palm her ass. "I like the way you think."

❧

The day is dragging. I've had two meetings already this morning, then nothing else on my schedule but building a couple potential plans for a new client to present later this week.

I've yawned five times in the past ten minutes. I'm exhausted. Sutton and I took advantage of officially having her place Dillon-free and ended up screwing in the living room, on the kitchen counters, and on the hallway floor. Only stopping to feed each other the delicious steak she had picked up for us.

It was exhilarating, but the rug burns on my ass and Sutton's knees are nothing we want to repeat. The night was in the top five best nights of my life, and not just because I was getting my brain fucked out of my head. But because of Sutton. Being with her, touching her, laughing with her, made every part of my soul sing with joy.

"What's that, your fourth cup today?" Jeff asks as I tip the pot to fill my cup while he waits behind me with his own mug.

"You would know since you've filled yours as much as I have."

He snickers down at his empty coffee mug. "Guilty."

"Why are you overdoing the caffeine today?"

"New baby kept me and the missus up all night with colic."

I hiss through my teeth. "Ooh, sounds rough."

"You have no idea." He takes a drink from his mug. "What about you?"

"Um... Up late."

"Doing?"

I purse my lips. "Stuff."

Jeff cackles. "Your better half to blame?"

"Yeah." I smile.

"I don't blame you. Enjoy the time together while you can because before you know it, you'll have kids demanding to sleep with you, destroying any idea of alone time you have."

"I—I don't think kids are in our near future."

"Smart." He claps me on the shoulder. "I wish Lisa and I would have waited a couple more years before popping them out."

"Really?"

"Yeah, I love the little fruit of my loins, but I also miss sleeping."

I open my mouth to respond, but my eyes catch on something I shouldn't be seeing. "What the hell..." I whisper to myself as Dillon the Douche hugs my boss before striding out of the office with a shit-eating grin on his face.

The confusion must show on my face because Jeff asks, "Do you know him?"

"Yeah," I mutter. "That's my girlfriend's ex."

"Maybe it's a coincidence," he says hopefully.

"Yeah, I doubt that. He didn't take the breakup well and has been more than a little difficult."

"Does he know you work here?"

"I don't think so."

"Shit," he hisses. "What do you think they were talking about?"

Mr. Avery glares across the office. "Shaw, my office. Now," he demands before turning around and walking behind his desk. Everyone's head swivels in my direction with looks of apprehension and intrigue.

"I guess we are about to find out." I set my mug on the desk closest to us.

"Good luck," Jeff says, giving me a thumbs-up.

I hold my head high as I move past my coworkers. Each one of them gives me a different expression that says "yikes."

The moment I step into his office, he demands I shut the door behind me.

I do as he says, then make my way to the stylish yet uncomfortable guest chairs in front of his desk.

"Do you know why I called you in here?" he asks, his tone lacking his usual jovial lift that I've come to expect.

"I can only assume it has something to do with the man who just left your office," I reply honestly.

"Yes, it appears you and Dillon are no strangers."

My heart rate increases as my nerves take over. I swallow. "You could say that, *unfortunately*. How are you two acquainted?"

"He's my godson."

My stomach drops.

Fuck. My mind races with every single shitty thing Dillon could have just told him about me. Lies and truths.

"So you can imagine my surprise when I saw you and Sutton, the woman who left Dillon at the altar, together."

"Technically, she didn't leave him at the altar. She refused to sign the—"

He cuts me off with a glare. "The way I see it, this means one of two things. Either you've been lying to me and everyone in this office about your relationship with Sutton. Or you were an active participant in the betrayal and heartbreak of my godson by helping his fiancée cheat. So, which is it? Are you a liar or a cheater?"

I ignore the sound of my blood rushing through my ears and the pounding in my chest as I tell him, "Our relationship is real."

He steeples his hands in front of him. "So you're a cheater?"

I clear my throat. "No, sir. Sutton and I didn't begin our romantic relationship until months after I began working here and long after their failed wedding."

A sneer-like smile graces his lips. "A liar it is."

I close my eyes. "Yes, but I don't see why my relationship status was ever relevant or even appropriate to be discussed."

"You made it relevant when you chose to lie."

I bite my tongue, not wanting to make the situation even worse by bringing up the fact that he and the board strongly implied that the position would go to someone who matched their lifestyles and ideals. Aka a person in a committed relationship. They all but said it in my interviews.

He breathes out through his nose, his frustration seeping through every pore. "Not only am I rethinking your recent promotion. I'm rethinking your entire future with this company."

I freeze, my heart feeling like it's going to explode. "Am I being fired?"

He shakes his head. "That has yet to be determined."

I nod. "I understand this doesn't look great—"

"Doesn't look great? That's not even half of it, Cooper. It looks like we hired a liar. The board won't be pleased." He leans back in his chair. "As of right now, you are on administrative leave until we make our decision."

"Okay." I swallow. "What does that mean exactly?"

"It means, collect your belongings and wait by the phone until you hear back from us."

I push myself out of the chair and make my way to the door. "For what it's worth. I've been in love with Sutton since the moment I saw her years ago. The timing of our physical relationship might have been an exaggeration, but the feelings weren't. I know your relationship with Dillon complicates things, but I hope you let my job performance speak for me instead of my personal drama with him."

He doesn't say a word. So I close the door behind me and head into my office to grab my belongings.

I don't have much in the way of personal effects. A picture of Nate, Viv, Sutton, and me taken from one of many trivia nights we like to frequent. My pencil case is filled with my favorite pens. And the stupid-fancy calculator I've never used once that Nate and Vivian bought me for my first day on the job.

Gathering up a few other items, I shove them into my backpack and turn off the lights without looking back.

From the moment I saw Dillon step out of my boss's office, there was only one place I wanted to be—one person I wanted to talk to, to see.

Sutton.

I have to know if she knew about Dillon and Avery.

The FTW building is beautiful. Nate and Sutton have both already told me that before but seeing it in person is something else. The cubicles aren't the boring old-fashioned kind that you can stick tacks into. They're black metal, giving the space a sleek industrial vibe.

"Welcome to FTW. How can I—oh, it's you." Hadlee's voice pierces my ears, bringing my attention to her.

"Hadlee." I nod. She is every bit as beautiful and awful as I remember.

"Cooper," she sneers. "Come to ask me for ways to get Sarah back?"

"Absolutely not."

"Then why are you here?"

"Sutton."

She rolls her eyes. "Her office is one floor below. You'll want to go past the cubicles and down the long hall. You can't miss it. Her name is on the door."

"Thanks," I mutter, taking off without another glance at her.

Her office is exactly where Hadlee said it would be. I knock twice on the thick door before she calls out, "Come in."

Sutton's long hair is draped over one shoulder while her eyes are glued to the computer in front of her. Her fingers move at a quick pace as she types away at the keyboard for a moment before looking up.

"Cooper!" She beams, pushing back from the desk and walking over to me. Her arms wrap around me, and she pushes up on her toes to kiss me. "What are you doing here?"

"I think I lost my job."

"What?" she gasps, pulling me by the hand until we round her desk. She pushes me into her chair and then sits in my lap.

"Yeah, well. The official word is that I am on administrative leave until further notice, but I'm fairly sure that's corporate for termination heading your way. Am I right?"

She hisses through her teeth. "It doesn't sound good."

"That's what I thought."

"What happened?"

"Dillon decided to pay my boss a visit."

Sutton pales. "To meet with Mr. Avery?"

"Did you know? Who my boss was?"

"Not until that night at his house... I saw a picture on the wall and put two and two together. I'm sorry, Coop. I should have told you right away. I know I should have. But we were so happy about getting rid of Dillon. I didn't want to ruin the mood."

"So instead of ruining a night or two of sex, you let me walk into work to be blindsided by this?" I spit at her.

Her face falls in a mask of pure guilt, and I instantly feel like shit for putting that expression on her face.

"I'm so fucking sorry. This is all my fault." Her chin wobbles.

I almost agree with her for a split second, but I stop myself. None of this is her fault.

"No. I'm the one who lied to my job about our relationship in the first place, which is what they're planning to use as my fireable offense."

"But I'm the one who left you in the dark about their family ties. If I would have warned you, maybe we could have figured out a solution before you were ambushed and put on leave."

"Maybe... But can we both just agree that Dillon is the asshole here?" I ask.

"As he is in all facets of life."

I let out a small laugh. "What am I going to do?"

"You aren't going to panic."

"How? I might have lost my income."

"I have more than enough to support us."

"Baby..."

"No, I don't want to hear it. If the worst happens and they are idiots and fire you over that little shit, I will support you as long as you need."

"I don't want you to have to do that."

"I know. But I will. Because we take care of each other. This relationship isn't one-sided."

I wrap her in a tight hug, inhaling deeply. Comfort washes over me as her scent fills my nose. "Thank you."

Her eyes soften and the lines on her forehead smooth out as she tips up and presses a featherlight kiss to the corner of my mouth.

"Go home, crack open one of those fancy IPAs from the fridge, and take a nice hot bubble bath. Use my lavender oils—that's important. It will make the entire experience more enjoyable."

"You being with me would make it more enjoyable."

"I know, baby, but I can't leave yet. I have an interview that I can't reschedule."

"Of course. I'm sorry. I wasn't trying to make you feel bad."

She silences me with another kiss, this one to my lips. It's not soft like the last, but it also isn't overly passionate.

"When you get in the tub, send me a text, and I will send you something that will make it one of the best baths you've ever had."

"Promise?"

"Promise."

I do as Sutton instructed.

I go straight home and pop open a cold IPA. The full-bodied flavor fills my senses as I make my way to the bathroom with an extra can in my left hand.

After finding Sutton's lavender bath oil, I crank the water on high and wait for the tub to fill. I pop the top off the oil and splash a few droplets into the water before removing my clothes and stepping into the near-scalding water.

Dropping my head back against the small pillow she has draped over the edge of the tub, I close my eyes.

My parents have not only finally accepted that I have chosen a career path different from theirs but are supportive of it. Hell, they even seem proud of me.

How proud will they be when I have to break the news I was fired?

What the hell am I going to do if I lose my job?

Am I going to have to dip into the savings I set up for my parents?

Go back to teaching?

I'd rather have Dillon third wheel every date with Sutton than go back to where I started.

Fuck. I groan, rubbing my hand through my hair.

What a lie. I'd rather do anything than have Dillon in Sutton's and my life, especially after he tried to end my career.

The only thing that makes this entire situation okay is her.

The fact that I found someone who'll stand by me through it all.

A woman who is strong, compassionate, and loves me like no one else has.

In a few short months, my feelings for her have grown from an intense crush to a soul-aching love that has me terrified of losing it.

If it comes down to it, I'll return to teaching. I'll do anything and everything I can to contribute to our life in any way I can. Even if that means going back to a job that was filled with stress and severely lacking in the pay department. I would do it, for us.

I lean over the side of the bath, careful not to splash any water onto the floor, and grab my phone from my pants.

Cooper

Home and in the bath. Now what?

Sutton

I have two videos for you to watch. One is an inspirational tale that I would love for us to aspire to be like, and the other is something special I made for you a couple days ago when you were out with Nate.

Two hyperlinks appear in blue.

Which do I watch first?

Whatever your sexy heart desires.

I click on the first link, only to be brought to a Hentai porn site with a video titled "Hot guy fucks hot babe." I chuckle at the video and fire off a text to Sutton before I press play.

You sent me a porn link…

Shrugs It's one of my favorites. I thought maybe it could inspire you a little.

Noted… I'm nervous to click on the next link.

Don't be. You are going to be INCREDIBLY pleased with what you find.

Intrigued, I ditch my plans to watch "hot guy fucks hot babe" and click on the second link.

This time, I'm not directed to an adult video site, which kind of has me bummed but also even more curious as it takes me to a Google drive with a folder labeled "For Cooper's Eyes Only."

Opening the folder, I click on the singular video file. I press play and find Sutton standing in front of her bed in nothing but a scantily, almost see-through teddy as her hands rub down her torso, then back up to her breasts, where she cups them and moans.

Holy shit.

Holy *fucking* shit.

Did she record a dirty video for me?

She looks at the camera, then licks her lips as she sits on the bed and spreads her legs wide open. The tiny panties she has on doing nothing to hide her slick entrance.

"Welcome to a very special Masturbation Monday." Her lips curl up into a smile as her sultry voice comes through. "I hope you enjoy the show."

I pull the wooden bath tray from the other end of the tub closer and prop the phone up as I slip my hands under the water to grip my cock. Sutton's fingers trail over her clit a few times before she plunges a finger inside herself.

"Fuck," I groan at the same time she does in the recording.

"I'm thinking about you right now. Thinking about your hands. Your fingers filling me as you fuck me senseless with them." Her face contorts in pleasure as she puts on the show of a lifetime for me.

I squeeze my cock, timing my fist to her fingers, imagining I'm there with her, feeling the inside of her hot walls tightening around me.

Sutton rolls her hips, fucking her fingers enthusiastically for the camera, for me. "I'm close," she pants. "Are you close?"

So close. I grit my teeth together, wanting to last as long as she does in the video. My balls are already painfully tight as I struggle to hold off.

Her legs begin to tremble, and her breathing picks up. "I'm coming."

So am I.

I let go just as she does.

Euphoria.

It's the only way to explain the intense pleasure and calm that washes over me and everything I am with her. Fuck, even when I'm imagining her.

I let my pounding heart rate come back down before I click back on the porn she had sent me for inspiration, and it's not even twenty minutes later that I'm palming my cock again, chasing after another orgasm.

An hour, two beers, and a couple of orgasms later, I climb out of the bathtub, relaxed and tired.

Chapter Thirty-Eight

Sutton

I can't focus for the rest of the day. I stared at my computer and tried to read the same three sentences about twenty times before I had to give up and close the file. The interview I couldn't reschedule was a mess. Well, more I like I was a mess and I'm pretty sure the candidate could tell my heart wasn't even remotely in it.

Every thought, every moment, is preoccupied with Cooper.

I feel as if I let him down.

He might lose his job over my mistake. And I might have just ruined his plans to help his parents.

I messed up by withholding the truth from Cooper.

I should have known better.

So it's my job to fix this mess I've created. I owe it to Coop.

So instead of sitting and staring at the surrounding wall, I make a call.

The phone only rings once, and before they can say a word, I ask, "Can you meet me at Shots and Ladders?"

It's not even two in the afternoon when I order my second lemon drop of the day.

"Hitting the booze hard?" Nate asks from beside me with his usual dimply smile.

"You would be too if your ex put your boyfriend's job at risk."

Nate's smile drops. "What happened?"

I relay everything Cooper told me to Nate.

"Why didn't Cooper call me? And why didn't you call Viv?"

"Because I needed booze to help not only wash away the guilt but also get my scheming mojo going, and it isn't fair to Vivian to bring her into an alcohol zone when she can't partake."

"I'm not partaking either."

"Yeah, but that's because you are a simp."

"I prefer the term sweet, supportive spouse."

"Noted," I tease before tossing back the last of my drink.

"Back to why you chose to call me instead of Viv. That's a bullshit answer, and you know it."

"Ugh," I groan. "Why do you have to be so smart? Okay, you want the real answers?"

"Yes."

"I called you because I needed someone who is team Cooper. Not team Sutton."

"But I am team Sutton."

"That's sweet of you to say, but if it came down to picking a team to be on, who would you choose, team Cooper or team Sutton?"

"Team Cooper."

"That's what I thought. I needed someone who would put him at number one, and that's you, not Viv. I'm Vivian's number one, so she would spin anything into my favor. I need the truth. Not my best friend's love."

Nate looks me over for a moment before he nods. "So what's the plan?"

"You tell me, Mr. Romantic Gesture. What can I do to make this better?"

He gives me a sad smile. "From the sounds of it, you've done everything you can. You are already planning to be Cooper's rock should the waves come crashing down on him. And that is more than enough."

"It's not enough," I argue. "He deserves more. Better."

"Sutton, he deserves you. That's all he wants and needs."

"Are you sure?"

"Yes. But if you want to mess with that dipshit Dillon, I am game. But don't for a second think your love and support isn't enough for Cooper. Because it is. And I know if you asked him, he would confirm."

"Okay," I agree because it's true. I know deep in my bones that Cooper doesn't blame me for any of this, but the problem is, I do.

My phone chimes with a text from Cooper. I instantly send him the video links I had prepared for him. It's the least I can do.

"Seriously, Sutton, are you going to be okay?"

I flash him my teeth in what's probably the least reassuring smile ever. "I should be fine."

Nate stands, paying my tab before slapping me on the back. "You're good for him."

I snort. "Yeah, tell that to his career."

"I mean it, Sutton. He's been really happy since you two got together."

"So have I," I admit. It's not a secret. But it's painful to know that same happiness is in the process of burning to ashes because I felt the need to give my loser ex closure.

"You need a ride home?" He twirls his keys around his finger.

"Nah, I'm going to get some food in me, then head back into the office to grab my stuff before heading home in a couple hours."

"If you need me again, don't hesitate. Okay?"

I nod. "Thanks for talking with me."

"Anytime." He waves and walks away.

I have no idea how to fix this situation for him. But I do want to try. For Cooper, I have to try.

Leaving Shots and Ladders, I find the nearest taco place and sober up.

Okay, I *attempt* to sober up.

I'm seventy-five percent sober when I make my way back into the office. The majority of the staff has already cleared out for the day, thankfully, because even with the greasy tacos soaking up my many drinks from earlier, I'm still slightly swaying as I walk. I blame the heels. My gorgeous, expensive heels. They weren't meant to take me on a booze break in the middle of the workday blocks away from my employment.

I'm halfway across the lobby when I notice a light coming from Mr. Tillan's office.

Instantly, I know I need to speak with him. I have to see what he can do for Cooper.

I walk faster than I would've thought possible mere minutes ago and knock on his door before cracking it open.

"Mr. T?" I call out.

"Come in."

I poke my head through and smile before walking into the massive office. Sitting behind his desk, Mr. T stares at a stack of papers. He looks up, a smile lifting his lips. "Ms. Hale, I thought you left hours ago."

"I had," I concede, flopping into one of the chairs across from his desk.

He puts down the paperwork he's been looking at, giving me his full attention. "Then why are you here?"

I sigh. "I have a problem. And I'm hoping you might be able to help because it deals with an individual we both know and love."

He sits up straighter. "Is this an official HR visit?"

"What? No." I wave him off. "It's about Cooper."

"My financial adviser?"

"That's the one."

"What about him?" he asks, leaning forward.

"Buckle in, Mr. T, because this story is a doozy."

I tell him everything—well, not everything. I leave out the parts about Coop and I banging like energizer bunnies, but he gets a good picture of the situation.

"So you want my advice?"

I shake my head. "No, I want your help in saving his job."

His face softens. "Sutton, I don't know how I can help in this situation. He isn't one of my employees."

His words sober me, and my eyes water. I have to look up and stare into the fluorescent lights for a moment to get it under control before I return my attention to Mr. T. Giving him a quick nod and a smile, I stand to leave. "Please, think about it."

"I will," he promises.

Chapter Thirty-Nine

Sutton

The drive home is a blur.

I don't even remember taking any of the turns because my mind is so caught up in fixing my mistakes.

My every thought on how to help Cooper. And my chest aches with the only real solution I could come up with.

I pull my car behind Cooper's truck and cut the engine. He's right through that door. The person I'd do anything for.

Leaving everything in my car but the damn tacos I had to buy him, I trudge up the sidewalk. My heart already aching. The front door opens, and Cooper's bright smile is there to greet me.

"Where have you been, baby?" He wraps me up in a hug. "I've been worried."

I hold out the grease-soaked bag. "I got you these."

"Sutton, baby, you didn't have to get me anything. Especially after that homemade video. That was enough to last you years without having to get me a gift."

God, I love his smile.

I love his laugh. His endless pursuit of new places and things to experience. I even love those stupid Clark Kent glasses that I'm not one hundred percent sold on him needing.

But most of all, I love his heart. His tenderness that's evident in everything he does, even the way he shows me every day how much he loves me.

Cooper takes the bag from me, setting it on the table. "What's wrong?"

This is it. I have to do it now. If I don't, I'll never do what's best for him.

I clutch at my throat, trying to find the right words to say.

"I think we should call it."

His jaw hardens. "Call what?"

"Us. This"—I gesture between us—"clearly isn't working."

"What isn't working? Where is this coming from?"

I give him a watery smile. "It's for the best. It might not feel like it in this moment, but trust me when I say you'll soon agree."

"The hell I will. You aren't doing this."

I glance toward the door. "Cooper, please don't make this harder than it has to be."

Hurt shines in his eyes. "Than *what* has to be? Say the god-damn words, Sutton, because if you are going to break my heart, you better be clear as fucking day about it."

I swipe away a tear on my cheek. "I'm breaking up with you."

"Why?" He grabs my hands and squeezes, imploring me to explain myself.

"Cooper..."

"No, tell me why?"

"Because I'm not good for you. You deserve more than someone who will rope you into half-baked schemes that hurt your career."

I yank my hands free of his, watching as they drop between us while I take two steps backward, retreating from his warmth and tenderness.

I fucked up. I brought him into my life and ruined everything for him.

And now I have to be the one to fix it.

Part of fixing everything for him is to remove the source of his problems—me.

The hurt vanishes as anger takes over.

Good. Let him hate me. I can learn to live with his hate.

"No," he barks, shaking his head. "You don't get to end this over something as ridiculous as my job. And you sure as shit don't get to take the blame for my lie that started long before we struck our bargain."

"Yes I do."

"No."

"It doesn't work like that, Cooper. You can't force me to stay with you because you don't accept that I'm breaking up with you."

"If you had a good reason, I would accept it. If you didn't love me, I would accept it. But we both know you do. And I love you. We can figure out my job stuff. That isn't important. You and I, we are important."

My heart pounds in my chest at a painfully quick pace. "Love isn't always enough."

"You really believe that?"

My chin threatens to quiver. "I do."

His face is a mask of anger mixed with defeat. "Don't do this, Sutton."

My hands shake as I step out the front door and walk to my car.

He follows me, staying two steps behind me. "Please."

My body hurts from holding back my tears as I climb into my car and lock the doors.

"We're over? You and me, we aren't something you can throw away whenever it gets hard. Run away all you want, Sutton, but you and I aren't over."

"Tell yourself whatever you want, but I'm done." Tears crest and fall as I back out into the street, refusing to give myself one last glance in his direction. I don't deserve to see him.

I don't bother to call or warn Vivian that I'm coming over. Instead, I use the emergency key she gave me to her and Nate's home, letting myself inside.

Flinging the door open, I announce, "I broke up with Coop."

"Sutton!" Vivian's scream pierces the air as I catch sight of my best friend's husband's ass. Vivian's positioned in front of him on the ledge of the couch, with her legs wrapped around his waist and her heels resting above said ass.

What are the chances I'd walk in on the same two people making sweet, sweet love—because that's what Viv and Nate do; they don't fuck, they make love—twice in one lifetime, in different places, nonetheless.

I wish I could say I avert my eyes immediately, but I don't. I stand there in pure shock, staring at Nate's nice ass. That is, until Nate leans forward, causing the both of them to topple over the edge and onto the couch.

"Oh my God." I run over to them, leaving the door wide open behind me. "Are you guys okay?"

"Sutton," Nate growls. "Turn around and close the damn front door."

"Oh." I scramble back to the entryway, shutting it quickly. I shield my eyes before facing them again. "Sorry, guys. But in my defense, who goes to pound town at six on a weeknight."

Vivian lets out an exasperated sigh. "Married people. Who live alone."

That tracks. "I'm sorry, if you want to finish, I can go sit in my car."

"Don't bother," Nate says, his voice laced with irritation.

The rustling of fabric fills the empty space, and I swear I hear what sounds like a kiss. Maybe they did decide to finish. Oh God, what if they are continuing while I'm in the room as a punishment for me walking in on them.

The temptation to find out is strong, but I'm too scared to peek out from my fingers.

The sound of footsteps padding down the hall fades until a door shuts.

"You can look now," Vivian tells me.

I scissor my fingers and peek through the opening to find my best friend sitting on the couch, a blanket wrapped around her like a towel. Her hair is a mussed-up mess. And I almost feel bad for interrupting her from getting dicked down. Almost. But I have bigger problems. I'm holding myself together by tattered threads.

"Did Nate go to get dressed?"

She shakes her head. "Cold shower."

I laugh, then wipe my nose.

"Come here." She opens her arms, and I run around the side of the couch and into her embrace.

I can't stop the tears the moment she wraps me in a hug.

She doesn't ask me anything or try to placate me. She simply rubs a hand through my hair and down my back, letting me cry until all my tears dry up.

"What happened?" she murmurs a while later, having put on some clothes. Cuddling under a different blanket than the one she had been covering herself with earlier, I snuggle in deeper.

"I realized I loved him too much to destroy his life."

"You aren't destroying shit."

"Viv, you didn't see the pure look of defeat on his face when he came by my office."

She sits there silently, her face soft and open as she listens to me.

"I did that. And I couldn't live with myself if I continued to bring him down with me."

"Bring him down with you? What are you talking about? You, my dearest friend, are above us all. You are an angel that fell from heaven and walks among us mere mortals, gifting us with your dazzling presence."

"Can you not. I need serious Vivian. Not hype-woman Vivian."

"No, apparently you need hype-woman Vivian, because I won't stand for you talking about yourself in anything but a positive manner. You are my best friend, my platonic soulmate. My first true love. You are amazing in every way imaginable."

"Viv…"

"No, you need to hear this. None of this is your fault. You are a gift to have in my life, and I am sure Cooper considers you to be the same."

"Okay."

"Repeat after me, I make others' lives better by being in them."

"Do I have to?"

"Yes. Now do it."

"I make others' lives better by being in them," I grumble. "Happy?"

"Very," she beams. "I know your faith in men has been practically nonexistent after all the dumb shit your dad used to pull growing up, but Cooper isn't him. He isn't going to let you down."

I wipe my nose with the back of my hand. "I know. I just don't want to let him down anymore."

"You won't. You'll learn from this tiny mistake because you are the smartest woman I know."

We sit like that for hours. Vivian making me talk about how awesome I am and refusing to take any Sutton slander.

It's 10 p.m. when Nate finally resurfaces from their bedroom. He strides into the living room wearing a pair of dark sweatpants and an old Fisher Landscaping hoodie. "Baby, are you and Sutton having a sleepover in the living room or in our room?"

"Our room, please." She flashes him her teeth.

Nate leans down and brushes a kiss across her lips. "If you need me, I'll be in the guest room."

"Goodnight," she says longingly as she watches him walk away.

Hopping her ass off the couch, she grabs a hold of my wrist and pulls me up with her. "Go make us popcorn and meet me in my bedroom while I go set everything up."

I salute her. "Aye aye, captain."

Grabbing the popcorn from the pantry, I sniffle and wipe my nose for the millionth time in the past hour before sticking the bag in the microwave, watching it like a hawk to make sure it doesn't burn.

I stop the microwave with thirty seconds to spare, then pour the hot, perfectly buttered contents into a bowl. After snagging a couple of waters out of the fridge, I make my way to Nate and Viv's room.

I feel kind of bad for kicking the man out of his own bed, but sometimes, a girl needs her best friend. And I'm thankful she's married to a man who understands that.

Walking into the room, I find Vivian already tucked underneath the covers on what I know isn't her side of the bed. Eyeing her warily, I set a drink on the nightstand closest to her before moving to the other side of the bed. "What are you doing over there?"

"I don't want to miss Nate."

"So you're sleeping on his side?"

"It smells like him."

"Creep."

She tosses a pillow at me.

"Hey, watch it." I move my body to protect the bowl of perfectly popped corn.

"Whatever, pass me the goods." She makes grabby hands at me.

I give her the bowl and climb underneath the covers beside her. "What are we watching?" I ask as she picks up the remote.

"As if you don't already know."

"Freddie?"

"Freddie," she confirms and presses play. And in no time, our favorite late nineties/early two thousands actor appears on the screen as we watch him navigate playing baseball and falling in love like our lives depend on it.

Halfway through the movie, I look over at Vivian. "You're going to make an amazing mom."

A warm glow washes over her as she smiles. "Thank you."

Chapter Forty

Cooper

Twenty-four hours.

That's all the time I'm willing to give Sutton before I march over to wherever she's hiding out and demand she stop being an idiot.

I was crushed last night when she drove away. But I thought she would come home after a few hours and we could talk about it some more. That she would come to her senses.

But she didn't, and my heart broke at the thought of not being with her.

She thinks we're done. That I'll accept that and walk away from her without a fight.

No.

Sutton is worth fighting for every day.

And I plan to do just that.

I had been lying in bed for three hours last night, alternating between staring up at the star-flecked ceiling and tossing and turning. Feeling too hot under the blankets without my little thief beside me. It was wrong. Everything without Sutton was wrong.

It wasn't until I was on my fourth hour of trying to sleep that my phone lit up with a new message.

I reached for my phone so fast, I knocked it off the nightstand. I glared at it for a moment, contemplating getting out of bed and picking it up. Instead, I got it into my head that I could attempt to reach it without climbing out of bed. With my legs on the bed, I reached down, stretching my torso and arms as far as I could. My fingers splayed out, inching further and further until I could almost reach it.

I grazed the case and slid the phone half an inch closer to me.

"Victory," I shouted, pulling it closer.

And then I fell.

My chin hit the rug, followed by my chest as my arms did nothing to help my descent to the floor.

The skin on my chin burned as I rolled onto my back, still clutching my phone in my hand.

My heart was galloping as I lifted it, hopeful to see her name.

Instead, I saw my best friend's.

Nate

> Please explain to me why I am currently lying awake in the guest room of my own home while my wife and unborn child are snuggled up in our bed with your woman.

A second later, another text appeared.

Or is she no longer your woman?

Cooper

Oh, she is still very much mine.

Does she know this?

Yes. Whether or not she has accepted it yet is questionable.

What the hell happened?

Dillon the Douche did.

Classic d-bag. But why is she here?

She spooked when things got rough. Oh, also, I'm at her house.

Why didn't she send you packing to your apartment?

Maybe she forgot I had one.

Or maybe she knew your lovesick ass wouldn't leave easily.

> True… Is she okay?

Define okay… She cried. That's about as much as I know because I gave her and Viv space.

My heart squeezed as I imagined the strong woman I love crying.

> Thanks, man. But also, WTF! Why didn't you text me the moment she showed up?

Well, first, she walked in on Vivian and me having sex. And then I had to take a cold shower. And then she was crying, and I felt like the last thing she needed was you storming over and demanding she speak with you.

> …She caught you guys in the act again?

The woman doesn't ever knock. Just barges in.

> Just like she barged into my heart.

Save the cheesy lines for Sutton.

> You think she'll listen?

We can only hope.

I waited all night for her without a word. No text, no call, no nothing. She hadn't come home for her stupid-expensive luxury skincare routine she did religiously or to trade in the ankle-breaking high heels she had been wearing when she left yesterday.

As the clock strikes 10 a.m., I'm still sitting on the couch, pouting as I wait, when I receive the phone call I've been waiting on from my office. Admittedly, I thought it would take them more than one day to decide my fate, but I guess not.

Putting on my favorite suit, I head into the office to meet with my boss to discuss their final decision regarding me.

I'm not feeling too confident when I walk through the building's rotating door. Familiar faces greet me with smiles and hellos, all seemingly unaware of the shitstorm that's my career.

Halfway through the lobby, on my way to check in with Mr. Avery's personal assistant, I hear my name being called.

"Cooper, wait up."

I spin around to find Mr. Tillan power walking his way over to me.

"I'm not too late, am I?"

The color drains from my face. "Did we have a meeting today? I-I'm so sorry, I must have completely forgotten. And actually, I need to be honest with you, I think I'm about to lose my job."

He studies me. "Cooper—"

"Not from any mistakes or miscalculations in my work," I quickly add. "But from a bending of the truth about when my relationship with Sutton began."

"Cooper." He places a hand on my shoulder. "I know. Sutton informed me of your predicament."

"She did?"

His lips form a somber smile. "She did last night. She also asked me to speak on your behalf."

"She did?" I ask again, stunned by this turn of events.

Mr. Tillan squeezes my shoulder. "She did. That girl loves you so much she was willing to light a fire under my ass to help you."

"She shouldn't have done that."

"Maybe not, but she did. And she was right. You're great at what you do, and your personal life and relationship status should have never been a factor in your career."

I swallow. "Thank you."

"Now, I want you to know I made a few calls to some colleagues of mine regarding your situation."

"And?"

"And they can't fire you over your relationship status. They have no other complaints on you, so they have nothing to use against you."

I let out a relieved breath.

"Don't get too excited. What they can do is demote you. Take away your clients. And make your life miserable until you decide to quit."

"Shit."

"Yeah, it's not ideal."

"So, what do I do?"

"You listen to the alternative offer I have for you."

Ten minutes later, I walk into my boss's office with my head held high, prepared to tackle whatever he throws at me.

Sitting behind his desk once again, he doesn't even glance up as I move across the room. "Please have a seat," he says, still not giving me the decency of looking at me.

I sit in the same chair across from him as I did yesterday. Only this time, I know what's coming.

I sit there for thirty seconds before he finally gives me the time of day.

"So, Cooper, I'm sure you are champing at the bit to hear what we've decided regarding your fate here at the company."

"I am, sir." I straighten my spine, gripping the armrests with my hands as I brace.

"To say I was disappointed to hear you had lied to us about your life outside of the company would be an understatement. But after a long and hard discussion with the partners, we have come to a decision that I am sure you will find more than fitting."

Blood rushes through my ears as he gives a dramatic pause before continuing on. "Do you want to say anything?"

"Will anything I say change the decision that has already been made?"

His lips form a thin line. "No, but—"

"Then I'm good."

He blinks at me, shocked that I'd turn down a chance to hear myself talk as if I'm like all the other finance bros who live for the sound of their own voices.

"Okay, then let's get to the meat and potatoes. Cooper, we have decided against termination."

I let out a relieved breath. I've never been fired from a job, and I don't want to have to explain why I was let go to potential future employers.

"Don't get too excited, son. We did come to a group decision that, while lying about your relationship might not be fireable, it isn't the behavior we want associated with an accounts manager."

I bop my head a few times. "I understand."

❧

After leaving the office, I run a few errands to kill time before her twenty-four hours are up.

The moment her grace period ends, I'm in my truck and on my way to her.

I don't knock. I throw open the front door to Nate's house and stride inside like I belong. Nate glances at the door from where he's sitting in the living room sketching. He tosses up a two-finger wave as I pass him, making my way down the hall to find Sutton and Vivian camped out under a pile of blankets in Viv and Nate's bedroom. Popcorn is strung out all over the bed, and there are half-empty water bottles scattered all over the floor.

"Cooper." Sutton jumps out of bed. "What are you doing here?"

I keep my mouth shut as I continue to stride to her.

Sutton places her hands on her hips as she waits for me to explain.

Stopping directly in front of her, I kneel, toss her over my shoulder, and wrap my arm around her legs.

"Put me down," she demands, pounding at my back.

"Not happening." I dip my chin at a grinning Vivian still lying in bed as she shoots me a thumbs-up and mouths, *Good luck.*

"Put—" *Pinch.* "Me—" *Poke.* "Down." *Punch.* Sutton's hands inflict as much torture as she can imagine on my back, hips, and butt.

Some of it has me hissing through my teeth as I walk out of my best friend's house and across the paved driveway to my truck.

I pull my key from my pants and unlock the doors. With one hand, I open the passenger door and bend to dump her into the front seat. While she's scrambling to sit up, I flip the child locks and shut the door, running around to the driver's side and climbing in as fast as possible.

She's already tugging at the door when I shut mine.

"What the fuck," she yells. "Let me out."

"No."

"Women don't like being kidnapped, Cooper."

"Really? Because all those smutty little books on your shelf suggest otherwise."

Her face reddens, and the corner of her lips curl up for a fraction of a second before she schools her features into a scowl that isn't meant to melt me from her cuteness, but it does.

I smile to myself as I put my key into the ignition. "Pout all you want, baby opossum, but you and I are going home to have a heart-to-heart."

Chapter Forty-One

Sutton

That son of a bitch child locked me in.

The nerve.

Not only did he storm into my best friend's house like a madman and kidnap me, but he locked me up like a toddler who's an escape artist.

And now he wants a heart-to-heart.

A heart-to-heart?

The man wants to have a cheesy teen-drama heart-to-heart?

What on earth is going on?

Well, too bad for him. I'm not in the mood to talk to him.

My decision was final.

If he has a problem with that, tough shit.

I wish my heels didn't make my feet hurt like I've stepped on a thousand nails, but guess what, they still do.

I hate that arousal flooded me the moment he tossed me over his shoulder like I weighed nothing.

He's like catnip to my libido.

Everything he does drives me crazy in one way or another.

I either want to strangle him or ride him like a horse. There's no in-between when it comes to us.

I angle my body away from him. He might've stolen me away from the comfort of Vivian's and locked me in the truck, but that doesn't mean I'm going to be grateful or even dare a glance at his dumb, handsome face.

We pull up in front of my house not even ten minutes later. Cooper places the truck in park and opens his door without a word before shutting it and rounding the truck to open mine.

Like the child he's treating me like, I cross my arms and refuse to get out.

I smirk. That will show him.

Except it doesn't.

His stupid-long arms reach across the seat and unclick my buckle, and then he lifts me in his arms, hauling me out of the seat as I squeal in irritation.

"If you think manhandling me like an oaf is going to get you anywhere, you're wrong." I pinch his wonderfully round ass. God, I love his ass—no, brain, no. Stop it. You will not think about his ass. He *is* an ass. Think about that. Think about how this man is not respecting the fact that you ended it with him... Right then, I know I have the perfect insult to throw at him. Something so good that he's sure to drop me straight onto the ground the moment it slips from my lips.

"Guess you and Dillon have more in common than I thought."

"Excuse me?" Cooper's grip on my thighs tightens as his steps pound up the sidewalk to the porch.

"Can't handle rejection, now, can you?" I taunt with a borderline evil smirk on my face. I'm channeling my inner bitch villain because it's the only way he's going to be free of me.

Cooper shoves his key into the lock and turns it with more force than is necessary before opening the door and slamming it behind us. Once inside, he slowly lowers me to the ground. His jaw flexes as anger blazes in his amber eyes. "Let's get one thing straight. You didn't reject me."

"Then what do you call me breaking up with you."

"Running. That's all you ever do, isn't it, Sutton? You run away without thinking things through." He swings his arms open. "You did it with Dillon."

Anger washes through me, along with a twinge of pain. He hit me where it hurts, just like I had to him. "This isn't the same as the Dillon thing, and you know it."

"Then don't compare me to that lying, cheating piece of garbage again."

I cross my arms over my chest. "You can't talk me into something I don't want, Cooper."

"I know that," he growls. "But this—us being over—isn't something you want. You love me. Love me so much you pretend to like the same things as me, love me." He moves and steps closer until there's only a foot between us. One measly foot.

One easily closed foot.

"And I—" His voice breaks before he takes a deep breath. "I love you so much that the world seems better, brighter, just by having you near me. My life before you was like looking up at the night sky and not seeing a single star. It was sad and lonely."

My breath catches in my throat. "And your life with me?"

"It shines. It's like the night sky is filled with millions and millions of stars, and I don't feel small in this vast galaxy. I know that there's something out there. There's something more, and it's you. There's wonder and endless possibilities as long as you're by my side. You've broadened my horizons in so many ways. You've made this world seem less lonely. My life's not so dark anymore because you brighten it. Please. Please don't take my light away again."

My nose burns as I try and fail miserably to prevent tears from pooling in my eyes. "But I'm bad for you."

Cooper shakes his head adamantly. "You are the best thing that has ever happened to me. I know you might not believe this, but I value you more than any job. More than anyone or anything in this world."

My heart aches with how much I want to reach out and embrace him. I believe him.

I don't know how he did it, but in a few short months, he's gone from my number-one frenemy to my number-one person. The one person I'm willing to do anything for, even cause myself misery if it means their happiness. I sniffle. "Even Nate?"

"Even Nate." A faint smile plays on his lips, and my chest warms with the overwhelming truth of his love and devotion.

I wipe my nose with a small, sad laugh.

"So, are we on the same page?" he asks, dipping his body so he's on eye level with me.

My chest heaves. "I think so."

"So that means you and I—"

"Are in it for the long haul."

His lips curve into the softest smile as happiness glimmers in his eyes. "Forever, baby."

I swallow the lump in my throat as tears blur my vision. "Forever."

His arms wrap around my back, pulling me into his powerful chest. The warmth of his body leaking into mine, burning away the cold that had settled into my bones when we were apart.

I want to stay like this forever. In his arms, where nothing can get in the way. But I have to ruin it by needing to ask the question lingering in the back of my mind.

I turn my head to rest my ear over his heart. The rhythm soothing me as I ask, "What are you going to do about your job?"

"It's already handled."

I pull back to look at his face. "What do you mean it's handled? What happened?"

His eyes are soft as they meet mine. "You did."

"Me?"

"You went to bat for me with Tillan. And then he did the same."

"Really?"

He nods, not offering me any more information.

"You still have your job?"

"No."

"What?"

"I ended up quitting."

"You did what?" I push away from him.

"I quit. Tillan called his friends, some who happen to be clients of mine or the company's, and others who have a close relationship with another firm."

"I don't understand. If he and other clients went to bat for you, why quit?"

"Because they got me a job at the competition's company and plan to follow me."

"Shut up. You quit and stole their clients?" I cackle. It's perfect. "Something tells me Mr. Avery wasn't so happy about it."

He grins. "Oh, he was pissed. He actually tried to demote me, expecting me to be happy to take whatever scraps of my job he offered me. You should have seen his face when I turned him down and told him I'd be taking my clients with me over to his competition because, stupidly, there was no noncompete in my contract, and the other firm doesn't punish their employees for not being romantically involved. In fact, they don't ask their employees about their personal lives, and they definitely don't use what happens outside of the job against them."

"Holy crap. He must have been flipping his shit."

"His face turned beet red. It was quite the sight. But once he started to yell, I left with a huge grin plastered on my face."

"I'm so proud of you."

"Thank you." He dips his head, pressing his lips to mine for a kiss. "I love you, Sutton."

I bask in the way his smooth lips slip over mine in the sweetest of kisses. "I love you too."

It had only been one day. One tortuously long day without him and those delectable lips. I never want to go that long without this again. Without him.

But Cooper seems to feel the same because he whispers, "You're my forever." Then kisses me again. His hands move down my back, slowly caressing every inch. He pours promise after promise into every kiss and touch.

Epilogue

Cooper

I close the door to Nate's pickup truck and give him a quick goodbye after our weekly "date night" before heading up the sidewalk to Sutton's and my house. It's been two months since Sutton tried to end things with me and I refused. Two months since we decided to give up my apartment permanently. One month since we decided we wanted to find a place not haunted by the ghost of Dillon Oak.

At least once a week since Dillon moved out, we had a random woman or groups of partiers show up looking for him at all hours of the day. At first, it was funny. But after a particularly long day with a visitor pounding on our door at 3 a.m., we stopped finding it so funny and knew we needed to get away from that house and Dillon's groupies.

It took us about three weeks to find the perfect house. And it was in walking distance from Nate and Viv.

With a bag of greasy street tacos from a random food truck in hand, I unlock the front door to find Sutton drinking straight from a bottle of wine as she sits on the kitchen floor, organizing our Tupperware into the cabinets. Boxes upon boxes fill the space. We moved in last week, only unpacking the essentials, and haven't touched a box since.

Her creepy-as-hell murder podcast is playing because my dumbass was so excited about getting home to feed her these tacos that I forgot to text her. A shiver runs down my spine at the memory of me walking in on her shaving her legs to the gruesome details of a woman's murder filling the bathroom. I wanted to puke at the information the host shared as Sutton tilted her head thoughtfully, hanging on to their every word.

Luckily for me this time, the hosts are talking about the police and their search efforts instead of going into gory details.

"Baby, I'm home," I call out, and Sutton lifts her head, blond hair spilling over her shoulders as a smile plays on her lips when she sees me.

I walk over to her, bending to kiss her.

She pauses her podcast. "What's wrong with your face?"

"Excuse me?" I ask my wonderfully kind and definitely not rude girlfriend.

Her face contorts in disgust as she gestures with her fingers at my face. "I asked what's wrong with your face."

I frown. "I don't think you're supposed to talk to people you love like that."

"No, I'm serious. Something is different." She taps her chin. "Perhaps one might say it's wrong."

I sigh because *here we go again*. "Listen, I know you aren't a fan of my new glasses, but you can't continue to act like I'm hideous."

"You aren't hideous," she clarifies, grabbing my shoulders to lean back and look me in the eye. "Those ridiculous frames are."

The frames in question are midnight blue at the top and lined with gunmetal gray around the lenses. They're the same shape as my old pair, which Sutton accidentally broke, much to her sadness, when she tossed them off my face in a lust-filled haze. Something she likes to completely forget about when it comes to trashing my new pair.

"Well, the frames that you have a weird attachment to are no longer being manufactured. So it's these or I force myself to wear my contacts every day."

"No," she squeaks out. "I like you in glasses."

"Then stop making me question your attraction to me."

Her bottom lip juts out. "I'm sorry. I'll try to stop, but are you sure you can't—"

"I'm sure. The company said they are no longer in production. So kiss your fantasies of seeing me in those particular glasses goodbye."

"But I met you in those glasses. Our first kiss was in those glasses. I fell in love with you in those glasses."

This woman actually has my chest squeezing at the memories we shared in that particular pair of glasses.

I throw my head back with a groan. "Fine, I will keep looking for them."

She beams up at me before grabbing my chin in her hand and pulling me back down to her lips for a loud, smacking kiss. "You are the best boyfriend ever."

"Yeah, yeah." I take off my jacket, throwing it onto the kitchen table.

"You're home early."

"It was a short but eventful night," I say, handing the bag to her.

"For me?" she asks, already opening the bag and pulling out a tinfoil-wrapped taco.

"Of course."

She moans with the first bite. "You are too good to me."

"Me or the taco?"

Mid-bite, she gives me a toothy smile. "You."

"See, that still didn't answer my question," I say, sitting beside her and pulling another box over to me before opening it. "You started to unpack without me?"

"Did you want me to wait for you?"

When I give her the side-eye, she laughs around another bite as I begin to pull the contents of the box out, setting them in front of me.

"You don't have to help."

"Like hell, I don't. This is our home. Which means I'm helping. Besides, I like spending time with you, no matter what we're doing. I just want to be with you."

She stares at me for a few moments, taking bite after bite while I place pots and pans into the cabinets. "This is why I love you."

"Because I'm doing the bare minimum in my home?"

"Because you care, too. You don't make it into a chore. You love me in the way I've always dreamed of being loved."

"And I always will."

We sit side by side, unpacking box after box with only the sound of Sutton's chewing and the clinking of pots and pans filling the space.

"What did you end up doing while I was gone?"

"Oh, you know. I just had some solid much-needed me time."

"Does that *me time* include your favorite pastime?" I waggle my eyebrows at her suggestively.

"If you mean masturbation, maybe. If you mean painting my nails, no. I prefer to have you do it now that I have trained you so masterfully."

Paint a woman's nails once when she's in a cast, and she never lets it go.

"Then what?"

"What do you think, Cooper?" She glances around the room.

I run my gaze over the stuffed room and wince. "I'm sorry I left you to go out with Nate."

She waves me off with a flick of her wrist. "Eh, it's fine. It needs to be done, and the sooner we get it done, the sooner you can fuck me on every surface."

"Ah yes, a house is not a home until every inch of it is covered in sex sweat."

She winks and gives me a look that screams *exactly*. "Anyway, you still haven't told me what you and Nate did tonight?"

"Oh, Nate and I went to some dingy hole-in-the-wall bar across town... to see a secret Muzzle Velocity concert." I smirk as I pull potholders and dish towels out of a box.

She places the bag of food on the floor, pushing it away near the pots and pans she was organizing, and stands. "Come on." She holds her bottle of wine in one hand and grabs my hand with the other, dragging me behind her around the mess of boxes to the living room before pushing me onto the couch and straddling my hips. Once she is comfortable, she says, "Okay, spill."

"So, Nate and I might have gotten wind that MV was playing a secret show for a special guest. A music producer."

Rumor has it that he and the band wanted to go under the radar tonight because things can get a little wild when their fans come out in the masses, and they wanted to wow the producer with their music and not the sheer number of screaming women.

Dillon gets a little sloppy when he sees women fawning over him. So none of their usual antics are ideal.

It was a solid plan.

They didn't advertise that they were playing tonight; it was hush-hush.

The only reason I found out was because Audra frequents this bar often, and one of the bartenders asked if she had ever heard of them.

Normally, I'd never do anything to screw with someone's career or livelihood, like Dillon did with me. But he had this one coming to him. And besides, this one last prank should be the universe righting some wrongs via my pettiness.

Day after day, Dillon's visitors would leave their numbers in hopes that Sutton and I would pass them on to him.

Obviously, we didn't.

We did, however, throw all the numbers into a pile of junk he left at the house, planning to throw it out while moving.

"Okay..." She tilts her head to the side, waiting patiently for me to tell her the rest.

"I might have taken all of those numbers the groupies had left and texted them about a top-secret show and how they would need to keep it all under wraps, but Dillon was excited to have them there."

Her mouth drops open as a laugh bubbles out of her, causing her shoulders to shake and her ass to bounce against my crotch. "You didn't. You really called the groupies."

I place my hands on her hips to still her movement because I really don't feel like popping a boner while talking about her ex. "I did. And you can only imagine the shit show that went down. The music producer looked very unimpressed from what I could see."

The man in question, a small bald man with sunglasses, was tucked into a dark corner, sitting at a small table with a reserved sign. He didn't look like anything special, but what do I know.

"I—" She wheezes between laughs. "Was—" Another wheeze. "The music producer."

"What?"

She clutches her chest as she pulls a rubbery-looking thing from her hoodie pocket and throws it at me.

I unfold the flesh-colored item to discover it's a bald cap. It takes me a moment to piece together what it means, but then it's like a light goes off. "Shut the fuck up. You were there?"

Tears fill her eyes as she explains how she called Dillon, pretending to be a famous music producer interested in Muzzle Velocity as one last prank. She also goes into detail on how she rushed out of the house the moment I left to assume the role of a balding man at the bar.

I'm in tears by the end of her story, clutching my sides as pain lances up my stomach.

"Did you see the woman with the knife?" She wipes away the moisture from under her eyes.

"Baby, I had a front-row seat to it."

The moment Dillon stepped onto the stage, women and men swarmed him. And much to my delight, more than a few were wearing the merch Sutton and I created.

At first, he smiled, welcoming their eager touches. But that all changed when they tugged at him. Dillon was jerked to the left before another fan pulled him to the right. Then someone got a hold of his shirt collar, and he was yanked backward.

His arms flailed, windmilling before he crashed to the ground.

Pieces of fabric went flying into the air as his fans screamed with joy. They circled around him, enclosing him as he pleaded for them to stop.

On stage, the band continued to play.

I enjoyed every second of it until I saw the knife. Nate and I had jumped up, ready to defend the man I hate.

Until I saw the unhinged smile on the woman's face as she raised a lock of hair up in triumph before walking away like she had won the lottery.

Nate and I had taken that moment as a sign that we needed to leave.

Sutton cackles. "That was my favorite part of the night."

"You're so twisted."

She circles the lip of the bottle of wine sitting between us. "I think I like the new glasses."

I quirk an eyebrow at her suspiciously. "Really? Because just a few minutes ago, you hated them. Said they were wrong."

She shrugs her shoulder, licking her lips in a motion that has my dick twitching. "Maybe I was wrong. Maybe they're growing on me."

"I think maybe you had a little too much wine," I tease, pulling the half-empty bottle from her grasp and placing it on the floor.

"Nah, I want to show you how much I love you, like you show me."

"You do. You show me every single day by being by my side. By being mine."

"And you're mine."

"Always."

She rolls her hip against mine. "Then let me show you how much I appreciate you in my favorite way."

I squeeze her ass just as her lips come crashing down on mine.

Her kiss is heaven. *She* is heaven. A piece that I never thought I would find.

I thank God every day that she struck that damn bargain with me. I can't imagine my life without her anymore. I can't imagine a future that isn't filled with her. And I hope I never have to. Fuck, I'll do everything in my power to ensure it.

"I love you. I love you. I fucking love you," I pant between each kiss.

She pulls her lips from mine and trails kisses down my jaw to my neck as her hands slip under my shirt, leaving my skin on fire in every place she touches. "I love you too, baby. But if you don't shut up and fuck me already, we're going to have a problem."

So I do.

Acknowledgements

This book was so freaking much fun to write. Seriously. I really let myself write whatever I wanted. Whether it was opossums to pegging. The sky was the limit. And for that this book was the wildest to write so far. Now that doesn't mean it was easy. I struggled at times, but I definably laughed at all my own jokes a little too hard. And I hope the joy I felt while writing Sutton and Coopers love story translates to you the reader. My hope for this book is that you get a craving to let your fierce and feral inner Creed lover free. Also, a bit of laughing and swooning wouldn't be bad either.

Brooklyn! YOU ARE THE BEST! You handled my massive tense mess up like a champ and didn't make me feel like a complete dope, which is a feat in itself. Even though I imagined you cursing my name as you changed everything to present tense. So, like I said before, you are the best and deserve all the caffeine in the world. Thank you for understanding my weird avoidant tendencies. My brain just doesn't brain sometimes, and you get it. I hope you know how much I ate up your notes. Your excitement and reactions bring me so much freaking happiness. Like seriously girl. You make me laugh so hard while editing. And make me feel like I really am funny! You continue to help me grow as a writer with every book we work on.

Tori- My fellow water sign. My book bestie. Thanks for matching my freak. Also, thank you for being so damn encouraging. And for reading anything I write, even when contemporary romance isn't usually your jam. I really hope you enjoyed every Twilight reference because I giggled to myself with each one saying Tori will love this. So, you better love it. I kid, I kid...or do I?

Loren- Once again, you make time for me and my books. It means the world that you take the time out of your busy life for me. You are the first person I created a dick-ionary for, so I hope you feel as special as you truly are to me.

Sawyer- Bruh, you are a pretty cool kid. I love you. Thanks for encouraging me to chase my dreams.

Special thanks to all the ARC readers. You guys are amazing! Thank you for helping me make my dreams come true!

And last but certainly not least. Thank you to you the reader. Seriously. It means so much to me that you would give my book a chance. I hope you loved it and will continue with me on my writing journey.

Dicktionary

Use this to guide you to the smut or to steer you away! Whichever your heart desires!

About Author

Registered Nurse by day romance writer by night. Bretta dreamed of becoming a writer since she was a little girl but finally wrote her first novel during the pandemic-imposed social isolation.
A self-proclaimed triple threat, Bretta loves to read smutty books and has an unabashed addiction to Coca-Cola. When she's not writing or caring for patients, you can find her daydreaming about her next book, making sarcastic comments, or being a mediocre crafter. She lives in Oklahoma with her hot mess son and a few furry babies.